THE
CONFESSION

Iain M. Rodgers

CrossModal

Published in 2019 by CrossModal

ISBN Paperback: 978-1-9161918-0-8
Hardback: 978-1-9161918-1-5
Ebook: 978-1-9161918-2-2

A CIP catalogue copy of this book can be found in the British Library.

Cover design by Graham Miles

Published with the help of Indie Authors World

IndieAuthors
World

For Bonnie, who seems to be my guardian angel.

Thanks for
buying my book.
I hope you like
it

Iain M Rodgers.

About the Author

Iain M. Rodgers was born in Glasgow. He sometimes has difficulty describing himself as a Glaswegian because for most of his life he has been pinged around like a pinball. The list of places he is associated with includes Glasgow, Manchester, Lagos, London, Sheffield, Dublin, Helsinki, Stockholm, Rotterdam, Amsterdam and Moscow.

His cover story is that he was a Civil Servant for a while, which got him into I.T. One day he decided to give that up, teach English in Moscow and try to write books. His cover story is a fabrication.

Every great dream begins with a dreamer. Always remember,
you have within you the strength, the patience, and the
passion to reach for the stars to change the world.
Harriet Tubman

1 - GOD SAVE THE QUEEN
(Glasgow - 1977)

A dark orange paper lantern, hanging from an elaborately decorative centre rose of the high Victorian ceiling, provided barely enough light to illuminate the languidly twisting coils of silver smoke that filled the room. The air was thick with the smell of cannabis.

Young men and women, a mixture of long-haired hippies and short-haired punks, were sprawled over the floor smoking joints and drinking from cans. In one corner of the large room, looking either like a witch or a puritan, an earnest young woman in a high-necked maxi-dress was kneeling to roll a joint on a low, half-broken side table. She did it carefully and ritualistically. Several people nearby watched with interest, as though her performance formed part of an important ceremony.

A guy with a guitar was slumped in a beanbag trying to play Leonard Cohen's famous blue dirge *Famous Blue Raincoat*, though no one was interested in his depressive mumbling. Eventually, someone decided he'd heard enough. A kid with spiky hair and an imitation leather jacket pierced with hundreds of safety pins and button badges skipped through the bodies strewn on the floor and pushed poor 'Leonard' off the beanbag.

"That's shite by raway pal." The punk sneered in a rough Glasgow voice. Then he shouted back over his shoulder: "Moira, put ra Pistols oan. Let's get some life intae ris party."

Meanwhile, Stuart and Richard were quietly discussing something in the corner opposite the young woman rolling the joint.

"You're all just wasting your time you know. All this marching and selling newspapers will never get you anywhere," Richard stated.

"History, man. History's on our side."

"History bollocks. You guys are just kids. You're just playing at this."

"Eddie's totally serious. Mibby worryingly serious." Stuart spoke with a slight Glasgow accent which, though mild, sometimes influenced Richard to imitate it to some extent. After pausing to think for a moment he added, "I guess ye could say I'm more interested in an academic way myself."

"I know that, man. See that PhD you're doing, all that theory shit, 'German philosophy from Hegel to Marx', I don't really get it. I wish I'd done some proper subjects myself; engineering say, instead of this politics and sociology crap." Richard thought morosely for a few moments before perking up a bit. "Imagine if, years from now, your education finally pays off and you find yourself in a half-decent job. Let's say no one even knows you're a commie. What would happen if you could reconnect with all your comrades from the Party and put yourself at their disposal?"

"What could you do then that you can't do now?"

"Who knows, man? But I bet you could do a damned sight more damage, or good I mean, than a hundred of these silly pot-smoking kids that think they're being so cool and radical."

"Mibby you're right, but you're not even a Party member. You're just a guy who tags along; a fellow traveller. You're not even interested in what the Party wants."

"You're right Stuart, I'm not. I'm not interested in all this posturing and posing, but, see if I thought I could do any good I would definitely do whatever it takes."

"Like fuck ye would."

"Course I would! And me not being a Party member would help anyway. I'm not on anyone's radar. I've never even had my picture taken on any of your half-assed marches or demos."

"'Half-assed marches'? Yeah, right-e-o! How come you've never even come on a march or demo, ya bastard?"

"Waste of time man. Take all those stupid asses that demonstrated to save every last job in the shipyards. All it did was make sure that the yards couldn't compete. Instead of saving jobs they made sure they all went."

Stuart was eyeing him with suspicion. They had argued on this subject a number of times already and agreed to differ. Richard didn't bother to bring the same old arguments up yet again but was dismayed that even Stuart didn't seem to understand him. He was well aware that nobody in the Party took him seriously. For one thing his background was against him. But, more importantly, there was an ideological divide between him and the others. If he had to explain to these Marxists in terms that would be acceptable, it was the difference between *Das Kapital* and *Der Grundrisse*. Properly reading either *Das Kapital* or *Der Grundrisse* was not something he had bothered to do, but he believed the difference between them explained the difference between himself and the others. Ultimately, he was reluctant to describe himself as a Marxist of any kind. An anarchist called Kropotkin had more attractive ideas. But that was something best not mentioned at all.

"Oh jeezus!" Stuart blurted out.

"What?"

Stuart jerked his head to the side in the direction of the door, which was being closed again after opening briefly.

"Line-up-Linda's just arrived. She's probably heading straight upstairs to get her legs in the air."

Richard knew Stuart didn't like Linda MacKerricher. He thought she was a slut. So she was; but Richard didn't see anything wrong with that. She was a liberated and independent young woman. In fact Richard found her crazily sexy. He cursed his luck in not catching sight of her – probably wearing those kinky wet-look boots and that purple mini-skirt. Liberated and "easy" though she was, Richard could never pluck up the courage to even talk to her, let alone join in one of the orgies she was reputed to take part in.

"So why would a posh cunt like you even want to help?" Stuart continued, snapping Richard out of the reverie that Linda MacKerricher had unknowingly evoked.

"Lots of 'posh cunts' are revolutionaries. Most revolutionaries are posh cunts in fact – Marx himself, Lenin, Guevara... you name it."

"Yeah, sure thing, Guildford boy."

"Fuck you Mr Kelvinside Academy." Richard knew that Stuart was as middle class as it was possible to be for a Glaswegian, but still had one over on him when it came to class-related, inverted snobbery. Richard's parents now lived in Milngavie, having moved up to Scotland from Guildford when he was about three. In the mindset of most Glaswegians, Richard was a toff – almost aristocracy.

"OK Guildford boy. So you like to tag along to the odd meeting. You like to slag off the hardcore members but will we ever see you put your money where your mouth is?"

"If I thought it could do some actual good I would. I mean the way society is just now... there's lots of things wrong. Systemic things. You know yourself how we've discussed it all; over and over again. Things that are wrong. Things that are wrong with the system itself and so can't be fixed by the system." He wondered if he was getting a bit drunk. He didn't usually use Glaswegian expressions like "You know yourself". He would normally say "As you know" or whatever the correct expression was.

"OK, agreed. So what do ye propose then?"

"Nationalise the banks without compensation. Step one."

"You can't just do that though." Stuart said with the sort of patience usually reserved for small children, "You can only do that after a revolution. Industries can only be nationalised after they've failed. Or by force, after revolution."

"Not true. Labour's in power now and there are already mutuals, co-operative banks, the National Savings Bank. Why don't they just expand that sector and take over the banking system step by step?"

Stuart shrugged. "Step by step hasn't worked. The Left has already tried Parliament. Every time they do something the Tories just reverse it next time they're in. Plus the Left never stick to their guns when they get into power; they always change. We've had Keir Hardie, Aneurin Bevan, Benn. Even Harold-bloody-Wilson was supposedly 'hard Left' and look what happened."

Stuart's attention was drawn to the door again. Richard looked too, hoping that Linda had come back. He was immediately disappointed. Instead of Linda MacKerricher wearing a mini-skirt and boots, someone wearing a duffle coat and a Partick Thistle hat and scarf was trying to push a bicycle into the room. It seemed that the Thistle fan was intending to ride the bike around the room as an amusing stunt. This was giving rise to a bit of an altercation because several of the punks were trying to prevent him. Their idea of anarchy in the UK did not extend to permitting people to ride bicycles in rooms.

"OK, let's agree, as usual, that only revolution will really change things. So how do you do it?" said Richard.

"How would you do it?"

"Just what I was trying to say a moment ago. You need something to trigger it, an act that causes significant damage to the existing system so that it's unable to function properly. Once that happens the socialists will rise up and the system will be unable to defend itself."

Stuart didn't say anything but nodded briefly in agreement. Then, remembering there were more important matters to attend to, he stretched his head back and began tipping half a tin of Tennent's Super Lager down his throat, seemingly oblivious as Richard continued his monologue:

"We're just kids right now, students. We know nothing. We don't know anybody who knows anything or has any influence. Even guys like Eddie are half-way to Walter Mitty; they're kidding themselves. But all this education we're getting might eventually be good for something. If we could keep in touch with the people we know who really want to change things and make a difference then one day we might be useful."

Stuart had stopped gulping the lager. His head lurched back down to its default position as he crushed the empty can into his fist. He studied Richard for a long time, as though he was somehow having difficulty recognising him. But finally a glimmer of comprehension flickered to life.

"What exactly would you do?"

"Sabotage. I mean something big. Something fucking big. Remember what I was telling you about Georges Sorel?"

"And you're volunteering...?"

"Sure, why not?"

"Count me in, man."

A wall of sound slammed through the room as The Sex Pistols' *God Save The Queen* blasted out. The punks immediately started pogo-ing in a frenzy, forcing the hippies lazing on the floor to reluctantly create space for them. The guy who had been singing Leonard Cohen songs left the room, meekly cradling his guitar to prevent damage. Stuart had to shout:

"We should go and see Eddie with this idea. He'll know what to do about it, or he'll know someone that does."

2 - EDDIE'S KITCHEN

"This idea of yours is aw very well but you realise it could put us aw in jail?" Eddie's mean, feral eyes stared at Richard accusingly through heavy black-rimmed glasses, making him look every inch the wee Glasgow hard-man he aspired to be. Richard had been invited round to his flat to go through the sabotage plan for the third time and it was becoming clear Eddie had little faith in either him or the plan. They sat in the cold kitchen to avoid disturbing Eddie's dad who was watching TV in the living room.

"It could, but this is what we're here for isn't it? Handing out pamphlets to people who chuck them into the first bin they walk past will never get us anywhere. We're supposed to be a revolutionary party not a pamphlet distributing party."

They sat in silence. Richard wondered if he'd pushed Eddie too far. Anyway, he was past caring. He looked round the cold, old-fashioned kitchen. There wasn't much there to soothe their nerves; an old-fashioned pantry, solid enough to withstand nuclear attack, had been painted yellow in an attempt at modernity. A worn-out Tricity cooker, covered in grease. Pitted brown linoleum on the floor. A ceiling pulley for hanging washing on. The council had vowed to build modern flats 'fit for heroes' but, somehow, they had created drab, grey schemes instead. Out in the street there were no facilities; no shops and nothing to do. Inside there was no comfort. Attempts to cheer up the interiors of these houses nearly always ended in tragicomic kitsch – in this case exemplified by the wallpaper with its repeated pattern of crowing cocks. Perhaps the cocks had provided a few moments of jollity once, but they had been crowing at least since the mid-sixties and looked a bit worn-out. To top it all, there was a lot of tyre screeching and occasional gunfire coming from the living room. The TV was blasting out at maximum volume to compensate for Eddie's dad's deafness.

"So what sort ay event do you think'd be sufficient tae trigger revolution in the UK?"

"It would have to be big, Eddie."

"So big it's impossible?" Eddie asked slyly.

It was clear Eddie thought he wouldn't or couldn't go through with it and was just looking for an excuse to avoid marching and agitating – the sort of party work that Eddie thought was essential.

"Eddie," Richard was trying to contain his anger. "Eddie, when Marx was writing he expected a revolution eventually, but he never lived to see it. Well, we've had dozens of attempts since then. We've got the USSR and China to show for it – OK, Cuba and stuff like that too. None of these were good or real revolutions. We still haven't seen what Marx was expecting. We need something better, more final. And it has to be in an advanced economy not a backward one. So if this puts me out of action for a while as far the Party's concerned – even if it takes my whole life – then so be it."

"Richard," Eddie was obviously annoyed too, "yur always making excuses. Nothing is ever good enough fur yuh. You think no socialist country ever succeeded in improving the lot of the people? Well yer wrong. The USSR is an improvement on the Tsarist Empire. Things huvney worked out perfectly but this is the real world."

"Yeah, but..."

"And don't forget the USSR's always been at war," Eddie said, ignoring Richard's attempt to interrupt. "They hud tae fight the revolution, then the counter revolution, then World War Two. Now we've got the Cold War. So they've been fighting proxy wars all over the world. But in spite ay aw rat thur still making progress."

"Yeah, but the USA's made greater progress."

"The USA did well frae both world wars by sucking the British dry. All I ever hear from you is how great these Capitalist countries are, nothing about the achievements of Russia or China."

Richard could tell Eddie needed more evidence of commitment before he could take this risk. He wondered if he should perhaps tell Eddie about his Uncle Bobby who, according to family legend, had gone to the USA and had tried to start up a union to improve working conditions. He was immediately arrested and soon after that died in prison. Reason for death – unknown.

But he decided not to bother. It was only a story anyway. It had all happened before he was even born. Furthermore, it proved nothing. He wasn't aware of any sense of following in Uncle Bobby's footsteps. Moreover, particularly now that he'd come up with this plan, he preferred his motives and beliefs to remain invisible in order to be more effective. So he decided to bite his tongue.

To prevent himself blurting out any story about his Uncle Bobby, he dug his nails into the palms of his hands and glowered at Eddie.

"They're more advanced Eddie, just like Marx expected. That's all."

3 - THE BLACK WORMS
(Moscow - 2012)

Years of nothingness had passed. The promises, the beliefs, the hopes, had turned to numbness.

Richard paused in the middle of pulling his left sock off and stared – confusion oscillating between fascination and horror. There were awful dark indigo bulges on the top of his foot in the flesh just beneath the skin. It seemed that parasitic worms of some sort had hatched out in his bloodstream.

Tentatively, he traced a finger over the bulbous nodes where their translucent, tubular bodies overlaid one another, half expecting to see them begin to writhe and twist deeper into his foot, or burst out leaving trails of filthy, contaminated blood. But as he examined them he knew they wouldn't. For they were not parasitic worms – they were something even worse – more portentous.

Varicose veins. He was starting to get varicose veins now! He sighed. Of course! Of course – this was just one more thing he was going to get as he got older. Varicose bloody veins! He shuddered at the ugliness of it – and sighed again. The inevitable was happening; as the inevitable always would. He removed the other sock.

And now he would have to face it. Another day had ended. Another night of sleeping alone in a strange bed would bring it to a close, leaving him to trust his subconscious mind to guide him to the next dawn, through whatever voyage of darkness or dreams that sleep would bring.

He glanced over to the far end of the room. The pale, naked creature he saw there made him flinch momentarily. But he consoled himself that being an unremarkable middle-aged man with mousey hair was a strength. It was a form of camouflage

The glance into the mirror had been unintentional. At home there would have been no mirror to glance into, intentionally or not. But, as usual, thanks to VirtuBank, he was staying in a hotel. This time he was spending a few days in Moscow, though for no particular reason, because the technical problem their client had reported had turned out to be trivial.

And this was how his adult life had been measured out – moving from one hotel to another, sometimes returning briefly home (if his flat near Baker Street could be called home) to seek out a few acquaintances to get drunk with.

But he was lucky. He was still here, and his life still had purpose too. The period of numbness was over. Now, at VirtuBank he had a glimmer of hope. He had stumbled into a job which gave him a real chance of achieving his dream.

He hadn't been in touch with his friends from college for years. The only people he had known since that time were workmates that came and went as he changed job. Even so, he was lucky. He was well aware that, by now, many of his lost or forgotten friends would already be dead. He knew that for certain. It was both surprising and obvious.

For example, he was aware, from the media, that so many of his teen idols had passed away already. Admittedly, film and rock stars seem likely to die younger than normal due to suicide or substance abuse. Nevertheless, a good proportion of them had also died in accidents or of natural causes, indicating that a similar fate would have befallen some, or perhaps by now, many, of the people he had ever known in the past.

So he was lucky. If he had been John Lennon he would have been dead long ago. But time was running out for him too. Had he cut himself off from any kind of normal life, that fateful day in 1977, for nothing?

The cause he had sacrificed his life for was worth more than the life of one man, but somehow he was not ready to accept his contribution to that cause would amount to nothing. He still wanted his place in history. He climbed into bed, weary and close to tears, trying to convince himself there was still a chance; that the promise he had made all those years ago was worth the misery and loneliness.

4 - IN PLATO'S CAVE
(Helsinki – 2013)

Andy Mitchell sat at his desk, staring at the paper in front of him. Somehow it had all become too much. Past failures crowded in on him. Even Richard. Especially Richard – he was going to be the biggest failure of all. What were they doing to him? What use was any of it? Everything he had ever done had unravelled.

After their meeting in Helsinki, Mitchell wondered what good would come of it.

Almost none, probably. He didn't blame himself for that aspect of this whole mess. He had followed the correct procedure. Well, as much as possible. He'd reported back to Skinner that the procedure didn't seem to work properly – it had been even worse than the previous time.

Skinner didn't seem to give a damn except that Mitchell hadn't got Richard's signature in the correct way at the proper stage.

But he had dismissed all that nonsense from his mind by now. Even if he'd got the signature in the proper way, what difference would it have made? Richard wasn't real any more. How could his signature be of any importance?

Richard hadn't been in touch since and everything was still in the drawer waiting to be collected. Perhaps Richard had decided to do nothing about this whole thing and keep himself out of harm's way. So much the better if he had.

Later, in the bar, it was clear at least no lasting damage had been done – in as much as Richard, or some husk of his being, had no recollection of anything he shouldn't know about.

Mitchell imagined how, to Richard, the world must be made of shadows projected into his consciousness. It must be a strange way to live. Like living in Plato's cave.

As he put his signature to the paper, it was suddenly blurred by a teardrop. The tear surprised him. But then he simply folded the piece of paper twice, put it in an envelope and tucked it into the inside pocket of his suit. His best suit that would soon be ripped to shreds, covered in black oil and soaked in blood.

***

The shadows of two men are walking together but on separate paths. Where is this place? We are floating in space. The brightness is too bright, the darkness too dark.

Mist begins to obscure the blinding brightness. Cloud-like wisps lightly tumble upon themselves, thickening into shadow, making everything incomprehensible. Slowly, it begins to rotate, like a dying galaxy.

Then nothingness.

Yet there is a sense of something new; something approaching.

Hidden by shadow, something disturbing is near and getting nearer. Vermiform, it oozes from the darkness. A colossus; tattoos on its long, limbless body glisten like rubies, emeralds, sapphires and countless other multicoloured jewels as it emerges. It moves by undulating lazily, pushing before it a head in the shape of a blunted lozenge. It hesitates, then goes forward again, zigzagging from shadow into ever brighter light, revealing shimmering fractals glittering on its surface. It is magnificent! A fallen angel. A Lucifer.

Its monster head, an expressionless mask, moves from side to side, seeking prey. Its metal eyes hunt.

Suddenly the head splits wide open, transforming into a gaping pink mouth, exposing fangs like curved needles.

Richard woke up. He was bathed in sweat. It was that dream again. Why did he keep having nightmares about a damned snake?

5 - BY EMAIL
(London - 2013)

Andy Mitchell was dead. The email said so.

"How can they be telling me this by email? It must be a hoax – a spoof email perhaps?"

Having just awoken from the nightmare about the snake, everything still felt unreal to Richard, so he found it hard to take in. A fake email from HR would mean there was a breach in the firewall. But a serious breach in security for an email like this wasn't at all likely. The message was real. Andy Mitchell was dead.

Richard reread it a dozen times wondering what could've happened to his boss. A heart attack? Car accident? The email didn't say.

He remembered the last time he saw him. It was while he had been staying in the Grand Sokos Hotel for a project. Mitchell had suddenly turned up in Helsinki and rang his room at quarter to midnight. It was summer, so it was still broad daylight. He had got dressed again, gone down to the lounge bar to meet Mitchell and they had drunk until three a.m. By then they must've been as pissed as newts. His recollection of what had happened was very hazy. To start with, the conversation had been normal enough. Mitchell had talked enthusiastically about music and playing bass for some band in his youth. But then he turned a bit odd. He became more and more morose. Suddenly it all came out as anger. He ranted for a while about what a bitch his wife was. He mentioned he was in serious debt.

He talked about being psychic, quite seriously. Then, bizarrely, he produced a pack of cards. He wanted to absolutely prove that he was psychic for some reason. Were they Tarot cards? Richard seemed to remember they were cards with letters on them... and didn't Mitchell start talking about politics or something at the same time? It was as though he was trying to prove Richard wrong every time he asked a question. Questions that had something to do with...? Richard couldn't remember. They were probably drinking that goddamned Salmiakki Koskenkorva – liquorice vodka. That would account for it. It had got quite weird and rather irritating, and the whole political thing had got really annoying in the end. Mitchell kept telling him to remember the facts, and repeatedly saying, "You need to wake up," just repeatedly saying "You need to wake up now," to whatever point he made. Well, they were both completely drunk. The standard of debate couldn't have been very high. It was probably a slur of barely intelligible babble.

Suddenly Richard had an uneasy feeling. A feeling Mitchell had said something important to him he'd completely forgotten.

And then he remembered the email Mitchell had sent him two days ago. He had dismissed it as jokey way of saying they had to go for a drink sometime. He read the words again with a feeling of déjà vu, or a feeling of having read them in a different life:

"Remember Helsinki? Have you made a decision yet? It's getting urgent. Let's arrange to meet soon."

It was only at that moment, now that Mitchell was dead, in fact *because* Mitchell was dead, that the strangest idea began to insinuate itself. Back in Helsinki, Mitchell had said something to him that was not only very important but very secret. But no matter how he struggled, he couldn't remember anything definite. *Why can't I remember the thing that I'm trying to remember?*

Richard shook his head, trying to shake away the presence of the dream serpent, the shadows of grotesque unreality that still swarmed around him; trying to imagine what Mitchell could possibly have said to him that was so important. Something to do with Osbourne Bank, perhaps – or another project? There was a more ominous possibility. The possibility that it was something to do with Zima. But that would be preposterous. Anything to do with Zima would have lit up in his consciousness like a neon sign. Where there should have been a memory there were just shadows.

So whatever this shadowy memory was, it couldn't be Zima. He tried to think what else it could have been. There was one more possibility. The possibility that Mitchell had never said anything important to him in Helsinki. That, like the snake, it was imaginary. So, finally, unable to bring to mind any substantial notion of what Mitchell had said, he dismissed it as the memory of a dream.

Richard switched off the laptop. He was annoyed though, that he'd read his emails just because a stupid snake dream had woken him. It was still only two a.m but now he wouldn't get back to sleep.

6 - VIRTUBANK SOFTWARE

The Bank of England, an ugly Georgian building consisting of an unfortunate hybrid of several incongruous elements, conceals the administrative machinery that once controlled an empire and continues to exert huge power over the global economy.

Walking near the building, along Threadneedle Street, you are aware of it only as a windowless Portland stone wall on top of which a disproportionately small Greek temple perches. From a greater distance, you would be able to see that the Greek temple has somehow been grafted to the front of something that looks like a French Hotel de Ville.

So, the Bank of England is ugly, but imposing. Fortunately though, the eye is somehow drawn away from it by other distractions. A statue of Wellington, on horseback, stands before the pleasant façade of the Royal Exchange building and, further down Cornhill, James Henry Greenhead, 1844-1896, forces traffic to bifurcate by occupying a position in the middle of the road on top of his stone pedestal.

In addition to Cornhill, six more streets scatter out at random angles from the intersection where the Bank of England is situated. They are surprisingly narrow – certainly not grand, continental boulevards such as those, for example, that radiate, in organised symmetry, from the Arc de Triomphe. They were not created for parading military might before cheering crowds. The might here is financial, not military, and so great is it that it must be concealed rather than paraded. Therefore, the streets are not (as Dick Whittington and his cat believed) literally paved with gold. Furthermore, the design is ramshackle and haphazard because they still mark out the positions where they were arbitrarily formed in medieval times.

In the vicinity of the Bank, the streets are crammed with more white stone buildings. Behind these, a little further away, glass skyscrapers rise up. All this would surely inspire feelings of awe in any who came here, or perhaps envy.

Richard emerged from Bank tube station and was confronted by the sight of all this history and glory. He felt a sense of disgust at the sight, both with the buildings and with himself for continuing to work here.

Yet capitalism was a necessary step on the way to socialism. Marx himself had promised this much. And, looking up, if not to Richard but to the impartial observer, the City seemed celestial. Fluffy white clouds were moving across a porcelain-blue sky. It was almost expected that horn-blowing cherubs would appear, unrolling scrolls of parchment so that some triumphant announcement could be made. You could believe that perhaps they would proclaim that here, right here, they were constructing the New Jerusalem which Ezekiel had prophesied.

It was obvious that heaven and the celestial sphere was an abstract dimension hidden just out of sight of most mortals, as the world of finance was.

Looking back at the Bank of England, it becomes clear the temple is at ground level and the wall it is built on is, in fact, its foundations. Everything else at that level is also subterranean. Black cabs and bright red buses crawl through these underground passageways, while swarms of pedestrians bustle along shadowy walkways. Above this, a better world exists in sunlight and splendour.

***

The headquarters of VirtuBank Software (UK) Ltd were in the heart of the City. No expense had been spared to express the image of cutting-edge technological prowess. The whole façade of the building was gleaming, precision-cut, plate glass, apart from six vertical stainless-steel tracks where transparent lifts slid up and down the exterior.

Richard stepped into one of these lifts from the reception area and, as the brushed steel doors closed behind him, he stepped forward and looked through the plate glass walls at the view. The small courtyard through which he had just passed held its usual throng of tourists and office workers; some looking up at the building, some taking photographs. It was an impressive enough building to merit a photograph.

From inside the building, members of the VirtuBank dev team on the fifth floor would be able to observe Richard, standing stock-still, ascending to their level as though by supernatural force.

Inside the lift, illusions of reflection and translucence bewildered the senses. The views of the surrounding buildings were mirrored back at the same time as other images were permitted to pass through directly, so that it was hard to tell what was real and what was reflection. The image of the skyscraper of St Mary Axe, popularly known as the Gherkin, floated upwards over the receptionist in an adjacent office while, turning round, Richard saw the more solid frame of the building itself looming above him. It shone like a sky-rocket.

Richard walked past reception, along a wide passage and into a large open-plan office. But he did not venture far. The hot-desks were nearest reception so that he, and other travelling consultants, would not disturb the office-based staff, many of whom, scattered randomly, were already bowed over their personal desks, or concentrating on their workstations. He sat down at one of the hot-desks and opened his laptop.

Darion, smartly dressed in a dark suit, came over, and was already wearing an expression of shocked disbelief by the time he was standing beside Richard's desk.

"What about that, my friend?" he said.

"I know."

"I was really shocked. Really!"

"What was it? Heart attack? Car accident?" Richard was still struggling to imagine what could have caused the sudden death of a perfectly fit and healthy man. Mitchell was only just in his forties.

Darion, a giant of a man with the strong lower jaw of a T-Rex, had a soft Greek accent that was ideal for expressing amazement.

"Suicide!" In his amazement, Darion elongated the third syllable of the word. His dramatic exclamation caught the attention of everyone in earshot and spread what seemed to be a ripple of unwanted emotion through them. Several co-workers nearby glanced up in apparent annoyance that their concentration had been disturbed.

"What! You're kidding."

"No," Darion said in a more neutral tone. "It was suicide."

It took a moment for Richard to think of anything to say. "Do you know what made him do it?"

"Nobody knows. Apparently the police said it was a 'brutal suicide'."

"God! I wonder what that means?"

"I don't know. Someone said he jumped in front of a train."

Steve Wong had been unloading his laptop onto a nearby desk. Now he came over.

"Yes, that's what I heard too. I heard he was in debt."

"But come on! Nobody kills themselves just because of a little bit of money." Darion's accent had grown a little thicker. He seemed indignant that Mitchell couldn't face up to mere financial problems. After all, they were all City workers. Money was easy to come by. Admittedly, it was easy to lose too, and never quite meant what you imagined it would. "He could've run away somewhere. What's wrong with Venezuela?"

The guys laughed a little. They knew that Darion had recently been to Venezuela and had had a whale of a time with the local girls. The economy there was smashed to bits and any foreigner was seen as a billionaire.

"Venezuela is a favourite place for dodgy geezers to run to," said Steve winking at Darion.

"You know, it's not such a bad idea, my friend. You can go there any time you like; they will welcome you as a hero of socialism and give you your own place to live."

"Wow! Really?"

"In a favela, or whatever they call the slums there, but it would be cosy, no worse than the others there have, and you should not have the bourgeois expectation of more." He winked at Steve to indicate he was being ironic and understood both he and Steve fully expected more. A lot more. After all, Darion was a securities expert for a specialist financial software company and Steve was a qualified accountant for that company. The tailored suits, fine cotton shirts and silk ties they both wore made it clear they were a cut above the likes of Richard, who nevertheless was also reasonably well dressed in a dark suit and silk tie. His were not quite so 'designer', though.

"Better than topping yourself, anyway," said Steve.

"Anything's better than that. Imagine his family!" said Darion.

"Last time I saw him, he seemed quite happy," said Richard. "He came over to Helsinki."

"There you go!" Darion asserted, case proven. "He was swanning around all over the place pretending to be a manager and getting paid for it. What the hell did he have to go and top himself for!?"

Everyone shook their heads disapprovingly and smiled a little. Darion was always joking but, whatever his troubles, at least Mitchell did seem to have had a pretty cushy, well-paid job. In the short time they'd known him, he'd acquired the nickname of "The Invisible Man" because hardly anyone ever saw him. It seemed he just travelled from place to place, doing very little except occasionally chatting to his subordinates. In the end, none of them were able to sympathise with what he'd done. They all considered it to be a selfish and unnecessary act.

"Christ!" said Darion, suddenly serious.

"What?" asked Steve.

"Don't you remember? Andy thought he was psychic. I wonder what shit he saw in our future." Darion drifted off, leaving the others wondering if he was still joking or not. Steve just shrugged and wandered off too.

But Richard was slightly disturbed by this. He remembered Andy mentioning this in Helsinki. And now he remembered that Mitchell thought that he, Richard, was also psychic.

And suddenly it slithered into a view. The thing that he had been trying to remember.

Mitchell had actually said, "When the stranger returns you must wake up." He could practically see and hear him saying it. Yet it was not Mitchell and it was not Richard. It was a kind of film of them talking together. They were just actors playing roles in a film. It could not have been anything real because, no matter how drunk he'd been, he would've recognised that phrase immediately. Unless, through drunkenness, Mitchell hadn't said it properly.

There was one more reason why it couldn't be true: if Mitchell was his contact, and he was now dead, the last hope of the plan he'd been waiting for had already disappeared.

7 - ADVANCE TO MAYFAIR

The meeting was taking place in a building in Mayfair belonging to Her Majesty's Government of Great Britain and Northern Ireland. Those present were Mark Osbourne, Jim Callan, Dr Joseph Skinner, Jack Logan, Graham Wood and Tom Brookes, all of whom had arrived almost simultaneously with great urgency and seated themselves around a tatty government-issue table. Last to arrive was Mark Osbourne, who took his place at the head of the table and began talking immediately.

"OK gentlemen, thanks for coming, sorry about the short notice. I guess you all know why by now. Anyone not heard the news?"

Everyone shook their heads except Tom Brookes, who looked round the table in alarm. What was going on that he wasn't aware of?

"What news?" Brookes blurted out.

"Mitchell just killed himself."

"What?"

"So we need to know why and clear up any loose ends he left lying around. He was handling several cases at the time of death, most of which are ticking along smoothly, I believe. The only item that gives me cause for concern is the work he was doing on *Winter*."

Osbourne paused for a moment as though expecting someone to contradict him. He looked down at his laptop and continued:

"So, let's talk about the suicide first. Any ideas?"

There was stony-faced silence.

"He left a note. I doubt if it means anything though. It seems utterly confused, quite frankly." Osbourne passed photocopies of the note around the table.

Callan read aloud: "I occupy this crevasse – the realm of nothingness which lies coiled in the heart of being like a worm, but existentialism is a false dichotomy, and therefore metaphysical hope is impossible. I have seen through the illusion. I know what it's like to be dead. I already know. When I walked into the room to see him I was dead then. He didn't notice but I knew.

"Anyway, as JFK said, 'Don't sing me no la la la tune no more I ain't gonna listen to that shit again.' By JFK I mean Jo Fucking King – but, my dear reader, no I ain't joking.

"Inside my mind I have seen into the soul of the universe and it is filled with A MILLION maggots of death. They breed. They are the EVIL in everything. THE e-vile.

"Now I just want to go there and be inside it. It will be me. I will be it. We will reign forever.

"I'll stand on the mountain that stands on me and I will see everything."

Callan had finished reading, but everyone continued to stare at their personal copy of the note as though they still expected to find some meaning in it.

Logan was the first to speak: "Christ! Mitchell wrote *that*? Are you sure? I mean..." he was lost for words. "I said cheerio to him Friday, going out the office. He said cheerio back. He was the same old Andy Mitchell I'd known for..."

Dr Skinner interrupted: "Some of that might not be complete gibberish; he's quoting Sartre – I think – and John Lennon. We should trace the quotes and see..."

Callan interrupted Skinner's interruption: "That's a fool's errand – we'll never get to the bottom of any meaning that might be found in a synthesis of Sartre and *Tomorrow Never Knows*. Was he on drugs or something?"

"Actually, yes. That seems to be it. We found significant traces of ChiroButyline-A in his blood. It's a tranquilliser that was banned worldwide about six months ago because people who took it for any length of time tended to commit suicide."

"Why would he be taking it then? How could he even get hold of it?" Callan asked.

"Both questions – we don't know yet. Second question – maybe he had been prescribed it some time ago but had decided not to take it, then for some reason had started taking it recently."

"I see. So it could have sat in his bathroom cupboard for years?"

"This is all speculation, but something like that is likely. However, if he had required medical help for any reason, he should have informed us. Needless to say, he didn't."

"Should have, yes. But of course it would be like waving goodbye to his career."

"But such cases are handled delicately to ensure people do volunteer this sort of information. We all know the rules."

"Of course we do, yes," Callan agreed.

"Hopefully, none here would hesitate to inform us if they required this sort of help." Osbourne looked around defiantly and received a murmur of affirmation before continuing. "So we have to be aware that perhaps there is some sort of foul play involved."

It took several uncomfortable seconds of grim silence for this information to be digested.

"If so, everything he was working on might be in jeopardy," Callan remarked.

"Yes, it might be," Osbourne agreed. "Bear that in mind when taking over his ongoing cases."

This ruffled a few feathers. Jack Logan, in particular, looked agitated or even annoyed. He had apparently guessed what was coming next.

"On that note," Osbourne continued, "Graham, Tom, I'm dividing the majority of Mitchell's cases between you – except *Winter*. Jack, you'll take over from Mitchell. It has to be you because of the aversion treatment. You're the only spare resource. Put in an appearance at VirtuBank but keep a low profile."

Dr Skinner broke in to say: "But Osbourne, Mitchell's work there was finished. There's nothing left to do."

"We just want to keep an eye on things."

"But how about Callan? Surely he can…"

"Can we just back up a bit?" Callan interrupted. "I have a question. How did he kill himself? Is it possible that someone killed him?"

"He threw himself under a train, Jim," Osbourne replied.

"Possible then – it's one of our favoured methods."

"The platform looks virtually empty at the time, according to the CCTV. Of course CCTV too can be tampered with in various ways, as we know."

"How many cases was he handling? Was he overworked?"

"No, definitely not. If anything, his workload was lighter than normal."

"Also, we all get tested for drugs once a month. He couldn't have been taking this drug for very long," Callan suggested.

Osbourne contradicted him bluntly: "We don't get tested for this stuff. It's banned and it's never been on the list."

"So why did they test for it in the autopsy?"

"A jar of the stuff was found amongst the mess that the train left."

"OK. But let's not jump to conclusions. I presume we're going to go ahead with a thorough investigation. Check for debts, mistresses, all the usual?"

"Of course," Osbourne said with finality. He looked down at his laptop again to make it clear the discussion on this matter was closed and he wanted to move on. There was another period of gloomy silence in the room as he did so.

"So what went wrong in Helsinki?" Osbourne was looking at Dr Skinner.

"I don't know. Everything went more or less to plan. Mitchell gave him the key and verbal instructions."

"But is *Winter* up and running? Is anything happening?"

"We don't know. We haven't heard anything yet."

"So probably nothing is happening. Any idea why?"

Dr Skinner glanced nervously at the expectant faces around the table.

"I, I mean Mitchell followed the procedure to switch phases. He got a signature and he followed the procedure to flip him back.

Then he gave *Snowman* the key and told him what to do with it. Maybe he was confused and didn't remember what the key was for. Phase transition is not easy."

"Other possibilities?"

Skinner shrugged. "Maybe *Snowman* doesn't want to do it."

"After all these years, I think that's unlikely."

Jack Logan butted in, "Yes, but maybe this is too hot to handle. Experienced operatives like Mitchell don't just top themselves for no reason."

Callan spoke: "But there does seem to be a reason in Mitchell's case: ChiroButyline-A. As for *Snowman*, the most likely explanation for his inactivity is that he couldn't understand what to do because you guys had just turned his mind inside out. Or imagine if he was in the wrong state when you gave him the instructions – he would probably be completely unaware of them when he flipped back."

Dr Skinner made a gesture as though he wanted to interrupt, but changed his mind. Graham Wood and Tom Brookes were looking bored now. All they knew about this was that they didn't need to know anything.

Callan continued: "It could be that he simply had no idea what to do with this damned key he found in his possession. He probably threw it away. He might have handed it in to the hotel, thinking it belonged to someone else."

"We could have that checked out," Dr Skinner said. "We could phone the hotel."

"I doubt if they keep records of people handing keys in to them, Skinner," Osbourne said. "But I think you might be onto something, Callan. Let's assume that it's true that he was in no state to remember verbal instructions and he misplaced the key or threw it away – what can we do about it now?"

"Give him the whole package again in writing," Callan said

"But how?" Osbourne asked. "Mitchell gave him the instructions verbally in Helsinki and we expected him to cooperate. As far as *Snowman* is concerned, nobody else was involved. Dr Skinner wasn't there and he was going to communicate only with Mitchell. So what are we going to do? How are we going to give him the instructions again?"

"Send them through the post anonymously," Callan offered.

"Why would he swallow that?" said Osbourne. "What's the scenario? Did Mitchell send them knowing he was about to…?"

"OK," Callan agreed, "No, that won't do."

Osbourne said, "We need someone who was already involved for this to be credible to him. We've got no one."

Dr Skinner hesitated and then said: "Apart from myself but, as we know, I've not been cleared to see him in any circumstances since the separation event, in case of fusion. So, yes, there's no one suitable."

"There is one other person," Callan stated.

"Who?" Dr Skinner asked. He seemed both surprised and worried.

"Mitchell told me about a girl that he used for errands. He told me he intended to use her to try to keep an eye out – "

"But this is completely irregular! How was he using this girl? Who the hell is she to – "

"I gave him permission. As it turns out, she could be just the person to keep this project on track."

"But, you're hardly authorised to have given per..."

Now Osbourne interrupted: "Please, Dr Skinner, spare us. All is fair in love and war. Let's consider this possibility."

8 - A MEETING IN THE PARK

A week had passed since news of Mitchell's suicide. Since then, Richard hadn't had a lot to do – perhaps Mitchell had been more effective at delegating work than he had been given credit for. This afternoon he sat at his desk watching everyone else work. The integration team were not at their desks. It was Thursday; they must be in the main meeting room. Rayhaan from pre-sales was screwing his face up at his screen. No doubt there was something about his power-point presentation that was causing him some concern. In pre-sales, you had to be careful of exactly what you said, and how you said it.

Richard's thoughts drifted back to Helsinki. That Helsinki trip had been quite a jaunt! He reminded himself of one particularly delightful event. A few days after meeting Mitchell, he had been sitting in the hotel bar minding his own business when some super-nice girl started chatting to him. They ended up getting blind drunk together. He recalled her showing him a tattoo on the top of her thigh, hitching up her skirt so he could read it (which was nice of her). He had a vague memory of rolling around in bed with her shortly afterwards. Unfortunately, he was so drunk he couldn't remember any details. He had no idea if she was good in bed or not, and it was unlikely he had been, the state he was in. "Rolling around in bed" was probably an all-too-accurate description of what they'd done. All he could remember about her was she had long brown hair and green eyes. She had a name like Mandy, or Elaine, or Ella or Maureen, or something. Well, she had some sort of name. Most people do, especially girls. In the morning she was gone before he'd woken up. It was a shame. And it was also a shame he was stuck in London just now. When you were abroad, staying in a hotel and on decent expenses, things like that tended to happen. Well, maybe not quite like that; she really had been something.

Time dragged for Richard. There were only a few other people around, all busy looking at their terminals. There was no one to talk to; they were not exactly transfixed by their terminals, but it was clearly their preferred way of interfacing with reality. Talking to any of them would be considered an annoying distraction. Even those of them that had been emailing him today.

It was time to take another look at today's emails. Nothing special there; the usual stuff about cakes in the kitchen for someone's birthday. Richard knew the cakes were all gone by now. He had one himself just to be sociable, even though he didn't know the person concerned. The core five lift was out of order... Don't use the sales dept printer until further notice...

There was an email from Mitchell.

For half a second, Richard truly believed it was from Mitchell. He opened it with a sense of dread, as though he really was going to be hearing from beyond the grave.

"Meet me at the bandstand in Hyde Park at three p.m. today."

There was nothing else. Just that. It couldn't be Mitchell, of course. It was someone else who had access to his email account. Who could that be? No one else should have access to Mitchell's account. It was almost more likely it was Mitchell.

Richard looked at his phone to check the time – two p.m. He would need to hurry. Scrambling to get his laptop switched off and packed, then wriggling into his coat, he left the building, heading for Bank tube. Bank would be better than Tower Hill, though a longer walk; the Central Line was more reliable than the Circle Line. The Circle Line is often delayed because it's the favourite one to commit suicide on.

Luckily, the tube was running well. Richard made it to Hyde Park Corner in plenty of time. He was waiting at the bandstand by 2:45. *Who am I waiting for?* he wondered.

It got to 3:05. No one had turned up. Richard had eagerly scrutinised every passer-by, trying to build a reason around that particular person; who they were, what their connection to Mitchell was, and why they would want to meet him. The girl in the mini-skirt who smiled at him would've been a particularly happy choice. Too good to be true.

A couple of squat, rough-looking Bulgarians had passed by too, giving his imagination a scenario that was less pleasant to contemplate. Richard told himself to keep a grip on his imagination as they passed him by without incident, spitting out their conversation in guttural tones, completely unaware of Richard and the wild speculation they had caused him.

Quite a lot of people passed by, with Richard's imagination, now suppressed, failing to relieve the boredom of waiting. There were loads of people cycling in London these days. Richard knew he was not brave enough for anything like that. He was not courageous; not physically; most of the time not even mentally. If someone criticised his work as incorrectly documented or badly structured, he would agonise for ages. That was what made him a good techie – fear of doing something wrong – even something trivial.

The girl in the mini-skirt was coming back. She looked vaguely familiar somehow, unless his memory was playing tricks from having noticed her ten minutes ago. She was in her late twenties, quite smartly dressed, with lovely, long blonde hair. Her shoulder bag looked expensive. All her clothes did, in fact. He speculated that perhaps she was Mitchell's daughter. She looked a little too cheerful and rather too well dressed, even glamorous, for that though.

"Hi," she said. " ... Richard?"

"Yes."

"Melanie. I sent the email from Andrew's mobile. I didn't know how else to get in touch."

Richard was still slightly taken aback. In spite of his speculation, he hadn't expected the girl in the mini-skirt to be the one. He couldn't get over the impression that he'd seen her before somewhere.

"Have we met before?" he asked

"Possibly," she said, more shyly than he expected, given her confident demeanour. But she continued without further explanation, "I have something for you. It's from Andrew."

Richard realised the expression of doubt that had clouded the girl's face must be a reflection of his own puzzlement.

"You did know Andrew, didn't you?" she asked.

"Andrew, yes. We called him Mitchell though. Andy Mitchell. I didn't know him all that well; only a few months. He was my boss."

There was a slightly awkward pause.

"So who are you then?" Richard asked.

"I was his girlfriend."

The vague idea they had already met persisted, but it was suppressed by another idea – Richard seemed to remember Mitchell had a wife. Yes, of course he had a wife. Well, it seems he had a girlfriend too. A hell of a girlfriend, in fact.

"You seem quite cheerful for a girlfriend who's just lost her nearest and dearest," Richard said bluntly.

"Ah." Her eyes looked down, showing that she was rather contrite after all. She hesitated a moment and then, after brushing her hand elegantly through her hair, the cheerful look returned to her face and her eyes looked directly up into his. "I was more of a girlfriend *experience*."

"A girl..."

"I work at Aphrodite's Secret." She snapped open her shoulder bag and took out a glossy card. "See," she said, offering the card.

Richard took the card. Out of a vague sense of embarrassment, he didn't look too closely at it, but a brief glance at the shiny black card with gold lettering was enough to let him know what kind of a girlfriend Mitchell had had.

"Anyway, take this too." She handed him a padded envelope. "He told me not to open it, and I haven't. He gave it to me with instructions to pass it on to you if anything happened to him. I had no idea that he had probably already decided to kill himself."

"Thanks." Richard felt slightly abashed. For some reason, it seemed like she had acted with the greatest kindness to give him the envelope. Still unopened, too. In fact, such was the level of altruism she had exhibited, it was Richard's turn to feel contrite;

he suddenly realised she needn't have bothered. He wondered why she had, in fact. Was that suspicious? *Am I being set up?* he wanted to ask.

"So what's in it for you? Why have you – " he blurted out.

She interrupted before he finished asking. "Oh, it's quite simple. When he gave me the envelope, it reminded me that he was pretty much irreplaceable as a customer. He gave me this." She showed him her necklace.

"Very nice." Richard was trying not to make it too obvious that his eyes had decided not to focus on the necklace but to look a little further down the top of her blouse. It wasn't just his eyes that were enjoying themselves; his nose too was enthralled by her scent. No wonder the poor bastard was in debt.

He couldn't get over the impression that he'd seen her before somewhere. "Did you say we've met before?"

"Yes, don't you remember? I had dark hair then. I was staying in a hotel with Andrew and ended up in the cocktail bar being chatted up by some nice gentleman."

Richard was still mystified.

"The Grand Sokos Hotel... I had green eyes too... contacts."

"Oh my god! Oh it's..." Richard was going to say "so nice to see you again", but in the circumstances he wasn't sure if he should.

"Andrew got me to fly over to see him. That was when he gave me this handbag. It's Miu Miu," she explained. "He was always giving me lots of little things like that."

"So you felt obliged to help him out because of that?" Richard asked, returning to the subject of the envelope.

"Not exactly. I decided it would be a good idea because, I thought that, seeing as we got on so well together in Helsinki, I thought maybe if I helped you with the envelope, you would quite likely be interested in seeing more of me."

Richard was surprised but delighted with this idea, but before he could express his delight she added: "As a customer."

9 - A WORD FOR WINTER

Karl Marx was right. In late capitalism, every human relationship would be based on money. Now that the idea was in Richard's head, it was pretty much irresistible. The idea of Melanie, that is, not the idea of Karl Marx being cynically correct.

So it seemed Melanie had simply taken the opportunity to advertise herself to a prime potential customer in return for helping Mitchell. Fair enough. He wondered if he'd paid for her services back in Helsinki. He couldn't remember handing over any money, but then he could hardly remember anything about that night. So maybe that was the explanation, and it hadn't been romantic infatuation after all, which was a shame. But he wouldn't mind seeing her again anyway, even on those terms.

Whatever the case, Melanie would have to wait until later. In fact, she might need to wait until he could afford a Miu Miu bag or two. She seemed to imply she thought he could be as good a customer as Mitchell had been in that respect. Unfortunately for her, that was most unlikely; he had a hard-enough job paying his normal bills, never mind trying to pay for an expensive 'girlfriend'.

Anyway, right now, all he wanted to do was open the envelope.

He watched Melanie walk off, back in the direction of Knightsbridge. For some reason, he wanted to make sure she wouldn't see him opening the envelope. That act was going to be too private. It was possibly even dangerous. By the time he judged she was far enough away, he was itching to get it open and have done with it.

Some burka-clad women were waddling towards him, and skaters suddenly appeared and sped off. He would need to head further into the park, into the trees. There he would be alone. Alone, and therefore vulnerable in a different way.

He began walking further into the centre of the park, looking for a quiet bench. He wanted to be sure no one was watching. He also felt he had to sit down to open the envelope. He was so nervous about it; it was worse than getting exam results. He could feel his heart beating. At last he found a quiet park bench.

The burka-clad women were well in the distance now, being overtaken by some joggers. He sat down. With trembling hands, he ended up accidentally ripping the envelope open so clumsily that it burst apart, sending a flash-drive and a smaller envelope spinning into the air. Fortunately, they were both white and easily visible. He scrabbled to retrieve them, quickly and anxiously checking the ground at his feet to make sure nothing else had dropped out. Nothing had.

He stared at the small envelope, almost as though it was beyond belief. Something that was impossible had finally happened.

The word was clearly marked on the small envelope. The word he had been waiting for. There it was... ZIMA!

"Zima" (in fact, 'зима' in Cyrillic) was Russian for "winter".

It was too good to be true! A wave of relief swept over him, as though he had been trapped, but the trap had sprung open, releasing him. He took a deep breath and let it out slowly. He had never felt such a feeling of elation and freedom. Soon the whole world would be free!

He opened the second envelope, but it was almost as though the second envelope was reversing the spell the first had cast. He was already becoming aware that, in reality, the word Zima had not liberated him; not yet. Instead he would be moving, in some intangible way, into a world of shadows and danger.

But at least he now knew. The sense of anticipation had been replaced by a calmness. Now he knew where he stood. He knew for certain he would need to do everything carefully.

The second envelope contained a key and a message from Mitchell.

"Richard, if you are opening this envelope it is because something has gone wrong for me. I left this message with someone I could trust, so they could pass it on to you. This is a copy of the key to my desk (#31). There you will find the remaining instructions. Too bad that we could not work together on this.

You blanked me in Helsinki. Please, you must proceed now. This is the only chance."

Richard blinked. "Blanked him?" He closed his eyes and tried to remember. For some reason, he put his hand to his forehead and immediately felt stupid and self-conscious about it. He was distracted by the image of himself posing thoughtfully. Suddenly the trees darkening in the distance were the Tulgey Wood in which the Jabberwock lived.

"As in uffish thought he stood."

He couldn't remember. There was nothing. No real memory at all of what had happened in Helsinki. He decided that it could not be important anyway. Everything was clear now; now he knew what he had to do.

All of this had taken years, and had been delayed by months by the misunderstanding or miscommunication, or whatever it was, in Helsinki. Now he could not contain his impatience – he wanted to get hold of those instructions immediately. He had to remind himself he needed to do all of this very carefully, but his thoughts were in turmoil. *What if I go back to the office with the memory stick and someone asks to see what is on it? Is there going to be anything on it or in the instructions that would be explicit or incriminating? If so, is it better to keep them (the memory stick and instructions) separate to reduce the chances that they will incriminate me?*

But the turmoil didn't end there. It swept around him like a maelstrom: *If I have to keep the memory stick and remaining instructions separate, how might I do it?* He weighed his options anxiously. He thought of taking the stick home first, before going back to the office, or putting it in a locker in a train station, or hiding it somewhere in Hyde Park, or even posting it to himself in an envelope.

But he'd waited years for this and didn't want to leave it anywhere until he knew what it contained. Now he had it, he somehow couldn't let go of it, whatever the risk. He was stuck with it, held in its power like Gollum and the One Ring To Rule Them All. It was his "precious".

He would have to go back to the office. Why was he so worried someone there might ask why he'd come back? Returning to the office wasn't such an outlandish thing to do. So what if he was carrying instructions that would sabotage the entire banking system? Why on Earth would anyone ask to see what he was carrying? No matter how incriminating the material was, no one would have any cause to ask to see it. Finally, he succeeded in reassuring himself he might as well go back and get whatever it was out of Mitchell's desk as soon as he could.

***

He was back in the tube, on his way back to the office. It was already building up to rush hour. The tube was busy. Richard held the memory stick in a fist made by his right hand and kept it in his pocket. Whenever he became desensitised to it through familiarity with its shape, he would give a little squeeze to reset his perception of touch. As though, if he didn't, it might really vanish. The idea the whole thing was, in any case, just a dream, also haunted him. Even the preposterous notion some particularly expert pickpocket would be able to steal it from within his grasp nagged him.

He had to do everything else with just his left hand. He kept his Oyster Card in his left-hand pocket so that it would be easy to get through the tube barrier.

10 - FOUR SEASONS
(Glasgow - 1977)

Richard had gone to meet Eddie in the Socialist People's Party bookshop on the top floor of a tenement building in Queen Street. As usual, there was no one there except whoever had volunteered to man the till. Today it was Linda McPherson, who had doomed herself to sit in the store for hours with little prospect of a paying customer.

There wasn't a huge demand for the sort of books stocked by the Socialist People's Party bookshop. They were mainly thin revolutionary pamphlets that preached only to the converted. Or, at the other extreme, academic tomes probably only read by the writer and his publisher.

Once, Richard's attention had been caught by one of these mighty works, bound in three hefty volumes – *A Revolution Betrayed: The History of the Soviet Union from 1917 to 1956.* He imagined it might be interesting to read this to get an insight, from a non-capitalist viewpoint, of what had gone wrong, and understand what had gone right. But after struggling through two pages of academic sociology-based language, Richard had slotted the book back where it belonged – to gather dust on the top shelf.

As usual, Eddie was dressed in the uniform of the party: a black donkey jacket and dark blue jeans. His thinning black hair was combed tight onto his scalp. His eyes blazed angrily through thick-rimmed black glasses. In his own mind, he had earnestly avoided following any of the current fashions. In doing so, he had spectacularly failed to avoid the fashion peculiar to the Socialist People's Party.

He went to open the back room and found it was locked.

"Hey Linda, we need tuh get through ra back."

Linda, in her guise as a post-feminist punk dominatrix, condescendingly unlocked the door to the back room to allow them through. She was in charge today. She scowled at them through her thick, dark make-up.

"Next time let me know when you want tae use that room," she said in a voice that could curdle milk.

"Sorry Linda. You know ra both ay us anyway," said Eddie.

Linda didn't think this worthy of a reply. She simply resumed her task for today of looking bored, sitting with her legs daintily crossed, on a chair next to the till. She flicked open a paperback novel and directed her bored attention to its pages.

Eddie ushered Richard into the room and locked the door behind them.

They sat down side by side at a table in the centre of the room. Eddie seemed very tense, as though it was he, not Richard, who was about to commit to this.

"Nice posters," said Richard. There were no windows in this room. On the far wall there was a row of four Soviet posters, depicting winter, spring, summer and autumn. Each poster had the name of the season in Cyrillic at the top and a transliteration in English letters at the bottom. They were evidently printed for tourists, though there was hardly such a thing as a Western tourist in the USSR at that time. When visiting the Soviet Union, Western visitors had to go via an official route as civil servants, trade unionists, in school parties, or some other form of official delegation. Individual tourists were a rare species.

"Archie brought thum back. He loves his hoalidays in Russia."

"He told me all about it. He even told me about the posters. He was dead chuffed with them."

"Yup. He likes his Russian culture."

"I guess it's harmless enough."

"Yeah."

The way Eddie said it reminded Richard that Eddie knew there was considerable doubt in his, Richard's, mind about the USSR and how harmless it was. In itself, that wasn't a great betrayal. There was doubt about the USSR in the minds of most people in the People's Party. The old-timers like Archie still hadn't shaken off their pro-Soviet tendencies, but many of the younger guys looked to China as the main hope of a socialist future. Some of them, like Richard and Stuart, didn't like any of the current examples of socialism.

"Must be terribly expensive to travel there though."

"Contacts via ra unions. It's all organised by his union. It's dirt cheap, apparently."

"Probably subsidised by someone." Richard didn't hide a slightly sneering tone in the word "subsidised". What was he, he asked himself. Some sort of "perfect market" apologist? Was it wrong for committed Party members to be subsidised? Especially when they were going on a high-minded cultural exchange to see one of the few working examples of a supposedly socialist country.

Richard felt embarrassed. He wondered if Eddie had noticed his sneering tone. To his dismay he realised he probably had, because Eddie was looking sideways at him; what he was saying amounted to a defence of Archie: "He has to go to a lot ay seminars while he's there, cuz it's supposed tae be an official visit, but he loves rat kinda hing anyhow."

"Not my idea of fun though." Richard winced to hear himself. Now why had he blurted *that* out? A lot of the stuff the activists did wasn't fun. It was to do with attending long, boring meetings; committee work. They didn't rush around doing exciting stuff. They didn't try to assassinate anyone or commit terrorist acts, but they were quite convinced that passing resolutions at their meetings would eventually lead to international socialism, to fairness and equality. Richard didn't mean to criticise this, only he wanted to short circuit it. He wanted something more direct. Something truly revolutionary.

"Anyway, wur here fur a purpose, Richard. You sure about this by ra way?"

Richard was aware that some of the Party members, including Eddie, doubted his sincerity. He was thankful that Stuart had vouched for him and convinced Eddie to take his plan seriously. Their first meeting to discuss things had gone well. This was the final hurdle. All he had to do now was avoid hesitation. Deep down he knew he was more committed and had clearer ideas about his objectives than any of the others, even Eddie.

"Dead sure. I don't need any more discussion about it."

"OK. We've been told what we need fur codes. We need things that you'll remember in any context, mibby years frae now. Things that will stick out but no' too much."

"OK. I know that already from the last meeting."

"You'll write them down, and stick rum in this envelope, but don't let me see rum. I'm no involved. I'm just goanie pass ruh envelope oan. As we discussed before, ruh first contact might be quite tricky. Someone just turning up out ay ra blue one day..."

"OK. So..." Richard wanted to check again if this was OK. "I need to be quite sure of one thing: that no one will know me personally. They'll know me only as a set of code words that matches a person who's going to identify himself and his location once a year (or no more than four times a year if things change quickly). I have to do this via a specific type of advert in a specific newspaper, as we discussed. This means a handler can locate me and then can identify himself to me using the first code word, or code phrase."

Eddie nodded, "Yes, that's the deal. Happy with that?"

"Everything seems OK to me. I only have your word that you're not going to look at the codes though."

"You don't need tuh worry about me, I canny do anything with the codes."

Richard was agitated. "But how..."

"Listen, whit mair can ah do? For whit it's worth, you can have mah word if you want it. You huv the word ae Eddie MacFarlane, the guy that's nivvur let anybuddy in the Party down." Eddie looked angrily at Richard.

"OK, Eddie, it's fine. This is a bit more stressful than I expected."

"Your handler won't have anything tae identify you by except these codes. And no one else will know them." Eddie seemed to be trying to say it in a reassuring way.

"I don't want to leave a trace of who I am."

"That's already agreed. Ah think ris wull work out just fine. The codes for the first contact just need to be quite exact so rut, wance we've goat a use fur ye, we assign a handler. He gets ra code words and then gets in touch with ye."

"It's all good Eddie."

"Ruh hing is, you may never hear frae anyone. This all depends on you getting into some sort ae position where yu're goannae be useful. It also depends on you no aborting when yu're coantacted." Eddie paused. He wasn't sure if he was allowed to say this but he was going to anyway. "By ruh way if you want tae abort fur ideological reasons dae it now, right? I don't want tae be part ay a complete waste ay time."

"No problem, Eddie. I don't know why you doubt me. I trust the Party. I'm in agreement with its overall objectives. As far as I'm concerned, aborting is only for operational reasons – if there's an obstacle. We can suspend and resume if we have doubts and only abort if we know for sure there's an insurmountable problem. We discussed it all in detail back at your place. We went through lots of different scenarios. We even did some role play exercises, as you know."

"Remember, frae now oan yu're no going tae be dealing wi' pals. There's gonnae be no Stuart, no Eddie, no naebuddy tae help frae now oan. I know ruh guy that I'm handing this envelope tae, but I don't know what kind of person or group that it goes tae efter rat. We have tae trust that it's someone competent."

"I'm sure it will be. I've never met anyone in the Party that was a fool." He hesitated and then decided he'd better say it. "One thing though, Eddie. As you know, I'm not interested in marches or any of that sort of agitprop shite. I want this to be something real. If I'm going to do anything, I want it to be something significant. I don't want to find that my mission is to unplug the photocopier or put some scratch marks on the boss's car."

"Fur this idea of yours to work, we have to hope that you end up somewhere useful."

"That's not looking too good at the moment. I might need to try to change the course of my degree a bit. Accountancy would be good but I don't fancy it. I might have to add in a bit more Economics."

"Ah wish ah could just casually say stuff like that. I struggled tae get a few O levels."

"Well, I'm not saying it will be easy, but I need to find something that gets me somewhere."

"Ah'm still worried. As soon as you get a decent job as an accountant, or whatever, you'll be wan ay 'them' – the bosses. You'll be driving around in a fancy car waving two fingers at yur old coamrades." Eddie's face was already starting to twist in anger at the thought.

"It's not like that at all, Eddie. This is more important than making a few quid for myself. I want to see a new kind of society. If an advanced country like Britain can give a lead, the world will follow. It will transform the lives of millions of people. The way society's organised just now, money and status are intertwined. In the society we want, the link will be broken. Do you see what I'm saying? Money ..." he gave a grunt of disgust. He'd said stuff like this before anyway. He didn't need to finish his sentence. Eddie knew what he meant.

"Right, OK, let's get oan wi' it. So this is what you need tae do. This is the list ay actions that need codes." Eddie pushed a form towards Richard. "You already have this list from our last meet. I'll go out tae ruh bookstore and leave you tae write codes that correspond to each of these actions. When yu're done, droap it aw in ruh envelope here and I'll come back in and get it. Take yur time. Yu've got aw day. I'm just going to go outside and chat to Linda while you get ruh codes written."

Eddie went back out to the bookshop and left him to it.

Richard already knew his words. Four of them were right there on the wall in front of him: Zima, Vesna, Leyta, Ocyen. He needed something memorable and knew this would work. For identification, he needed phrases that would jump out. Hopefully the ones he had decided on were ones that he could remember no matter what, but anyone else (who overheard by accident) would presume to be just some sort of literary quote. He took out his copy of the codes that he'd decided on and copied them neatly onto Eddie's form:

Identify handler: *When the stranger returns you must wake up.*

Discuss: *You will remember me again when we meet one day, though we have not met.*

Identify operation: *Zima* (Winter)

Suspend: *Vesna* (Spring)

Resume: *Leyta* (Summer)

Abort: *Ocyen* (Autumn)

He read them all one last time. He was happy enough. He folded the form neatly, put it in the envelope and sealed it. He stuffed his own copy back into his pocket. He would burn it later.

11 - FOCUSSED

He was a young man then. Now what was he? Nearly sixty! His life had gone past like a dream. He'd got into IT, then banking software. He had never settled down anywhere.

More years had passed than he had expected. He felt like one of those Japanese soldiers hidden in the jungle from the forties until the seventies, not realising WWII was over – except this war, the Class War, was not over. It hadn't even started. The memory of choosing all those code words had faded to a blur. It all seemed not quite real any more. The codes themselves were firmly imprinted in his mind, even though, for many years, he had given up on ever hearing them. He even wondered if they had been totally serious at the time. Well, they must've been, because here he was: about to take the biggest risk of his life to put their plan into action.

In fact, he hadn't climbed very far up the ladder to a position of any particular power. He hadn't climbed to the dizzy heights he might have imagined as a student. Even Stuart's progress had been greater – university lecturer, or whatever he was. That part of the plan had been a complete failure. In the end it was just luck that had put him into an IT job in the banking industry, where he believed he could carry out his plan. Where he was now, he was too lowly to attract much attention, but he had real opportunities to do damage – he was trusted to deploy software for an important private bank. If only the Party realised what they could do with him, and if only they had the right resources to exploit the opportunity. He had access to a weak point in the banking system. He could deploy software that could sabotage an important private bank. He could deliver a psychological blow that would spread uncertainty and panic among some of the richest and most powerful people in Europe.

He'd almost given up on getting anything from the Party when now, at last, it had become obvious that the financial system, still recovering slowly and painfully from the financial crisis of 2008, would not survive a further shock. At last they had sent him the package he'd been hoping for.

He'd lost touch with Stuart and Eddie years ago. Of course, losing touch was part of the deal. The last he'd seen of Eddie was an angry face, mouth wide open, shouting. Eddie's enraged face shouted out of a photo in the *Evening Times*. That was Eddie: he had a short fuse. The accompanying story was that he, and several others, had been arrested on a demo in support of the miners during the miners' strike in the eighties. The strike had failed. After that, the old-style socialism that Richard had grown up with, but never really believed in, had died worldwide.

Richard could remember the photo of Eddie almost as though it was projected into space in front of him. The furious anger of his face shouting out of the newspaper was iconic of those times. So many of the activists back then were angry young men. Angry, but not well focussed. Richard speculated that, deep down, Eddie wasn't motivated by a desire to change society; he merely wanted to exorcise his own demons. Give vent to his fury at the world.

But Eddie was never more calm than he was that day when Richard handed the codes to him. That day they had both been focussed on achieving something.

12 - A REAL CAMPAIGNER

To begin with, Eddie had been shocked Richard had come up with this plan. He was also somewhat suspicious of his motives. Eddie sometimes doubted if Richard was even a socialist of any sort. Stuart had vouched for him, though, and Stuart knew him better than anyone. Stuart was rock solid. A real campaigner.

So Eddie had decided it would at least be worth discussing the plan.

After the discussion back at his flat, Eddie had been quite convinced that Richard was genuine and capable too. That was why he'd gone to the trouble of getting in touch with contacts that could make it happen. After the final meeting, he'd begun to have doubts again. But it was too late by then.

It hadn't been too late at the moment Richard handed him the envelope. At that moment, all he had to do was nothing. Richard would never know he'd sabotaged the plan. But even though Eddie had his doubts, on balance he thought it was worth the risk of going through with it. His own personal risk was very limited. So he handed the envelope over. Before he did, Eddie did something to ensure that, even though Richard would have no idea who his handler was, at least his handler would know Richard. He slipped a photo into the envelope.

Eddie had noticed something about Richard – he didn't quite seem to live in the real world. He talked about things as though they were academic or theoretical. Maybe that's why he was so calm when they were sorting out the code words. Maybe the reality of the situation was hidden inside a whole abstract fantasy.

Eddie didn't live in any fantasy world. He'd had a tough upbringing. He lived in a rough part of Glasgow. He knew every time they went on a march or handed out leaflets, there was likely to be someone who wanted to give them a good kicking. He also knew that what could happen to Richard might be a damned sight worse than taking a kicking from a few fascists.

13 - INSTRUCTIONS

Though it was not yet five p.m. it was already quiet in the office. Most of them would leave early to try to beat the rush, or go for a drink so that the rush hour had died down before they actually set off home. The rush 'hour' in London starts around four p.m. and goes on until around seven p.m.

As Richard opened Mitchell's drawer, he was aware Jim Callan was approaching down the corridor of the open-plan office. His heart sank. Should he close the drawer quickly? A brown envelope was the one and only thing in there. Should he try to pick it up before Callan saw him? It was too late for that. In any case, he was only looking into a drawer, for Christ's sake, not stealing the Crown jewels. Just keep calm.

Jim Callan was not someone who would just come and casually talk to you. He would always plant himself strategically before you and puff himself up a bit before starting a conversation. He did that now.

"I thought that was Mitchell's drawer."

"Don't know. It's a hot-desk. I had the keys."

Callan eyed Richard malevolently. Whatever he did, Callan always did it confrontationally. There was a long, intense silence as though Callan was a judge in a reality cookery contest and was about to vote Richard out.

"The hot-desks are over there." He pointed to the area behind reception, near the managers' glass cubicles and the break-out room.

"I guess they moved them. I was given this one ages ago. Maybe they did it by mistake," Richard offered.

"What you need it for anyway?"

"I kept some tax forms and things here for safe-keeping while I was away in Moscow."

Callan paused again, preparing to escalate the level of confrontation. But this time he seemed to realise it was none of his business anyway. He relaxed slightly, perhaps to catch Richard off-guard.

"How was Moscow?"

"Expensive. Painfully expensive. The per diems barely covered our food. We were all teetotallers by the time we were done."

Callan allowed himself a little smile at this. All the consultants drank like fishes when they were away from home. "I mean how did the project go?"

"Not bad. The project's still ongoing but they're into phase three now. I'm back in the UK for a bit."

"What's next for you?"

"Nothing next as yet. I'm still at Oldhams, for a good while."

"Did you know that project will be finishing up soon?"

"No?" Richard's heart missed a beat. If he was moved on from Oldhams, what was the point in having the memory stick?

"Be careful." Callan looked pointedly at him.

Richard felt an involuntary spasm in his cheek. He wasn't very good at this, he realised.

"There are a few redundancies coming up. Consultants need to be chargeable."

"Don't worry, I know that."

With that, Callan decided to withdraw. Richard watched him move slowly and purposefully back up the corridor and re-enter his frosted glass cubicle. Callan was another of those on-contract project managers that rarely made an appearance in the office and seemed to have the vaguest workload. For some reason, Richard didn't like him. He waited until he was sure Callan was settled into his cubicle before quickly picking up the envelope. Then he went down the service elevator at the back of the building to avoid having to pass Callan's office.

Christ! If I'm made redundant, the plan's over, he thought.

14 - THE BRIDGE

People swarmed towards Richard and bustled past. Most of the swarm was heading south, as he was, pouring out of the City, streaming across London Bridge and disappearing into the station named after it. But some of the most agitated and determined ones were, for some reason, going against the flow.

A seagull swept through the air, holding its wings out rigidly to be carried by the wind. Richard imagined what the seagull, looking down, would think of the human folly it observed.

And suddenly Richard too was high above it all, looking down on himself and seeing his stupid mistake with chilling clarity.

He was trapped. He could see the bridge spanning the Thames from north to south and the river itself beneath, running west to east. He could see himself, by now halfway across, being carried along with the flow of humanity – just another anonymous member of the multitude on the left-hand pavement, busily progressing to the South Bank. To his right, traffic flowed freely in each direction, and on the far right-hand side other members of the agitated nest bustled past each other.

His attention focussed on the person he knew to be himself. He could see through this person's coat and into the pocket where the memory stick was clutched in his fist.

What if someone accidentally jostled him? What if a pickpocket decided that he was an easy target?

What if the members of the swarm, still blandly unaware of intentions, somehow sensed the threat to their hive and turned him?

He would lose a memory stick that was worth around a fiver, but was irreplaceable. He would lose his chance to change the course of history.

He saw the melee developing. From above he watched the swarm converging on him. Then, looking through his own eyes, faces full of fury. But that was from a future which, although it was foreseen, had not yet happened.

And then he felt a twinge of guilt. These were people, not members of a hive or nest. These were the very people he intended to destroy. Wealthy bankers, City workers, spoilt middle-class Londoners with pleasant jobs that all relied on financial services.

In his guilt he realised they would be justified in turning on him. It wasn't likely; nevertheless he tried to think of a way of escape. But of course, there was no way of escape. He began to realise he was no more trapped here on the bridge than anywhere else. He would be vulnerable wherever he went. He just had to get home as soon as possible.

All he had to do was get himself, his laptop bag containing both envelopes, and the memory stick in his pocket, back home. But it wasn't easy when every passer-by might somehow realise you were a ticking time bomb.

And then a surge of rage boiled up within him. It wasn't easy when you gave in to feelings of guilt. He gripped the memory stick 'l he felt it would cut into his hand. These were the very people 'om guilt or pity was wasted. They had to be destroyed for 'l of humanity.

15 - DREAMS

' into a seat on the Jubilee Line. The train was
taken him several stops since getting on at
ition himself to obtain such a prize. He had
wes to outsmart any of his competitors in
ical chairs.

Things like that gave your life a false sense of purpose. London was very good at giving you a general sense there was a buzz around and you were involved in its excitement. It gave you opportunity to think you had accomplished something. In fact, all it had to offer was illusory nonsense. Years could go past before you realised your life was actually empty.

But who said life had to have any meaning? Well, now, it did have meaning.

Today he was on the Jubilee Line because he had decided to walk from the office across to London Bridge tube station, as he sometimes did, hoping the walk would relax him. But it hadn't helped at all; instead he had felt an increasing sense of panic and paranoia while walking through the crowds of people, that someone, perhaps everyone, knew what he was up to. Slumping into his seat, and giving the memory stick another squeeze to make sure it was still there, Richard finally began to relax a little.

A lot had happened in the years since he was an activist. Everything had changed. He wondered if he still wanted to go through with it. Of course he did. Things were worse than ever nowadays. The attempts that capitalism had made to save itself had proved futile.

Capitalism was failing to satisfy the advertising-induced greed of developed countries. Nevertheless, it was claiming itself to be successful. Successful in raising the living standards of poorer nations. This process had been given the label of "globalisation".

Successful? The world population was projected to peak at fifteen billion. Imagine fifteen billion people trying to live in the style of the USA! It would not be physically possible for the planet to provide the raw materials. It was doomed to failure. Catastrophic failure.

Meanwhile, the banking and financial systems, perhaps in combination with IT, were concentrating wealth and power into the hands of fewer and fewer people worldwide. The funny thing was that, because of taxation, this wealthy elite actually felt they were supporting the rest of the population, instead of it being the other way around. The wealthy elite were now so wealthy compared with the rest that they paid a significant percentage of total taxation, and therefore believed they supported, rather than exploited, the masses. They seemed to have overlooked the fact that the cause of this was the masses not being paid enough due to their exploitation.

Eventually, there must be a breaking point. Either the elite would break away from the rest of the population, deliberately using social spending and welfare as a means of suppressing them, or there would be revolution. That, he reminded himself, was why he was not a Social Democrat. Welfare abuse was their raison d'être.

He was no longer an activist either. He had been sleeping. In fact, Richard was a card-carrying member of the Conservative party. His reasoning was that since capitalism would destroy itself through its internal contradictions, he should help it along as much as possible. It was like being an actual socialist without the hypocrisy, he reasoned. Or, actually, it was like being a capitalist – with both hypocrisy and irony.

"Stanmore!" a woman's voice joyously exclaimed, waking Richard from his daydream.

"This train terminates at Stanmore," the invisible woman continued.

The breathless glee with which she said the word "Stanmore" led Richard to assume it was one of her favourite places and she was very much looking forward to going back there. The Jubilee Line had an invisible woman to tell you what stations you were at, or were approaching. Soon the invisible woman breathlessly cried out "Baker Street".

He was there. Baker Street. Almost home and safe to take a look at what he had.

"MIND… THE GHYEP!" a stern male voice boomed out from the walls of the station repeatedly as Richard pushed his way out of the carriage onto the bustling platform. The robot man warning everyone to "mind the gap" had obviously been educated in Eton or some such place. The calm, robotic repetition of this advice conflicted with the chaotic flurry of the crowds of people who gave no indication they were minding any gaps whatsoever.

During every tube journey, commuters were accompanied by invisible people offering all sorts of advice and warnings. The Jubilee Line woman was particularly posh and enthusiastic. Other lines had imaginary people of different temperaments or social backgrounds (the woman on the Docklands Light Railway serving Canary Wharf was surprisingly common compared with her customers).

Advertising vied for your attention too. There was a bombardment of excitement, beauty, witty advice, things to do, places to go. Your brain had to process visual information where what was real mingled with images from TV screens and posters, and auditory information where real people were shouted down by electronic people who had more important things to say.

In the shiny, synthetic, Brave New World of the near future, real and imaginary lives would become difficult to separate. People already existed as avatars; there was already a *Sim World* where people were becoming real millionaires for activities they undertook in an imaginary, computerised existence. Bitcoins too were accepted as a genuine currency and were increasing in value (though the Chinese had recently put a slight dent in that value). There was the Twitter-sphere. There was the whole Facebooking world of bullshit friendship. Richard himself had more than a hundred Facebook friends, though the only people he knew well enough to drink with were a handful of work colleagues.

In the near future, dreams, reality and simulation would intermingle freely (and all that before we even start to 'experiment' with drugs). What was to become of actual freedom? How would anyone know if they were really doing what they thought they were? How would people know if they really wanted to do the things they did or were guided by companies trying to make them behave in some way that would be beneficial to company objectives? People primarily existed as consumers to sell to, not as individuals or members of society.

Richard stepped through the heavy, darkly lustrous rosewood doors at the entrance of his apartment block, and then traversed a greying black and white marble floor. He pulled a manually operated lever to open the gold-coloured trellis doors of the lift and took the gracefully slow journey to the second floor. The lift travelled upwards inside a dusty, gold-coloured cage within a quarter-turn staircase. The solid wooden balustrade of the staircase was still polished like new; shiny and smooth to the touch. He was lucky to be able to afford to live here. VirtuBank paid well.

VirtuBank paid well, but not so well that Richard could live in the style for which the building had originally been designed. Richard liked to use the lift, though it was old and slow, so he wasn't reminded that, though they had once been sumptuous, the carpets of the staircase were threadbare. The solid wooden balustrade was pitted and scored. In places it was patched with sections of mismatching wood. The elegant, family-sized apartments had long since been butchered – downsized, downgraded, divided up and converted into studios or one-bedroom flats. Each of the resulting dwelling places had been separated off from its neighbour by flimsy partition walls.

He entered his shabby, one-bed apartment. Here, all trace of the building's original magnificence had been erased. Here, it was obvious that it was worn out, dirty and even disgusting. If it wasn't for the memory it had been a five-minute walk from Baker Street and the entrance hall had made some effort at keeping up appearances, you might presume you were in a slum.

He stepped over a fresh scattering of junk mail and bills. He could collect that together later and add it to his growing pile of uninteresting, unopened mail. Right now he was eager to find out what he had.

16 - NIGHTMARE

It turned out that what he had was a password to the folders on the memory stick. What he had on the stick was some software and detailed instructions for its deployment.

Using his laptop, Richard began studying the instructions carefully. It looked like a good job, as though it had all been written to VirtuBank standards using their templates. All the correct documentation was there. They had also carefully imitated the Chennai English of VirtuBank's own developers. There was a covering letter:

> *"Kindly find attached software patch PRX20-INT-101. This is a priority stand-alone patch with no dependencies. It fixes internally discovered software issue INT-101. Install immediately. Kindly requesting to carefully follow all below mentioned instructions and attachments, having firstly read through them, further to standard practices.*
>
> *... etc. etc...*
>
> *...in case of doubts kindly revert."*

He paused to think. It was clever that they had made it seem like it fixed an internal issue and not any issue the bank had discovered. "Priority" and "stand-alone" sounded good too. Fewer questions for the bank's testing team to ask.

So, it seemed they had finally understood what he would be capable of doing – Operation Zima was what he had hoped for. He would have to install this software, which would harm the bank somehow. But was that good enough? His intention all along was to trigger revolution and destroy capitalism. Was Oldhams quite as important as that? Of course, it was his own enthusiastic messages that had signalled to them it was, but perhaps he had been over-optimistic. Now the software was right here on this USB stick, things felt different. He wasn't prepared to risk his neck just to cause some inconvenience to one medium-sized bank, albeit a private bank that held the assets of some very wealthy people. Then again, whatever this was going to do, he had no one to complain to, or seek confirmation from. Mitchell was dead. He could send a message asking for help, but the message cycle took months. In any case, help had never been part of the plan.

Why on earth did they need him anyway? he wondered. The instructions didn't explain any of that. He was annoyed at how little the instructions explained. He had been left to guess at what was going on.

But then he decided he was just making excuses to himself. Now that the plan was a reality, it was suddenly more frightening than he had anticipated. He continued to read carefully. When at last he turned to the final page of instructions, something caused him to frown.

At the bottom of the page in bold, enclosed in a red text box, was an advert for water-damaged rugs. Above the box was a note in large, bold text:

"Publish this advert in the usual way. Do not wait for the next date in the cycle. Publish immediately, with no alterations."

Why would he have to do that? And did they expect him to copy this into the paper without even knowing what it said?

He spent thirty minutes decrypting the message hidden in the advert. It read:

"Continuing with plan as stated. Contact now only required if Ocyen or Vesna."

He sat back and stared in disbelief at what he had decrypted. There should be no need for this message. What was going on? What on earth was this supposed to achieve?

Above all, why would Mitchell ask him to use code words, albeit encrypted, in his message? Perhaps it would be safer, now that he had the software, and now that Mitchell was dead, not to send any more messages at all?

But he had no choice. It was an instruction from his handler. He had to follow whatever instructions he was given. He logged in to his *Evening Times* account and bought a full-page advert for water-damaged rugs, for sale to trade only.

***

Richard remembered Eddie's prophetic words. He hoped they weren't true:

"The thing is, push comes to shove, you won't have the bottle, Richard. It won't be as easy as you think."

He was back in Eddie's kitchen. Back breathing in the smell of chip fat, hearing the bittersweet jingle of a distant ice cream van making its way through the Council Scheme. Just Eddie and him, sitting on greasy wooden chairs either side of a small, fold-down table. It was the first meeting to discuss his plan.

He cringed to remember his lame, though sincere, reply:

"What about when we threw the newspapers in the river?"

"Oh sure, that was you. It was all your idea. But that was just opportunistic. If I remember right, you were a bit drunk, staggering down the road with yer pals when suddenly the opportunity presented itself. One in the morning, big pile of *Telegraphs*, no one around but us."

"Fair enough. It's just an example."

"Here's ruh hing. What effect did it huv? No effect oan anythin'. Even if you'd stoapped the entire production of the *Telegraph* fur ivvur, what effect would that huv? Some sort ae sabotage is not goannie help us. Society's stroanger ran nat."

"I don't agree. There's a thin skin of civilisation. Scratch the surface and things get ugly. Take me for example. You always say that I'm pretty middle-class, and you're right. But the thing is, I'm not happy. The thing is, there are thousands, maybe millions, of people like me. If someone could trigger something... get the people to wake up... who knows what could happen?"

***

He had to be careful. This was all about detail. He checked everything again. The software pack really did look as though it had come from the dev team in Chennai. No difference at all, unless maybe the sequence numbers weren't genuine?

Well they wouldn't be unless they had managed to get fully qualified and capable programmers into Chennai.

There were probably other details that looked correct at first glance but would be fake.

If this pack was referred back to VirtuBank's team in Chennai to be double-checked, it would be obvious it was fake.

His task would be to get this into the bank and ensure it didn't get detected during testing or documentation and referred back for any reason.

The first problem was the software had to just turn up on-site and get installed. It wasn't a download from the patch site. It bypassed that whole system and he needed a cunning excuse to have it accepted on-site. The first thing he would have to do was come up with that excuse.

17 - TRADE ONLY

Every year, Richard put a large advert in the local newspaper back in Glasgow. The advert was designed so that as few people as possible would be interested: fire-damaged goods; water-damaged furniture; second-hand (and obsolete) electronic goods. For sale to trade only. He put his own phone number as the contact. If anyone did happen to be interested in the advert and rang him, he would apologise and explain that someone had already agreed to buy the whole lot. He never had to apologise to very many disappointed customers.

The adverts were placed on one of these days – January 25th, April 25th, July 25th, October 25th – so they would be easy to track. The method of passing messages was very simple. Richard could write anything he wanted to make the advert look genuine. The messages hidden there were decoded using serial numbers that were part of the advert itself. Therefore, so long as he had all the letters of the alphabet somewhere in the wording, he could send any message just by "pointing" at the letters using his serial numbers. It was that simple in principle. The serial numbers printed on the advert had to be transformed using a mapping algorithm, but it was still a simple technique. It would be easy for an expert to decode. But why would anyone ever suspect these adverts were not genuine? They would surely never come to the attention of any decoding expert.

Starting on July the previous year, he had put adverts in on every possible day. The more often he placed the adverts, the more paranoid he was that he would expose himself. Nevertheless, he was really convinced he was in the right place at the right time by now, and he was surprised no one had reacted yet. His messages had become ever more urgent. His last message read: *"Still at VirtuBank. Opportunities with access to main servers at several major financial customers."* His full contact details were there as usual.

He had checked his coding and decoding again and again, wondering if he had made a mistake, so convinced was he that he should have been contacted this time. There was no mistake. He had posted that last message to the paper three months ago but had still been ignored. He had expected an immediate response.

Every time this had happened, he had gone through the same feelings. Elation in placing his advert. Anticipation while waiting for a reply. Disappointment that, yet again, nothing had happened. Each time the disappointment was more numbing, the possibility of ever doing anything more remote.

This time he had been so disappointed that he had not bothered to repeat his message on 25th October, 2013. Yet that was the time when they finally reacted.

18 - RISK ANALYSIS

Richard remembered, sometime in the mid-eighties, walking up and down the rows of gravestones looking for his father's headstone one sunny day in the hills near Milngavie. His dad had died suddenly, of a heart attack. Richard was on holiday in France when it happened. No one had managed to contact him, and the funeral had to go ahead without him. He flew up from London as soon as he could and found the stone where he laid flowers a few years previously. Now both his parents' names were inscribed.

There was something funny about how death always seemed to take you by surprise. Death was inevitable, but every time it happened it was shocking.

His father had been the last living link to Uncle Bobby, the first real socialist he'd ever heard of.

They were all socialists, of a sort, of course, everyone on that side of the family. Family, friends, neighbours. Almost everyone in and around Glasgow was. The industrialised Central Belt of Scotland, blackened and scarred by heavy industry, had fought back to produce people who wanted to create a cleaner, brighter future – Keir Hardie, Manny Shinwell, Uncle Bobby.

They had all hoped that socialism would be the answer, apart from his dad that is, but their efforts had been absorbed by democracy or deflected by the establishment or blocked by the law. Actually, Richard never knew if his father was a socialist or not. Richard assumed he wasn't, somehow. He seemed very sceptical of socialism. He was also ambitious. He had got a better job and taken the family down south for a few years until they returned to Glasgow after Richard's maternal grandmother died.

Stories of Uncle Bobby – in fact his Great Uncle Bobby – were legendary in the family. But Uncle Bobby, for all his good intentions, had ended up dying in prison. An unknown failure.

Richard didn't want to fail. He wanted to avenge the memory out of principle.

He went through the software instructions again and again. He had to be sure this was for real and could be done. He wondered why he had been so slow to realise Mitchell was telling him to wake up. His failure to react must have made Mitchell uncertain of his intentions, which would explain why he had not gone straight on to give him the operational instructions. Unless he had done that too, and those instructions had been waiting in his drawer ever since Helsinki. That might explain why, this time, he had not disguised the word "Zima" in any way that made the message ambiguous.

Richard felt such a fool for not reacting immediately – when Mitchell might have helped or given him more information. Now, whatever he had to do, he would have to do by himself, totally alone.

For some reason he couldn't control his doubts. He didn't like the idea of doing this with no help and no clear instructions. Furthermore, such a lot had changed since this whole idea started, back in the seventies. Technology, politics, everything. Would this operation still be relevant? Was deploying this piece of software his only task? What would it achieve? Would it be something destructive enough? Would it be worth the risk?

19 - AN UNEXPECTED VISITOR

The doorbell rang. It was a loud shrill ring that made Richard jump. Not now! Why would the bell ring now? In three years of staying at the apartment in Glentworth Street, he had never heard the doorbell ring. He had never had a visitor. Why on earth was someone ringing the doorbell right now, at the very moment Operation Zima was initiated?

He hesitated, wondering if he should answer or not. The memory stick, the instructions spread out all over his desk, his home computer, switched on and still showing the PDF of the Chennai team's covering letter. It was all evidence and all incriminating. With trembling hands, he grappled to clear it all away.

The doorbell insisted on ringing. The fact it kept ringing was all the more suspicious and worrying. Had he been set up? Were the police already there to question him? Or, if not the police, who?

He felt his heart thumping. His mind was racing. What really happened to Mitchell? He didn't seem to be the suicide type. Perhaps he was pushed under the train? This person ringing the bell...?

For Christ's sake, get a grip!

It took him a minute or two, but everything was tidied away at last. The bell was still ringing every now and then, but Richard still didn't want to answer. He wanted to get away from the flat, but there wasn't a practical exit apart from the front door. He could sneak out the kitchen window onto the emergency exit. He considered that for a moment. What if he just didn't answer?

The damned bell shrieked at him again. Finally he gave up. He decided it would be better to see who it was. Anyone that persistent would keep trying, and it would better to meet them at the front door rather than clambering down the fire exit.

He pressed the intercom.

"Who is it?"

"Zima."

The reply startled Richard. This was not on! No one knew; no one should know!

"Mister Zima? I don't know you. You have the wrong apartment."

"No, Mr Slater, I am not Mr Zima. I am Mr Weber. I need to talk to you about Zima."

"I don't know what you mean."

"Please, Mr Slater, I do not wish to intrude. Meet me in five minutes in the café on the corner of Melcome Street and Baker Street."

Richard felt a wave of relief and gratitude sweep over him. At least the stranger was not trying to get into the flat.

"OK. In five minutes. I think there is some mistake though. I don't know you."

"You will remember me again when we meet one day, though we have not met."

Those words! Those words were quite exact – exactly like the second cipher Richard was supposed to remember. But Richard already knew there was something wrong. The ciphers were supposed to be delivered in order: Identification; Instructions; then possibly Discuss or Suspend, Resume or Abort. He was relieved he did not have to invite the stranger into the apartment, but still it meant he had to go out, leaving all the stuff he had just acquired inside the apartment. What if the person ringing the bell was trying to lure him outside so someone else could search the flat?

The memory stick was still lying on the desk! He snatched it up and dashed around in an almost comical hurry, trying to think of a good hiding place. What about inside the coffee jar? That would have to do. He poked it down into the middle of a half-full jar of instant coffee. The paperwork went into the middle of a pile of other paperwork and then he headed out to the café.

20 - WEBER

"Klaus Weber."

"Richard Slater. Pleased to meet you."

Weber took a sip of his coffee before replying, as though he needed the time to consider his response.

"Well, I'm glad that you say you're pleased. Though I don't believe you. In fact, neither of us believes anything about the other. So, how are we going to do this when neither of us are to be trusted?"

"I have no idea what you're talking about."

"Of course not. But we have some mutual friends. Do you remember Stuart Douglas?"

Richard wished he had learnt how to play poker, or at least how to keep a poker face when required. He had no idea if his face had given away any clues, but he did indeed remember Stuart Douglas.

Back in the day, they had spent many hours arguing about dialectical materialism and stuff like that.

"I know him pretty well. I imagine he'll be retiring soon," Weber stated, not bothering to wait for confirmation of whether Richard knew him before continuing. "I expect that, after all this time, you might be wondering if it's worth the effort? You probably even changed your mind about your belief system..."

"A man may not know his own mind," Richard replied dryly, but when Weber showed him an annoyed face, he felt obliged to explain. "It's a quote from *The Egyptian* by Mika Waltari."

"I want to keep this meeting brief. Very brief. We have no time for quoting literature. So let us assume that you want to go through with the original plan. What we need to do is establish credentials so that we can trust one another and take it from there. Would you agree?"

"I suppose so. Though I have no idea..." He was cut short by another Weber frown.

"I have a photograph to show you." Weber reached into the breast pocket of his coat and pulled out a photograph. He showed it to Richard, taking care not to wave it around indiscriminately, so that only Richard could see it, though there seemed to be no reason for such care.

Richard saw a much younger version of himself looking out of the photograph. He must've been nineteen, maybe as much as twenty-one in the photo. Standing next to him was Stuart Douglas and, beside Stuart, Eddie. They all looked scruffy, young and defiant. There was a poster with a clenched fist in the background. The poster used to hang on the wall of Stuart's student flat. Richard remembered the place fondly. It was a sprawling old Victorian house in Glasgow's Kelvinside. The epitome of radical chic, it was more or less a squat with all sorts of people coming and going without bothering to contribute to the rent. People would simply hand over their keys on a whim to acquaintances. Hardly any of the assortment of hippies, free-loaders and naïve young people realised that Stuart paid a substantial rent to the owner, or that that money came from a wealthy actress who believed she was making a contribution to the socialist cause. How utterly decadent and pretentious it had all been. But so much better than the dull, organised squalor students went through for no apparent reason these days.

"So you have an old photograph of me. What do you want now? An autograph?"

"You probably need more time to consider what you want to do. That's understandable." Weber took a gulp of coffee. "We don't need to rush into anything, but I think it's worth our while having a proper talk sometime soon. Somewhere less public and in the open. I'd prefer the park."

"Which park?"

"Any park. Regent's Park is nearer for you though."

"OK."

"Shall we meet at the Clarence Gate entrance on Sunday?"

"What time?"

"Ten a.m. One more thing. Take this card. It will get you into the Turkish baths in Porchester Gardens without paying. Go there tonight and stay for half an hour. It is a club for homosexuals. Don't worry, no one will bother you and I will not meet you there. All you have to do is drink for free in the reception area for half an hour and then leave. Of course, if you want to make friends or use the facilities there, you are free to do so. It is a very exclusive club with good standards of behaviour."

"What? Wait, why do I have to go there?"

"If you don't do this before we meet again it will be very dangerous for you. In fact, our present conversation may already have put you in danger. You must do it." Weber pushed the plastic card towards Richard.

Richard took the card obediently.

Standing up, Weber tossed a ten-pound note onto the table and left.

Once Weber had left, Richard almost felt sorry he had been so uncooperative. This had been a chance to piece together a few bits of the jigsaw. What if something were to happen between now and Sunday? What if Weber were to decide to top himself too?

***

That evening, Richard made a visit to the club as Weber had told him to. It was only much later that he found out why he had to do it – Weber liked to ensure that anyone he met frequented, or at least visited, the Turkish baths in Porchester Gardens. It was good cover. It explained why he met so many random men. The fact the club was not exclusively gay explained why he could meet straight men randomly too.

Standards of behaviour were indeed good, as Weber had mentioned, but (and again, Richard only discovered this later) Weber detested homosexuals. Fortunately, he had found a way of disguising these feelings, or rather, of using them to his advantage. He was known as a sadist. Indeed, on the occasions when he had to, he took great delight in meeting some young boy or other and taking him to the private rooms to administer a good beating. No one questioned this. Weber had noticed, with disgust, that it was within the acceptable parameters of homosexual behaviour, along with pretending to be a dog or other animal.

21 - ALLOCATION OF RESOURCES

That Friday, Richard went to see Anita, the Resource Allocation Planner. His luck was in: Anita offered him a project at a tier-one bank in London – Royal Commercial Bank. The project had been running for a few months, so it was still early days for a bank of that size. It was even better than Oldhams; ideal for his purposes.

"It's a big project, Richard. There are a number of different roles that you might be suitable for."

"Such as...?"

"There's a role for Technical Support to the Financial Reporting Business Analyst. You'd be making sure that the BA documents get converted into proper functional specs, etc. There's also a Release Management role – software deployment, and so on."

"I'm not sure," he said. He didn't want to seem over-eager. Normally he would much prefer the BA role, but if he was personally responsible for Release Management then deploying the Zima software would be so much easier. "Can I think about it?"

A look of annoyance hardened Anita's face. "I have to ask you to decide fairly soon. There's a whole list of people trying to get themselves assigned to this project. It's a biggie, as I'm sure you realise."

"I quite fancy the Release Management role for myself actually," he blurted out.

"Discuss it with Germain," Anita said, relaxing back into her seat. "He's Project Director for this one. He wants you to meet him on the bank's premises at one p.m."

***

Clouds slid down from the sky, disappearing into the ground in front of Richard as he approached the RCB HQ by traversing a small plaza in which fountains played. When he was really close he was able to observe himself approaching. He looked busy and business-like, the clouds surrounding him and still slipping downwards behind his reflection. And then it was all gone; the sky, clouds, and Richard himself all simply vanished as sliding doors opened briefly, revealing the interior of the building.

Without changing pace, he entered and was swallowed up into its vast atrium. He turned slightly to look upwards through the plate glass, taking a last glance at the clouds and sky. They had resumed their normal aspect; instead of slipping down the mirrored exterior of the building, they were back where they belonged, high above the ground making an imaginary heaven for imaginary angels.

Richard joined a quarter-hour-long queue of externals trying to get temporary permission to enter the building for similar reasons to himself. That is, they were all consultants or contractors who had some business at the bank. Richard wondered how many disparate systems the bank must be running that regularly required this number of external people. Eventually, he had his temporary pass and someone was on his way down to accompany him to the meeting room. It was a young bank employee who made his excuses and left Richard to open the meeting room door himself. Seemingly, the young man had urgent business of his own.

"Richard! I asked Anita to assign you. Take a seat."

Richard shook hands with Germain Stoltz and did what he suggested – sat down. Round the table he recognised Dmitri Vassilov, whom he had met on the Moscovsky Zakrit Bank project in Moscow, and Maria Woo. The guy with the short hair and missing dog tooth was new to him, as was the lady with the very dark make-up and hair tied up in a tight bun. They turned out to be Michael Turner and Kinga Harmati.

There was silence, during which the people round the table nodded at Richard and then resumed their task of doing nothing in particular.

"We're just waiting for Frank," Germain explained.

At that moment the door opened and Frank stepped into the room.

"Speak of the devil! Sit down Frank, we're just about to begin." Frank sat down, acknowledging the glances of the others.

Germain continued: "I just thought this was an opportune moment to gather a few of you guys together and give you a brief overview. I know some of you are already on the project" – he looked towards Frank and Dmitri – "but I just want to give you an idea of the big picture here. Things are going OK so far. We produced a scoping document and the bank have agreed to sign that off. That should happen..." he prompted Maria to finish his sentence.

"This Tootheday," said Maria, having difficulty pronouncing the word "Tuesday". She had been in London for at least ten years, but her accent was still quite strong.

"Yes, Tuesday. So that's pretty good going. Thanks to everyone involved there." Everyone round the table looked pleased. Even those, like Richard, who had had nothing to do with it. "The bank have been very reasonable too, which helps." He paused and decided to draw inspiration from the ceiling, leaning his head back and clasping his hands together on top of the desk.

"The thing is the bank is still in quite a bad muddle. They haven't fully recovered since the crash. You probably know from the news that they had to split off their Indian operation and they had to sell off 300 branches here in the UK. They're desperate to get their IT systems consolidated around our software so they can get back into India and the rest of Asia. Everyone is very aware that that's where the growth will be..."

Richard found himself drifting off into his own thoughts. RCB was almost the perfect target. It was too good to be true. He couldn't shake off the idea he was being set up. How had Klaus Weber come by that old photo? Why had he turned up at the very moment when he had been awakened by Mitchell? It was suspicious. It was frightening.

"Richard, you'll be answering to Alexei Petrov."

Richard was startled out of his reverie. Answering for what? What had he done wrong!

"A-Alexei?" he stuttered.

"Alexei Petrov. Do you know him?" The Project Director had broken off his conversation with the ceiling and was looking directly and expectantly at Richard.

Richard racked his brains for an answer. No, he didn't know him. The answer was "No." All he had to do was say "No".

"No." Just to be sure he was telling the truth he added, "I don't remember working with him, at any rate."

"OK, well Dmitri can take you to meet him straight after this meeting. Dmitri will be working closely with you and you will both be under the guidance of Alexei as Chief Technical Architect for the project."

Many of the technical people working for VirtuBank in Europe were from the ex-Soviet Union. During Soviet times, quite a few of them had been top mathematicians or physicists working on the space program, missile defence or something similar.

The Project Director resumed his explanation of the situation at RCB, warning some of the bank staff were now in a tricky position, having lost former colleagues they might have relied on for help, as well as IT systems that had still not been properly replaced. He advised them to play this to their advantage and to push things through as quickly as possible, rather than allow it to become a hindrance.

Of course! thought Richard. *If everyone's in such, a rush that gives me an even better opportunity to push my false software through. As soon as the software is installed it will be easy to persuade the bank staff to do only the most rudimentary user acceptance testing.* Thanks to the Project Director, everyone round the table basked in a warm glow, feeling confident they would achieve their objectives on time. Especially Richard, whose personal objective would trump everyone else's.

22 - APHRODITE'S SECRET

A man may not know his own mind, Richard thought, twirling the black and gold card from APHRODITE'S SECRET (Exclusive Gentleman's Sauna) round and round in his fingers. He hadn't planned on seeing Melanie, but he felt the events of the afternoon were worth celebrating in some way. What better way than this? Besides, it would be a perfect way to find out a bit more about Mitchell.

Finding out if the whole Mitchell thing hung together – that was the reason why he was now paying the taxi driver for the journey to the club. That was the real reason. Mitchell or Weber? Which one was for real? Mitchell was convincing. Weber had not given the proper identification code. He had mentioned "Zima" out of context. He had mentioned it as though it was an introduction, not as an operation, and he had not offered any instructions for the operation. Weber was probably some sort of imposter. If Melanie had more information, he would be able to confirm it. What he would be able to do about it was another matter.

It was hard to believe Mitchell had committed suicide. Perhaps Weber... perhaps Weber had killed or even tortured him. Richard shuddered. Perhaps that was how Weber had got hold of the codes? Would a professional killer be able to torture and kill someone and have the evidence wiped out by throwing the body under a train somehow? He didn't know if or how that would be possible, but he knew he would need to be very careful with Weber.

As the taxi drove off, Richard speculated that perhaps he had not brought enough money. He had £500 in twenties in his pocket but he had no idea how much a girl like Melanie would cost. He had an idea that it was a lot though.

He had no particular qualms about what he was doing. It was the capitalist version of an ideal of feminism he'd grown up with. Back in the day, back in the squat in Kelvinside, feminism had been all about freedom. Relationships had been all about free love and one-night stands. But things had changed. Free love was never quite as free as it purported to be. Everyone was jealous of everyone else. Even girls like Line-up-Linda often turned out to be wilder in reputation than reality. Linda liked sex, yes, but as Richard had eventually found out, not quite in the random gung-ho gangbang way that everyone had assumed – or hoped.

This was some sort of throwback to those times. Except that, as Marx predicted, all human relationships had become financial.

Aphrodite's Secret was in the middle of nowhere, just off the North Circular Road. More precisely, it was in the middle of an industrial estate which was quite deserted at this time of night. There was darkness all around apart from a cosy little scene in an oasis of light.

Included in the oasis of light, just to the right, was a parked Bentley with a personalised number plate. The blank grille of the Bentley's face neither smiled nor scowled. It was inscrutable. On the left-hand side, an Aston Martin maintained a sickly expression on its visage, as though expressing disgust.

Behind and between the two sports limousines was an impressive red awning adorned with gold trim and tassels. This overhung a plush red carpet. A red carpet that melted beneath Richard's steps as he approached the entrance. It was as though he had floated there, drawn like a moth.

Thick glass doors emblazoned with decorative gold lettering slid apart effortlessly and Richard drifted through them into the space beyond. Here, the dull thud of music throbbing from the interior quickened the pulsing of his blood. He felt almost faint with anticipation. But he had yet to get through the wrought-iron gate protecting the reception area. Beyond reception, a waterfall gurgled cheerfully down a false cliff, in the middle of which was a not-so-secret, secret door. It was all very snug and reminded Richard of a Santa's Grotto he had the wide-eyed pleasure of visiting as a child.

A buzzing noise indicated the receptionists had released the electric lock of the wrought-iron gate for him, and he obliged them by opening it and letting himself in.

"Have you been here before?" a blonde receptionist dressed in a clinician's white coat asked him. It was a genuine white coat that would be worn in a genuine clinic, not a cheap thing that you would wear to a fancy-dress party, and certainly not a "naughty nurse" uniform.

"No," said Richard.

"The entrance fee is £80. Drinks are free, apart from our bottles of Moet Grand Cru, and the rest is negotiable."

"OK."

"What shoe size?"

"Erm. Nine."

"OK. This is your locker key. Take this bathrobe to change into and wear these sandals after you change."

Richard wandered to the rustic door dreamily. The dull thumping clarified itself and transformed into proper music as he opened the door. The lighting was intimately dimmed but he was able to see the immediate features of the club quite clearly. There was a wide entrance to changing rooms with lockers just to his right, and directly in front, a raised circular platform on which two stunning girls, naked except for a layer of glistening oil, cavorted within a narrow cone of light.

There were other guys in the changing rooms. Some of them belonged to stag parties and were quite drunk. None of them were alone. Suddenly he felt quite lonely. He changed, gloomily wondering if Melanie would even be here. He hoped she would be.

By now the stunning, oiled-up girls had stopped cavorting and had been replaced by a couple of equally stunning "schoolgirls". The schoolgirls skilfully carried on the tradition of cavorting. They slunk around, each undressing the other with over-acted passion and enthusiasm.

The bar was straight ahead of him, raised above floor level by three shallow steps. He headed off to see if the drinks really would be free. But achieving this goal was not as easy as he had expected. Every few steps another spectacularly sexy, scantily clad woman would approach him.

Each of them seemed eager to know his name, and where he was from. He supplied this information courteously but somewhat warily. Some of the girls thought he had nice hair, others said that he had nice eyes. Many of them were concerned that he looked sad and needed to be cheered up. He politely fended each one off. It wasn't easy. He made a mental note of several of the girls in case he decided to change his mind, but for now he only wanted to see Melanie, and he had a reason. He could already see though, that nearly all the girls here were quite as pretty as she was and they were all dressed in just underwear or were completely naked. Naked, shaven, some with large fake boobs, some with real ones. Pale white girls, black, brown, blonde, brunette...

"Rum and coke please." Richard had made it to the bar. From this elevated position, he looked round and surveyed the scene. It was strange to recall that, from the outside, this building was simply a windowless industrial unit, intended for use as a warehouse or factory; a lot of effort had gone into creating a theatre in which the imagination was encouraged to reign like a decadent potentate.

The main room, in which the bar was situated, was large but partially segmented into more intimate spaces by the arrangement of snug seating areas – opulent, high-backed, curving shapes that lent themselves to being occupied by panther-like females. The openness of the room was also interrupted by tall, highly decorated pillars that pretended to support intricately baroque mouldings that swelled upwards, and swooped and dripped downwards. The restrained lighting enhanced the feeling that intimacy would be protected and private. Men, cosseted in luxurious towelling robes, laughed and joked with their new female friends; some standing, some sprawling on large couches – Roman Emperors at an orgy, surrounded by concubines and both guarded and threatened by the panther women, some prowling, some reclining.

Beyond the bar's oval-shaped counter, visible through a wide, round archway, a loose web of shadow undulated across the walls slowly and randomly, for the light in that room originated from the sapphire depths of a small pool. In this mysterious domain a naked girl relaxed, or perhaps simply displayed her wares, by floating with her long black hair spread into inky tendrils on the water's gently rippling surface.

That she was holding her arms out, as though crucified, further enhanced the sensation of something ethereal, something beyond even the realm of magic, being demonstrated. She was performing a miracle. Richard could see the miracle – her perfect body suspended in a column of light.

He looked around to try to see Melanie. *Perhaps she isn't here!* Loneliness suddenly stabbed at his heart and seeped through him like a hollow pain. What was he getting so upset about? He was surrounded by beautiful women. Any of them could make him feel less lonely. Perhaps he would go over to the swimming pool soon, or perhaps he would go and look for one of the other girls he'd already made a mental note of. His heart was beating fast at the idea. Yes, he had decided, he would do it! But there was one final obstacle. It was the only thing stopping him now – he was spoilt for choice. He couldn't decide which one to approach. He sipped some of his syrupy drink. It had just enough alcohol to give it an edge. There was no hurry to decide yet.

There was a kind of three-dimensional map on the apex of the bar showing the facilities. As well as the stage and the pool, there was a Turkish steam room and a Finnish sauna. You just had to go through the archway to which the apex of the bar pointed. Maybe he should take a walk there too. Not yet; soon.

A voice behind him said: "Hi, I saw you coming."

It was Melanie! At once Richard felt less lonely.

She was completely naked apart from high heels and a pair of pink cashmere leggings which came up to her thighs. She stood on tiptoes and leaned over the bar to ask for a drink, and Richard noticed she had a tattoo of an ankh on her shoulder. The lean that she did was obviously carefully choreographed to ensure that her naked breasts thrust out over the bar while her bottom and long legs would be nicely displayed to whoever was interested, which would include most observers. Her action was not lacking in grace or charm, but Richard found it distasteful, as though he expected her to behave with more decorum when they were together.

Free love was never free, not even when you paid for it. You always felt insecure or jealous for one reason or another.

"Just an orange juice please," she told the barwoman, who delivered the order in a tall glass with a black straw. She had a whole row of juice lined up just ready.

"Well, I'm glad to see you."

"I bet you are!" she replied, turning to him and reaching into his gown.

Richard stopped her. She turned away again, suddenly uninterested, and sucked at the straw.

"I'd like to talk to you," he said.

"OK. We can talk."

"About Mitchell."

"We can talk about Mitchell," she said, her long lashes pointing downwards as she examined the straw carefully. "Let's go somewhere more private though," she suggested, looking straight at him. It was that radiant, angelic face again. When that face made suggestions, they were rarely denied.

"OK."

She took his hand and led him through the arch and along a corridor. There were numbered doors on either side of the corridor, like a hotel. At length she stopped outside one of the doors and knocked. There was no reply, so she reached up to the hook adjacent to the top of the door and took the key. She pushed the unlocked door open and locked it behind them.

The room was sumptuous in a fake way. All of the elaborately carved wooden furniture was made of moulded plastic. Heavy duty, good quality plastic. But still – plastic. There was a huge, fake Louis Quatorze bed with a fake crystal chandelier hanging over it like the sword of Damocles.

There was a nice little side table on one side of the bed with a nice little table lamp, all in fake walnut, and there was comfy fake sofa on the other side of the bed. The walls were covered by a material that resembled silk, and although there was no window behind, one wall had full-length curtains along its whole width. You could imagine that they would slide open at the press of a button to reveal a balcony overlooking the ocean. You could imagine many things in this room.

"Why did Mitchell give you his mobile?" he snapped.

"Oh, this is so boring. Why can't we just have some fun, babe?"

"Don't call me babe. Answer the question."

She sat down and looked sulky. This wasn't getting anywhere.

Richard sat down on the edge of the bed and looked at her crossly. They were having their first tiff. A fake one, of course.

"Listen Melanie. I'm quite happy to be a good customer of yours if you like. I have nothing better to do with my wages. But I'd like to be able to trust you."

She perked up a bit. She didn't reward him with the whole radiant face act, but she definitely stopped the sulky face act.

"I can tell you if you like."

"Go on then."

Having promised to be a good customer, Richard wondered what he'd let himself in for. He wondered how much this fakely magnificent room was costing him right now, and as for diamond necklaces and designer handbags, he had to admit he still hadn't bothered to find out what they would cost. He hadn't done his research. For all he knew, he might have already blown all the money he brought with him just by stepping into this room.

"Andrew was really, really nice to me. Sometimes we really were like girlfriend and boyfriend. He just told me he was in trouble and he wanted me to have his phone for safe-keeping. So I did. I didn't expect him to kill himself the very next day."

"I see."

"Can't you see that he was really in love with me?" She turned to him, her face suddenly distraught, tears falling from her beautiful eyes.

Richard didn't doubt it. She was lovely, she was sweet, she was an emotional roller coaster. He remembered how lonely he had felt as he tried to find her just a few moments ago.

"Did you love him?"

"No, not really."

The sincerity of her answer convinced him she might be telling the truth pretty much the whole time.

"No, I liked him a lot, and I'll really miss him, but..." she tailed off and started crying again, holding a tasselled cushion up to her face to catch the tears.

Richard wondered if he should go and put his arm round her to comfort her, but he couldn't do it. He would feel such a fraud, although perhaps the fake room would welcome another fake addition to its collection of fakeness.

Instead, he just waited until Melanie had stopped crying.

"Do you still have the phone?"

"Yes, of course."

23 - DESIGNS

So now he had Mitchell's old phone too. Of course, he had not resisted Melanie's charms either and had to use the cash machine in the reception area to make up the full payment. It had all been worthwhile though. The phone, Melanie... the whole thing. Richard was quite pleased, though some £900 had disappeared from his bank account during the evening. Nearly a month's rent! Paying the rent when it was due would not be easy, but he would just have to cross that bridge when he came to it.

Richard didn't have much to occupy himself with on Saturday. He moped around his flat thinking about Melanie, wondering if he should pay her another visit.

Melanie wasn't like those other girls in the club, the ones that had approached him with their stock questions and insincere flattery. When she looked at him, he felt she really understood. They had talked at the bar for a while before he left. They had talked properly.

It was a long time since he'd had anything like a proper relationship.

In the heyday of hippiedom, even Richard had managed to find a bit of "free love" and quite a few one-night stands, but he soon realised how empty those relationships were. Over time, as attitudes changed, the one-night stands fizzled out. In fact, it was starting to get more difficult to get sex of any sort.

A possible explanation for all this was that, like so many of the beliefs he had internalised and that had formed his personality, the basis had by now been proven false. A few years ago, Richard had been shocked to read an article on the web about Margaret Meade. The anthropologist, whose works had laid the foundation for the very idea of free love, an idea which had been so eagerly taken up by the hippies, feminists and counter-culturalists of the sixties, had been the victim of a hoax. Another anthropologist, Derek Freeman, proved the young girls who had given her the information her work was based on had simply lied to her for their own amusement.

In spite of the article, and his personal failures in this regard, Richard still couldn't shake off his belief in free love as an ideal. It seemed to him an essential part of being a leftist libertarian. The fact the only place where the ideal of free love really existed was in "sauna clubs" such as the one Melanie was a "member" of was, therefore, of little concern to him.

What was so wrong about paying? He hadn't done so before, but he hadn't particularly thought of doing so before. Until now he had swallowed the third-wave feminist propaganda that it was exploitative and sordid. More to the point, he hadn't realised girls like Melanie might be available.

Where the sexual revolution of the sixties and seventies had failed, the free market stood ready to provide a solution. Richard had no problem with this. He'd never got to go with Linda MacKerricher, but only because he'd been too polite or shy to try. So why, now the opportunity had arisen, should he be squeamish about paying for something, or rather someone, he really wanted?

His bank account couldn't withstand another onslaught, though. It would have to wait. He decided to go and have a look round Selfridges. It would be worth finding out if he could afford to buy designer handbags as presents.

The answer, he soon found out, was no. It turned out designer handbags were a serious consideration.

A bitter debate took place in his mind. Richard wouldn't admit to himself the underlying reason for the debate was sour grapes. The subject of the debate was "handbags".

Handbags... there was almost no limit to what had to be spent to buy a really good designer handbag. After a certain point, the money wasn't going toward increasing quality. It was going toward snob value – the more you spent, the higher that value was. Why was that necessary? Because these items were bought to massage the ego, and there was no limit to how much the ego needed to be massaged, because the very shallowness of character that required a handbag to heal it made it impossible to build something more enduring and real onto that character.

In spite of winning the debate with himself, for some reason he found himself trying to calculate what he could cut back on so that he could get into the handbag-buying league, to compete with his deceased rival for Melanie's attentions, Mitchell.

24 - WATCHING FOOTBALL

Sunday came at last. Richard knew it was his duty to go to meet Weber. He wanted to feel powerful before this meeting, so he put *Siegfried's Funeral March* on full blast. After a few minutes he switched to *Ride of the Valkyries* but then decided the ominous music was not helping. He tried Mendelssohn's *Hebrides Overture* but switched it off despondently and roamed round his flat starting useless tasks without completing any of them. He didn't want to see Weber again. Right up until the last moment, he kept delaying, hoping to think of a reason for not going. But in the end, there was no reason, no excuse.

It was obvious to Richard that Weber was just trying to get information from him. Weber had not used any of the "wake up" phrases Mitchell had. Weber must be somebody dangerous. Yet here he was preparing to go to the park to talk to him. The problem was that, the more dangerous Weber might be, the more necessary it was to keep him away from his flat and, for Christ's sake, not mention Mitchell to him! He had to play along. He had to go to the park.

The park was only a few blocks away. Weber could wait for him if he wanted to meet. Sure enough, Weber was there already when Richard turned up five minutes late.

"I suggest we walk towards the playing fields. There should be fewer people there," said Weber.

Richard nodded solemnly. Why not? he asked himself. The thought then crossed his mind as to why not. Well, anyway, it was still a totally public place. He could run, cry out. He would not be in any real danger.

The noise and oppression of Baker Street faded away as they made their way past the pond and into the interior of the park. In the park, everyone was happy and carefree. Liberated.

Weber wanted to talk about holidays as they made their way to their imprecisely specified destination. Richard supplied a few unwilling replies to his questions. He was able to assure Weber he had a nice holiday in Croatia that year and was most impressed by the Dalmatian coast. Dubrovnik had been wonderful. Klaus, for his part, highly recommended Vancouver. It was his first visit to Canada, but he had already promised himself to go again.

The sound of distant shouting became louder as they approached the football pitches. Teamwork is not a stealthy activity. It requires the participants to shout instructions at each other and there were at least ten games taking place, including one on a pitch just a few yards from the bench Klaus was heading for.

"So, here are the playing fields at last. Let's sit." Weber took a small hip-flask from an inside pocket of his coat. He unscrewed the little cups from the top and set them down on the ground in a series of precise movements. "Cognac?"

"Not for me, Weber."

"Call me Klaus. You don't trust me, do you?"

"I don't trust anyone."

"If I could believe that, it would at least be of some comfort to me. My fear is that you are more trusting than you imagine."

"What the fuck are we doing here, Weber? Scouting for a new striker?"

"'Klaus.' We're being discreet. We have things to discuss. One thing, anyway."

"And what's that?"

"Зима."

"Zima?"

Weber suddenly seemed weary, as though the effort of answering was draining all his strength.

"You are supposed to know what it means. If you don't know, I can't help you and we have both been wasting our time. Not just the last ten minutes. Not the time that we've wasted since I rang the bell of your flat. Years of our time."

Richard considered this. It might be true, but for the fact there was already a Zima contact. The original contact, and best, had already provided him with actual instructions. Furthermore, this new guy had not followed the correct protocol.

"OK, Mr Slater. I think I see your dilemma. You don't know who I am. You are prejudiced against me. I need to help you overcome this, and since I am sure of who you are, I can lay my cards on the table."

"Go on."

"This photograph shows you with Stuart Douglas and Eddie MacFarlane."

"Yes. You showed me that already. By the way, how did you get..."

"Eddie was convicted of a terrorist act in 1994."

"I lost touch with Eddie years ago – late seventies."

"Very good Mr Slater, very good indeed."

"It's true."

"I can tell you more about Eddie's conviction if you wish."

"Why not?"

"Yes, why not? Eddie tried to petrol-bomb the HQ of Lloyds Bank."

"Really? A petrol bomb would do nothing of significance to Lloyds."

"He was taking part in a demonstration objecting to Shell Oil's activities in Nigeria. They were targeting the bank's AGM. Some demonstrators bought shares to gain access to the AGM itself. The rest of them wanted to make a more public protest outside the HQ."

"You said they were demonstrating against Shell Oil. What the fuck were they doing at Lloyds Bank?"

"Silly me, I should've explained. Lloyds was Shell's bank."

"Oh. I see." Richard knew this was quite a common tactic. Activists tried to isolate companies by targeting their suppliers, banks etc.

"Anyway, the fact is that Eddie threw petrol bombs at the door of Lloyds' HQ."

"It was just a gesture, I imagine. A futile gesture."

"Exactly. It was exactly that, a futile gesture. A misjudgement. Other demonstrators threw paint bombs. They were charged with vandalism. They understood the purpose of the demo was publicity, not revolution. Eddie got ten years, later reduced to seven, for terrorism."

"Poor fucker."

"So you sympathise with him?"

"Oh, have I fallen into your trap?"

"Don't worry. It's a free country. You can sympathise with whoever you like."

"Just so long as you never do anything, eh?"

"Let me get back to the main point though. The photograph shows you with Stuart and Eddie for a good reason."

"It was a long time ago."

"Yes it was, but the reason lives on, as you know."

"I'm sorry, I can't help you with your plan... Klaus."

"Zima is your plan. It is you who needs help, and I who am offering it – as you know."

"What help do you think I need?"

"Tell me what help you want and I can arrange it."

Weber's words were icy. But Richard was determined not to be intimidated. That question confirmed that Weber was just fishing for information. He had no idea about Zima.

They sat in silence.

An argument had broken out on the nearest pitch. There was a lot of extravagant gesticulating and shouting between several of the players. Then someone took the initiative of simply taking the free kick, and the players who had been doing the theatrics had to quickly drop their posturing and resume the game.

"I should get back home, things to do."

"Mr Slater, I don't wish to embarrass you with reminders of youthful idealism, but we both know that this was once very important to you."

"Once."

"...and we both know that it still is important."

"If you say so."

"Take my card. Call me when you are ready. One last thing Richard – if you are in any doubt about what to do, make sure you do nothing."

But as Richard wandered off, without bothering to watch Weber retrieve the two cups with the same precision as he had placed them on the ground, he was already planning to burst into action like a jack-in-the-box.

25 - GHOST TRADERS

Richard was on his way to another of RCB's offices on the Thames. He was going to meet Alexei Petrov and Dmitri Vassilov for an introductory meeting with the bank.

Two small revolving doors, side by side, offered him a choice of entry to the building; a glass and marble-clad edifice which towered importantly above him, making him feel like some sort of tiny insect. He decided on the rightmost of the small doors and crept into it. As an insect, he had to retract his antennae to squeeze into the space.

But during the process of allowing himself to be inexorably transported inside the building by the automatic revolving door, he discovered the segment he was occupying was not as small as it had seemed in comparison to the building, but large relative to himself. Large enough to make him feel important, but not so large as to be intimidating.

Suddenly he didn't feel quite as insect-like or insignificant as he had on the outside of the towering structure. During the process of being transported into the interior, he had grown back to his normal stature and was already no longer creeping in, but arriving heroically. Now he knew how Alice had felt when she kept changing size, and a fair idea, from his initial impression, of how Gregor Samsa had felt on discovering his metamorphosis into a cockroach.

He found himself in a huge marble hall where two reception desks sheltered against the far wall – one for employees, one for visitors. He tried the visitors' desk, though he was, temporarily at least, some sort of employee.

He was quickly given a visitor's badge, and sat reading the in-house magazine while waiting to be collected. Soon Dmitri came down to collect him with an Indian colleague in tow. Dmitri introduced him to Srini, "Development Team Liaison Lead" from Chennai, who had flown in for a few days and was going to sit in on today's meeting. Then they went up a beautiful, wide flight of marble stairs leading to the mezzanine floor.

There, a surprising thing happened. Surprising to Richard, at any rate, though by now the others had experienced it at least once. On opening a heavy wooden door they found themselves contained within a glass corridor which, in turn, was contained within the original, much larger, hallway.

There, they had to play a game, swiping their security passes, so they could pass through a set of three small, or rather, human-sized, doors. Each time they swiped they were allowed to pass further along this small, or rather, human-sized, glass corridor to the next door. The rules of the game permitted only one person at a time to occupy an individual compartment.

The object of the game was to prove to the security system and CCTV cameras, which were now trained on them, that they were to be allowed into the building. The CCTV was sending images of all three back to a team of security people somewhere. Finally, they all finished playing the game and were rewarded by being allowed into the large hallway itself, which had evidently been constructed with an evil ogre in mind, judging by its dimensions.

The building they were in had been created by knocking two separate, older buildings together, and adding modern facilities to them. Therefore, there were a lot of unusual floor levels and features.

Full-length, floor-to-ceiling windows to their left showed a vast trading floor one-and-a-half storeys below. On that floor, huge curved desks were arranged in intersecting circles, almost like Olympic rings, except there were more than five continents in this world. There was a small gap in each ring, allowing entrance to the trader who was supposed to work there. Each desk contained between five and seven CRT computer screens.

There were no traders there any more; the whole operation had been shut down several years before.

It looked as though trading had stopped suddenly and unexpectedly, for no apparent reason, like a banking equivalent of the Mary Celeste. The bulky, now-obsolete screens had not been moved from the desks they stood on when trading stopped but they were blank: switched off or not even plugged in.

However, still alive with light, and spanning the whole length of the far wall, was a huge, illuminated map of the world. Beneath it, every major currency, and many lesser-known ones, were stating their rates relative to sterling, at that exact moment, also in light. What had once been state-of-the-art was a museum piece, and perhaps even more impressive as such.

It was another of those buildings with a lift that liked to give advice and information to its human occupants as it went about its business: "Fifteenth floor," sang the lift, then added in a grave tone, "Doors opening." Just then, the doors slid open, revealing the fifteenth floor as predicted.

The attempt to give human voices to machines irritated Richard. In the end it made him feel less human himself. It reminded him he had been educated to believe that he, too, was just a machine. A machine made of chemicals instead of electronics; nevertheless, just a machine, in danger, one day, of being made obsolete. Inevitably too, one day a malfunction would cause his machinery to fail completely. It was something that could happen at any moment.

They continued along another wide corridor and opened the door to the conference room. A further wonder confronted them.

A panoramic vista of the river, looking down over London Bridge and south toward The Shard, opened up. Richard felt almost as though he should not take another step forward or he would plunge headlong into the brown, sluggish water of the Thames, so immediate was its presence. Once again, size was relative. This time, the room they were in was, in fact, enormous and contained a huge, oval table just to their right, but the view of London overwhelmed the senses and initially made the room seem tiny; as though they had opened the door to find themselves perched in mid-air, on a thin ledge overhanging the river.

Richard stood near the window so he could drink in the view.

The river curved toward them from the east, on their left, and then twisted away to the right, toward Westminster.

The river was brown but not as filthy as it once had been when London's East End had been an industrial port. The old docks and sooty, coal-fired industries were long gone. Today the sun was shining on a bright new London. The river was a playground. Just to the right was the London Eye; a huge Ferris wheel for happy tourists to ride. Down there, pleasure boats were seeking out childish adventure, their eager snouts pointing expectantly to where they intended to go.

A chain of barges, laden with filthy containers full of waste, ploughed its way laboriously upstream, throwing up furrows of brown mud that proved transient and melted back into the river's glistening coils.

Beyond the Shard, low clouds were drifting past, at eye level, making it seem that the meeting would be taking place in the sky. Richard breathed deeply, as though taking in fresh air from clouds he could reach out and touch. He felt their power and majesty infuse him as he stood there overlooking the entire "South Side of The Sky". A plane, high to their left, heading west to Heathrow and making its way beneath a vast mountain range of cumulus, put into perspective the enormous scale of the prospect that was laid out before him. Buildings and streets spun away into the far distance, meeting blue skies on the horizon.

26 - IN THIS THE DEVIL IS

They sat down, huddled together at one end of the enormous beechwood table, occupying the seats nearest the door, to await the bank's representatives. They were still five minutes early. Richard wryly recalled the time when he was on a project in Germany and had arrived five minutes early. Instead of being viewed favourably for making sure he was on time, he was mildly reprimanded. In Germany, you wasted time just as much by being too early as too late. Punctual meant being exactly on time.

Soon the bank's staff arrived and also took up residence at the nearest portion of the enormous table so that at least a third of it was in use. After brief introductions they attempted to talk about the technical tasks facing them.

It was difficult to make progress. RCB had made an effort to express their enthusiasm for the project by sending a very high-powered team of senior managers. Unfortunately, they were so senior they had long ago lost sight of the minutiae of working procedures and could only understand their business at the most abstract level. VirtuBank would require a much deeper level of analysis if the project was to succeed.

In software, it was common to remind everyone the devil was in the detail. But it seemed to Richard that perhaps, up here, looking out at The Shard and the silver clouds beyond, everybody believed themselves near enough to God not to be concerned about the Devil. Pride and Satan would be ready to trip them at the first opportunity.

This meeting would only serve to enable some of the participants to recognise each other and their roles, or perhaps as a starting point to other more meaningful meetings. Richard began to pass his time looking out at the view and daydreaming. He was thinking of an article he had read in a newspaper some time ago, asking why the bank bailouts were costing so much money and why so little progress was being made.

When the meeting finished, they went back downstairs to their desks, past the screens of ghost traders, back down the marble staircase.

27 - ZOMBIE

Once shown to the desk and workstation allocated to him, Richard postponed any work he had been given. He had to think about how to get his Zima software installed.

He could simply install it himself, of course. That is, he could install it on the test system himself, no questions asked. He would have to tell Alexei and Dmitri, too, just so they knew (that was usually a formality). But then it would need to be migrated to another server for VirtuBank's test team to do acceptance testing. Then it would be migrated again onto another server for UAT – User Acceptance Testing by the bank's test team, and finally it would be migrated to the live system. The whole process would take a minimum of three months. In any case, the live system would not go live for at least another six months. At each and every stage, questions would be asked. Various people would check the installation instructions and accompanying documents. So the documentation needed to look right, which it did, and it needed to come from an official channel, which it didn't. It couldn't just turn up via Richard himself. Somehow he needed to make it look like it had been sent to him officially.

The proper way of receiving software was to go to the VirtuBank download site and download it. Would he be able to hack into that site and put the software on there? Not a chance.

The only other way was email. He had already received lots of proper, official packs and patches by email because sometimes the dev guys bypassed the download site if a software pack was particularly urgent or, occasionally, for other reasons.

So he could quite simply attach the software and its instructions as a zip file to one of the emails he already had, change the wording of the email to match the documentation of the patch, and send it to Alexei or Dmitri to ask for permission to install.

But that wouldn't work either. If anything went wrong and there was an investigation, it would be obvious that the first email containing that particular zip file had originated from his laptop. That would happen if anything at all went wrong – not just the unthinkable.

Of course! The answer was obvious. If he could send the Zima software from another laptop, that would be that. Well, no, it wouldn't be "that". The software still wouldn't originate from anywhere. The software would just come into being in an email from someone's laptop. It would just frame whoever that poor bugger was. But that would be better than being in the frame himself.

So the plan would be to get his zip file sent to the relevant parties via someone's laptop. He was aware hackers knew how to do this. They would use a virus to turn an unsuspecting person's laptop into a "zombie" they could take control of. Or they could use "spoofing" – change the IP address that something had actually been sent from to a different one. Richard was also aware he had no expertise in these things. He didn't intend to take the risk of using techniques he had no experience of when his neck would be on the line. KISS – Keep It Simple Stupid, was always the best policy in IT, no matter what you were doing. Even if what you were doing was an act of cyber-terrorism. Especially then.

If he could just get hold of someone's laptop for a moment, and if he had the email ready to go, that would be ideal. It would only take a few moments to send it to himself and the normal mailing list. He racked his brains.

Ask to borrow someone's laptop? That would be preposterous. He would be immediately marched to the front door by security where he would discover that he had been kicked off the project and fired. He could steal a laptop. He would need to steal it while it was still logged on though. Otherwise he would need to know the password. Richard was not a magician. How could he do that?

He spent thirty minutes making sure he had put everything onto his memory stick so he would be ready once he could think of a decent plan. He was vaguely considering setting the fire alarm off and stealing someone's laptop as the building emptied. So far it was the best plan he'd been able to come up with. He would also need to be first back into the building so he could replace the laptop. Or else he would need to stay inside the building the whole time, hidden somewhere, with a good excuse ready in case a fire marshal found him and asked what the fuck he was doing.

He went home that night still thinking about his options. None of them were great.

***

A week went past. He hadn't come up with a decent plan yet and nothing much was happening on the project. He had filled in some forms and had his photo taken to get a permanent building pass. He had sat in on a couple of routine meetings with Dmitri and Andrei. Apart from that he was left to vegetate for most of the time.

Steve Wong turned up on-site.

"Hey Steve, what you up to?"

"I just thought I'd pop over and liven up you lot of techie geeks and dullards."

"This area's reserved for technical wizards and people that are doing proper work. We don't want a whole load of bean-counters coming to annoy us here."

"Are you saying you don't like people who can count? Perhaps you're jealous of abilities beyond your comprehension?"

"Jealous? We get the computer to do the trivial work."

Steve decided to break off the banter with an observation. "Well this is a nice cosy little room they've given you lot. Where I am, we're all in a big open-plan room with all the big shots from the bank. It's like being in a goldfish bowl surrounded by hungry tom-cats." Steve was always paranoid about what the bank's staff were thinking about him. "Where have Dmitri and Alexei gone?"

"I think they're in a meeting in the other building. Anyway, what really brings you here?"

Steve assumed a polite and conspiratorial tone, as though he was discussing a matter of great diplomatic delicacy.

"I just thought I'd come over here and, politely, invite the new boy to lunch, so I can introduce him to a few of our colleagues."

"New boy?"

"Srini."

"Is he new? I thought he was Development Team Liaison Lead."

"Do you practice being autistic? New to you lot I mean. Hasn't he just been moved here this morning? We should try to make him feel welcome. Culture shock and all that. Half the guys don't even know he's not still in India."

"Good idea! Shit Steve, we didn't even think of that. Andrei just stuck him in the corner and left him there."

"And neither of you have even said hello to each other. I wouldn't expect a bunch of semi-autistic techies to behave differently."

"Actually, I doubt if he will come, but you can try I suppose." Richard thought it unlikely that Srini would want to go to lunch and risk the wrath of his gods. He noticed that he had brought a plastic container and had no doubt it contained a vegetarian meal he had prepared himself.

"So that's him at the desk in the corner with his back to us?"

"Yeah."

Steve trotted over to introduce himself in his best public school manner, and explain his plan to Srini. Srini waggled his head from side to side in reply and then stood up to shake hands with Steve.

The conversation continued for a while with both Steve and Srini making improbably polite gestures. Steve stood straight, with his head inclined as though respectfully bowing as he spoke.

Richard attributed some of Steve's extreme courtesy to his Asian background. An Asian upbringing would also account for Srini's bashfully polite mannerisms. Richard believed Steve's impeccable conduct and politeness had been additionally polished at an English public school, though he had never attempted to confirm this.

To Richard's surprise, Srini picked up his coat and the pair of them made their way back toward him.

"It's curry day in the canteen today," Steve said to Richard, as though further explanation was required for the fact Srini had decided to join them.

"Oh! Excellent!" replied Richard.

"Very excellent," said Srini, grinning.

As Richard picked up his coat to join them, he noticed Srini had left his laptop on. With several applications still open! This was it! The opportunity! He went toward the lift with them, trying to think what to do with the laptop. As the lift door opened, he decided to act.

"Go ahead guys, I'll join you downstairs, I just need to..." He couldn't think of an excuse, other than "switch my laptop off," and he didn't want to say anything like that – it would remind Srini! So he just gesticulated in a vague way. To his dismay, Steve and Srini had paused to wait for him to finish saying what he needed to do. The lift doors were already closing! Richard stuck his hand through the doors and held his other arm out to usher them in.

"Be with you in five," he said.

He was by Srini's laptop in an instant. He already had everything prepared on his memory stick. He plugged it in to the USB socket and waited anxiously to see if the laptop would block it. It didn't.

Outlook was already open, so he copy-pasted his pre-prepared email from the memory stick into a new email and then attached the Zima zip file. He added a subject line, typed his own name in as the recipient and copy-pasted the usual names into cc. Was that it? Had he remembered everything? Email body, attachment, name, cc, subject. Yes. *Hit send quickly before Dmitri or someone from the bank wanders in and catches me using Srini's laptop!*

He hit send.

That was it. Oh wait! Srini would be likely to look at his sent emails at some point during the day. Why hadn't he thought of that until now? What could he do? He opened the sent folder, about to delete the last email. Better still, let's just keep it but lose it. He looked to see what folder structure Srini had in Outlook. He recognised the folder names as names of various projects. He moved the email from the sent folder to one called "Dynamo". Dynamo was a failed project that had been abandoned several years ago. The ideal place to put the email. Now it was pretty much lost until anyone wanted to find it. If anyone did, they would see it had been sent by Srini, and Srini would not be able to deny it.

Richard couldn't believe his luck. He hadn't just sent the software from any old laptop; he'd sent it from the laptop belonging to the Development Team Liaison Lead. It was perfect. If anything went wrong and the software was traced, it would seem as though the software genuinely originated from the dev team. If anything went wrong, investigators might spend ages trying to track who in the dev team had tricked Srini into sending a software pack directly from his laptop, but there would be no way they could connect it to the real culprit. In fact, the more Richard thought about it, the more perfect it was. It might seem as though Srini had accidentally sent some old software belonging to the Dynamo project. A project that had died off years ago. It would be a dead end.

Of course, Srini might be sacked for his carelessness, but that was nothing in the scheme of things.

"So did you manage to..." Steve mimicked the gesture Richard had made at the lift.

"Oh yes, very thoroughly," replied Richard.

The guys round the table laughed at this as though it was hilarious, then returned their attention to gobbling up their curries, while exchanging their usual argumentative banter.

28 - PLEASED

On getting home, Richard felt surprisingly drained. The stress of the email had tired him out. He felt guilty too. Srini was a really nice chap. He didn't deserve to be framed. Well, anyway, it wouldn't matter unless there was an investigation for some reason. In which case, Richard realised, he hoped he had not made any mistake, but had framed Srini successfully.

He was flicking from one TV channel to another aimlessly, unable to relax or concentrate properly. Suddenly he remembered that he had only taken a cursory look at Mitchell's phone. He went and fished it out of his coat pocket. There were no stored messages of any importance, so he started looking through the contacts.

He had no idea what sort of information the phone might have that would be of any interest. Perhaps he had only asked for it to be nosy. Perhaps, just because he could. "A man may not know his own mind", he reminded himself, or was it, "A man does not know his own mind"? What did it matter? There was very little difference. In any case, the quote was a translation from Finnish.

Well there she was: "Melanie". Melanie was in Mitchell's list of contacts. Of course, she would be. After a few diamond necklaces and fancy handbags, he would be an extra special customer. Richard was tempted to call her. Why not? He felt so stressed out and lonely right now, it would be nice to see her tonight. He would have to dig into his savings, of course. He could do that.

He dialled.

"Andrew!" he heard Melanie's surprised but delighted voice.

"Oh sorry, no, it's Richard."

"Oh God. Richard?" she sounded utterly confused.

"Yes, I'm sorry. I didn't think. I'm using Mitchell's phone. I'm really sorry."

"Oh." There was a pause. "Oh, it doesn't matter. I... I was just confused for a moment. I forgot... you had the phone. I forgot he's... Anyway, why are you ringing?"

Richard was relieved she wasn't angry or upset.

"I was thinking about coming to see you."

"Oh! I see! Well, yes, of course. You don't need to ring. Just come to the club. I already told you what nights I work."

Richard was disappointed that she was treating him like an ordinary customer, someone who should turn up on her workdays instead of someone who could call her and arrange to see her. What could he expect? He decided he better not spend another £900 to be just another customer.

"Oh, maybe it's not such a great idea. I can leave it for another time."

"Oh no, don't. Come round tonight after eight. I'll be really pleased if you can."

So Richard changed his mind back. After all, Melanie would be pleased.

29 - CAT FIGHT

In war they'll stick a rifle in your hand, and then it's kill or be killed.
Richard was still worrying about framing Srini as the taxi made its way toward Aphrodite's Secret. Still trying to justify his actions to himself. *But the difference is that no one stuck a rifle in my hand. I'm not a conscript, I'm not even a volunteer. I picked up the rifle all by myself. I even invented the damned weapon.*

As the taxi drove steadily along a dual carriageway, orange light repeatedly flashed onto his face in a slow, hypnotic pattern that implanted encoded messages directly into his mind.

And after several iterations of this treatment, the thought that occurred to him was this:

Why should I give a damn?

The passing light continued to alternately brighten and darken his face. He stared, unseeing, straight ahead. *My own neck is on the line, I don't care about that, so why should I care about Srini or anyone else? All that matters is that this succeeds. Everyone involved is expendable.*

He opened the fairy-tale grotto door of the club. Standing immediately before him, just a few feet away, was Melanie. She was carrying a pile of fluffy white towels which she was taking to the ladies' shower area. As soon as she saw Richard, she dropped the towels onto the floor, revealing she was clothed pretty much as previously, in nothing but a pair of thick woollen stockings. She threw her arms round him and squealed happily.

"I'm so glad you decided to come. I was worried that you'd changed your mind."

"The driver went the wrong way."

"Anyway, it's still only eight-thirty. We have plenty of time."

She said it as though Richard didn't need to worry about the fact that, in Aphrodite's Secret, time was literally money.

Once they were in the room, Melanie turned round to him and put her arms up around his neck, holding her hands downwards, lazily crossed at the wrists. She stood on tiptoes, and held her pretty face up to his.

"So what would you like to do with me?" she inquired.

"Can I kiss you?"

"Since it's you, yes. But it's 'girlfriend experience'. It costs extra."

"Oh, I didn't know. Is it a lot?"

"That depends," she said coyly, "on what you think is a lot."

"Well, how much?" Richard knew he was being played. He was being made to seem miserly or cheap, and all the while she was sucking his bank account dry.

Perhaps she had noticed that she'd pushed too far, or perhaps what she said next was genuine, because she said: "Just this once, just for you, I can do it for no extra," and they kissed.

After they had made use of the bed which, in spite of its fake aspect, served very adequately for its purpose, they talked. Melanie told him how badly she wanted to get out of the club. She hated working in this "horrid place" and had hoped she might save up enough to be able to afford to live a normal life one day.

"A normal life in a normal job?" Richard asked.

"No, silly. A normal life as a normal home maker. Maybe one of my rich guys will have me one day."

"Do you think that's likely? Don't you think most of them are married anyway?"

"Yes, they are. You're not though, are you?"

"No, I'm not. But I'm not rich either."

She seemed to sulk at this, as though he was lying to her.

"But if I was I would love to marry you."

"Goodness! Did you just propose to me?" she giggled.

"Oh, I didn't mean to."

"But I might say yes, if you did."

And at that moment, for the first time, it struck him that in many ways she was still a carefree child. She could earn a very good living from well-mannered gentlemen in the club without experiencing any of the everyday worries normal people struggled with. She was not to be taken seriously – that would end in disaster. It was unfortunate, in a way, but she was merely a plaything, and right now she wanted to play. Melanie allowed him to roll her onto her back, and prove, once again, the bed, whatever its failings in terms of authenticity, was functionally able to fulfil their requirements.

They agreed to meet at the bar to have a drink before Richard had to hand over the money.

At the bar, two of the girls were getting in each other's faces. It seemed that one had taken the other's regular customer. Pretty soon they were clawing at each other and trying to pull one another's hair. An American customer sitting on a high revolving stool thought it was too good to be true.

"Wow, do they have this every night?" he asked Richard eagerly.

"I doubt it. They would be on the stage if it wasn't for real."

A couple of burly security guards arrived briskly at the scene. They took one girl apiece and lifted them away from one another.

"Sorry gentlemen," said one of the bouncers. The struggling girls were soon removed from sight of the customers. Richard wasn't sure if the bouncer meant he was sorry about the fight or the fact they'd broken it up.

"You see what I mean?" said Melanie. She had hung back, near the ladies' shower area, until everything calmed down. "You probably think this is a nice, classy place with lots of nice girls, but really they're all bitches."

30 - BLACKMAIL

"That package I gave you. Was it useful?"

Richard froze. Why was Melanie asking about that? And why "package"? Why not "envelope"?

"Why do you ask?" he managed to say in a strained voice.

"Oh, nothing. I just wondered about it. It just seemed..." She trailed off. Her eyes studied him anxiously and then she turned away, looking round the room. Perhaps she had noticed that she'd scared him. Suddenly, she gave an exclamation of surprise. Her hand alighted on his chest as though to steady herself.

"You see that girl over there?" she asked, her voice an excited whisper.

"Yes."

"The little madam with the pointy tits. As usual she's wearing that leather mini-skirt with a gap at the front, so she can show off what a cute little thing she is." Melanie stared at the girl. Richard wondered if she was jealous of her or attracted to her.

"Hmm, she is indeed a cute little thing," he said, appreciatively. As well as the ridiculous mini-skirt that wasn't a skirt, she was wearing high stilettos that were almost impossible to walk in. Apart from those two items, she was entirely naked, showing off the smooth perfection of her skin.

Melanie flashed a disapproving glance at him, but returned her attention to the girl and continued: "A couple of months ago one of her clients hobbled out of here and had to go to hospital to get the welts on his bottom treated."

It took a moment for Richard to try to process the information; his brain was otherwise occupied. He managed to tear his gaze away from the girl and looked at Melanie in puzzlement. "Wait, what are you saying?" he said.

"I'm saying she whacked him so hard with a riding crop on his bottom that he needed hospital treatment," Melanie said, clearly exasperated that she was trying to tell him something about this vile girl and all he could do was stand there drooling at her.

"No way!" Richard found it hard to believe that the girl in question would hit anyone, let alone put them in hospital. Anyway, why would you turn up in hospital with whip marks on your bottom? The story was made up. "Surely you wouldn't do that? I mean, go to hospital – what would you say to the quack?"

"I think he went to a private clinic. But you're right. It must've been pretty bad for him to do that."

"Well I wouldn't go to hospital. What would I say?"

"I don't know what you would say. Are you thinking of asking her for the same treatment?" Melanie asked, pretending to be cross.

"No, no, of course not."

Melanie was obviously amused she'd got him slightly flustered. She smiled to herself but, continuing the story, the smile disappeared: "Then he went to the police to press charges for assault. The hospital probably advised it."

"I can understand that. If the injuries were that bad..."

"So you would do the same?" Melanie twirled a strand of hair in her fingers and looked at him.

"No, I mean I..."

"I know what you mean," Melanie said darkly. "Never mind that though. Want to hear what happens next?"

"Go on."

"She'd made a video recording of the session. It shows her whipping him with a riding crop and it shows him asking her to hit him harder, and thanking her for each whack."

"Shit, so it was all his own fault?"

"Not exactly. The little bitch only showed so much to the police. The warm-up bit with the ending edited in. She and some of her friends get to watch the full video. They, ahem, 'enjoy each other's company' while they watch the bit after she hides a vibrating egg inside that sweet little pussy of hers and starts making him scream and beg to stop."

"He screams? Why did no one stop it?"

"There's a special room downstairs for this kind of thing. It's soundproofed so it doesn't upset the other customers."

"Wow! Why didn't he just take the crop off her and get the hell out of the room?"

"Don't be silly, she'd tied him up just before inserting the egg."

"How come the police didn't realise she'd edited it?"

"Well edited. I don't know if she did it herself or had professional help. She's quite a clever girl you know. University degree."

"But what happened wasn't consensual at all. It really was assault."

"Apart from the video there's no evidence. But it gets worse. She started blackmailing the guy too. He's not married but he has a good job. She's been getting a tidy sum from him every month since."

"That's pretty mean."

"It could be worse. I guess she could blackmail him into a repeat performance if she chose to."

"I guess so." Richard had to admit the girl was wildly exciting to look at.

"She's not the only complete bitch in here, Richard. So just watch your step!" Melanie smiled at him and tossed her hair back.

31 - THE HERO

Richard was worrying about what to do if and when the Zima software was deployed.

He imagined, not for the first time, the crowds in the streets. There would be riots. There would be bloodshed. He imagined himself, actively involved, calling for calm, re-establishing order. A new, socialist order.

What if it failed? The software itself could fail. The revolution, even if triggered, could fail. Would he have to flee? Where? To Venezuela? Would Melanie come with him? No, of course not! She was the sort of woman that wanted all the pleasures of a consumer society. In spades, in fact. Maybe in diamonds.

Women, he speculated, or rather men's lust for them, is what drives capitalism. If he wanted Melanie he would need money, or at least power.

But that was where there was a glimmer of hope. *If I succeed, I'll be a hero of the revolution...*

So the options were two. First that the Zima code would sabotage the bank and cause a bit of a problem, but not a sufficient problem to trigger a revolution. In spite of his precautions, there was a chance the bank would eventually discover what happened. To be on the safe side, he might have to run for it or face a hefty jail sentence.

Or, secondly, the Zima code would do what it was supposed to do and rip capitalism wide open, so that it could finally be replaced by a true socialist system. In which case, he could step into the limelight as a hero. Ta da!

He was no longer a youthful, optimistic activist. He thought of the consequences of ripping capitalism wide open. A lot of greedy bastards would lose everything; serves them right. But maybe even people with nothing would lose everything too. They might lose the few lucky opportunities the current system offered. They might lose their freedom.

32 - HONEST BROKERS

Richard had arranged to meet some of the others back at VirtuBank HQ so they could go for a pizza at lunchtime.

As he strolled into the fifth floor reception area, the HD TV behind the desk was showing Bloomberg TV, as it always did. The TV, together with a scattering of financial magazines and newspapers on the desk, were supposed to impress upon any visitor that VirtuBank knew everything there was to know about finance and took a keen interest in it.

The story showing on the TV concerned the disgraced CEO of the Co-op Bank. It had turned out that he knew almost nothing at all about banking.

"I expect he was so high on cocaine most of the time that he didn't even realise he was supposed to be running a bank," a jovial Richard said to the receptionist.

The receptionist had her back to the TV so she probably didn't know what he was talking about, but smiled politely anyway.

Steve was already hanging around waiting in the dev area. He exchanged pleasantries with Richard before getting down to business:

"What about the Arsenal?"

"They overdid it as usual. Should have won easily. Sucker punch wasn't it?"

"Can't wait to wind up Michael Turner."

Richard looked round at all the empty desks in dev.

"Where are they all?"

"Who? Dev? All gone."

"Gone? What happened?" Richard already guessed what happened, but he felt he had to ask.

"Redundant. It's all gone to Chennai."

Dmitri emerged from out of one of the side meeting rooms and joined them.

"Did you say dev has all gone to Chennai?" he asked.

"Yes," Steve replied.

"God. More and more is going over there. Do you think it will stop with dev?" Richard asked.

"Who knows? Those guys are seven times cheaper than Europeans."

"But eight times more shit than we are," Dmitri stated.

"It certainly makes communication more difficult," said Steve, diplomatic as ever.

"Those guys are not developers; they are bureaucrats," Dmitri growled.

"Good, here's Michael," said Steve. "Let's go."

***

"I had some good news today," said Michael Turner, slicing off a piece of American Hot and stuffing it unceremoniously into his face. He had just spent ten minutes fending off banter on the subject of the Arsenal's latest result. It seemed he wanted to remind himself of happier matters.

"Oh?" asked Steve.

"Yes." He munched for bit until he was able to continue, "My endowment policy paid up."

"Wow! Lucky you!"

"Yes. Originally it was supposed to pay off the whole mortgage, but anyway it's going to take a good sixty grand off. Means I can start making some serious inroads into the remaining sum from now on."

"Sixty grand is a fair old chunk, I imagine."

"It's not bad. Anyway, now that the kids are grown up, we can downsize and buy something smaller any time we like."

"That's the thing," said Richard, "all this stuff about endowment policy mis-selling was a load of bollocks. Whatever anyone says about them, they were better than nothing."

"A lot better," agreed Michael. "Too many people these days haven't got anything at all in place. They have 100 per cent mortgages and no repayment plan at all. That was the real mis-selling: selling people mortgages with no repayment plan."

"Everyone knew that endowment policies were a high-inflation hedge. They worked well when inflation was high. Once inflation came down, the whole idea struggled a bit, but I think to call it mis-selling was bollocks," said Richard.

"Call me paranoid," Steve interjected, "but I sometimes wonder if the people who really screw up the financial system try to create a smokescreen so that no one notices the most dodgy activity."

"Could be. Like, what do you mean?"

"If you assume that the big players can manipulate the markets – and why wouldn't we assume that? Because all these recent scandals show that they try to. Even though they always claim that the markets are too big and too liquid to be manipulated, the very fact that they try shows that they must think it's possible. So if they point the finger at a bit of dodgy insurance, if they accuse endowment sellers of mis-selling, etc, etc, that ties up the regulators, the press and the stupid-ass politicians who all go looking in the wrong place for problems."

"Nice conspiracy theory," said Michael Turner. "Anyway, I'm just damned glad that I took out that policy."

"So what's the answer? Do we write to our MPs and ask for more regulation?" Dmitri asked. They could tell from his cynical tone that he did not believe that to be the answer.

"Maybe. Maybe just more competition. These guys are still all too big to fail. Break them up so that they're not too big to fail and they have to compete with each other," Steve said. But he shrugged his shoulders, resigned to the fact he had probably not come up with the right answer.

"Maybe there needs to be better regulation instead of more regulation," Dmitri offered.

"Ah! Motherhood and Apple Pie. The solution to everything!" said Michael Turner.

"Anyway Steve, what's going on with the Trade Finance Interface?" Richard asked. "I'm supposed to get involved on the technical side at some point."

"If I told you that I'd have to shoot you," Steve replied.

"At least that would be an end to my worries."

"In fact, we still haven't got the ball rolling yet. I can get you invited to the meetings if you want to sit in."

"Yes, do that. It would be good for me to know what I'm doing for once."

"It would be a pleasant change," Steve agreed.

"Someone told me that Darion's already paid off his mortgage on that place he has in Canary Wharf." Michael Turner's thoughts had drifted back to the topic of mortgages, and he sought confirmation of a rumour he had just remembered.

"I think Darion does well, but not that well. He still has a mortgage, but it's pretty tiny compared to the value of the place," Steve replied.

"So he's not as mad as he appears to be."

"Darion's very astute in fact. He can churn numbers around in his head with the greatest of ease."

"What's his area of expertise?" Dmitri asked.

"Securities."

"He's young to have done so well. Is he from a rich family?"

"I don't think so. He does well with his own stock-market dabbling, also when he bought that place he used to have a girlfriend who got him a great rate on his mortgage."

"Oh, so he didn't borrow the money from Wonga?"

Steve sniggered.

"He definitely didn't borrow the money from Wonga or any other bunch of thieving loan sharks. As I said, he's astute, and you don't need to be too astute to know to avoid that sort of borrowing."

"That's another damned disgrace," Richard couldn't stop himself from interjecting angrily. "That's another example of actual mis-selling. Preying on the poor and desperate. How can it possibly help anyone to borrow at those rates?"

But Dmitri was more concerned about Darion's ex-girlfriend and ignored Richard's question, asking: "So what happened to his poor girlfriend who got the great mortgage rate?"

"Oh don't worry. When they split up he paid out for her share. He worked it out properly so she didn't lose out. She did OK."

"The system does work. It just needs honest brokers," said Michael Turner, digging in his pocket for his share of the bill. Lunch was over.

"Make sure he isn't using that twenty note with the elastic string again," said Steve.

33 - REJECTION

"Shit. Complete shit," Alexei was saying.

"What's shit?"

"This software pack."

"You're kidding, right?" Richard laughed.

"No. I'm not kidding. It's really awful. The worst shit."

"Well then, can you be a bit more specific?" Richard didn't want his Zima pack rejected on a whim. If Alexei wanted to reject it he would have to give a proper reason.

"What are these guys playing at? Why didn't you reject it yourself?"

Richard fought to keep his cool.

"The documentation says it's a core fix for this release."

"I don't care what kind of a fix they say it is. Look at this. They've sent three Java modules that have to be deployed in Websphere instead of just attaching a new subroutine to the hooks we already have in place."

"So it makes it more difficult to deploy?"

"Not particularly, if anything it makes it too easy. But I have no idea what might be in these routines. They could do anything and no one would know. There is no source code, just jar files that don't have to be compiled but run as soon as deployed. I want source code and I want to compile and test it on the test server myself. We disable the compiler on the live system for a reason, you know."

Richard's heart sank. He didn't want to push Alexei further. There was a danger that Alexei would start to figure out exactly what was going on. In five minutes, Alexei had seen a danger Richard had not considered in several days. No wonder he had been a rocket scientist.

Deployment of the Zima pack had fallen at the first hurdle. His whole project was a failure. His dreams of pushing the pack quickly through user acceptance testing and into the live system had just turned to dust. Mitchell was dead and there would be no replacement for the pack.

34 - RETHINK

Richard was back at his flat wondering what he could do now. Was this the end? Was this all he had to show for his hopes? It couldn't be! There must be some way of salvaging something.

Perhaps, if he could imagine what the software was supposed to do, he could write the code himself.

But that would not be easy. The code would have to do something official, like transfer currency rates from an external feed into the bank's database, which would stand industrial-strength testing by several highly experienced test teams. On top of that, it would also need to have in-built functionality to sabotage something. Functionality which was undetectable during testing, but which could be triggered when required, and would work perfectly first time and every time thereafter.

The software pack would have to be of a reasonable size compared to its official function so that it didn't look suspicious. He tried to imagine what sort of chaos a relatively small piece of code could wreak that would make the effort even worth attempting. He thought of the recent LIBOR case. Even banks deliberately manipulating LIBOR for their own personal gain had not been sufficient to damage capitalism in the slightest. The effect was probably to suck money from ordinary people with mortgages into the coffers of the bank, and thereby into the bonus schemes of the people at the top, but the effect on the workings of capitalism as a system was negligible to the point of being undetectable.

As for the software he had received from Mitchell, what could one little program do? It seemed the Zima software mimicked an interface that passed currency rates from A to B. So what could it have done that would have caused damage? Would sending out wrong currency rates have any significant effect? What if it was pushing future rates in the wrong direction to distort the yield curve? That could cause wrong decisions in the markets. But it was highly unlikely anyone would be tricked by this. The trouble with market capitalism is that someone, somewhere, might still make the right decision in spite of any particular set of misinformation. In this case, almost everyone would have the correct information and any strange results at a particular bank would be ignored during trading and then investigated.

In any case, he realised, the interface was an inward interface. No information was sent out to any external bank or organisation, not even a receipt or acknowledgement message. So the program would only affect what was going on in that particular bank. That being the case, all the correct information known and acted on by every other bank would outweigh any misinformation coming from the single bank affected.

So, what if he could modify an interface somewhere that did send out a response? He might get it to send out viruses or modify software by software injection. These were areas that Richard had very little working knowledge of, but he knew it would not be possible. He was aware that all banks had specialist security teams that did regular stress tests. Thinking about it, he began to wonder why he had had such faith in Mitchell. He imagined that Mitchell must have had a strong team of hackers behind him. Even so, there was no guarantee they were strong enough.

At that, he gave up trying to think of an answer. The whole thing had been a crazy risk with little chance of success.

Yet now, more than ever, he felt that something had to be done. Western culture was soft and decadent as well as unfair. The soft mush that passed for entertainment on TV was mind rotting. Rock and pop music had once seemed dangerous and challenging; now it was infantile drivel churned out to a formula. Food was full of additives and sugar so that it acted as a physiological comfort even if as it left you hyperactive or diabetic. Every human experience had been diluted and diminished. If only technology could be properly harnessed, it should be possible to broaden the experience of the masses and to create a fairer society. He wanted this. Nearly everybody wanted this, even if they were not fully aware of it. There must be a way of achieving it.

35 - QUARRY

Richard had been sent to Hemel Hempstead. He had to meet Carmina Fernando the following morning to discuss some technicalities concerning the back-end database, and had been sent to stay at the Holiday Inn overnight. Didn't they know that Baker Street to Hemel would only take him an hour? Well, at least he would get paid expenses for being away from the office, and get a decent cooked breakfast, so he wouldn't complain. Unfortunately, Hemel was not the most exciting town in the world. Sitting in the hotel bar, watching the football on TV, he was bored stiff.

Melanie crept back into his thoughts. He wished he could see her.

Clearly he was not going to have enough money for her tastes, though by normal standards he was well paid. Clearly he was not going to be a hero of the revolution. He went back up to his room and moped around wondering what he could do.

He had brought his unopened mail with him, and left it scattered on the dresser. He was in the habit of allowing mail to remain unopened for days, even weeks before opening it. He found it such a chore these days. There was never anything interesting in it; just bills or unpleasant trivia. The mail could wait a bit longer; he wanted to think about Melanie.

Deep down he felt both ashamed and annoyed he had to pay to see her. There was one part of the set-up that didn't shame or annoy him – that it was a form of free love. Even though Margaret Meade's *Coming of Age in Samoa* had been completely discredited, it didn't matter to Richard.

He still adhered to those values.

After all, human nature was not fixed, it was flexible. The Swinging Sixties was proof of that. Behaviour could change. People acted as though free love was possible and different lifestyles were permissible.

The same applied to other political ideas. It didn't matter whether Marxism had failed or not. The USSR and China were only attempts at a Marxist society. Furthermore, it didn't even matter if Marxism would always fail, because Marxism wasn't the only possible model for Socialism to adopt. Whatever model of society would be used to create a true socialist society, all that mattered was that it was possible and that it would improve on capitalism. All that mattered to him was that revolution was the way to trigger the changeover.

The only annoying thing about having to pay to see Melanie was that he couldn't afford it, not that it was in any way immoral or wrong. The only thing to be ashamed of was that he was not attractive to her – his money was the only attraction.

He wanted to see her again but he didn't have £900 to spare. What caused him to do it, he didn't know. He only had the vaguest notion of what he intended to do. A vague notion which nevertheless inspired him to call for a black cab around two a.m. Melanie would be finishing around three a.m. He was on his way to Aphrodite's Secret, but this time he had a better idea, one that would only cost a couple of cab fares. He specifically asked for a taxi with dark tinted windows so no one could see inside the cab.

When they got to the club, Richard asked the cab driver if they could wait near the entrance. The cabbie wasn't too happy with that idea, but was happy enough to put up with it. The meter was ticking along quite nicely.

"Shit!" he said aloud. After they had been waiting ten minutes, he realised the girls were coming out of a back exit and getting straight into cabs or cars. Richard hoped he hadn't already missed her.

"Let's go over there to wait," he said, pointing to a spot where he could see the cars and taxis as they came out of the exit. He had wanted a cab with tinted windows just in case anyone recognised him. But now, in the glare of the headlights, he felt almost naked. Naked and exposed, with shadows creeping slowly behind him. Creeping away in the opposite direction from the light that some-times shone on his face so brightly he had to screw his eyes up.

Another fifteen minutes passed. He could see her coming out the door now. She waited near a couple of Biffa bins while a car pulled up beside her. She waved happily at whoever was driving and jumped in.

"Follow that one."

"Mate, I'm not happy with this. What are you up to?"

"Don't worry about it, cabbie. I can pay £50 extra if you follow that car back.» Richard saw that the meter was already reading £350. This wasn›t going to be very much cheaper than making a proper visit to the club!

"Make it £100 and we›ve got a deal,» growled the cabbie.

"OK, £100. Just don›t lose them."

The driver obliged. At that time of night, with so little traffic on the road, it would quickly become obvious what they were doing. Would that matter? Richard wondered. He also wondered what good any of this was doing him. He had wanted to follow her home to see where she lived. But since her friend was driving, it seemed likely they would go to the friend's house. Unless she lived in a shared house with the friend? But whatever the scenario – what was really the point of knowing where she lived? Too late to worry about that now. He had just wanted to know. Maybe he had just wanted to know if she was married or had a boyfriend. He didn't know what he had wanted to know.

The strange thing was the cab was taking pretty much the route they would've taken if he'd been going home.

My God! She's going to visit me! thought Richard. He felt ridiculously happy at the idea she would want to visit him. At the same time he was kicking himself for not being at home. But common sense told him that was too good to be true anyway.

The car drove down Baker Street, just a few yards from Richard's flat in Glentworth Street, then it carried on into Soho and parked.

Melanie jumped out, holding her phone to her ear and looking round expectantly. Her face lit up, looking back along the pavement, and suddenly she was in the arms of her lover. Another young man approached and stood nearby. He stooped down and grinned into the front window of the parked car.

Then the driver got out of the car. It was another girl of Melanie's age. She struggled with her hem for a moment, managing to tug it down to the tops of her thighs, before making clippy little steps toward the pavement. This was not what Richard had hoped for. He had not known what he had hoped for, but this was not it.

"OK, let's get back to Hemel," he said.

36 - FALSE ADVERTISING

Back in his hotel room, Richard felt more lonely and desperate than ever. He wished he had never tried to follow Melanie. What was that ever going to achieve? he wondered.

He was angry with Melanie. He was more angry with himself.

The envelopes on his dressing table were waiting to be opened. His conscience nagged him for procrastinating. All he had to do was open the damned things and see what was there. Bills, junk mail, instructions to all residents to remember not to let unknown persons follow you through the entrance, notifications of road-works, other joyless crap that sapped your energy. But the time had finally come when he had to do it. He opened the envelopes and read each one. The first three were bills, then a bank statement, then a newsletter from the Conservative Party, then the local news-paper from Glasgow – *the* newspaper...

He always got a copy so that he could double-check his advert, but it was hardly worth it this time because, this time, he hadn't bothered to put the advert in. He decided to flick through the paper anyway, just for the sake of it, just to alleviate his wretchedness and boredom. He flicked through, glancing at all the usual small-time trivia those papers were filled with.

Something that looked like one of his adverts was there after all!

That's funny, perhaps they made a mistake and re-ran the previous one. He decided to check to see. After all, he didn't want to be charged for an advert he didn't need. Suddenly his heart was beating faster. What if someone else knows about my adverts? What if someone else put this in?

He was in such a state of confusion that he found it difficult to decode. But it was already clear there was something there that could be decoded: a message – a message that was unfamiliar.

"VirtuBank making redundancies. Possible last chance to act. Likely to be at RCB soon. Prime tier 1 target."

The words were absolutely true. But the words were not his words. He continued to decode until the full message was clear.

"VirtuBank making redundancies. Possible last chance to act. Likely to be at RCB soon. Prime tier 1 target. Making plans to take action alone if not contacted immediately."

He stood up, pacing the room. Emotions burst through his brain in stabbing pulses that made him sick and dizzy. It was as though the newspaper had read his mind. But the final part of the message was not true at all! He never had any intention of acting alone. He would have no idea how to act alone. Who could have done this? Why?

He sat down again and checked the date of the paper. This advert had gone into the local paper on 25th October. Two days later, Weber had rung the bell at Glentworth Street.

So had Weber got in contact with him because of this false advert? Would Weber have put this advert in?

Richard ripped open the remaining envelopes, somehow expecting to find another clue as to what had happened. There was nothing unusual in any of them. No more clues – but clearly someone else had known about his coded messages and had decided for some reason to put a false message in. A false message that was almost totally accurate. A false message that predicted something he himself had not known – that he was likely to go to RCB.

37 - OUT OF DARKNESS

Richard slept badly that night. Mitchell and Weber were swimming round in his troubled thoughts. And Melanie. How did it all fit together?

And suddenly Eddie jumped out of the darkness, his face contorted in anger, shouting.

Eddie! Eddie had been in prison...

Memories of Eddie were indistinct now. The angrily shouting newspaper cutting had overwritten earlier, more personal memories. He remembered Eddie was a strong person, but how strong? What could've happened to poor Eddie while he was in prison? Had he given away some details of the plan there? So perhaps Weber was some Mafia boss with connections to someone who had been in prison with Eddie...

And Melanie, for Christ's sake! Melanie was a prostitute! She was almost certain to have connections to organised crime. What proof was there Melanie was genuine? What proof was there she was giving him instructions from Mitchell? What proof was there even Mitchell was genuine? Was Mitchell killed so someone could take over the real operation for criminal purposes? Instead of installing software that would destroy the capitalist system, perhaps he was being duped into installing something that would simply switch a large payment into a private bank account...

Who, back at the Party, decodes the messages, and for whom? Whoever that was could put a false message in... But why would they bother, why now, after all these years? The only person doing the decoding should be his handler – Mitchell... or Weber.

Furthermore the message wasn't very much different from anything he would've put in himself. Except, perhaps, for the bit about acting alone.

Richard racked his brains, wondering if somehow, he had prepared the advert himself and forgotten about it. No, he remembered very clearly that he had made the conscious decision not to bother with another advert. Besides, he didn't know about RCB on 25th October. He couldn't have said he was likely to go there.

Eddie, or someone in the Party, must have given him away. He made up his mind he should go to see Eddie. He was somehow quite convinced that Weber was Mafia of some sort. The fact Weber had come to see him so soon after the advert first appeared must be significant. But Melanie too had appeared at that time...

The meeting with Carmina didn't go too well. Richard was exhausted. He had probably only had a couple of hours sleep in the end. Carmina asked him if he was feeling OK and he seized on the opportunity to say that he'd better go to see a doctor. He didn't feel well at all, in fact.

What he really wanted though, was to go and find Eddie as soon as possible.

38 - EDDIE

Richard hadn't been in touch with Eddie since his student days. He had flown up on the Friday night without giving a moment's thought that it might be difficult to find him. He had expected to go to the bookshop in Queen Street and trace him through someone there. But the bookshop was closed down. It had probably closed years ago. Now he had no idea how he was going to get in touch.

By chance, he found some people from the Party hanging around nearby, handing out pamphlets. After overcoming their suspicions, one of them had given him the address.

Cambuslang – it came back to him now. That was where Eddie had lived in the old days. He hadn't moved. Somehow it hadn't occurred to him Eddie would still be living in the same flat. Richard had moved around dozens of times in the intervening years. Also, his memory of Cambuslang had faded slightly. He had almost forgotten the meaning of the term 'Deprived Area'. He felt distinctly uncomfortable getting out of the taxi at Eddie's address.

Especially because, instead of using a normal taxi company, he'd used the company that VirtuBank normally used. It was more of a limousine service than a straightforward taxi company. VirtuBank had to keep up appearances to its customers.

Richard had kind of become accustomed to getting in and out of limousines on his way from one shining glass building to the next, or from one gleaming airport to an equally gleaming hotel. Even though he was always impressed by the buildings the banks owned, he was hardly aware he spent most of his time living and working in glass palaces in the sky. The most evident glass here was the broken glass scattered over the pavement. A few of the houses nearby had boarded-up windows. These sorts of areas used to be fairly dangerous. Even back in the old days, he felt a bit out of place coming here. Now he was definitely an outsider. And what was funny – the more derelict and deprived an area was, the more likely it was that some bunch of bampots would defend the territory. As though, if they didn't, there would be an influx of people eager to take up residence. Sometimes poverty can be worn as a badge of honour. Criticism of poverty is taken as an insult – as though you are criticising the people themselves. Even encouraging aspiration of any sort is presumed to be a threat to the feeling of working-class solidarity that is supposed to exist. That way, lazy councillors and trade unionists had a job for life in an area like this.

He went up the close and rang the bell. After a while, noises behind the door indicated someone was preparing to answer. In the old days, Eddie's dad used to live here too. It was usually he who came to the door. But surely his dad wasn't still alive...

The door opened a crack, to the full extent of the chain.

"Eddie? It's Richard."

"Richard?" Eddie's face, peering into the space beyond Richard, was confused.

"Richard Slater."

Eddie's eyes finally looked directly at Richard instead of hunting round behind him to ensure he was alone. "My God! Ah thought ye were dead man! Long ago. Hang oan. Ah'll open the door and let ye in."

After fumbling with the chain for a while, Eddie got the door open and showed Richard through to the living room. Richard noticed Eddie stooped slightly and walked with a pronounced limp. They sat down; Eddie in what was obviously his personal chair and Richard in one nearer to the window.

Eddie was looking at Richard with puzzlement. Finally he asked, "So whit brings ye back here efter aw riss time?"

Richard couldn't tell Eddie the truth, but he hadn't prepared himself to answer this very obvious question.

"I... I suppose it was just that I was passing through," he said lamely. He had passed through Glasgow hundreds of times since he'd last bothered to see Eddie. They both knew it. There was an awkward silence. He could see Eddie looking at his shoes. They were nothing fancy, just Timberland, but they were a mistake. Richard realised that, to Eddie, in his cheap moccasins, living in a council flat in Cambuslang, they would seem like a posh designer label.

"Ah see," Eddie replied tonelessly.

Richard wanted to steer the conversation toward what he needed to know.

"Ah heard you were in prison fur a while?" Richard was embarrassed to note that he was already imitating Eddie's accent. He hadn't meant to. At least he'd asked the question now. This was the subject he needed to discuss. He needed to know if Eddie had wittingly or unwittingly let any information out.

"Whit of it?"

"Just..." This was impolite. They should chat about something else first. "Nothing," he said lamely. He needed to at least make it clear he wasn't being judgemental, certainly not in a negative way. "I was sorry to hear about it. I hope it wasn't too bad anyway."

"Well... ah suppose ye could say it wiz just abutt as bad as ye might expect."

There was another excruciating silence.

"Do you hear from Stuart at all?" Richard hoped that mentioning Stuart might bring back memories of happier times. Or at least times when they had things in common.

"Nope... ah fell out with Stuart quite a while back."

"Oh."

"He wuz nothing but a useless swotty shite. No fucking use at aw tae anybuddy thut needed help. Swotty bastart." Eddie's voice grew louder and angrier with every word. Suddenly his anger subsided; another idea had occurred to him. "How about you, Richard? Did you ever get round tae doing any aw ra hings ye said ye would?"

Richard had no idea what to say. He couldn't let Eddie know that Zima was up and running. He was tempted to, though. Poor Eddie; it might be of some comfort to him.

"I'm still..." he couldn't say it, not even to Eddie, "I'm still..."

"ARE YOU FUCK!!" Eddie shouted. "Are you fuck still anyhin!"

Richard was stunned, but Eddie had still not finished with his outburst.

"Look at yuh, there wi' yur designer label shoes, coming here in a fuckin motherfuckin Mercedes, fancy fucking claithes oan..." Eddie's voice was strangled with rage and bitterness.

Richard took a deep breath, trying to control his anger. Eddie used to get quite violent in the old days. He was almost grateful he seemed to have ailments or injuries that would make him less able to fight physically.

"Eddie! Eddie! Calm down."

Eddie sprang to his feet. Immediately, surprise and pain registered on his face. He stumbled onto the floor, breathing hard and clutching his ankle.

"Are you OK?" Richard got up and helped Eddie back into his seat. He sat down himself and waited until they had both started breathing more evenly before deciding that he'd better ask what he had to ask. As soon as he'd done that, he could go.

"I came for something quite important. I need to know if you passed on any information about me and that envelope that I gave you."

"Whit?" Eddie spat the question out.

"Do you know anything at all? I think someone out there who shouldn't know, does know."

Eddie just stared at him, suspicion in his eyes. That same hostile stare, through heavy, black-rimmed glasses.

"It could even be some criminal gang or something like that. People that could've got to you when you were inside."

"Whit? Whit makes ye think that?"

"I think something's going wrong with that whole envelope plan." Richard couldn't think what else to call it except "envelope plan". It was vague, but not vague enough.

"That whole plan wuz years ago man. Nothin' ever came ay it."

"Something's coming of it now, but I don't know what."

"Ah never knew ay any ah the details in the envelope and ah never said nothin' to anyone in prison... or anywhere else."

"I'm a hundred per cent sure that someone out there knows."

"I'm a hundred per cent sure that ah never telt anyone."

"How'd you get your limp?"

"Aye, that was prison aw right. One ah they bastarts didnae like commies."

"So how did he know you were a commie?"

"Are you daft? Everyone knows ah'm a commie. Ah'm proud ay it. Ah tell everybuddy. But ah don't tell secret information and ah never even knew what yuh put in the envelope."

They sat in silence. That was that then.

"Can you tell me who you gave the envelope to?"

"Ah'm probably not supposed to tell anyone that either. But ah can tell you that it makes no difference really. No one could trace who it would go to ultimately. We were a Trotsky-ite party but anything that required serious funding, like your envelope, probably ended up in the Soviet Union. Who knows who got hold of your details when it all broke up.

"Wow. I'm so fucking naïve. I never even thought of that." Richard looked out of the window. A couple of drunks were staggering along the road. It looked as though they were performing an ungainly and sinister dance.

Eddie was scribbling something on a piece of paper.

"Here, go un see Stuart. He might finally be uv some use. Even if only to gie ye a telling aff for ever being uh socialist. That's aw rah help he wuz tae me when ah ended up in jail. Who knows, he might think you're worth lifting a finger for."

"Thanks Eddie, appreciated." Richard took the paper with Stuart's address and phone number. That was that then. There was nothing left to say. He waited a moment to see if Eddie would say anything. He was trying to think of something else himself, but there was nothing. Finally he said, "I'll let myself out." He left Eddie sitting in his chair. Eddie didn't turn round or say goodbye. He just looked straight ahead at the blank screen of his TV.

39 - SOVIET STUDIES

Stuart was Professor of Soviet Studies at the University of Glasgow. He lived in a sandstone flat in the West End, in an apartment not dissimilar to the one they shared as students. Now he had a whole apartment to himself – though it was smaller than the sprawling multi-occupation squat had been. The living room, instead of being furnished with the cheap, garish artefacts of the late seventies and full of punks and hippies, was tastefully decorated and full of books.

Richard had made the tactical decision to start the conversation off in the way he would have back in the old days. He didn't want to make the same mistake he had with Eddie. It would be even less likely Stuart would be able to help him in any way. It would be even more difficult to bring up the topic of "the envelope".

"So, how's my old comrade then?" Richard asked, affecting a jovial tone.

"'Comrade'," Stuart repeated, spitting the word out as though it tasted bad.

"I had an idea you had drifted away from all that stuff. Eddie told me you fell out."

"Yeah, I'm not much of a comrade any more. We all grow up I guess."

Richard was completely taken aback. It seemed the old days were well and truly gone. It confirmed his fear it wouldn't be easy to talk. Richard only had the vaguest idea of what he could ask of Stuart anyway. The only common ground he had was their intellectual attachment to a socialist ideal. If he was going to be able to talk to him, or trust him in any way, he had to get onto that common ground.

"But surely... surely there was an intellectual basis that still stands?"

"I'm head of Soviet Studies nowadays. I'm a fucking expert in all that shite; written papers; given speeches. All that poisonous shite that we used to play with like it was a new toy."

"So, your expertise serves to enable you to attack rather than defend the way we used to think?"

"Richard, you probably don't want to hear my views. This is why Eddie fell out with me."

"But none of us were pro Soviet Union anyway."

"That's right; we used to think the Soviet Union was a bad example of socialism. But it wasn't just that the Soviet Union was a bad example of socialism. It was worse than that."

"How so?"

"We used to go around thinking 'if only it wasn't for Stalin, the USSR could've been a great success.'"

"Pretty much, yeah."

"But of course, once we bothered to read up properly instead of just browsing a few propaganda leaflets, we would say 'OK so Lenin's hands were pretty dirty too – if only it wasn't for Lenin, the USSR could've been a great success'."

"A lot more people believed in Lenin. It was Stalin that really screwed things up for the USSR."

"Really? How about Lenin's idea of 'the dictatorship of the proletariat'?"

"I can't remember all that stuff nowadays," Richard lied. He didn't want to get bogged down in an argument about the USSR.

"Let me remind you," Stuart said, smugly confident in his expertise. "Marx had presumed that Socialism was a further advancement from capitalism. That, therefore, the first countries to become socialist would be the most advanced capitalist ones."

"Yeah, OK."

"So when Lenin took control of the Russian Revolution, he had to change the narrative to fit the facts. He decided that even a less-developed country, such as Tsarist Russia, could become socialist. All that had to happen was that it had to be led. There had to be an elite to lead it. This elite had to be a dictatorship, that would, as true Socialism developed, wither away. The state, at first all-powerful, would wither away."

"Yes, it comes back to me now. The more left-wing, true socialists, like us, believed this was a terrible mistake. A betrayal of the real principles that Marx had in mind."

"But even that was untrue. Marx himself was not too careful when it came to principles of individual freedom. It's hard to imagine how any country could have taken the ideas that Marx laid out and made a success of them. I think it was lucky that it was not a more advanced country, because if it had been they could have crushed external opposition and internal dissent even more easily."

"So you're actually glad that the socialist experiment took place in a weak country so that capitalism was able to re-assert itself?"

"Yes, otherwise there might have been no escape from the downward spiral."

Downward spiral. This wasn't going too well at all. The awkwardness was just as bad as it had been at Eddie's flat. Richard was stunned into silence. He hadn't expected Stuart to be ideologically opposed; he had expected him to be, like himself, doubting, or looking for an exact interpretation... but not to be diametrically opposed.

Stuart had stood up and was hovering his finger over the bookcase at the back of the room. "Here we are," he said, "this is from the *Rheinische Zeitung*, January 1849, Marx's own newspaper. Marx says: 'There will be primitive societies that are not yet capitalist that need to be destroyed.' Charming eh? Destroyed. Were the pogroms that some of us presumed to be inherited from Tsarist Russia, intellectually part of Marxism itself?"

Richard didn't know what to say. "Destroyed." What did it mean? Was it an invitation to starve millions to death, as Stalin had done, or did it mean something else? He sat there in silence, feeling foolish, wondering what to say next. In the old days he was well up on his Marxism, or so he thought. He could give Stuart a decent argument, though they were on the same side of the fence, usually only arguing about points of detail.

"Anyway, I'm guessing that you've given up on all that stuff by now, like the rest of us." Stuart was almost challenging him.

"Apart from Eddie, of course." Somehow, Richard didn't want to include himself among the believers.

"Apart from Eddie."

Richard thought about Zima. That was what he was here for. How could he bring it up? What purpose would it serve? He had hoped for some sort of help from Stuart, even if it was just moral support. This was quite unexpected; Stuart was completely changed.

"But no, not really. I suppose I haven't thought about things for a long time. Just talking with you now brings back stuff that I haven't thought about properly for ages, but I haven't given up on it". At some point he would need to talk about Zima. It was wrong to do it, but he needed help.

"Hopefully nothing ever came of that envelope that you handed over to Eddie. I remember that I was almost as keen on that idea as you were. Thankfully I never quite got round to being a man of action. Too busy thinking about stuff. Once you start acting on something it forces you to stop thinking."

Richard had a feeling that this was a direct criticism. Was that what had happened to him? Certainly he no longer thought about anything in any theoretical way. He had prepared himself to act and he was going to act.

Stuart continued, "Remember, back in the day, how we used to have such serious discussions about the RAF?"

Richard smiled, "Yes, the Red Army Faction; the Baader-Meinhof gang. Quite a few of the Party thought of them as genuine freedom fighters."

"Something I could never see."

"Me neither."

"They were more like spoiled kids who happened to like fast cars, guns and sex – and who doesn't? The whole pseudo-intellectual babble that they came out with to justify their actions was just self-delusion."

"Remember how we used to have a laugh at some of their statements?"

"Yeah, we used to satirise them as though they were an art movement." Stuart's face broke into something resembling a smile, but mirthless. Grim. "That was how their declarations read. Like some sort of new wave art movement." He leaned forward and put on a silly German accent: "Protest is ven I say zis does not please me. Resistance is ven I ensure vot does not please me occurs no more." He could still quote Ulrike Meinhof verbatim.

"It was very German. Continental."

Stuart ignored this remark because he hadn't finished his comparison of Ulrike Meinhof with Salvador Dali. "That was Ulrike Meinhof with what she thought was a clever slogan. She was probably part of the same performance art group as Salvador Dali," he joked, continuing, "Dali's slogan was, 'I like it, murder, because this is courage. It is anti-bourgeois'."

"Yes, slogans, that's what the Chic Left used to be good at back in those days. It's odd how random slogans seemed to have so much meaning to so many people even when they turned out to be superficial or meaningless in any practical terms."

"I always felt quite sorry for some of them, Ulrike Meinhof in particular. I could never understand how a mother of two children and successful journalist got caught up with the RAF. Anyway, the Stasi didn't mind them one bit. That's the trouble: quite often well-meaning and 'innocent' people like that get caught up in a wider struggle. They get used as pawns in a big geopolitical game that is being played out between the great powers."

Richard thought of himself. Did this apply to him? He certainly felt like a pawn. Was Stuart aware of something he wasn't? Was he giving him a direct warning, or was he still just generalising? He was about to bring up "the envelope" again but Stuart had thought of a new variation on his theme...

"I say that they're pawns but quite often they have a greatly exaggerated sense of ego too. I think Baader and even Kim Philby probably fell into that category."

"Not sure about Philby, but I know what you mean."

"... and his buddy Maclean. Did you know, when his cover was blown, and he had to escape to Moscow, Maclean had the cheek to object? He'd spend years helping the Soviets and undermining the West but when it came to the crunch he personally wanted no part of living in the USSR. Cheeky fucker."

"What if there could be a real revolution?"

"OK, what if there could?"

"Would you be supportive?"

"The thing is, when I was young I used to think of Marxism as being just more of what I wanted. A more pure version. But as I grew up I came to realise that it was a different thing altogether. Socialism in the UK had been based on Methodism, or ideals based in religion – perhaps Puritanism. It agreed with ideas of social mobility provided by capitalism. It agreed with liberal ideals and freedom of speech."

"And Marxism doesn't? Not even the purer versions?"

"'Purer versions,'" Stuart mocked. "No, that was another mistake. Leftist parties were always looking for something pure. Splitting themselves into smaller and smaller groups because of some finicky detail of theory or policy. On the other hand, a lot of leftist parties and groups made unholy alliances with all sorts of opposing or unrelated groups. The Molotov Ribbentrop agreement might be the biggest example of that. Baader-Meinhof itself was strangely blind to the fact that they were not remotely on the same side as the PLO – which should have been all too obvious when they got ejected from the PLO training camp in Jordan. Somehow it wasn't obvious to them. They went on to support the Black September attack on the Munich Olympics."

Richard had no reply. He stared at the rows of books lining the walls wondering how Stuart found time to read them.

Stuart had thought of a new angle of attack. "Eddie thinks of the Party as a Trotsky-ite party because, like a lot of undereducated 'libertarian' socialists, he thinks that Trotsky was better than Stalin. 'If only Trotsky instead of Stalin...' they bleat. But let me quote from the delightful Mr Trotsky: 'We must put an end once and for all to the Quaker-papist babble about the sanctity of human life.' The hard Left threw the baby out with the bathwater when they abandoned religion-based Socialism. Of course, I'm not a religious man myself..."

"But you're not a socialist any more in any sense?" Richard asked.

"I'm some sort of capitalist liberal if I'm anything. I don't like labelling myself. Like everybody else..."

Richard was annoyed now. He seized an opportunity to argue against what he guessed Stuart was going to say, even if he had to put words into his mouth. "Like everybody else – no alternative – neo-liberalism. But don't you think it's gone far enough now? Don't you think that the rich will go on getting richer and richer until we're right back to where we were at the start of the twentieth century with a tiny elite capitalist class and a huge poor working class?"

"OK. Let's say that's a danger."

"Then Marx was right about one thing – capital. Wage differences, even huge ones like the difference between a top banker and a cleaner, are irrelevant. It's ownership of capital that creates insurmountable, innate differences between classes. Income earned through wages is temporary and taxed quite highly."

"OK. So let's say capital is the problem." Stuart had the intellectual's irritating habit of conceding a point to you just so he could show you how difficult it was for you to gain from it. "Let's say that the fact that capital is concentrated in the hands of a very few people is the problem. It's easier to redistribute income rather than capital. The people who own capital have all the power. They will not give up that power. The owners of capital won't give it up just to be nice."

"Exactly. That's why the status quo has to be destroyed. There is no other way. When something is standing in the way of progress it has to be destroyed. They say that if the dinosaurs had not been wiped out by a chance event there would have been no way for the tiny mammals that they shared the planet with to evolve into human beings."

"Maybe the dinosaurs themselves would have evolved. Maybe they would have evolved into something even better than human beings." Stuart grinned but Richard took his point seriously.

"Come on. There was no pressure on them to change. Capitalism is not under pressure either just now. It's ossifying. Things are getting worse."

"I don't know, Richard. I only know that Marxism failed once…

several times in fact." He decided to change tack. "Anyway, you didn't come back just to have an academic chat. Or did you? I should charge a tuition fee."

"No. I went to see Eddie earlier." Richard had still not addressed the fact that it would be even more difficult to discuss "the envelope" with Stuart than Eddie. Stuart had nothing to do with it. What was he going to ask for?

40 - WISER

Richard decided he'd better take the plunge. Suddenly he said, "Remember our plans?"

"Plans?"

"To stay hidden until we were in a position to do something useful for the revolution?"

Stuart laughed. "Yes, I remember that."

Richard could see the puzzlement on Stuart's face. He understood why he was puzzled. Stuart was wondering why he was bringing this up again even though he'd already mentioned it and dismissed it just a few minutes ago. In a moment Stuart would realise that he'd carried on with that reckless plan and conclude he would want to have nothing to do with it. Richard would have to handle this carefully.

Richard remained stonily serious. "I remember you thought it was a good idea at the time. Did you go through with it?"

"If I did, I wouldn't be able to say, would I?" Was Stuart amusing himself at his expense?

"I guess not. Unless..."

"Unless what?" Stuart was obviously tiring of this childish game. His face was impatient.

"If you had signed up for it, what would you do if it was all going wrong?"

"I have no idea. What could I do? I don't recall there being any contingency plans. It was a one-way ticket to desolation. Once you were committed you were on your own. No help, no backup... nothing."

Richard felt lost. It was all true.

"That's why I didn't go for it," Stuart added.

Richard was annoyed now. Why hadn't Stuart warned him of this if he had been able to foresee it at the time? He was even more annoyed at himself. Was Stuart so much cleverer than he was? Why hadn't he thought of this too?

Stuart hadn't finished. "Another thing is, I imagine the Party would be heavily infiltrated by MI5 slash MI6 as well as being controlled or influenced by God knows what terrorist group – perhaps the IRA, perhaps the PLO, at best the Soviets. As innocent, idealistic students we might have found that we'd inadvertently wandered into the front line of the Cold War."

The trouble is, I did go through with it. Richard imagined himself saying it. He imagined what would happen now it was out in the open. He imagined the feeling of relief he would feel. He imagined the moments of silence while Stuart tried to understand what he was saying.

Instead he said nothing. He'd come within a step of blowing away years of total secrecy. He shuddered. It was the same sort of feeling you sometimes get when you stand on a clifftop and imagine that, if you just take a step forward, you would be able to fly. The same sort of feeling of thankfulness that you don't do it.

And it has gone totally wrong. I need some sort of help. The unsaid words echoed in his mind as he stood up and made his excuses to go before the demon in his head tempted him further. So, instead of saying them, he found himself in the hallway while Stuart went to the front door. Instead of asking for help he found himself saying, "Yes it's a very different world now. Everything has changed. I'm glad that neither of us went through with that half-baked nonsense." He stood back while Stuart opened the door.

"We're older and wiser than that now," Stuart affirmed, as he started to shut the door behind him.

41 - THINGS TO CONSIDER

Osbourne was holding another meeting.

"Let's get straight down to business. We have to decide what's gone wrong with *Snowman*. Establish why he's still not doing anything and try to come up with something that will finally get him active."

The others sitting round the table were Callan, Dr Skinner and Jack Logan. Callan was first to reply to Osbourne:

"It seems to me that he's just going about his normal business as though nothing is happening – but I know for a fact that this time he has received our instructions."

"So what's wrong? Has he decided not to do anything after all? After all these years! Do you think that's possible?"

Dr Skinner replied to this: "It's quite possible. There are several things to consider. Firstly that Mitchell killed himself. Put yourself in his shoes. If Mitchell, who has just introduced himself as the handler, has killed himself, he must be wondering just how hot this project is – "

"Wait!" Osbourne interrupted. "Surely Mitchell didn't introduce himself as anything. Wasn't he supposed to take advantage of *Snowman*'s dual-state condition to pass instructions in state A that he would act on in state B?"

The penny dropped. Callan agreed: "Bloody hell! That's why we gave him the instructions verbally in Helsinki. Mitchell was supposed to convince him it was his own key and implant a memory. But when he did nothing we sent the girl to him, specifically mentioning Mitchell. We screwed up."

"We certainly did," Osbourne said.

Callan sought clarification.

"So we've stupidly made him think that Mitchell is the handler and, now, if anyone else has contacted him in the meantime, he's simply going to believe…"

Dr Skinner interrupted: "I can't agree. Don't you remember the email from Mitchell that we found? Mitchell dropped a much too heavy hint. That was a grave mistake. So surely it's more to do with Mitchell's suicide? He's simply too scared to do anything. He's got cold feet."

But Osbourne wasn't going to give up yet.

"Well, maybe, but even if that's true, the problem is that Mitchell has become linked to him far too strongly. All we need to do to rescue the situation is come up with something to break the link."

"OK, it's easy to say that," Skinner said angrily. "But unless someone has a time machine, it's impossible by now. What's done is done."

"Don't exaggerate, Skinner. We don't need a time machine. We just need to break the link," Osbourne said.

"I have an idea," Callan said. "Discredit Mitchell."

Osbourne nodded sagely, but Dr Skinner was not satisfied.

"This is something of a leap in the dark. In reality we don't know why he's not doing anything. I'm worried that something else has gone wrong."

"Can you think of any other possibilities?" Osbourne asked.

"No, I can't, but if we go on fumbling around in the dark and making mistakes, as we have been doing, there is even a danger that our phase-switching technology could be in danger of being discovered and reverse engineered," Dr Skinner said, his face strained and haggard.

"This was always known to us." Osbourne said, "It only becomes possible if any clues…"

"Clues such as *Snowman* displaying unusual variations in his behaviour," Skinner said irritably. "It's possible. If things are going wrong, it's likely. We don't really know his state of mind now."

"We're doing our best to keep him under observation without letting anyone know he's being observed. If we try to observe him too closely, that could be a bigger clue to our opponents than any changes in his behaviour."

"But if our opponents were to suspect anything they would not hesitate to use the most extreme methods at their disposal in order to discover our secrets. If we stop now at least we protect those methods for use another time."

"And what if this happens that time too? No, I want to go on. We have gone this far and I see no point in withdrawing now."

Dr Skinner looked grim but said no more.

42 - SCANT EVIDENCE

As the plane took off from Glasgow Airport, Richard knew he would never see Eddie or Stuart again. For all these years he'd imagined that they were still somehow with him, united by strongly held beliefs, in spite of the fact they had never been in contact. But that illusion had been shattered.

He got back to London late on Saturday night. The door of his flat was ajar. He hesitated but, overcoming a feeling of dread, pushed it open while stepping back and bracing himself in case someone burst out. His eyes searched anxiously, expecting to find everything in state of chaos. Everything seemed to be as he had left it.

"Hello?" he asked tentatively.

He stepped through the door and switched the light on. Along the hallway all the doors were shut. He walked to the kitchen and turned the handle carefully, trying not to make a noise. He pushed the door just enough to reach inside and switch the light on, half expecting to feel his wrist roughly grabbed or for the door to be yanked open to reveal someone with a knife or a gun.

But no, the kitchen too was just as he had left it. He repeated the process as he searched the whole flat, creeping quietly from room to room with the unsettling feeling that it was he who was the stranger in someone else's house. After checking each room carefully, he concluded no one was there. Nothing appeared to have been damaged or moved. So, either no one had been in, or someone very professional had been in. But surely a professional wouldn't leave the door open? So, no one had been in. He had left the door open himself in his hurry to catch his flight and, by some miracle, no one had come in and ransacked the place.

He was exhausted. Meeting up with Eddie and Stuart had been a psychological drama. The open door was the last straw. He thought about reporting it to the police, but there was nothing to report. It would just be a waste of time and he was tired. So he went to bed and slept fitfully, wondering about Mitchell, Weber and Melanie and what the plan was now. Wondering if anyone at VirtuBank knew he had tried to deploy the Zima code, that it had failed because of Alexei, and if any of that mattered.

***

He was following Melanie home again. It was raining and he couldn't see anything distinctly. Bright streams of sodium-lit rain ran down the windows. The cab driver was hidden in contrasting shadow.

They were passing close to his flat again. This time the car turned into his street and stopped. Melanie got out of the passenger's side. A man got out of the driver's side, leaving the door open for Melanie to get back in. As the car moved off the man put up an umbrella and turned toward Richard's cab. His face was lit up in the headlights. Mitchell!

The cabbie stopped and asked Richard if he was getting out.

"Wait."

Richard looked up, through the streams of sodium yellow. A light went on in his apartment. Someone was there, someone who walked with his right shoulder down. It could only be Mitchell.

A snake came looping down behind Mitchell, its head inquisitively thrust forward. A snake, hanging from something unseen, uncoiling toward the back of Mitchell's head.

Richard woke up. That god-damned snake was haunting his dreams. And now it had roped Mitchell into its shenanigans for some reason. He looked at his alarm clock but was too tired to register what time it was. In another moment he was asleep again.

Around noon he got up. He made himself a coffee. The memory stick had long since been removed from its temporary hiding place in the coffee jar and had been used to send the email. Then it had been wiped and thrown into the Thames. All the paper copies of the documents had gone too, burnt. Once Richard had sent the email, he didn't need any of that stuff.

What about the phone? Was that what someone had broken in to look for? If so, they would have had no luck, because it had been in the pocket of the coat he had been wearing the whole time. Richard went to his coat and got it. He sat playing with the phone for thirty minutes or more. He couldn't see anything of any significance.

43 - PURPOSE

Richard couldn't live without purpose; he was trying to clear his mind to come up with a new revolutionary plan. Perhaps, he wondered, he could go back to the Party, get them to find a new handler and rework the original plan. Perhaps he should try to organise a more overt type of sabotage; in other words, terrorism.

So now he was doing something he hadn't done for some time, though it used to be a regular habit. He was trying to focus his energy.

It might seem to an outsider he was praying, or practising yoga, but this was something he felt he'd invented himself. He knelt in the middle of his living room, with the palms of his hands pressed together. To distinguish it from praying, he held his fingers splayed apart with the tips of both forefingers resting against his lips. The tips of his middle fingers pressed against the tip of his nose and he breathed deeply and hard.

He was not physically strong. There was no point in doing exercise; there was no point in learning martial arts or how to use weapons. But he wanted to be mentally strong. He was trying to summon up the hatred he felt so he could make himself unfeeling while imagining the destruction of capitalism.

Since his meeting with Stuart, Richard had realised how out of touch he'd become in his knowledge of Marx and Marxism. In any case, he was not really a Marxist; he was a post-Marxist revolutionary anarchist. He'd been reading up again, re-reading biographies of Lenin, Mao, a few Marxist pamphlets and a few anarchist ones. He'd also read some green activist pamphlets. He'd bought the book by Piketty in the hope that it would point the direction that a post-Marxist revolutionary should go in. He hadn't read it yet. But somewhere in among the stuff he'd been reading there would be someone to connect with to help revise and revive his plan.

If he could he would probably have to work his way into a terrorist group. Perhaps an Islamic group. It seemed they were easily able to commit acts of terror. Although they seemed less successful in actually changing anything, especially of making the sort of changes he wanted. Instead of individual acts of petty terror, they needed to be directed toward full-blown revolutionary change.

He thought of the people he had known in the banking industry. If there was a bloody revolution, it was possible that every one of them would be killed. He might somehow be caught up in the killing himself. Would it be possible for him, supposing he was somehow called upon to do it, to kill one of his work colleagues in furtherance of the revolution? Callan or Mitchell (if he was still alive) would be possible; easy in fact to kill them. Something about both of them was just detestable. But what about Steve...?

Richard stood up. He stretched his arms up to the ceiling and breathed in. What had to be done would have to be done.

He walked over to his CD collection and chose something to play. He slipped the CD into the player and began to listen to the measured solemnity of the opening bars of Tannhäuser by Wagner, apparently Hitler's favourite composer. That didn›t make it bad music.

Richard had taken to listening to classical music. Pop and rock were no longer progressive, subversive or radical. They evoked memories of childhood and adolescence, stirring up feelings of nostalgia, often tinged with melancholy, but nothing more. Nothing remained of the original modern, revolutionary spirit. That spirit had been left behind in the sixties and seventies when the music was new.

So now he challenged himself by listening to Wagner and Beethoven. He had heard that Lenin did not permit himself to listen to Beethoven because it made him feel emotion. So Richard was Lenin in reverse – he felt less emotion listening to classical music.

What, he asked himself, had made him into this dangerous lunatic?
Nothing.

Besides, he was not a dangerous lunatic. He was a thoughtful, considerate person. He wanted to trigger revolution but not aimless, excessive violence. Lenin had ensured that the Russian Revolution would be a failure by his fanaticism and insistence on violence. Hitler had subverted a once-socialist party through violence. The modern revolutionary Left acknowledged the mistakes of Lenin and Stalin. They were inspired more by Trotsky or Che Guevara or even Gandhi.

Richard wanted to be someone cool-headed enough to get the job done, not somebody ranting uselessly while police observers took photographs and filed reports.

Lenin had been deliberately encouraged back into Russia by German authorities eager to see him wreak havoc on their enemy.

The revolution that had already begun was sabotaged by Lenin's actions; not helped by them. Lenin had deflected the revolution from its objectives. What might have happened if there had been a true revolution?

The crux of the matter was resources. If resources could be more evenly and fairly shared among people – among all the people of the whole world – there would be less pressure to fight over them. Warfare would be a thing of the past. He remembered arguing with Quinton about it in the pub.

"OK, any fool can say that," Quinton had said. "Especially drug-addled millionaire songsters like John Lennon. The fact is that countries have borders. Inside those borders there's stuff that people want. Those countries need to keep what they have – they don't want to give it away for nothing. You know what the answer is? It's not some sort of imaginary, impossible socialism – it's trade. Same goes for people. The people who happen to have their money safely tucked in a vault or safely invested in shares are quite willing to give it away – if you have something to offer them."

"Oh that's not the same thing at all. That's not what I'm talking about."

"Only because you're talking complete bollocks, mate," Quinton concluded.

But there was something that interrupted his thoughts. Some sort of distraction that turned his attention away from analysing the possibility of true revolution.

Dangerous lunatic. That's how the newspapers would describe him. Especially if he failed and was found out. Dangerous lunatic or mad loner, take your pick. Maybe both.

He wasn't a mad loner – he had friends.

There again, he had to remember one thing, as he had re-affirmed just a few moments ago. If required, and there was a clean and easy way of doing it, he would have no hesitation in killing any of them. He had to remind himself sometimes that what he would be called on to do might be something brutal. He would have to be strong enough to do it. If, for example, someone required him to give access codes so a building could be blown up with all his colleagues still in the building, he would have to do it.

And, after all, none of his friends were really friends. They were all work colleagues. His relationships with them had simply been created by expediency. By capitalism's need for people to cooperate in the workplace.

Richard had moved from one company to another many times. Each time it happened he would keep in touch by phone for a few months, but sooner or later the phone calls fizzled out. Friendships would always become meaningless.

He had no doubt he could allow everyone he knew to be blown up or killed by an act of terror if it was for the right reason. It was just that he couldn't focus on the right reason, and even if he could, he had no means of achieving it.

44 - BREAKDOWN

Richard moped around his flat for the whole of that day and the next morning. His attempts to refocus himself were getting nowhere. He had called in sick. He wondered if perhaps he really was sick. Perhaps he was having some sort of breakdown.

The doorbell was ringing again, for only the second time since he had moved into the flat. What was going on? Weber again? He picked up the entry intercom. In contrast to the previous time the bell had rung, he didn't care who it was. He felt empty and defeated. All his causes were lost and nothing mattered any more.

"Richard?"

It was Melanie! Richard was dumbstruck.

"Richard, can I come in?"

Richard was even more dumbstruck to hear excitement in her voice.

"Yes, of course." He pushed the button to let her in and listened to make sure he could hear the buzzer at her end. The buzzer sounded, followed by the door rattling open. He listened until he heard the door clatter shut again before putting the receiver down, and then opened his apartment door expectantly. His heart was beating hard. He could hardly wait for the stupid lift to deliver Melanie into his arms.

Finally it began to appear, rising slowly in its dusty cage. Then Melanie stepped out through its gold-coloured doors.

As she approached, he went to kiss her on the cheek but she waved him away, flapping her tiny hand in irritation.

"Something terrible has happened."

Richard looked at her dumbly. He had only just realised she wasn't excited; she was worried.

"I've parked downstairs in a resident's slot. I left Sally in the car. She's in a bit of a state."

Richard still couldn't find words.

"Sally?" was all he could manage.

"We need to go down and help her up here, but first I'd better tell you what this is about."

"OK, sit down."

"No, no time. Listen, Sally just told me something about Andrew. She got herself a bit high on something at the club and then she told me that she thinks he only pretended to kill himself."

"What?"

"She thinks it's an escape act so they can run off with the money."

"What money?"

"The money they're going to steal from VirtuBank or its client using some fake software that Andrew Mitchell tricked some silly fools into using."

Richard sat down on the sofa. He felt slightly sick.

"Which silly fools?"

"The fool that delivered an envelope to another fool who could open that envelope and find some sort of software."

"Oh fuck. She knows about some sort of software? She knows about you and me? Are you sure?"

"No, I don't think she knows about us; she knows about Andrew and someone that he tricked."

"My god, Melanie, obviously that's us. What are we going to do?"

"Let's get her up here first."

The image of the two of them trying to chop this girl into tiny pieces and flush her away in the bathroom flashed into Richard's mind.

"We need to find out what she knows and what we were involved in," Melanie said. "I already know some of what she knows. She told me."

"Why did she tell you this?"

"She wants to cut us in if we make sure the plan goes ahead."

"There are only two problems. Mitchell really is dead and I ..." He stopped himself from saying "can't deploy the software".

"Well we don't really know he's dead..."

"But – " Richard didn't want to say any more than he already had. Melanie shouldn't know anything about this. All she should know is that she passed a message on. She shouldn't know about Zima or software or that he had already tried and failed to deploy it. Obviously this Sally person shouldn't know anything either. "What has she said then?"

"She was expecting to see a huge amount of money pop up in a joint account in Switzerland and so far nothing has appeared. She wants to get the money by hook or by crook. Whether he's really dead or alive is not her main concern. Her main concern is that the money hasn't turned up like he promised."

"Hang on! Why did she tell you any of this?"

"She knows I was his favourite. She thinks he swapped accounts into my name and I'm going to collect."

"If you were his favourite why weren't you the one involved in the first place?"

"No idea, Richard. Maybe she thinks I was. As far as I knew I was his favourite but he never promised me any of this, honestly.

But anyway, let's get her up here and find out if any of what she's babbling on about is true. We need to do it while she's still high. If we can get her conscious again."

On the way down to the car, Richard said, "How long have you known her?"

"She came from Jezebel's in South London about a week ago."

They got to the car and managed to revive Sally enough to walk her to the lift and slump her onto the small couch in the main room.

Melanie sat down beside her and took her hands. She began rubbing them gently between her own.

"Sally, Sally, listen."

"Mmph," Sally murmured drowsily, half opening her eyes.

"We're going to try to help you get the money. Richard was a friend of Andrews's. He knows what to do." Melanie looked up at Richard uncertainly.

Richard wondered if she was looking for support – as though she wasn't sure if this was a clever enough lie. It was better than anything he had.

"He promised..." Sally mumbled.

"What Sally? We're here to help. What did he promise?"

"'s on my phone. Villa in Spain. 'count in Schwisserlan..."

"It's OK. We can help you."

"He promise… you promise too but..." She shook her head vigorously like a spoilt child refusing to eat.

"Show me on the phone," Melanie suggested.

"'s in my bag."

Melanie rummaged in the bag and retrieved the phone. Richard stepped closer and watched her begin searching it.

"Where is it? What do we need to know?"

"Get it working and the money goes straight in there."

"Where?"

"Schwisserlan. Get it working an I give you one or two mill."

"Get what working, sweetie?" Melanie said softly.

"Deh sofware. Should be there now. Den I go Spain an meet him."

"Aren't you just telling us porkies, Sally? You're making this all up, aren't you?"

"Look in the folder Melly. Look in the Spain folder."

Melanie found the folder and looked. Richard leaned in and looked too. It was all there, pdfs of a joint account in Switzerland, documents relating to the purchase of a large villa in Spain. A deposit of ten per cent had already been paid, but the next payment was due in three months' time when the main structure would be complete. Richard took the phone and plugged it into his laptop. He copied the folder and gave the phone back to Melanie. Sally had begun to snore gently.

Melanie stood up and whispered to Richard.

"We've got to get rid of her now, babe."

The image of chopping in the bathroom flashed back through Richard's head but Melanie continued: "I'm going to give her some Rufanol so she won't remember things properly. Then one of Aphrodite's regular cabbies will take her back to the club; get her in the back entrance. They can sort her out from there."

Fifteen minutes later, that was done, and Richard found himself alone with Melanie. He was still wondering what she had known previously and what she knew now.

"What do you think, Melanie? Do you think any of that was true?"

"How can it not be?"

"Mitchell is really dead. I'm pretty sure about that. It was announced officially."

"Fuck, they'll have caught me by now! I'm still in a resident's spot!" Melanie said suddenly.

"Oh damn! Yes, it's too late now. They'll have given you a penalty."

"Fuck! Well never mind that now. What about Andrew, Richard? How do you know he's dead? Did you see a body? Did you see any official documents, or just an email?"

"No."

"There you go then." She smiled sweetly and looked archly at him.

"Let's think about it a bit." Richard realised his mind had gone blank. That smile, the way she had changed posture, reminded him he would rather stare mindlessly at her breasts than do any sort of thinking. A plan popped into his head, though it was unrelated to anything that had happened that evening. "Coffee?"

"No thanks. You go ahead, I don't drink home-made stuff," she said, throwing herself back down on the sofa.

"I can perc it if you want. I have some proper ground coffee and a percolator."

"Sorry, I'm a bit of a snob when it comes to coffee. I have to have the proper stuff. I get my coffee fix in Myrrha's every day at three p.m. precisely. Coffee and cake."

"Myra? Sounds a bit sleazy. Named after Myra Hindley?"

"No," she giggled. "She's one of those Ancient Greeks that had an incestuous relationship with her father. I don't know why they chose that name. But it's a nice place. Near Claridge's. I used to go to Claridge's but Myrrha's is better for coffee, actually."

Claridge's not good enough! What next "actually"? Richard kept his thoughts to himself and flopped down beside her without voicing his secret criticism of her habits.

"I wonder..." Richard began. "Do you think he's alive and on the run?" It was time for him to ask a blunt question. "Was he a criminal, Melanie?"

Melanie looked at him with astonished eyes.

"Andy was one of the nicest customers I ever..." The look of astonishment faded away and turned to disappointment.

"But if this stuff of Sally's is real, he must be a bit dodgy to say the least. At best, he forged those documents to fool poor Sally."

"Yes. Oh shit. I don't know."

"Whatever the case, he was either fooling us or Sally. You know, the club must be crawling with all sorts of dodgy people." Richard thought it better not to add "including you and all the girls who work there," though a little devil sitting on his left shoulder was whispering to him that he should.

"Andrew gave me lots of extra money for being my special customer and I thought his money was all legit." She paused, seemingly unsure if she should tell him this: "Most of the time we're coked out of our minds in the club. Sometimes we don't know who's nice and who's not. Everything is just a big game."

Richard contemplated this. He didn't know whether to believe her or not. She was still just a child in so many ways. Less than half his age. How had he been so stupid as to entertain the idea he could have her somehow? How had he thought that he could love her, she could love him or they could have any kind of real relationship at all?

For some reason he heard himself saying, "Would you like to stay with me tonight?"

Melanie just nodded.

45 - A SHADOW

Logan was satisfied. He had hesitated over whether they should leave the flat in a mess, leave another clue or leave everything unchanged. They had finally decided to make it look professional; as professional as possible when leaving a door open "by accident".

The break-in had confirmed there was still no real cooperation between any handler and Richard. Richard was still flapping in the wind uselessly. So "Sally" had to do a bit of role playing.

Logan could only hope that, at last, Richard would feel the necessary sense of danger and urgency. He could only hope he would finally be pushed towards his contact and whoever that was would no longer be able to ignore him. If not, Richard would not live long enough to waste any more of his time.

46 - WAKING UP AGAIN

"I think I'm in trouble, Stuart." Richard was back in Glasgow. He was standing in the hallway of Stuart's apartment again. There was no alternative: Richard had to hope Stuart would want to help an old friend. Of all people, Stuart would understand his predicament. Of all people, he would be most sympathetic. The question of whether he would be able to do anything remained open.

Stuart allowed Richard to step into the hallway.

"It's about that envelope."

"That was all years ago!" Stuart replied, closing the door again.

"But nothing came of it until recently."

"God, I thought by now that would be all over and done with. I thought you would've just declined to do anything."

"Yes..." Richard's eyes darted round in confusion – declined to do anything – why hadn't he thought of that? That was the answer. But no, it was too late for that. He was roped in. "Yes, something came of it recently, and clearly..." He hesitated. Why did he never have any choice in what he had to do? He shouldn't talk about this with anyone, but he had to. "Clearly, something has gone wrong."

"What sort of thing?" Stuart was looking very concerned now.

"I don't know exactly. All I know is that..."

Richard woke up sweating. Melanie was gone. Another worried dream. He thanked God that it was just a dream. He hadn't gone back to Glasgow; he hadn't said anything to Stuart. There was no way Stuart could've done anything to help him. He got up and started making himself a coffee. It was six-thirty. He might as well have breakfast – he couldn't sleep any more. He went to his laptop and started looking through Sally's folder.

These dreams meant his subconscious must be trying to tell him something. How much sense did they make? They were telling him he couldn't involve Stuart. He knew that already. What were they telling him about Mitchell?

In any case, Richard didn't believe dreams could tell you more than logic. He had to think properly, not rely on some nonsensical dreams. Nevertheless, the dream disturbed him. There was no time to bask in the warm delight of having shared his bed with Melanie. The dream had stolen that pleasure from him. God! Why did I end up in bed with Melanie? I had more important things to do.

Sally's folder was full of evidence Mitchell was some sort of scammer. Even more worryingly, he might still be alive! Emails sent to her, hotel bookings in his name after the fateful date – no definite proof though. What was more definite were the legal documents relating to the purchase of an expensive villa in Spain.

If Mitchell is still alive, how and why did he manage to fake his suicide? Because he's a criminal and he wanted me to take the blame for whatever that software did. What if Mitchell is MI5? That's even worse! That would mean he was trying to set me up for some reason; probably to expose me as a Party member and saboteur.

Richard shuddered to think of the consequences. Why on earth had he believed Mitchell and not Weber? Dead or alive, Mitchell was the false Zima contact; not Weber.

Richard went through the Zima plan to try to get it clear. How was it supposed to work? How could it go so wrong? How could Stuart Douglas now be so indifferent about the whole thing when it had been, at least partially, his idea and originally he had seemed quite enthusiastic.

For a while it even seemed that Stuart wanted to do the same. The memory of Stuart saying "Count me in man" was imprinted on Richard's memory. And why wouldn't he want to be 'counted in'? They had both felt strongly there was something rotten at the heart of the system they wanted to do something about.

But now he was alone.

The plan should have been very simple, and yet he had ended up with two handlers and somehow hadn't figured out Weber was the real one.

He found Weber's card and sent a text to him. It was seven a.m. on Sunday. Weber might still be sleeping. He hoped a text would be a polite way of waking Weber up. He hoped he could trust Weber.

Richard struggled to imagine why he had found Mitchell so convincing. It was Weber who had given him more of the correct ciphers, though not the "wake up" one. All Mitchell had given him was some software. Both Weber and Mitchell knew the Zima code word. How could anyone who was not part of the set-up know the word "Zima" or its significance?

47 - BAYSWATER

Richard's cab stopped outside 127 Leinster Terrace. It seemed that running a cell was a job with good perks. Leinster Terrace was in Bayswater, one of the most upmarket areas of Central London. The exterior of the flat was Georgian stucco, with cornices and pillars, all painted white, resembling an elaborate wedding cake. One of the first-floor flats had the curtains open and there was light coming from some of the rooms. All the others had curtains or blinds drawn and were still in darkness. Richard hoped Weber had got his text and was already up and about, expecting him.

Indeed, Weber was already dressed. He opened the door of his apartment to let Richard in.

If the exterior of the building was impressive, the interior was sumptuous. While Richard was used to glittering offices and four-star hotels, as well as the fake luxury of Aphrodite's, he was not used to quite this level of opulence. He passed through a hallway, lined with genuine artworks, into the living room. After the revolution we'll all be living in Bayswater, he joked to himself, somewhat bitterly.

"Weber, I've been a complete idiot."

"Very probably," replied Weber. "Sit down and make your idiocy comfortable." He began a wheezing chuckle and Richard sat down. Weber seemed superciliously complacent for someone who had been woken up to meet a virtual stranger at eight a.m. He still gave off the air of someone who held all the cards and was totally in control of the game.

It was very easy to feel comfortable in Weber's living room, unless guilt gave rise to contrary feelings. It was a precisely created room where every detail was beautiful and artistic. From the antique rosewood furniture, through the genuine old masters in genuine gold-leaf frames, and then to the silk wallpaper, your eyes would dart happily from one lustrous object to the next... gold, silk, silver and so on... right down to the antique pewter coasters waiting on each of the side tables for crystal glasses of vintage wine. There was a hush of self-satisfaction about the room.

"I might as well tell you everything, because I have nothing to lose."

"Go on."

"Up till now I didn't believe you. I don't know exactly why, but I believed someone else. Someone else who claimed to be the Zima contact."

Weber sat down too. He seemed a little unsteady on his feet.

"Someone else? The Zima contact? How is this possible!?" he whispered.

"I don't know. But just hours before you made contact I was contacted by someone else. He gave me a pack of software to install at the bank I'm working at. He gave code Zima. Operation Zima was to install the software he gave me."

Weber screwed up his eyes.

"The word Zima is known only to you and me," he stated dryly. "No one else ever knew it, no one else ever needed to know it. Other sleepers have different code words. Some people don't need code words for their activities."

"If you say so."

"Did you ever write it down somewhere? Did you ever get drunk and tell someone? Who knew the word?"

"Mitchell knew it. Someone called Mitchell." Richard wanted to unburden himself – tell Weber as much as he could. Richard's whole world had dissolved. There was nothing left to lose and now Weber was the only person he could trust.

"Mitchell?"

"Yes."

"Who is Mitchell? MI5?"

"I have no idea. I thought that he was just a colleague, my boss at VirtuBank. He committed suicide but I think that was just a pretence. He's probably still alive." But what if that wasn't true? What if Mitchell was genuine and Weber was false? It was too late to worry about that now.

"Did you tell Mitchell the word?"

"Of course not. I never told anyone. I never wrote it down. It's easy to remember."

"Yes, but perhaps it was easy for you to let it slip."

"No, I don't think so. But maybe Mitchell didn't know the word, maybe Melanie... He committed suicide and just after that..." Richard racked his brains. "Melanie gave me the envelope with the word."

"Wait. This is impossible for me to follow. Try to tell me in logical order. Maybe our cover is blown, maybe it's not. Maybe having our cover blown won't matter anyway. Just tell me logically and I can decide."

"Oh shit! What you said just now; you're right. Mitchell came to Helsinki with the specific purpose of getting me drunk!" Richard blurted out.

"Why did you believe that this Mitchell was the contact and not me?"

Richard was stumped. Why was that? He just had a feeling... no, wait! It was more than that! "You didn't use the identification cipher first. You mentioned Zima and then the cipher that you wanted to discuss, but you were supposed to identify yourself first."

Weber frowned at him. "I had no instructions to tell me that. I thought I could use the ciphers in any way that made sense. No one said that they should be used in any order."

Richard placed three fingers of his right hand on his temple, his thumb nestled against his cheek. The gesture half-hid his face and he half-hoped he could completely hide his stupidity. He sat like that for a minute, trying to think. He had been such a fool! He had kept the codes in his mind in this order, but there were never any instructions about how to use them.

"Then it was all a terrible misunderstanding!"

"Just tell me everything logically and chronologically."

The calm and precise way Weber asked sent a shiver down his spine. Weber was cold, reptilian. Could he trust him after all? He had no choice now.

48 - COGNAC

Weber poured them both cognacs. It was ten a.m. Not an ideal time for a drink, but this time Richard accepted willingly. He had explained everything. He no longer cared if the cognac was full of Polonium. It tasted like cognac, it had alcohol in it. That was all that mattered.

"Perhaps the damage is limited. Perhaps we can make use of events to our own advantage. It's sometimes surprising how things work out," said Weber at length. "I had no particular plans for you Richard, because there is no urgency for what we want you to do. I can tell you that the operation I am conducting is bigger than you think."

Why is he telling me this? Is it because I'm already dying from the poison in the cognac?

"Go back to your apartment. I will try to find out more about Mitchell. You are correct; he may be MI5 or he may just be a criminal."

Richard hesitated.

"If you want I can come with you," Weber offered.

"No, it's OK. I will go alone, of course."

"I want the phone. Drop it through my letterbox ASAP."

"OK."

"Is Mitchell, or anyone else, aware that you tried to deploy the Zima software?"

Richard thought for a moment. "I don't know."

Weber seemed to expect more from him. Richard put his head in his hands and tried to think clearly.

"Probably not," he said, looking up expectantly at Weber, like a child, to see if he'd given the right answer.

49 - MELANIE

Melanie didn't need an introduction card to know who she was talking to. She talked to a lot of guys at the club, of course, but not all of them wanted to know stuff like this. For a start, it was suspicious that a customer of Aphrodite's would want to talk about anything at all, let alone try to find out about other customers. It was obvious someone connected to Mitchell's opponents had decided to ask her a few questions. He was quite good at it, made it seem casual and friendly, but she knew what he wanted and she knew exactly what story to feed him. Mitchell had helped her with the role she was supposed to play. She was still upset that apparently he was a fraud and Sally was his favourite but, anyway, in this situation Mitchell's help was the only weapon she had.

What made it easier to tell these lies was that they were nearly true.

Richard really was a kind of boyfriend now. She'd allowed that to happen because it made things easier. She might need to let him down easily once this was all over. In fact, she might need to give him some clues it would never work out before it came to that.

Mitchell really had come to the club as a customer. There was no need to let them know Mitchell didn't just pay her for her skills in bed but to participate in his "schemes". She really had worked here long before Mitchell became a customer.

These pillars of truth helped hide the lies.

But there was one lie she would absolutely not to admit to. On no account could she tell anyone that Mitchell hadn't given her the software.

She hoped it wasn't too obvious that she was easy to find and told her story so willingly. She had to remember that Richard wasn't the only one in danger; they all were.

50 - REALITY CHECK

Richard was on the phone to Melanie. He wanted something in his life that would comfort him. But why had he been so presumptuous as to call Melanie? Already the call was going badly. Why was she being so awkward tonight? He paced up and down his kitchen holding his mobile to his ear.

"I really liked that you stayed with me that time. Why can't we do that again?" he asked.

"Oh, are you saying I should work for nothing?"

"Work?" That word really annoyed him. "Oh, was it such an effort then? Do you have any idea what real work is? What you do isn't work, it's..." he was lost for words. He was going too far. He had been on the point of saying "disgusting", but he mustn't say it. He didn't want to fall out; quite the opposite. But it was already too late.

"You have no idea, Richard. You have no idea what my life is like, or why I do this work. And it really is work." Her voice was bitter.

"OK. I'm sorry, I just thought that we were becoming closer and you could come and see me... Like a proper relationship..."

"No. I can't commit to anything with a client... I'm sorry Richard. You don't know what it's like."

A client! That word twisted in his stomach. But it was true. Besides, they hardly knew each other really. There was silence.

"Richard, I have things to do. I have to hang up now, I'm sorry."

There was another moment of silence. He wanted to say something. All he could think of was: Wait! Can I see you at the club? But it remained unsaid. What would the point be of saying it? Of course he could see her at the club. Anyone with a few hundred pounds to spare could see her at the club.

She hung up.

51 - PSYCHIC

"Let's say Mitchell is MI5. Why has he not already turned you over?"

Richard found himself sitting once again on one of the opulent sofas in Weber's opulent apartment. He hadn't even considered this question. Under the steady gaze of Weber's cold grey eyes, he had no idea what the answer was.

He wasn't the only guest. Two young men from Weber's gay club were playing together in one of the bedrooms. Weber hid his contacts in plain sight by having as many visitors as was reasonable for a homosexual with an insatiable appetite.

Richard wondered what had possessed him to come over here again. Would Weber finally get round to poisoning him this time? The trouble is, he realised, if he had refused to come over that would be suspicious anyway. He had no choice. Furthermore, it seemed Weber was the only friend he had in the world. Everyone else was gone.

"I don't know," he replied.

"Here, take the phone back." He pushed the phone across the coffee table. "We've already had a good look through it. I've had all the names checked out. Nothing of interest. But at least it shows that we're working together now."

"Do you know any more about Mitchell?"

"I know why he was brought in to dig around in VirtuBank."

"Can you tell me?"

Weber sighed.

"I don't need to. But perhaps I will anyway. I've realised that the things that have gone wrong with Zima have been caused, not by a lack of security on our part, but by the fact that the two of us have been keeping things so secret that neither has known what the other is doing."

That was a fair comment, Richard thought.

"First, let's think about why Mitchell has not turned you over already. We need to decide if you need to make a run for it or not."

Richard hadn't seriously considered the idea of making a run for it. But with Weber mentioning it, it suddenly seemed more real than previously. It even seemed inevitable. His flat in Glentworth Street was nothing like as magnificent as Weber's apartment, but he was well aware he was very lucky indeed to be able to live there. He would have to give that up. Where could he run to if he was wanted for attempting to sabotage a bank? What skills did he have that would allow him to earn a living in some godforsaken part of the earth that was out of reach of the long arm of British justice? None. He was an IT geek, that was all.

"Let's first think about the Zima code. How do you think Mitchell got the word 'Zima'?"

"I have no idea."

"Have you asked your girlfriend?"

Weber saw the confusion on Richard's face so he added, "That Melanie that you've been hanging around with."

Richard was open-mouthed.

"How did…?"

"I run quite a big operation, Richard. In the interests of the openness that I spoke about, I will tell you more about that operation presently. Meantime I can tell you that I have had people observing you for a while now. We also found her name on Mitchell's phone and saw that the number had been dialled recently – it had been dialled since you received the phone."

Richard was still open-mouthed, but Weber continued: "It turns out that she knows something about Mitchell that you never knew. Of course, you, me and anyone with half an ounce of sense would assume that he was an expert interrogator."

Richard was indignant. Weber noticed and, perhaps feeling that he was being harsh on Richard, added, "But no one would ever imagine that he had another skill unless they saw for themselves." He paused for dramatic effect. "He was psychic."

"He was psychic?" asked Richard incredulously.

"That's what he told everyone."

"I know. He told me too. But no one is really psychic." He was beginning to wonder though. "Are they?" he asked, feeling naïve and foolish yet again.

"Melanie told us that he knew how to do hypnosis. Did you know that?"

Richard struggled with confusion. "No. What does it matter?" Panic was building up inside him. Melanie! Why had he never got around to questioning who she was? Was Melanie Mitchell's accomplice or just another unwitting stooge? If she was an accomplice, she had betrayed him from the start. But even if she wasn't, she would be likely to betray him if she ever got to know about Weber. Now it seemed that Weber, or his people, had been in contact with her.

"Women make such fools of us. You know what Mitchell did? To show off to Melanie, he performed a trick on another customer at the bar in that club of yours. He made the customer believe that he was psychic by hypnotising him."

"Hypnotising him into believing that he was psychic?"

"Not exactly. He hypnotised him, and then proved that he was psychic. He got the guy to tell him a few facts, his age, car reg, stuff like that, under hypnosis. Then he woke him up and proved that he was able to read the guy's mind by giving back the information that he had just discovered. Melanie told us that the customer was totally convinced that Mitchell was psychic."

"When he told me he was psychic, I wasn't convinced at all."

"But he didn't need to convince you. He needed you to be comfortable with the idea that he could know things about you that were not expected. That made it easier for the hypnosis to work. All he needed to do was get you a bit drunk, drunk enough for you to allow him to hypnotise you. Then he might play a game of some sort – lettered cards, Scrabble tokens, whatever. It seems you're not as aware that you are giving away something secret if you spell it letter by letter instead of saying it in full."

"So he got me to spell out ZIMA!" Richard remembered they played some sort of card game. It was funny that he couldn't remember any of the details.

"Yes. He probably didn't know what Zima was or anything. But he suspected you could be an infiltrator prepared to cause some sort of – "

"But why would he suspect me, or anyone? I was sleeping for thirty-odd years!"

"Ah, yes. It's no coincidence that he turned up just as I appeared on the scene," Weber said, sheepishly.

Richard had never seen Weber look sheepish before. Smug, complacent, avuncular; never sheepish.

"You see, and this is what I was referring to previously, I run quite a big operation. I tie a lot of strands together and make sense of them, fashion them into something effective. In the big picture you were quite forgotten, in fact. I have funding for my operation from a big organisation – you can imagine – an official government department. The problem is that, if they have a change of heart there, funding might dry up at any moment, and there are always arguments about the worthiness, efficacy or need for my operation. I rely on the old guard for support – ex-KGB and the likes; proper Soviets who are disaffected with what happened to our international power and influence."

Richard didn't like the sound of this. He was always well to the left of any Stalinists. He didn't want to be associated with any funding from those Red Nazis.

"We have quite a few people working in development in VirtuBank India."

Richard wondered if Srini was one of them.

"It seems that we may have too many people, because VirtuBank management seemed to spot something was wrong. One of my guys must have done something that alerted them. They must've sought advice, probably from a private software security firm, probably from a government advisory service, perhaps even MI5. I don't know exactly. Anyway, I presume the result was that Andy Mitchell was brought in to shake a few branches and see what or who fell out. He spent a few weeks in Chennai and then came over here. You are in danger of being shaken out of the tree."

"Wow! Where does that leave us?"

"I don't know. Falling out of a tree can be an unpleasant experience, Mr Slater. You might need to make a run for cover."

"I don't want to start running if I'm on one of the top branches." Richard tried to make a joke of Weber's mixed metaphors, but only succeeded in annoying him.

"Yes, yes, Mr Slater, you are nowhere near the top of the tree. Let me tell you that."

Richard tried to get a handle on the big picture. He couldn't imagine how some disaffected old communists in the former Soviet Union would still have influence in this way. Nor, he imagined, would they be able to run a slick operation. He pictured the chaos he'd seen in Moscow in the nineties when he was working for Bizkore, an ERP software company, previous to VirtuBank. Soviet Communism had proved to be unworkable. Politically, all that remained of the Soviet system was a shambles.

"You say it's a big operation. Would they be able to pension me off? What support can I get from your guys if I need to run for it?"

Richard couldn't believe he was saying this. When it came to the crunch, everyone had to look after number one. For all those years he'd been waiting to act, altruistically, for what he thought was the common good. But throughout those years he'd been handsomely rewarded by the capitalist system for his contribution. Now he wanted to be bailed out, at any cost, by the adherents of another system he didn't support, just so he could continue to live in the style to which he was accustomed.

52 - SUNSET

"Let's think a bit more carefully about whether that will be necessary," Weber replied. "We still haven't established what Mitchell was up to or whether he was working alone or in a team. Neither have we established what they were trying to achieve and, if Mitchell is still alive, or his team still active, why you haven't been turned in already. If he hasn't done it already, perhaps it's because he doesn't need to, doesn't want to, or doesn't know that you haven't done anything yet."

"He doesn't know that I haven't done anything yet!" Richard repeated almost happily. "That's probably it!"

Weber looked at Richard slyly.

"Can you be sure? What makes you think that?"

"I'm not sure. But there are two reasons. First that the Zima program that he gave me has not been deployed anywhere yet. It all depends who he told to look out for it. Someone made the whole thing disappear."

"Wait, wait, wait." Weber's face was screwed up as though he was being tortured. He had only just realised something. "You sent the Zima zip file because Mitchell gave you the code word, not because you had decided to act alone?"

"That's right."

"And the stuff that you sent was not something that you had been creating for this purpose? It was something that Mitchell gave you?"

"Yes, isn't that what I told you?"

"Maybe you thought that's what you told me, maybe you did tell me that. It didn't sink in. Somehow we... somehow I thought that the software you deployed had been written by you, and you deployed it because I..."

Weber seemed to be trying to solve some sort of quadratic equation in his head. Finally, he seemed to arrive at a solution. He was clear to ask another question.

"So you only sent the email to one person and he deleted it?"

"No. There were others cc'd. In normal circumstances those people aren't really involved or interested. They're in the list more or less by convention." Richard realised that these circumstances were not normal. Mitchell might have any one of the people in the cc list as the lookout. If that was the case, they had their evidence and he was done for.

"Anyway, you said there were two reasons."

"Yes. The second reason that I don't have a finger pointing straight at me as yet is that I sent the email from Srini's laptop."

Weber slumped back in his chair. Richard was alarmed for a moment that he had slumped back disappointed about where the finger was not pointing, but it turned out that he had slumped back in relief. The tension had been released. He was finally able to relax and do some thinking about the big picture, rather than worrying about Richard.

"I want you to go to Moscow as soon as possible. Can you arrange for that?"

"Yes, I can ask for a vacation; I'm due one. Better still, I might be able to get VirtuBank to send me there on business."

"See what you can do. I want my people to meet you. It might only be for a few hours, it might be for a day, but take a week off anyway. Can you do that?"

"No problem at all. I have a current visa because of Moscovsky Zakrit Bank."

"I wonder if it's a coincidence that Mitchell's plan is quite similar to the real one? I guess it's just inevitable that it would be. It's a bit like Apple and Samsung both using white oblongs as a 'cool' design feature of their products – there are so few alternatives."

Richard wasn't listening too carefully any more. This was his opportunity! Weber would sort out the whole mess involving Mitchell. Weber understood what he was capable of doing. Weber would be able to get him the right software. Richard would be a heroic figure in the new society following the revolution. Maybe Melanie would see him in a new light after that. But why should he care? There would be hundreds of girls just as cute as Melanie that would be interested in the man who reshaped the world.

53 - INSANE

Richard had arranged to be sent to Moscow to follow up on Moscovsky Zakrit Bank. He had to get authorisation from Callan. Callan, of all people! Why was Callan suddenly in charge of what goes on at Moscovsky Zakrit Bank, he wondered? Anyway, Callan had rubber-stamped it and here he was, back in Moscow. In the summer, Moscow had been too hot – sometimes almost thirty degrees. Now, as he had expected, it was too cold – on Sunday evening when his plane landed, it was minus five. Quite warm for Moscow in the winter, but still too cold.

But things were looking up. Either that or the bank had some serious issues and wanted to ensure they got the best possible attention. They had put him in the Hotel Ukraina.

The Hotel Ukraina, Richard already knew, was built as one of Stalin's "Seven Sisters" – Soviet skyscrapers in the neo-Gothic style. This particular sister stands proudly in a bend of the Moscow river which, at that time of year, was frozen solid.

Taking his cue from the hotel's logo, Richard could easily imagine the building surging upwards in incremental stages towards the heavens. But in more prosaic moments, he saw it as a clunky series of cuboids of diminishing sizes, set one on top of the other, onto which a spindly, star-tipped spire had been placed, with the principal tower flanked by four lesser cuboids on either side, each adjoined to form a more or less coherent whole.

But no matter how he thought of the architecture, he appreciated that it was a building of outstanding historical importance, refurbished to the highest standards by the Radisson group. There could be only one reason for being sent to a hotel like this; someone somewhere believed he was going to do something wonderful enough to justify the expense.

Behind the Ukraina, ultra-modern skyscrapers of the Moscow International Business Centre sparkled, reflecting sunlight from their gleaming surfaces; evidence of how well the Russian economy was doing now its huge resources of oil and gas had been plugged into the capitalist system. Turning to the right was the Gazprom HQ on the opposite bank of the river and, near that, the white parliament building, known as the House of the Government of the Russian Federation – the building that Boris Yeltsin got his own tanks to fire on.

Richard had almost forgotten the immense feeling of size and power that Moscow exuded. According to Muscovites, after the fall of Rome to the Visigoths, civilisation had fled to Constantinople and then, they insist, to Moscow after Constantinople had in turn fallen to Islam. Moscow was therefore the "Third Rome". The oil was flowing and the rouble was strong. It was the most expensive city in the world. Even VirtuBank, normally so generous in spending their clients' money, had refused permission for him to take a taxi from the airport to the hotel. It had taken forever for his train to get from the airport to the centre. It had trundled along at a steady pace, initially passing through a frozen landscape of icy, skeletal trees on the edges of darker evergreen forests, and then through satellite towns of drab Soviet tower blocks whose tiled cladding was so poorly finished that what the architect had intended as straight clean lines splurged out in a ragged mess of crooked concrete.

From the terminus, his taxi had taken him round the Garden Ring Road – a boulevard, originally tree-lined, that had been widened to eight lanes in each direction in the 1930s and no longer had any resemblance to a garden. Instead it was normally chock-full of traffic belching fumes and often reduced to a crawl. Shiny black limousines with tinted windows were a common sight. If, as reported in the UK press, these impressive vehicles belonged exclusively to the Russian Mafia, then there were a lot of members in the Mafia. Almost everyone who owned a car was in the Mafia.

After having his bags scanned by a security device at the hotel entrance, he checked in and gone immediately to his room to unpack. Now he was sitting in the bar gloomily nursing a ridiculously expensive vodka with fresh pineapple. He wondered what the week had in store for him. Almost certainly, Moscovsky Zakrit Bank must have some nasty issues with their software. Why else would they agree to him coming over here at the drop of a hat? Why else would they put him in such an expensive hotel? It felt more like a threat than a reward. And then, there was his ulterior motive. What were Weber's people expecting of him? Even more worrying, had he gone insane? He smiled at his own joke. What had possessed him to go for vodka and fresh pineapple at £25 a go? It was half his per diem. He swigged it back and ordered a whisky to calm his nerves. The whisky was a mere £9. He was sane after all.

***

Walking to the underground station on Monday morning, it was noticeably colder – probably minus twenty. Wind, slicing through the snow-covered streets, cut straight through his multiple layers of clothing. On days like that, you appreciated the effort your nostril hair made to keep your lungs from freezing but wish it would make a better job of it. He got the Moscow Underground from Kievskaya to Kuznetskiy Most. He was quite looking forward to meeting Yevgeny, the bank's technical lead, again. In the summer, Yevgeny had been the one that had helped smooth out all the problems. By the time he got to the bank, he'd convinced himself Yevgeny had probably been promoted on the strength of his efforts that summer and surmised he had been eager for Richard to come over so that they could organise a new team to extend the project. Of course, he was almost forgetting he was no longer primarily interested in VirtuBank's business objectives. Whatever happened at Moskovsky Zakrit Bank, he would need to keep a foot in the door over at RCB.

It turned out Yevgeny had left and gone to another bank. Yevgeny was almost the only person not paranoiacally suspicious of everything VirtuBank did. In terms of paranoia levels, Vadim was the worst of all. Richard's heart sank when he discovered it was Vadim he would be answering to this week.

Vadim wasted no time in assigning a dull clerical task to Richard. "Please, check this spreadsheet to ensure that the modules are correctly installed," were the first words he said to him.

"Well, of course they are. They wouldn't work if they weren't."

The stony expression on Vadim's face did not alter. "We believe there is a discrepancy between what has been installed and what is documented. Perhaps we are paying maintenance for components that were never installed."

"Then we should check the MSCF, the Master System Control File, instead of a spreadsheet. This spreadsheet is just a document."

"Then I will try to arrange security clearance for you to do that."

"Thank you, you should do that. There's no point in checking this spreadsheet. We can compare the MSCF with the original contract if you like but this spreadsheet could come from anywhere. I have no idea if it's accurate."

"I prepared it myself."

"Even so, it is not definitive."

Three days crawled past.

Sometimes Richard was able to brace himself for the cold and venture out. There the pale blue, almost white, sky was clinically crisp and clear. Moscow, in winter, with its wide streets and pastel-coloured buildings, is a city lit by heaven.

But unfortunately, Richard was only occasionally and briefly able to get out to experience light and freedom. Most of the time he had to stay in the office awaiting instructions that never came. The interior of Moscovsky Bank's offices were gloomy and far too warm.

Midway through Wednesday afternoon, Vadim told him he might as well take the afternoon off and do a bit of sightseeing. Richard was worried that perhaps this meant Vadim thought he was not achieving anything. Perhaps he would report back that he was unsatisfied with his work? Perhaps he would arrange for him to fly back immediately? He was relieved when Vadim told him he would arrange for an informal meeting tomorrow. Then he would be free to take Friday off and fly back that evening as arranged. At least he was still in Moscow, still available to meet Weber's people when required.

He had checked his Dropbox every few hours every day. There was no message from Weber or his people. This was worrying too. Was it all going to be a waste of time? The possibility niggled at him. But there was nothing he could do except try to relax and be ready when required. That cold Wednesday afternoon, he took the Red Line (officially named the Sokolnicheskaya Line, though everyone uses their colours to identify lines, rather than names or numbers) to the University.

The University, another of Stalin's skyscrapers, sits high on a hill with spectacular views over the city.

Richard had visited Sparrow Hill several times when he had worked at Moscovsky Zakrit Bank during the summer. On Saturdays there had been wedding parties up there: happy young couples posing for photos or waving from white Lincoln convertibles garlanded with ribbons and flowers. Now, on this bleak day, there were no signs of any weddings. Only a handful of people stood around in small, aimless groups. He walked to the stone balustrade and stood with his back to the University, staring out at the infinite white sky and, beneath that, stretching round in an immense semi-circle to the horizon, the view of Moscow.

The 81,000-capacity Luzhniki Stadium lying directly before, and slightly below him, captured his attention first, until he challenged himself to pick out more distant landmarks. Rather than the cupolas and domes of churches, or the spires of any of the Seven Sisters, a jumble of anonymous apartment blocks occupied most of the scene. These linear shapes in assorted tints of cream, beige and grey were monotonously specked with black arrays of windows.

Nevertheless, Richard was able to find some of the most well-known places of interest within this monotonous jumble and congratulated himself on being able to do so. Beyond the stadium, made tiny by distance, stood the Cathedral of Christ the Saviour with its golden domes and pristine white walls. Somewhere on the far side of that lay the Kremlin, hidden except for three tiny golden domes crowning white towers belonging to the Ivan the Great Bell Tower.

The skyscrapers of the Moscow International Business Centre huddled together to the right. Coming further round, two large smokestacks, brightly painted in red and white, stood out, with the Ostankino TV Tower, in white distant haze, just visible between them. Shukhov Tower too, like a latticed wickerwork carafe, was recognisable in the distance, to the left.

Richard turned and looked at the University for a moment. On top of the massive main monolith, its fifty-seven-metre spire was transmitting dreams into the atmosphere, creating its own reality. The building stood alone in a substantial forest of evergreen trees, and Richard had the impression it might be the last man-made structure you would encounter in that direction; that beyond it there was only forest and wilderness until you crossed the Ural Mountains, journeyed all the way across the Siberian Steppe, sailed across stormy seas and arrived in Seattle.

He noticed he was now alone. The groups of people who had been standing nearby had vanished. He turned back to face the city and rested his gloved hands on the stone balustrade to lean forward. Only now did he appreciate the extent of the parkland that sloped steeply down to the frozen river. Furthermore, it was only beyond that, quite some distance away, that there was any sign of urbanisation.

Snow began to fall again.

It suddenly struck him that Moscow felt eerily detached, and that the Gothic behemoth behind him and the wilderness it masked were its edge. As snow continued to fall, colour drained away, leaving only a ghostly vestige of what had been there before. It seemed that the entire megalopolis was abandoned and devoid of habitation.

Richard reminded himself again of Hitler's plans for Moscow. Hitler had wanted the entire city razed to the ground and flooded to create a vast lake in its place. Moscow was to be erased from the map. Erased from history.

54 - DEAD ZONE INCIDENT

It was Friday. No message. He was bored with being a tourist. He decided to take an hour or two to explore the real Moscow before checking his Dropbox again. He chose a Metro station at random and went to explore the area. Petrovsko-Razumovskaya was the Metro station he ended up choosing. He got out and walked around the grubby stalls and cheap shops nearby. He was deep in thought and didn't notice that he'd wandered quite a distance from the station into a long narrow street, with nothing much of interest in it. He was about to turn round and go back when he noticed something curious, and having nothing better to do...

There was a woman walking about twenty yards in front of him. He noticed her because of the strange way she was walking. Dressed in dirty tracksuit trousers, trainers and a mangy fur coat, she was lurching from side to side as though drunk, but more exaggeratedly. Her head was tilted upwards, her eyes searching unseeingly. As Richard approached, he noticed that she was waving some sort of belt or leash around. Then, when he was just nine or ten paces away, she suddenly spun round and stopped, staring at him. He noticed the leash was dangling from the neck of a dead cat which she held by the forepaws in her right hand. The cat's body hung limply, its head twisted round to one side.

Richard stopped in his tracks, undecided if he should try to go past the woman or wait for her to continue. He could see anguish and anger on her raddled face.

But before he could decide what to do, he realised that two men on the opposite side of the road were taking an interest. One of them began to cross the road, making an effort to walk straight, but staring malevolently at Richard the whole time, head thrust out. The other one, who was dressed in a leather biker's jacket that had probably been rescued from a landfill, just continued to stare at him. Richard realised that he was going to end up in the middle of a triangle with the cat lady in front of him, one of the men on the opposite side of the road and one behind him. He decided he had better move, and began to cross the road at an angle, to get in front of the cat lady and the biker and continue on his way, but as he did so the man in the biker's jacket moved unsteadily to the side, as though anticipating Richard's escape route.

Richard hesitated, glancing at the cat lady on his left and the biker man on his right, undecided. The other man was now moving further to the right, where he would like to go to retrace his steps.

"Schto teey deealisch? O tebya ni tvoyey prablemiy?" The biker said in slow, guttural slur. By now he was standing almost in front of Richard, sideways-on, with one fist held out behind his back as though he was preparing to launch an almighty haymaker.

Richard didn't answer. He didn't know what the man meant. It didn't matter what he meant either. He just had to get out of the situation. For some reason he didn't want to run – perhaps it would seem undignified, even cowardly. He glanced round. The others were moving toward him. What the fuck do they want with me? he wondered. He didn't run; he walked briskly, intending to go past the man, staying on the road to avoid getting too close. But Biker Man scuttled sideways along the pavement like a crab. Suddenly his face tightened into an angry scowl, giving Richard a moment's notice to skip sideways just as he swung out. Richard was surprised the drunk only just missed him. He felt a swish of air that indicated the punch had missed by centimetres, not by a foot or two as he had expected. Either the guy wasn't drunk or he was such a fighter that drunkenness didn't diminish his abilities.

Then he was running as fast as he could. The ice and snow made it difficult to run flat out. He ran straight down the middle of the road to start with and then crossed over to the pavement on the cat lady's side of the road. He kept running hard for three blocks without looking back. There was no sign of a good place to run to. No bar or restaurant, not even a shop and no side streets. He looked over his right shoulder. No one? He had feared, or expected to see Biker Man running just a couple of paces behind, to his right. There was no one there. He turned a bit more, aware he had to slow down a bit to do so. Aware of the danger – if they were close it could be a fatal mistake. But he turned his neck as far as he dared without slowing down too much. No one was close.

He turned right round and did something that he hadn't tried since childhood – he skipped backwards for a few paces. No one had followed. He could just make them out, still standing more or less where they had been when he had decided it was time to run. There was no need to run any more. He stopped and slumped against a lamp post, breathing hard. The cold air was unpleasant to breathe in so deeply. After a second or two to get his breath back, he continued on his way.

He got back to the hotel to find that Mitchell's phone had been stolen from his room. He reported it to reception. They blandly reassured him the chambermaid had probably tidied it up somewhere and they would check and get back to him in the morning. Richard thought it quite likely that the chambermaid had tidied it up. Tidied it up and sold it. Anyway, he didn't need it. When he got it back from Weber, most of the apps had been wiped. The contacts were all gone too. But he had already made a backup of the contacts anyway.

The phone was the least of his worries.

There had been no message from Weber or his people. He checked his Dropbox again. His flight was tomorrow at noon. He would have to be at the airport at ten a.m. and leave to get there at nine Weber knew his flight times so it seemed there would be no meeting and the whole trip had been a waste of time, both for the Zima project and for the Moscovsky Zakrit Bank project.

His phone rang.

"Richard." It was Callan. "Don't go to the airport tomorrow. There's a problem with your visa. Some bloody fool cancelled your visa because they got a message from Moscovsky Zakrit Bank saying you were no longer working on their project."

"What! They told me to take Wednesday and Friday off, that's all, and I was there on Thursday for another pointless meeting."

"I know. They were trying to tell us you weren't at the office but there was a mix-up in their English. Don't worry about it. You were chargeable the whole time. The point is your visa's been screwed up now and if you go to the airport or try to leave Russia, you'll be arrested."

"So what should I do?"

"We're going to try to get the visa sorted out ASAP, but it's an irregular situation so it might take some time. Moscovsky Zakrit Bank were paying for your hotel. We can't afford to keep you there so you'll need to move out into the accommodation we've arranged for you."

Richard's heart sank. He wondered what sort of grubby apartment in what sort of slummy area VirtuBank could afford to put him up in now that he wasn't chargeable.

"OK, I guess I have to do what I have to do." Richard couldn't hide the disappointment in his voice. He looked round at the fixtures and fittings of his five-star room and wondered what he would be looking round at in a few hours' time.

"So, the apartment is 112 Butyrskaya. A taxi from the rental company will come and pick you up tomorrow morning. The driver will show you round and ask for a signature for the keys. He'll need to take your passport too."

"Take my passport?"

"Yes, it's standard procedure since we can't show them a proper visa."

"Fuck." So now he would be totally trapped. He was not going to do that in any circumstances. He would give the driver a photocopy. That was just as good, and there was no need to mention his intention to Callan either.

"The driver will be there at eleven."

"OK," Richard replied, but he wondered what would happen if Weber finally contacted him tomorrow morning. Would Weber let him postpone their meeting until he had his flat? He had all the time in the world to see Weber's people now he couldn't get out of Russia.

55 - SECRETS REVEALED

Richard was in his little apartment near Dmitrovskaya Metro Station. It was a typical Soviet apartment from the Khrushchev period – badly finished and rather small. There was an entrance hall, a lounge/diner/bedroom, a tiny second bedroom, kitchen, bathroom and toilet. The whole lot fitted into an area of approximately sixty square metres.

He'd got used to the fact the apartment wasn't great. It wasn't that bad either. It looked a crumbling mess from the outside, but it felt fairly solid. It was small but he actually had more space than in the Ukraina, and more privacy. Just not so much luxury or service. In fact, no luxury or service whatsoever. He was finding it a nuisance having to make meals and tidy up.

He lay on the sofa bed listening to the sounds of the city. The day was crisp and clear, the sky cloudless and blue. He had opened the window slightly because the sun was pouring in and the heating was on full blast. The heating was on full blast because there were no thermostats in the flats. In winter the heating went on when the authorities decided it was time. When it was on, it was on, and it would stay that way until spring.

Somewhere out there a siren was making its eerie wailing sound as it drifted through the streets. Eventually it faded away to be replaced by the noise of a dog barking in the distance, and then just a general wash of traffic noise.

Richard could feel the bright, crisp air from the open window awakening his spirit.

On days like this the hidden treasures of Moscow would be revealed – from behind sullen grey buildings the turrets of colourful cathedrals would peep out, holding aloft golden onion domes which glittered in the sunlight. In the parks where the snow was clean, ethereal pastel-coloured buildings would be floating in whiteness, veiled by copses of silver birch.

If anyone wanted to contact him, they would give him reasonable notice, wouldn't they? So right now he had time, and he had the whole huge metropolis of Moscow available to him just by entering the wormhole of Dmitrovskaya Metro Station.

He took the Metro to Chekovskaya and started walking down Tverskaya Ulitsa towards the Kremlin. Yesterday's snowfall had already been cleared away, though a further light fall overnight was still melting in the sunlight, making the pavements wet. The authorities were always quick to clear the roads and pavements of snow in Moscow. In fact, often you would see men on the rooftops making sure the snow was shovelled down to street level, from where it could be cleared away before it became hazardous. Muscovites don't consider snow to be a good thing. After a few moments of beauty it turns black and ugly. It's a danger. They get rid of it as soon as possible.

Tverskaya is a wide street, six lanes in each direction, thrusting all the way from the outer ring into the very heart of Moscow – the Kremlin. In that area it is festooned with overhanging fairy lights that swing across the sky from lamp posts. The apartment blocks either side are imperious oblongs of the Soviet period. The façades of these edifices, interspersed with rows of regularly spaced windows, are elaborately decorated with marble pillars and ornamental balconies. All in all, it is a most suitable route for tanks and intercontinental ballistic missile launchers to parade along, which they do every year on Victory Day – the ninth of May.

But as ever in Moscow, the intended effect of magnificence was lessened somehow, in this case by rusting air-conditioning units and satellite dishes hanging from the fronts of the buildings. In spite of the clear blue sky and crisp air, the street seemed oppressive to Richard. The buildings formed walls on either side, amplifying the roar of the traffic. The lamp posts, made of cheap rusty steel, too old and tired to stand up straight, leaned slightly at various random angles. Everything seemed to lurch and sag awkwardly, creating clutter. A haphazard tangle of telephone wires and trolleybus cables overhead seemed to pull the sky closer down, trapping him like a bird in a cage.

As he continued down the sloping street, past the Department for Physical Culture and Sport, Richard noticed mist rising up from the wet pavement. Large patches of the pavement had already dried out completely. He was intrigued and stopped for a moment to consider how this might be possible. He could see that it was confined to a fairly regular area in front of the building. The sunlight was no stronger here than elsewhere, and there was nothing focussing or reflecting it onto this spot. There must be heat coming up from below, perhaps from underground rooms.

It caused him to wonder. What other secrets were still unknown to him? What had he yet to discover about his own plight, for example?

56 - A PLACE WITH SEVEN GATES

Savelovskaya Station is one of those good old-fashioned ones that squats in its own, nondescript filth. The main station brings floods of commuters in from the suburbs who then proceed to pour into the sleazy passageways and filthy tunnels that lead down into the Metro.

Richard passed several sex shops as he picked his way through the puddles. It wasn't easy to avoid walking through the puddles when there were such crowds of people swarming around you, moving at different speeds and in different directions. And it was not pleasant, especially as his shoes were not totally waterproof and his feet soon began to feel damp and cold.

He wasn't sure where the entrance to the Metro was, but the driving sleet made it difficult for him to keep his head up to look for it. It turned out to be just past a crappy looking bingo place. Not a bingo hall, just a bingo place; where the shop-front window had been replaced by a panel illustrated by cards and tumbling money; where they enticed you into its fluorescent-lit interior by having a loudspeaker clamouring at you with the numbers that were being called out.

The entrances down to Metro stations were very often paved with solid granite steps. In Savelovskaya, the steps were made of decaying concrete. He plodded glumly down them, into a long tunnel, following in the wake of an annoyingly slow old man he was unable to overtake due to the people coming up towards him on his right and some rusty metal runners to his left. These runners were common to many underpasses and were fastened over the top of the steps for people with prams and anything else that could be wheeled up and down. But it was often easier to lift things because they were too steep and too wide, so there was no space to place your feet between them without running the risk of getting a foot trapped underneath. In which case it was likely you would trip over with your foot still firmly wedged, causing you to suffer some horrible injury.

The scene inside the tunnel was no improvement on the passage-way he had just left. There was shelter from the sleet but it was even more crowded here, and the wan glow from industrial light units made everyone look sickly. An old woman, standing sideways-on to the general flow of people, with her back to the wall, held out an icon in her cupped hands. Her head, covered by a black shawl, remained stationary, facing downwards as if in prayer. People swarmed round in front of her, passing by without a sideways glance. No one gave her any coins.

A little further on a dwarf, his face hidden inside the hood of a heavily soiled white coat, held up a hand-written sign and repeated the same phrase incessantly, "Pamagitey meehyay pazhalsta, pamagitey meehyay pazhalsta... (help me please, help me please)."

The underpass was lined with small kiosks selling various things. Some of the kiosks were missing, making the passageway wider at these locations. However these recesses were darker and even filthier than the main thoroughfare. Alcoholics favoured them as a place to meet and share drink.

At one of these recesses there was a series of three steps leading slightly upwards. Here a heap of soiled clothes had been discarded and lay scattered over the steps. It was only on noticing there was a human head facing out from the bottom of the heap that it became apparent this was a person who was lying where he had collapsed. His comrades showed no interest in him but continued to seek the same state of oblivion.

At last Richard made it to the escalator and down to the platform. He found what he thought would be a less crowded part of the platform from where he would have a good chance of getting onto the train. It wasn't the rush hour but sometimes, even at this time of day, you had to be quite pushy.

Most stations were built to a similar overall design to this one. There was a large central hall into which escalators ran. On either side of the large hall there were supporting columns. In this station these were square and around eight feet wide. Passing between the columns, you would get to the platform which was about 160 metres long – room enough for eight full-sized carriages. Richard was standing almost two-thirds of the way from where the train would arrive.

Distant rumbling warned that something was approaching. At the far end of the station, what had looked like a solid black oblong, starkly contrasting with the white marble walls, was beginning to grow less distinct. A grey haze had started to develop within it. As the rumbling grew louder, the oblong began to glow internally. It was no longer solid. It was dissolving. Now you could see deep into the previously unseen interior. An entrance had opened, into a deep tunnel. There, an eerie white light slipped and slithered along entrails of electric cables strewn along the walls. Motes of dust seemed to dance and vibrate in the light, which was becoming stronger and stronger until finally it was concentrated into a row of six powerful lamps in a horizontal line – four grouped close together in the centre and two more, further apart, on either side.

Behind those lamps, if you could bear the searing pain of looking through their intensity, a dark structure was forming, and, emblazoned in the centre of it, the horned shape of an "M". A demon in the shape of a huge metallic serpent burst out from behind the light and rushed into the station, howling as it came.

Then reality was re-established. On entering the station, the demon had revealed itself to be the usual, battered-looking blue Metro train. Row upon row of carriages thrust out of the tunnel, one after another, still howling, trying to decelerate.

Suddenly a siren blasted noise everywhere. It came clattering off the smooth marble walls with deafening intensity, alarming urgency. Richard became aware of a swiftly moving shadow to his right, just behind him. He stepped forward towards the onrushing train. At the same moment as this instinctive reaction, he felt something jolt against his back, moving from right to left, and then the train rushed past him, on his left, carrying with it the deafening blare of the siren. He was aware of some sort of soft thudding noise and turned to see most, or all, of the people waiting on the platform had contorted their faces into peculiar expressions. Some of them seemed to be screaming soundlessly. Then the crowded platform lurched and heaved in slow motion, backing away from the train which continued onwards, howling and shrieking in fury. For a brief moment a man was flying in the air just above, and in front of, the train. He flew sideways, twisting frantically, and then was gone.

The train had managed to stop by now and the noise of its siren had been replaced by a discordant sound that swelled back towards Richard. The sound, a kind of hymn to horror, of women screaming and men shouting. The wave of sound, eerily quiet compared with the siren, washed over Richard as the carriage he was standing next to swung round crazily and swept upwards towards the roof, pulling the whole of the train with it. He felt something hit his head and wondered why everyone was hanging, upside down, from the ceiling. Then everything went black.

***

"Chai, koafee? Visky?"

Richard had grown accustomed to the fact he was in a small room now, and had to answer some questions for some reason. He remembered being helped into a car, and helped out again. It had been impossible to tell what the Russian voices were saying to him. The faces were no more hostile, and no more friendly, than usual. The faces had told him things and had probably tried to explain in English, but he hadn't been able to understand any of it. Everything seemed muffled, as though he was deep underwater. As he was being helped out of the car, he had realised they had taken him to a police station of some sort.

The first question was easy, even though it was asked in Russian. The words were almost the same as English – tea, coffee or whisky?

"Chai pazhalsta," Richard replied. At least he knew how to say "tea please" by now. He looked round. He was surfacing; the sensation of being underwater was fading away.

He was sitting in front of a large, paper-strewn mahogany desk in a room with a window whose view, through thick metal bars, was of a blank wall just a few metres away. How had he got here? He rubbed his head. There was a lump, and what felt like dried blood in his hair.

"I should go to hospital to be checked up, maybe?" he asked.

The man answered slowly: "Dwoaktor calms, weal de-cyade. Eef you woah keay thane ay yask qvayschuns." Richard translated the man's thick accent; though he hardly spoke any Russian, he knew how to decipher even the thickest accent.

The doctor is coming. He will decide. If you are OK I will ask some questions.

The policeman put a brown plastic cup of steaming black tea on the desk in front of Richard. He seated himself behind the desk.

Richard looked at the tea, and at a pile of official documents stacked at one side of the huge desk. He had already realised the policeman was wearing an important-looking uniform. The significance of an important-looking uniform and a huge desk began to impress itself on him. The policeman looked a powerful and imposing figure. For some reason he felt extremely sorry for himself. He was concussed and probably dying, but they were going to interrogate him and charge him with... with what? With spying, sabotage, with causing a train crash?

He'd had some sort of dream when he was unconscious.

There was a long corridor. He was passing along it. At regular intervals there were wood-panelled doors on either side, opposing each other. A patterned, mostly green, rug ran the full length of the corridor, but not the full width, so a margin of parquet flooring was visible on either side.

Halfway along the corridor the carpet was making undulating, wave-like movements, sometimes quite violently, like something alive tugging to be free but flailing helplessly, and sometimes smoothly, with control and power, like a snake.

As they walked over and past this disturbance, Richard remembered feeling a strong, cold draught. He imagined the curtains in the adjacent room would be streaming inwards like the arms of a ghost blindly reaching for something or someone.

Finally, he was ushered through one of the side doors. Into the room where he was now.

"Alexandrovich! Pa-idtee – Come!" the policeman barked out, adding English to his Russian for Richard's benefit. He was looking past Richard as though he wasn't there. Richard turned to watch a man let himself into the room.

"In case you have concussion I must give you check up," he said.

"OK," said Richard.

The doctor stood in front of him and looked into his eyes one by one, then shone a light into them. He held one finger up in front of Richard's face.

"Look," he said, and moved the finger slowly from side to side. "You are OK," he announced. "Probably are a little shocked by incident in Metro."

"Oh, good." Richard was genuinely relieved, but he still doubted it was true. He didn't feel OK.

The policeman spoke to the doctor in Russian.

"Our detective inspector wants me to stay to act as interpreter," said the doctor. "He has a few many questions."

"OK," said Richard, wondering if he was going to be asked a few or many questions.

The policeman and doctor spoke together in Russian again. Then the doctor turned to Richard and said: "He wants to know if you saw the man."

"No, he came from behind. I think he tried to push me in front of the train."

"At least one witness has said you pushed the man – the deceased."

"No, he came from behind."

There was a brief consultation in Russian and then a new question:"Can you explain how he managed to fail to push you if that is the case?"

"No, I don't know. I think I felt a presence behind me, or perhaps there was a shadow." Richard shrugged. "I took a step forward just in time. A second later and I would've been dead. I guess that's why I fainted."

"The CCTV has already been reviewed. We know if you are telling the truth."

Richard felt confused. He had told the truth. Were they not satisfied with his answers? What else could he say?

"We also have witnesses. Many witnesses. Some say you pushed someone in front of the train."

"But I didn't!"

"I am told this man deceased. If pushed you, you will have been charged with murder."

"But I..." Richard wasn't completely sure what the doctor had meant – his English had suddenly deteriorated. Had he already been charged with murder?

"Did you push him?" the doctor asked.

"No, of course not. He came from behind. I think he tried to push me."

"Who was he?"

"I don't know."

The doctor and policeman looked at each other knowingly. It was obvious the policeman could understand what Richard had said although his spoken English was weak and his accent was all but indecipherable.

"So you saw him?"

"No."

"But you just said you don't know him. You must have seen him to make this statement."

"Oh." Richard was confused.

"If you did not see him how could you know you don't know him?" the doctor demanded. The policeman smiled in satisfaction and relaxed back into his seat a little.

"I didn't mean that. I just mean... I saw him when he was thrown in the air. Just very briefly."

"Why you did not say that to begin?"

"No, but, it makes no difference. I didn't really see him properly."

The policeman smiled, "Woah keay," he said, and then spoke to the doctor.

Richard stared dumbly into space as they talked together. If he had been charged with murder, or was about to be, he would lose his job. He would lose Zima. His life would be over. He wondered how bad conditions in a Russian prison would be. Suicide. Suicide might be the only escape. He thought back to how they had all criticised Mitchell that day. But perhaps sometimes...

"OK, this is enough. The CCTV is similar to your story and it confirms what you and the majority of witnesses have testified. But you should be careful how you talk." The doctor paused. "And you are free to go."

Richard sighed in relief.

"Thank you." Richard was surprised the ordeal was not worse, especially as he had not been precise, and the situation required precision. In his experience, Russians liked absolute clarity.

"Just one more thing."

In the movies there was always "just one more thing" – it was always this thing that caught you out, thought Richard.

"Oh?" he said lamely.

"We need to complete the formalities." The doctor paused to ask the policeman about this.

Richard had just realised something. They would ask to see his passport! When they found his visa was invalid, they would arrest him.

"Yes, you are witness in this case. We need signature on witness statement which will be in Russian. Then name and address."

"OK," said Richard, wondering what he could do. This was going to complicate things. They might hold him in jail for weeks or even months.

"We need to see your passport of course. Let us begin with that."

Richard handed it over, trying to look confident, hoping that perhaps they wouldn't check it too carefully.

The doctor took it and handed it over to the policeman. After spending some time looking at the photo page, he copied all the relevant information from that page carefully onto the witness statement Richard was about to sign. He went to the photocopier and photocopied the photo page and then flicked through to the visa page. He took a photocopy of that page too and sat down again.

He was carefully stapling together each of the photocopies and the witness statement.

"Nayem ee aahdrecc."

There was a moment's silence before Richard realised the policeman was asking, in English, for his name and address. Just as the doctor was opening his mouth to repeat the question more clearly, he replied:

"Richard Slater, 112 Butyrskaya Ulitsa, Building Seven." He fumbled in his pocket for a taxi card which he handed over. He'd copied his address on the back of it in case he ever got lost. The policeman copied the address and handed the card back.

"Pleyecc sayn," he said, thrusting the paperwork towards Richard and holding his thick forefinger down on the paper to indicate the dotted line for Richard's signature.

He hasn't looked at any of it. I'm going to get away with this, Richard thought, signing as indicated.

But the policeman had already begun leafing through the passport again. He came to the visa page again. He was frowning. He looked very carefully at the page while picking the receiver of his phone up with his other hand. He jabbed the keypad of the phone and said a few terse words to someone on the other end. After listening to the reply, he put the receiver back down and said something to the doctor.

The doctor spoke: "He says you must enjoy working in Russia to have a visa that's valid for three years."

"Yes, I do. Of course I do."

"Thyenk yew foar yoor cawoperaytion. Yewa woah keay to gow." The policeman handed the passport back to him as Richard deciphered, "Thank you for your cooperation. You are OK to go."

57 - GAMES PEOPLE PLAY

Richard didn't know what to make of it. Either the visa was OK or the policeman missed something. If the visa was OK, it could only mean that Callan had lied to him. Or that it was Callan who had missed something.

Once again Richard was stumped. If Callan was playing a game with him, then why? Because he wanted him to be stuck in Moscow for some reason? Not just stuck, trapped!

But now he was free to go. Free to go anywhere. Free to go home!

Unless, of course, it was the Russian police who were playing a game with him.

58 - SIGNS OF SIGNS

Richard booked a flight to London as soon as he got back to the hotel. Before going to bed he checked his Dropbox for what he expected to be the last time.

A message had come through.

59 - BRUTALIST

They had been driving for miles. It had given Richard plenty of time to think about his fate and to start to become anxious. He had to keep reassuring himself everything seemed to be going to plan. His flight would be taking off in an hour and he would miss it. That hardly mattered. It was just a bit annoying the message hadn't come through five minutes earlier – before he'd booked the flight. The message had read: "Black Lexus will meet you outside Hotel Ukraina at nine a.m.". They couldn't have known he wasn't staying at the Ukraina any more, but that didn't matter either; he had gone there to meet them. The limousine had turned up right on time and an athletic man in a dark suit had sprung out of the front passenger seat to introduce himself as Nikolai Yakimenko. Richard was ushered into the back seat and introduced to another, rather genial Russian called Vasily Kirov. Then they set off, down

Novy Arbat Ulitsa, heading straight through the centre; over the Moscow river; past the Kremlin to their left, then down some huge Soviet-style boulevards, eventually leaving Moscow behind and charging south for mile after mile. He wasn't introduced to the driver but he soon noticed the others called him Gleb.

"Mr Weber tells us you are an associate. Am I correct?" Nikolai asked.

"An associate?" Richard tried to remember the cover story Weber had given him. He was a customer, not an associate.

"Yes, of Mr Weber," said Nikolai.

"No, well... I buy things from him. Russian artwork. For rich London clients."

"But you are IT worker? No?"

"Yes. This is just something I do on the side. It was just by luck that I knew some wealthy bankers that wanted Russian art, and I knew Klaus. So I put two and two together and started helping him make sales."

"Yes. Good. That makes sense."

Of course it makes sense, Richard thought. *It's what Weber told me to say. But if push comes to shove I couldn't tell an icon from an iPhone, Kandinsky from cannelloni.* He hoped there would be no more questions. Weber had told him he should have a cover story, and he should keep to it, just to prove he would not offer any more information. Not to anyone.

The car had turned off the main highway and was picking its way through some dreary Soviet satellite town. They were going much more slowly now, the driver looking this way and that, as though uncertain of the exact location.

"Will we be there soon?" Richard asked.

"Soon enough."

Somehow the terse way Nikolai gave this answer made Richard shudder. What was he worried about?

As the car drove slowly up a wide boulevard, through rows of large apartment blocks on either side, Nikolai began speaking. He seemed to be telling a joke – the others listened attentively with a sense of anticipation. Richard couldn't understand any of it until suddenly some words jumped out at him:

"So now you're fucked."

There was a puzzled silence, a calm before the storm, until Nikolai repeated the punchline in Russian.

Then the storm raged – a loud and violent noise filled the car, each man trying to outdo the others in volume and intensity. The driver was shaking, leaning forward, blasting a foghorn of laughter into the windscreen.

Vasily turned his laughing face directly into Richard's and nodded enthusiastically, his face contorted with mirth. From his open mouth a fetid mixture of cigarette and garlic assaulted Richard.

"Zoh nauw yoower faakt," he parroted.

The car pulled up in front of a graffiti-covered tower block at the end of the boulevard. Someone had spray-painted a question, in English, on the front of the building: "Who now will preserve our lands for the white races?" It was an oddly well-conceived question in terms of grammar. Richard wondered who had written it and why. Especially as it was unlikely that any English-speaking person would ever see it. Russia was not exactly a melting pot, it was almost exclusively white. The people that Russians termed "black" were, ironically enough, Caucasians.

The tower block stood on its own in the middle of a white waste-land of frozen snow. Behind it, two hundred metres away, there was a distressed looking perimeter wall made of whitewashed concrete, topped with barbed wire. Beyond that, quite a distance away, rows of smokestacks tipped with red and white hoops pushed grey clouds into the icy white sky. In the opposite direction, lining the boulevard which they had driven through, were neat rows of massive apartment blocks of the type that would have been depicted as impressive and futuristic in propaganda magazines such as *Komsomolskaya Pravda*. They now looked a forlorn sight.

It was difficult to discern the original purpose of the building. It was a brutalist concrete structure, boarded up with steel shutters on the ground and first floors. At ground level, the exterior walls were decorated all over with the ugly scrawl of graffiti. Most of the windows of the second and third floors, which were literally a stone's throw from the ground, had been smashed by vandals. The square main tower was thirty storeys high. The lower two floors gave the entire building an "L" shape, with the base of the "L" horizontal to the ground. Confidence in futuristic architecture and technology was expressed by the fact the base of the "L" thrust out from the tower some thirty feet above ground level. This was accomplished by a parallel array of asymmetrical V-shaped canti-levers. Perhaps the building had been a hotel with a restaurant or, even more likely, a conference hall. But it was an odd place for a conference hall, the middle of nowhere.

The driver killed the engine and all three of Richard's hosts sprang out of the car at once. Nikolai held open the passenger door for Richard to clamber out; stiff after sitting so long. Gleb went to the side of the building and started fumbling with some keys to open a series of padlocks which kept a small steel door chained shut. This little door was probably a service entrance beneath and just to the side of the main entrance. They were not going to attempt to go up the wide steps of the main entrance. Those steps now existed as a rotten, rusting sculpture of twisted metal rods to which irregular fragments of concrete clung. The entrance itself, now hanging in mid-air above this diseased skeleton, had been blocked off by steel shutters.

"Let's wait for the other prisoner," said Nikolai in English.

Other prisoner? thought Richard. His throat felt dry. He didn't want to ask the question aloud in case his voice gave away the fear that was overwhelming him. He just had to stay calm. As Weber had told him – this was all just a little get-to-know-each-other session. He had also mentioned that perhaps there would be a test too. He had been unable to inform Richard about the nature of any such test, just that it was a possibility. Ludicrously, Richard had pictured himself sitting at a desk filling in a multiple-choice questionnaire. It seemed the type of test they had in mind would be a bit more robust.

"Mashchina zdyes – Vot ana," Gleb replied in Russian.

To Richard, Gleb's thick, guttural voice seemed threatening and alien.

A black BMW 7 came gunning down the street towards them and swerved to a standstill alongside their Lexus, throwing up slush and hard lumps of ice from its tyres. The doors burst open and four men manhandled a fifth out of the car. The fifth man had a sack over his head.

"What's this?" asked Richard anxiously.

"Let's go." Nikolai took hold of Richard's arm and bundled him through the little door.

"But what's going on?" Richard didn't try to struggle. The hard, insistent grip of his escort was enough to warn him that this one man alone would easily overpower him if he attempted to resist, and there were three of them assigned to looking after him. Richard had never been strong or athletic. Years of working in IT jobs had further reduced his physical capability. When he was abroad he sometimes attempted to potter around in the hotel gym, but it only served to remind him how weak and unfit he was. There was no point at all in resisting. If there was some sort of problem, he would have to hope he could talk his way out of it.

The lift was small. Richard and his party only just fitted in with everyone crushed together. The rickety lift doors shuddered closed just as the other group burst through the side door, battering it against the wall with a loud bang which echoed round the bare concrete of the stairwell. The man with the sack over his head was still struggling with his captors for some reason, as though he hoped just one more effort would enable him to escape. Richard glimpsed blood dripping from the bottom of the sack and onto his shirt. Apart from anything else, the poor bastard must be freezing in this empty building. The lift doors closed on this macabre scene, but the lift didn't move.

"Kaput?" Vasily asked.

"Then we will walk," Nikolai replied. "But it not broken. Temperamental, like woman. Kak zhenshina." He banged his fist against the control panel and the lift began its creaking journey to its destination.

Gleb's mouth widened and split open, toad-like. He was grinning.

The doors opened onto floor fifteen. The number '15' stencilled on the originally grey walls of the block was almost completely obliterated. The entire wall was covered by obscene spray-painted images, scrawled Cyrillic writing, and the English word "FUCK!" repeated randomly. They squeezed out of the lift and waited in silence. A drip of water was the only sound. Amplified by the bare concrete, it marked the passage of several seconds before the silence was broken by a scream coming from one of the floors below.

A lot of shrieking began echoing up the stairwell and reverberating throughout the derelict shell of the building. The man shrieking sounded frightened. Had they ungagged the captive and taken the sack off his head? Why? Perhaps they were expecting him to talk now?

They waited at the top of the stairwell as the noises of struggling and shouting grew louder. At last the group arrived at the top of the stairs. What Richard saw sent a chill through his guts. The man no longer had a sack over his head. He was badly beaten, with blood dripping from his nose and mouth.

But the strangest thing was that Richard felt he knew him from somewhere. A dream, a recurring nightmare? For a moment, Mitchell's idea he was psychic came to mind and then he remembered. This poor bastard was Mitchell's replacement at VirtuBank – Jack Logan.

60 - THE RABBIT HOLE

Jack Logan was right there in Moscow. But for how much longer was he going to exist?

Richard had barely recognised him from the time when they were supposedly working together because Logan hadn't even bothered to introduce himself, let alone get involved in RCB. Richard only knew his name because Steve had pointed him out one day. What on earth was Jack Logan doing here in Moscow, and why were these thugs interested in him?

Logan continued to struggle as he was manhandled along the corridor by four other men. Herded along by his three companions, Richard followed with leaden feet moving automatically, having been disconnected from a brain numbed by dread. His head felt light like a balloon. It floated along on a cord attached to his body, looking down on it with only air and emptiness for thoughts.

Sometimes, as Logan thrashed around, his bloodied head turned enough for Richard to see his vacant eyes. It was clear Logan no longer hoped for anything and yet he still battled against his captors.

Devil's music accompanied them – every sound reverberated electronically along the passageway and came pulsating back through the ventilation shafts as demonic mocking. Richard's feet moved forward, detached from his will, plodding out a slow beat. They made their way through the darkness towards the only source of light – a thin wedge of jaundiced light which leaked out from a side door near the far end of the corridor onto the bare concrete floor and connected to a single bright stripe on the wall opposite.

Once through the door, they found themselves in a large room where they were met by an explosion of lurid colour. Fluorescent paint, slobbered over the windows like vomit, formed crude and disgusting images which were illuminated, like stained glass, from outside. It was a cathedral of obscenity.

There were two numbered doors in this room. Logan was pushed into room 1507, and Richard guided into 1506.

This room was smaller and it was cold and dark. The sunlight in the big room had made it comparatively warm. The only light in this room was from a bare bulb in the ceiling, though here too, the windows were still intact. But they were much smaller than in the big room and they had been blinded by blocks of black and red paint, overlaid in some places with patches of purple. The paint was too thick for light to penetrate and had been applied with no distinction between window and wall, squirted on so thickly that it dripped like black or bloody tears. It was like being inside a macabre version of a Mark Rothko painting. A representation of death.

"Help him with his coat," Nikolai said.

Without saying anything, Gleb helped Richard out of his coat and carefully rolled up the sleeves of his sweater and shirt, exposing his right arm. He turned to Vasily, who handed something to him. A moment later, Gleb was holding a hypodermic syringe carefully upright, focussing his eyes on the tip, from which a thin stream of liquid squirted.

Richard felt his heart thumping. He was hyperventilating too. But at the same time, he felt as though the whole thing was happening to someone else.

Gleb injected the entire contents into Richard's arm, then rolled his sleeves back down and helped him back into his coat. Richard remembered Laurel and Hardy used to perform similarly careful acts of comedic humiliation using custard pies down trousers instead of syringes in arms.

"So, please sit down," Nikolai said, waving his hand to indicate a metal chair in the middle of the room. It was the only item of furniture in the room.

Richard's mind was numb. He looked at the chair stupidly, as though he had never seen such an object before and had no idea of its purpose. He sat.

Vasily and Gleb left the room while Nikolai paced back and forward. Richard could hear noises from the room next door.

Faint, insinuating noises. As he waited, the idea that something he needed to know was eluding him slithered into his mind. There was something he had to remember. Something hidden inside something else. Or masks; one face masked by another, with the face behind the mask being different from the person it should be. He had to remember to hide something from Mitchell, from Weber, from everybody. Even from himself.

Gleb returned carrying two chairs, followed by Vasily carrying a third. They arranged the chairs in front of him and sat down, Nikolai in the middle, directly facing him.

"We will..." Nikolai paused until a scream from the room next door subsided. "We will question you here and now. We believe the man next door may be connected to you in some interesting way. If so it would be best if you tell us of that connection before he does."

All three of them were observing him dispassionately to see how he would react.

"I..." he struggled for something to say. He wanted to find an excuse to perhaps relieve Logan's suffering.

"Or how about Mitchell? You knew him better than Logan. What can you tell me?"

For the moment he couldn't think. He couldn't think who he was, who he was supposed to be, or if there was any incriminating connection between himself and Mitchell that Weber should not be aware of. Of course, he and Mitchell were both MI5 and... what was he thinking? By coincidence they were both VirtuBank employees. Mitchell was perhaps MI5, or a criminal, or both. He, Richard, was a revolutionary socialist that Mitchell had tried to trick. But Weber had rescued him. So what was this about? The screams from the next room were horrific. He tried again "I... I..." He couldn't think what to say.

Somewhat pathetically a voice asked: "Can you get them to be quieter? I can't think." It was his own voice.

"I'm afraid they have a job to do. We don't want to disrupt the work of our dedicated colleagues, do we?"

"Of course not," Richard agreed feebly.

"Please, don't forget that Logan will soon be telling us all about you. You should volunteer your information now. We need to know your connection to Mitchell."

Richard was in a blind panic. He didn't know what he could say about Mitchell. Why were these people so interested in Mitchell? He looked round, wild-eyed as though he might find what to say scrawled in the graffiti. Weber had already told him to stick to the art dealing story no matter what. All he could come up with was: "I have spoken to Weber about Mitchell. He knows everything."

"Really? Everything?" Nikolai asked.

"Yes, Weber must've told you this. If you don't believe what Weber tells you, do you really have his interest at heart?"

Vasily snorted. Gleb grinned his toad-like grin.

"We will come to that presently."

"OK. Look. What do you need from me? You know Mitchell and I worked for VirtuBank. I still do. You know my connection to Weber. What else do you want?" He had decided to try to be defiant.

"What else?"

"I expected you to tell me something about your side of..." He had nearly used the word "operation" but that word would have dangerous connotations. He decided the word "thing" would be more suitable. "...Of things. I expected..."

Richard trailed off. He couldn't imagine what he expected.

Vasily stood up and wandered off to a corner of the room. He pulled a packet of Ziganov Black out of his jacket pocket, selected a cigarette, and started smoking. Perhaps he was bored. Perhaps he couldn't stand the smell of rottenness that pervaded the whole building.

No one seemed to mind that Richard wasn't saying anything, nor did they say anything themselves. There was silence. The only sound was that incessant, echoing noise of something dripping.

The dripping indicated that the temperature in the building must be above zero. It certainly didn't feel like it. Richard had been sitting still for some time and was shivering convulsively. The dripping continued, the echoing seeming to grow louder, replacing all thoughts of anything. Then, gradually, from the next room, the sound of sobbing came through the silence. Logan was already broken. But it wasn't enough. Another scream showed that the workers were still dedicated to their task.

"I didn't expect this," Richard said quietly when the scream died away, and the sobbing resumed.

"OK. You win, Slater. I will explain." Nikolai signalled to Gleb, who disappeared for a moment and then rejoined them, standing near the door. Perhaps he had gone next door to ask the neighbours to keep the noise down. If so he was successful. The sobbing and screaming were replaced by some scratchy gramophone music.

Nikolai continued: "Weber is a fool. He is trying to run your operation for the good of all. But his whole organisation is infiltrated. No one is interested in the good of all any more. We are only interested in ourselves. Do you agree?"

Richard had to keep trying to think who he was, who Weber was. Perhaps it was the cold, but he found his thoughts sluggish. It seemed to take him ages to get his mind to work at all. "I help Weber sell artwork, nothing else. We are both only interested in that mutually beneficial trade."

"No, no. I won't have that answer. That is not a good answer. We will need to start treating you in the same way as Mr Logan next door if you give answers like that. As you well know, I'm not talking about some imaginary art persona. I'm talking about Weber. You know who and what Weber is." Now Nikolai too stood up.

"I don't know what you're talking about. Just let me go. You have the wrong person..."

"OK, like that. Let's forget about Weber. Let's even forget about Mitchell. Who cares about them anyway? Let me tell you a bit about myself. You see before you a disappointed man. Disappointed. When I was younger, I narrowly missed out on some golden opportunities. When that drunk fool Yeltsin was in charge, I was still young and idealistic. I didn't look after myself the way I could have, and I didn't take chances that offered themselves to me. But now, now I finally have another chance. You are that chance. Perhaps my last chance."

"You have the wrong person."

"You know I don't."

"What can I offer? What do you want? Artworks?"

"If this is how you want to negotiate. If you want to make an offer that is a good beginning – but let's talk about software."

"Software!?" Richard hoped he hadn't overacted the surprise in his voice. Of course he could talk about software. That was his job. His real job. Shit, he wasn't doing this too well. Pretty soon he would end up going through whatever Logan was going through.

"Yes. Software. I want you to change the program code Weber is giving you. Just make a simple change. From now on you don't do what Weber wants you to do. You do what I want you to do. Do you understand?"

Richard thought. If he tried to do what Nikolai wanted him to do, would that make things better or worse? It was very simple. He couldn't do what Nikolai wanted him to do. Weber controlled all of that. He didn't have any say in what Weber's software did or how it worked. But should he admit that? He knew everyone who is tortured cracks eventually. When should he crack? What story should he give? Was there a story that would help? If only he had some way of modifying the software, he would be able to help Nikolai and get out of here. But he had nothing.

He was vaguely aware of the dripping sound again. The room was much darker. Wherever he moved his eyes it was lit up, but only with torchlight. Nothing else seemed to be happening. Richard was aware he had been saying something to somebody in a voice that was thick and treacly, though what he had been saying was unclear, unknown. All he knew was that he had talked. Nikolai reappeared from out of a long tunnel.

"Please. Take this. We are going to leave you alone now. Call me if you want to help me."

Richard looked round blankly. Nikolai had produced a phone – his own stolen phone – as though by sleight of hand.

The three men left the room silently. Richard continued to sit in his chair. He wondered when the poison would kick in. He wondered if it would be painful. But after a moment he realised that nothing much was happening. He realised that whatever the injection did had already happened, and now he was coming out of it. He continued to sit in his chair, not daring to believe he would be able to stand up. Then he stood up.

What now? Logan! He staggered to the door feeling strangely elated, wondering why he was staggering. It didn't matter much. He seemed OK. Just a bit drunk or something. He crept into room 1507, not knowing what to expect. A record was still turning on the gramophone player. The needle was stuck at the end of the last track, making the arm twitch. The noise it made was the sound of finality – a scratching click that repeated over and over. Logan was lying on the floor, eyes open, glassily staring at the ceiling. Richard checked for a pulse. The body was already cold and dead.

Then he noticed a faint smell of burning coming from the corridor.

***

Richard wondered where the smell of smoke was coming from. He pressed for the lift but then thought better of it. In any case, the lift seemed to be really broken by now – there was no sound of movement. He rushed downstairs. On each of the lower levels he noticed stacks of junk piled up, often spilling out of the front doors of the apartments. There was a lot of smashed wood, but there was paper as well, bits of carpet, smashed tiles and porcelain. Some of it looked like drums of toxic waste. On one floor there was a whole stack of large gas canisters. When he got down to level three he realised he was doomed. The whole staircase was boarded up with steel shutters.

Then, for a moment, there was a glimmer of hope. He noticed, half-camouflaged by graffiti, there was a steel door in the shutter. He tried the door. It was locked. The glimmer of hope died.

He couldn't tell how big the fire was. If it was confined to one of the rooms on the floor below, he might still have time to get out before it was too late. It might still be worth the effort of searching for a way out. But the wisps of smoke were already getting thicker. Ominously, the fire was beginning to make an angry crackling sound. It would probably begin working its way upwards to the other floors soon. Would he have time to wait for the fire brigade or would he be overcome by smoke? If he could find somewhere that would remain smoke-free, perhaps he could give himself time. That would mean giving up hope of finding a way out. Richard could never understand how concrete buildings could burn like raging infernos, but they seemed to be able to. The fire would be able to spread through any cracks it could find. Ventilation ducts, conduits for cabling. There might be just enough dust and flammable material to allow it to spread.

The piles of oil drums and gas canisters on level five!

Richard looked out of the stairwell window. It was too small to climb out of and too high up to jump from anyway.

61 - ZENITH

His phone started ringing.

"Who's playing?"

"Weber! I'm in a burning building. I…"

"Answer the question, Mr Slater. Who's playing?"

"I don't care, Weber. I know it's you and you know it's me, and I was just nearly killed and..."

"I apologise, Mr Slater. We Russians like to play rough sometimes. This was just a little test to see how you would react."

"A test?"

"So, who's playing?"

"Zenith." Richard had to say "Zenith" if he was able to talk and "Spartak" if he wasn't.

"Good. That's better, I like to follow protocol. If you don't follow protocol every time, you might make a mistake when it's important."

"OK. Now that we've followed protocol, can we hurry up?" Richard was starting to panic.

"I know where you are. I can get you out. You still have time."

"OK. How?"

"Go to the top floor, floor thirty. Go into suite 3003. You will see that the local hooligans have had a lot of fun vandalising the building. In the bedroom there is a wooden ladder. It is propped up against a ragged hole that goes all the way through to the roof. Climb up the ladder onto the roof. When you are there you will see a contraption that these kids built to keep themselves amused. It's a rope that hangs over the side of the building. You have to grab hold of the rope and throw yourself off the top of the building."

"I have to what?"

"Make sure you hold on tight and the spooling mechanism that the rope is attached to will slow you down when you get near to the ground."

"You're kidding me."

"When you get down, go towards the housing blocks. The main street is Dachnaya Ulitsa. At the end you will come to a commuter station – Fryazino. The train goes to Yaroslavl Station. There you can get the Metro home. No, I'm not kidding. Hold on tight."

"I will if I can. This was all just a test, you say?"

"Yes. Lucky you didn't call or mention the wrong people."

Richard thought it was lucky he had no people.

62 - LEAP OF FAITH

The snow fell gently.

Standing on the thirtieth floor of a derelict Soviet tower block in the freezing cold does not leave you much time for weighing up your options. He had examined the amateurish contraption but hadn't decided how it would work, or even if it would work. It was quite clear that the thing was built for thrills, not safety. There was a rope wound round one large drum, linked by a motorbike chain to a cog wheel and then by another cog to another large drum which had a rope attached. This rope was played out over the side of the building. Both drums were parallel to each other and both ropes hung over the side of the building. It seemed that as the rope round the first drum wound down, the rope round the second drum would wind up. Richard considered that it might be safer to try to climb down using the second rope. But it was thin and made of nylon. Not easy to grip or climb on. Secondly, there was no play left in it. If you held on to it, it would simply unravel a bit and probably leave you dangling somewhere near the twenty-ninth floor. Then you would need to climb down the rest of the way, hand over freezing hand, trying to grip on to a cold, thin, nylon rope. And then – what if the rope ended at the fifteenth floor? The first rope was thicker and made of hemp. It had a thick knot that you were clearly supposed to grip onto – but so what? How did the contraption save you?

Richard's hands were already freezing. He would have to do what Weber had told him to do. That was the recommended method. Pretty soon he wouldn't be able to grip the rope hard enough – or his hands would be so numb he wouldn't be able to tell if he was gripping it at all. It would mean leaning over the edge of the building and stretching to the limit of his reach just to take hold of it. What if he lost his balance? Just thinking about doing that made him draw in his breath. He took a moment to compose himself. After a last look at the amateurish contraption supposed to prevent him from plummeting to his death, he reached forward and stepped over the side.

He was falling like a brick. Confusion and panic surged through his mind, followed by dismay. Somehow he must have failed to catch the rope. Yet his fingers were gripping the knot so tight they were numb. He had hardly enough time to wonder if the line had broken before his shoulders were yanked almost from their sockets. He had suddenly decelerated.

He had not realised that his eyes had been shut tight. Now they were wide open in terror. The ground was spinning and lurching wildly. The building loomed towards him and then span away.

He had stopped only thirty feet from the top, swinging loosely like a pendulum. The nylon cord alongside, under tension, was vibrating rapidly. There was a noticeable upward motion in it.

He had hardly enough time to wonder what was happening, what he could do, and how much longer he could hold on before he became aware the upward motion in the cord alongside had ceased. Immediately, he was falling again. The wretched device was a test of strength, and he was not a strong man.

The contraption was dropping him down roughly thirty feet at a time. It was torture for his arms. But those didn't need to be strong, he could try to let them relax, just so long as he was able to hold on with his hands; that was all that mattered. He gritted his teeth and tried to concentrate all his strength into his hands. There was some small comfort in the fact that each time he dropped, the pendulum he was part of grew longer and swung less violently. Finally, just below the second floor, the torturous jolting ended. It was clear that this time he really had stopped completely. With his aching arms stretched to their limit above, Richard dangled there, unable to see what was directly below. Now the only thing he could do was let go and hope. He let go and fell. The rope knot he had been holding was pulled upwards, vanishing between his upstretched fingers.

He landed on a steep wedge of snow-covered earth heaped up against the side of the tower, pushing his feet to the right and causing him to slide then roll. He tumbled down the wedge of earth, getting covered in snow, and finally came to a stop, sprawled on his back, looking upwards. He lay there, mentally and physically exhausted, until the rope he had held onto was back in its original position. He briefly wondered if the kids that had made this home-made attraction had a more elegant way of coming to rest, as he picked himself up and brushed snow off his clothes as best he could with his trembling arms. Thick smoke was pouring upwards from at least two floors on the left-hand side of the building. The fire was burning fiercely. He had to get away before those gas canisters went up. Besides, presumably the fire brigade would be here any second now, and the police. He started to run.

He was halfway along the Dachnaya Ulitsa when he heard the first explosion. He stopped and looked back. Another, bigger explosion took a huge chunk of prefabricated concrete out of level four. The tower started to topple slowly, pivoting over the largely missing fourth floor. Two further explosions marked its end as it collapsed into an upward rush of swirling smoke and dust.

Luckily, the building had been like a snaggletooth in an otherwise heavily populated development. The falling structure and other debris didn't cause any damage to the inhabited buildings nearby.

By now straggles of people were running into the street to look, or leaning out of windows. The fire burned black and orange, like rubber or tar, creating lurid, dancing shadows. Richard hoped that no one would notice him, an obvious foreigner, smartly dressed and yet covered in dirty, wet marks all over his clothing. He didn't want to have to explain what he was doing here. He slunk away and made it to Fryazino Station.

63 - RADIANT FUTURE

He was exhausted. He checked his watch. It was nine p.m! Where had the time gone? The car journey had probably taken around two hours, but that meant they must have been in the derelict conference centre for about ten hours.

The train crept along. Indistinct in the darkness, ghostly crenelated walls slipped past. Impossibly huge pale walls, punctured all over by hundreds of vacant squares; blind eyes empty of hope; mouths crying out without purpose. The walls were rows of tower blocks, probably from the Brezhnev period.

The carriage was unheated and not very comfortable, but at least now they had picked up a bit of speed and were rattling along. The swaying motion seemed calming, even though it was jerky and irregular. The dim yellow lighting was growing dimmer. Alone in this carriage, he felt strangely calm considering what he'd just been through. He had nothing to do, but he didn't want to think about what had just happened. He wanted to get home, home to the UK.

He noticed the train had slowed to a snail's pace again, making long metallic scraping noises and marking the completion of each plaintive scrape with a percussive jolt as it slowly crept over some points. His mind seemed fuzzy and contented. It was cold but he didn't seem to feel it.

His head jerked. Shit! He suddenly realised he was falling asleep. In Russia in winter it was dangerous to fall asleep. You might never wake up. He remembered reading a tourist advice brochure in the hotel; the thing to do was to stand up. He dragged himself to his feet, feeling heavy and drowsy. Even the panic of realising that he could die of cold had not shocked him out of his lethargy. He had to focus, wake up. Try jumping. He stood up straight and jumped a bit.

Feeling more alert, he sat down again, gradually becoming aware there was a strong smell of fat and rancid milk.

They were no longer moving. They had stopped completely, in the middle of nowhere. It soon became clear they were waiting at a station, although it seemed to be a place of such insignificance that the station had been given a number instead of a name. There was no platform, but a straggle of people were trudging through the snow towards other carriages, after avoiding his with some angry gestures of complaint towards the door. He then noticed there was a sign on the exterior of this door – presumably a warning the carriage was out of use. He moved into the next carriage and noticed the horrible smell was gone. It was also nice and warm. Armed only with a few hints and tips he had read from guidebooks he was a stranger in a strange land.

***

At last they were at Yaroslavl Station, where he could transfer to Komsomolskaya on the Metro.

In summer, Moscow had seemed a great place, and as safe as any major city. Not quite the happy playground that London was, but pleasant and safe.

Richard had been particularly impressed, as everyone is, by the Metro. As all the tourist guides pointed out, it was much, much deeper than the London Tube, with stations that were far larger, and decorated like underground palaces.

Komsomolskaya station was one of the most magnificent, but now, travelling back from his ordeal, it took on a sinister aspect. The lighting seemed dull and dusty, struggling to reach into the recesses of its huge subterranean halls and passageways. Light served only to create shadows and a sense of foreboding. The effect on mood reminded him of the dark sinister city of his childhood – Glasgow. Glasgow and childhood. So long ago. So different from the modern world. Back then, Glasgow had been a place of blackness and grime, a place where cold, gentle rain was always falling from grey skies. A place where dark skeletal cranes stood idle in the docks and shipyards. Rotting away.

In the cold, dark conditions, poverty was unbearable. No wonder it became, and remained to this day, a hotbed of radical Socialism – Red Clydeside.

The modern world was no improvement though. Just as grim, and more dangerous. There in the Moscow Metro, he recalled that two female Chechen terrorists had killed more than forty people in the 2010 suicide attacks. There had been other, less effective, attacks too; one just last week. The terrorist threat was obvious wherever you went in Moscow. There were screening devices in use at the entrances of all international hotels. There were screening devices at the entrances to the major shopping malls and department stores. There were screening devices, though sporadically used, at the entrances of most stations, including the Metro. *These were the times we lived in*, he thought. Unrelenting danger and misery punctuated by brief periods of promise. Perhaps if the driving force for progress was no longer in the hands of the few, but distributed among the many, then there would be no need for the vicious fighting over resources.

Komsomolskaya station was one of the finest examples of the "radiant future" style. Radiant Future: a propaganda expression full of optimism. He took a long escalator journey towards a vaulted room where immense lustres hung in space. Then, after walking through this room, a different set of escalators took him down to another marble hall where metallic serpents howled.

At around the same time that the station was being built, in 1932 and 1933, huge efforts were being made to increase production. At the same time, seven million people were deliberately starved to death. This was the reality of the command economy. Decisions could be taken at the top for the completion of some magnificent master plan. Those at the bottom could have no influence even if the plan was crazy. Socialism was not supposed to be about dictatorship. Marx had never specified precisely what sort of economy would replace capitalism, but surely a bureaucratic command economy was not what he had in mind.

It was likely that Stalin had beaten his old adversary, Hitler, in the number of people killed for ideological purposes.

Thoughts of Hitler reminded him again of Moscow erased from the map. What a terrible crime against civilisation that would've been. Luckily, Hitler had failed, though at the expense of extending Stalin's popularity. He had failed where Ivan the Terrible had succeeded. Ivan the Terrible had destroyed, and erased from the map, the city of Sarai, the Mongols' Russian stronghold near the Caspian Sea. A place that had been forgotten after its destruction in the sixteenth century. A place whose existence was not known to history until the thirties. A place which contradicted the view that the Mongols were entirely barbaric. But history is written by the victors. To be on the right side of history, you had to be a winner.

*∗∗

At last he was at Dmitrovskaya and heading upwards on the escalator, back to the safety of his apartment. An announcement was being made. The speaker system turned the announcer's voice into that of a metallic automaton, making it seem that something urgent and menacing was being broadcast. The message was coded, being made in an indecipherable language – Russian. Richard, on the run from a race of cyborgs, knew that the message was telling the other cyborgs that they were tracking him and would intercept him as soon as convenient. The announcement ceased.

The escalator continued its journey towards its destination. Near the end, the voice of God began making another announcement; the metallic voice of God, echoing wrathfully in the halls of the howling steel serpents.

And suddenly music began playing. Romantic, nostalgic music, like something from the love scene in a sixties spy movie. It was

The Snows of Spring from an old Soviet movie, in which the hero died in the war against Hitler. The heroine never married. In the village to which she returned, there was no one left to get married to. Richard didn't know any of that, but felt the sadness of the music in his soul.

The music faded away behind him as he walked through the glass doors and back into the cold.

***

The area round Dmitrovskaya Metro station was utilitarian during the day and, whenever the police were unable to keep a presence, somewhat menacing at night. Tonight the police were nowhere to be seen.

At the station entrance, a zombie staggered towards Richard. The zombie swigged from a bottle of vodka, and stretched a hand out, hoping for money, but did not attempt to follow when Richard walked briskly past.

A little further on, some down-and-outs were huddled round a small fire. The fire was contained inside a brazier but even so the police, when they turned up, would not be tolerant of this act of arson, even in this temperature. One of the group broke off and went towards the exit of the station. He approached some people who were coming out but they waved him away angrily and he returned to warming himself by the fire. Apparently, keeping warm had to be his priority, even above getting money for black-market vodka. Yet it seemed his only reason to remain alive was to drink, even though that was what would inevitably kill him, for no one who made or sold this stuff cared what sort of chemicals went into it, so long as they were cheap. He didn't seem to care either. His existence was another life without choice.

At last Richard was back in his apartment, safe and sound. His phone rang.

"Who's playing?"

"Spartak will win 2-0." Richard just couldn't be bothered with Weber right now. This answer gave him twenty minutes respite. If it was really urgent, Weber would say to him, "No, the Premiership," and he would have to listen.

"OK."

64 - THE JOY OF LIFE

Weber was using his satellite phone. He hated using the satellite phone because it was the only thing he did that a normal person or an art dealer wouldn't do. The Bureau insisted it was safe. But he never assumed the British to be stupid. Enigma had been a long time ago, but it was a good lesson that you could never know what your adversary knew about you. It could be that they knew everything and it was convenient for them to let you keep giving them more. But Weber had to assume that his people were not stupid either. If they said it was OK and they wanted him to use it, he had to use it.

"This was too much, Nikolai. I expected you to shake him up a bit but really I did not expect this." The receiver buzzed with Nikolai's answer:

"So what did you expect? You asked me to check him out. We did that. We found something that might be interesting. Slater and Mitchell were working together."

"What do you mean? What on?"

"On Zima. The link was Zima. That's all we found. It was all a jumble. Something about Helsinki, something about VirtuBank. He asked me not to trust Mitchell. It didn't make sense but there is some link."

"Is that all?" Weber was disappointed that Nikolai had over-dramatised. "Interesting." He'd actually found nothing interesting. Why had he said that? Was Nikolai trying to catch him out now?

"It seems to be all. Just Zima. It was about Mitchell's false software, wasn't it? We knew it already. No other link."

"Of course there was another link between Mitchell and Slater." Now Weber decided to play with Nikolai.

"What?"

"They were colleagues. How about Logan? Did you get anything from him?"

"No. He was a zombie. He seemed to have no memory of anything. He must've taken something. I don't know why he didn't try cyanide. Our guys fooled around with him for a while and just killed him in the end."

"Couldn't you wait a bit? You mean you killed him there and then?"

"When were we supposed to kill him? Should we wait until he's in the old folks' home and has Alzheimer's?"

"OK, fine, it was OK. But I hope you're not going to go round killing everyone we need to interrogate. Thank God you didn't decide to kill Slater. Slater might still be valuable. Don't think that because you're over there in Moscow your actions will have no repercussions here. I don't like anything that might make my opponents allocate more resources to..." Weber didn't dare finish his sentence. The phrase "looking for people like me" remained unspoken.

There was more buzzing in the receiver: "If you delegate something to someone expect them to do it as they see fit."

"OK. You did well anyway. I think he's clean, don't you? I've already sent a taxi straight from the airport to collect him. Have you been monitoring his calls?"

"He hasn't made any calls to anyone."

"So nothing there. No attempt to call 112 either?"

"As I say. Nothing."

"That's good. It shows he's trustworthy. He might even be quite good at this. Maybe we should get him back over there for some training?"

"I don't want to have anything to do with him. I don't want to see him again and I don't want him to see me."

"OK. I wasn't quite serious. If he has a purpose, this project will be it. No hiring, firing or pension plan. But make sure you understand that he's not expendable. Make sure everyone understands that. Now that he's checked out OK, I might have a use for him sometime."

***

Half an hour after that call, Richard's taxi dropped him off at Hyde Park corner. Weber was waiting for him. Richard knew he would be there, of course – that was the arrangement – nevertheless he hadn't thought why Weber would want to see him. As soon as he saw the expression on Weber's face he became anxious, for it was only then he realised Weber wasn't meeting him for a pleasant chat. He was going to be asking him about Nikolai, finding out what he'd said to him and probing for any differences in the information he'd given Weber in Leinster Terrace and the information Nikolai had obtained in Moscow.

As they began walking away from the traffic, the only thought revolving again and again through Richard's head was: "What did I say to Nikolai? What does Weber now know?"

"So how did you like Moscow?"

"It was OK."

"I believe you met Nikolai?"

Electronic echoes played devil music – *Luzifers Abschied* by Stockhausen. Richard's feet moved like lead. His head felt as empty as a balloon. He felt something rather than remembered it – an experience that was imprinted into the physiology of his nervous system.

"Yes."

"And what did you talk about?"

"I don't know. I have no memory of it." It was true he had no memory of what he had said, but the point was he knew he had said something. Weber could probably activate the right physiological processes to get him to confess to anything.

"Don't be impertinent."

"I'm not. They injected something into my arm. I have no idea what I said to Nikolai. I don't even know if I was talking to him or somebody else."

"Very well then." Weber seemed to come to a conclusion. "I can only imagine how traumatic that was, but welcome to my world. I'm sorry if they played a bit rough."

"Rough! I thought they were Mafia."

"The Mafia are pussycats by comparison, Mr Slater. This is what you're dealing with."

Richard began to relax a bit. For a moment it seemed Weber's mood was mellowing. But he was mistaken: "They are my people. They are Bureau employees who were supposed to interrogate you politely and check out your connection to Mitchell. I know you have a connection to Mitchell."

Richard felt an ice-cold dagger rip through his entrails.

"Connection?" His mind churned.

"Yes, exactly." Weber said coldly.

"Yes. Of course you do; I told you all about Mitchell," Richard said, trying not to betray any emotion, though his heart was pounding. He hoped Weber had not noticed that, in his confusion, it had taken him longer to reply than was necessary.

"Yes, of course you did," Weber said.

There was a long silence. They were almost at the fountain now. There were lots of people near the fountain: children and toddlers running round it, laughing; an Arab couple with a pram; several people seated on the benches that face inwards, surrounding it; others approaching or walking past casually. Weber stopped and Richard, who had taken another step, turned to face him.

"Nikolai told me he had an interesting talk with you about various matters, including Mitchell, and Logan."

Richard fought against the pounding in his temples. He knew he had to appear calm. He had no idea what he had said to Nikolai about Mitchell and Logan. His thoughts fizzed randomly, and he realised that attached to the name "Logan" there was nothing. Nothing was something he could talk about freely.

"I know nothing about Logan. That was the first time I've ever met him. If you can call what happened 'meeting'. I believe he was Mitchell's replacement at VirtuBank. What on earth was he doing in Moscow and why did your people kill him?"

"For now I'd prefer if you let me ask the questions. In due course I may be able to give you some information. Agreed?"

"Do I have a choice?"

"No, of course not." Weber chuckled, but his face had hardened before his next question. "Mitchell. What was he up to? What was he involving you in?"

"I've already told you all I know about Mitchell. I don't know what he was trying to do with me. I have some ideas but… Anyway, it's good that both Mitchell and Logan are gone now if they were trying to usurp Zima in some way. Though the way they got rid of Logan was unpleasant to say the least."

"Mitchell was MI5, as you suspected. I had the software he gave you reverse engineered so we could see what it did."

"Oh? What did it do?" Somehow Richard felt some sort of guilt about Mitchell's false Zima software. Perhaps that he'd been so easily duped by it.

"It diverted funds from the bank into his personal account."

"What?" *So Sally's story was true!*

"Yes, just that. Diverted funds: large sums, from the bank into a personal account in Cayman Islands."

"Incredible." Richard had already decided he would have to play dumb about this.

"Yes, incredible."

"So it turns out that he was just in this for himself? Just a criminal?" Richard remembered what Nikolai had said about modifying the software. He wondered if he should mention it, but thought better of it.

"He was definitely MI5 originally. Probably got corrupted somehow, ended up a criminal. And you would have been his bungling accomplice if the software had fired up."

"I would have rotted in jail for years for something I knew nothing about."

"Yes, exactly. Lucky I turned up in time to rescue you. In the scheme of things, the little misadventure you just had in Moscow was a walk in the park."

"Your people killed Logan though. They didn't just hand him in. They tortured him and killed him."

"These things have to be done. I did not authorise that, nor do I condone it, but I trust the judgement of the Bureau in these matters. After all, he was still MI5 and probably still taking an interest in us, or rather, you. My people shook you up more than they should have but all in all it was a neat operation. I can tell you Logan's death didn't even make it into the national papers back home. The international press knows nothing about it. The only reportage was from the local papers who reported the collapse of the building and have been very critical of the council for not demolishing it some years ago. The papers are concentrating on the scandal of allowing persons unknown to store canisters of gas, oil, tar and even hazardous chemicals, near to inhabited family homes. Their story is that someone was running a profitable business there due to local government corruption. The fact that an unidentified body was found is not even mentioned. I imagine that everyone thinks it is just another junkie or vagrant who lived in the building and no one cares."

"I don't know what to think. I want to help with the operation as much as possible but I never imagined getting caught up in anything like this."

"Go home and relax, Mr Slater. You did well."

65 - WAIT AND SEE

Weber was happy. Nikolai was right; in any objective sense, Richard was expendable. But in the bureau, they had a joke; sometimes the most expendable people were the most useful. He just had a feeling Richard might be useful, so why get rid of him now? At least he was loyal; that was clear. He had noticed Richard was relieved Mitchell was out of the way, which confirmed what he'd said to Nikolai during interrogation. He had a certain inner strength too – he was able to listen to Logan being tortured and killed in the very next room without flinching. Not everybody could do that without cracking up and confessing to anything and everything.

It was good too that Logan was gone. No one could tell that his injuries had been inflicted shortly before the building collapsed. Anyway, the actual cause of death would be the heroin injection.

No one had quite figured out what Mitchell was up to. He was confirmed as MI5 by the Bureau, but had he really gone rogue? Did he really expect to get away with such a simple trick? Could he really be stupid enough to expect his software to divert money straight into his own account?

Then there was Melanie to consider. From what Weber had heard of her, she was able to persuade men to acts of folly. Maybe she had persuaded Mitchell in some way.

66 - OSBOURNE

Osbourne sat at his desk with his head in his hands. The *Winter* project had reared its ugly head once again. Was it worth the risk of letting Richard go to Moscow? How could he protect him?

It was annoying that this relic from the Cold War was distracting attention just when they should have been concentrating on the Middle East. But for now this was his priority. It would be foolish to waste years of effort by dropping the ball now. He reminded himself that Hamilton, long before he had become Sir Hamilton, had been quite certain it would be worth putting resources behind this. There was a real possibility of someone coming up with a plan that would fit Richard's scenario. In which case the people behind that conspiracy would need to be caught. He remembered having an argument with Hamilton at the time. He had wanted to simply arrest Richard or have him put out of action, but Hamilton was quite clear he believed Richard's idea could be activated independently of Richard. In which case, with Richard being the only conspirator known to them, their only chance of stopping a catastrophe would be to get Richard involved and use him to trace the others.

They still knew very little. It had taken ages to push Richard into the guardianship of his proper handler. They knew from the fact he was on his way to Moscow that it was likely he was in contact now, but they had still been unable to establish who he or she was. The Steering Committee had told him to give Richard more time. He'd come up with the dodgy visa idea and asked permission to have him watched.

They should have been watching him even more closely in London too, but there was a limit. No one he'd been in contact with was of any interest. They'd wasted a lot of resources watching him closely last year until it was deemed too costly. They'd gone back to the original plan after that.

Other than that, nothing was happening. There were no suspicious messages on his mobile, no suspicious calls had been traced, no emails of interest. Perhaps it would all begin to happen when Richard went to Moscow. But he would be going to Moscow alone, with no idea what was going on.

He had decided to ask Logan to go. Logan might not be able to protect Richard, but if Richard was contacted in any obvious way, he might be able to pass back details without relying on Richard. In the worst case, he would be able to act as a decoy if he was set up properly. Osbourne hadn't hesitated to take the precaution of doing exactly that. This was something that even the hardest bastards in the Service hated to do, but he had to do it this time. He had to keep Richard in the game.

67 - LOGAN

As he watched the syringe being inserted into a vein in his arm, Logan wondered if it was time for him to bite his tongue. It was clear to him at that moment that Callan had used him as a gambit. He felt the warmth spread throughout his body. There would be no need for him to break the other implant after all. They had decided to kill him. Soon he would be dead.

As the warmth spread, he cursed Mitchell for the suicide that had brought him here. If Mitchell had wanted to die, he could have had it done in Moscow and made himself useful in the process.

When he was asked to go to Moscow and wait for instructions to observe Richard and help if possible, Callan had reminded him that if anything happened, he was to squeeze the implant in his earlobe. The drug would give him almost total amnesia within an hour. That was a grim reminder for Callan to give him. His amnesia would protect anyone from getting at his knowledge, but it wouldn't stop them trying. In spite of being used to the idea of this possibility, he had shuddered to think of the techniques they would use.

If things got too bad, he had another implant. It was a last resort. Even though total amnesia was already a "last resort" in that it would be no way to live. But he wasn't supposed to give in too easily. He knew he would have a duty to use the second implant only when his interrogators had wasted enough effort on him. He would have to bite hard into the middle of his tongue. That assumed he would still have teeth to bite with, or still have a tongue to bite into.

Nobody knew for sure the best way to behave in these

circumstances, but Logan believed it was best to struggle and make as much noise as possible. Make the interrogators believe they were being effective. An act like that would not make them back off in any way, but it might be worth doing. It might be its own reward in a sense.

Furthermore, Logan had consoled himself with the thought that it was routine for anyone who had been given these implants to be reminded of them before a mission. Nevertheless, he had not been looking forward to going to Moscow. Something seemed wrong.

68 - REMARKABLE PEOPLE

"Coming for a drink tonight?" It was good old Steve Wong.

"Yeah, OK. Why not?" Richard replied. "Just a quick one."

"Good luck on that; Darion is coming."

"I have a will of iron."

"Yeah, well just join us for a quick little drink then. We're going to be sensible. Michael Turner and Quinton will be there. They will keep things sensible."

Quinton needed no second name, though Michael Turner had to be specified exactly to avoid ambiguity.

"Good, when are you going?"

"Well, now would be good. It's gone five."

"Blimey, I've been skivvying so hard I didn't even realise. Go on ahead, I'll meet you there. Where are you going?"

"The Hung Drawn and Quartered."

"OK."

Richard pushed his way through the crowd towards Steve. The rest of the party were already there and had formed themselves into a protective corral against the jostling of adjacent corrals. As he arrived, Darion spotted him and signalled to turn round again. He swigged the remains of his beer and went towards Richard.

"Too busy here. We're going to try The Slicker."

"Jeezus, I thought we were a bit too proletarian to get in there."

"Hey, don't worry my old peasant friend, stick with me, I can get you in."

They pushed their way back to the exit with Darion leading the way and the rest of the group following in the brief wake he created.

The Slicker was a recently opened watering hole set in the stone basement of one of the City's oldest buildings. It was decorated with oxidised metal artefacts which reflected subdued lighting in unexpected ways onto random people, giving their faces a seraphic, or occasionally demonic, appearance.

There was a wall of frosted lager glasses stored in the chiller behind the bar. A barman in a smart black uniform slid the glass door of the wall back and removed one. He poured Richard's Lapin Kulta into it, transforming it from opaque to translucent.

The ambience in The Slicker was ultra-modern, stylish and calm. The velvety darkness was comforting and exclusive. Better still, they had a fantastically wide range of continental lagers on draft, served ice-cold into chilled glasses. The range included Lapin Kulta from Finland and Zagorka from Bulgaria, which Michael Turner favoured.

Suddenly Richard's heart sank. A figure had detached itself from somewhere in the depths and was heading straight towards him. It was Jim Callan, and he didn't look happy.

"Richard," he said bluntly, planting his feet firmly and drawing himself up in customary fashion.

"Jim," Richard replied, hoping he had not sounded too unenthusiastic.

"I notice you've taken rather a lot of odd days off lately."

"What's it to you anyway?" Richard grimaced that he'd inadvertently been so rude to JC. JC was quite a big shot, even though Richard wasn't aware of his exact job.

The reply was terse. "I happen to be your boss now. I've taken over from Logan. I'm also responsible for Moscovsky Zakrit Bank."

"Oh, I see."

"You even took a day off when you were in Moscow."

"No I didn't. The only time I took off was when they told me I wasn't needed. There was no real work to do anyway, but even so it was no picnic over there. It was tricky." That was absolutely true – it was no picnic at all.

"That's not what the customer said. They weren't happy."

Somehow Richard felt guilty, though he'd done nothing wrong.

"But the worst thing, the worst thing of all, was making a run for it and coming back here before we got your visa sorted out."

"But it turned out there was nothing wrong with my visa."

"Pure luck I guess. Russian work visas can be utterly Byzantine. We were convinced there was a problem and you should have waited to get it fixed."

Richard was annoyed that he had successfully used his initiative and now was being told off for it.

"Who said there was a problem anyway?" he asked accusingly.

Callan seemed momentarily taken aback, as though he didn't know the answer to the question.

"Listen, if you need help come and see me. And watch out, for Christ's sake! Watch what you're doing. I want to see you soon in any case. I'll arrange a meeting in my office. I'll send you an email in the next couple of days when I can squeeze you in." And with that he turned round and headed back to where he had come from.

69 - POND LIFE

The last person Richard would want to see if he needed help was Jim Callan, so that wasn't going to happen. But it was annoying that Callan was threatening him with some sort of apparently compulsory meeting. It couldn't possibly be anything important or he would've just called him in. A couple of beers later he was starting to feel less uncomfortable about having to see Callan in his office, though he had to keep reassuring himself that it was nothing important.

Richard took a gulp of his Lapin Kulta and reprimanded himself for choosing it. It was just another example of the false choices offered by capitalism. Here were hundreds of choices of lager from all over the world. The only problem was they all tasted pretty much the same. Richard knew that was because the product itself was made by two or three huge brewing companies that churned out beer as though it was an industrial chemical. Real choice, in the form of small independent brewers, was not available because they were completely unable to compete; they couldn't afford the advertising required to build a successful brand.

He took another gulp to reassure himself of his conviction. Lager was one of those products that were made deliberately bland to appeal to a wider range of people. Thanks to the distorted world of capitalism, there were even products that were identical but just had different labels stuck on them to appeal to different market sectors. Another related point was that globalisation was making everything the same everywhere.

Even worse was the fact that, by making too many things too easily available, capitalism reduced the value of experiencing them. This applied both to things, such as mobile phones, and experiences, such as holidays abroad. At one time a mobile phone had a certain snob value. That had long gone. At one time a holiday abroad was a type of adventure. That had all been sucked out of the experience. In any case, "abroad" was no longer as different from "home" as it used to be. Globalisation again.

"Richard."

"Huh?" Richard had been so deep in thought he hadn't noticed Steve approaching.

"What's going on man? No meditating in public, it's a disgusting habit."

"Sorry, I just drifted off."

"Well drift back. Let's go and talk to those girls."

Somehow, Steve was good at talking to girls. Perhaps it was his polished manners that fascinated them, but Richard sometimes found himself left on the sidelines while Steve held forth. So he was half-glad Steve was intercepted by Michael Turner, who pulled him aside to say something confidential.

Suddenly a loud, assertive voice behind him was saying: "Of course, the pond life don't even realise what's hit them. Our systems can react to any change in prices at least a thousandth of a second quicker than anyone else. A thousandth of a second is a lifetime in arbitrage. We can make a trade worth billions in that time and even if we only syphon off a tiny fraction of the margin – "

"It's like a licence to print money," said another voice, interrupting enthusiastically.

Richard glanced behind him to see two large gentlemen in dark pin-stripe suits standing at a high table. They were holding forth with a pair of leggy blondes, trying to impress them. The party had bought themselves a bottle of Louis Roederer Cristal, which was upside down in their ice-bucket, awaiting replacement.

Richard knew that they were talking about automated arbitrage.

Where the hell does that money come from? he thought to himself. Those two bastards are boasting like a pair of schoolboys, but actually they're not doing anything clever at all. The only clever bit is getting hardware and software to run fast enough. They probably pay the IT guys normal, crappy wages and then take all the credit and money themselves. He looked at them again. They probably weren't even in that line of business anyway. They looked more like old-fashioned, open outcry traders to him. They probably worked as car salesmen who just dressed themselves up to look impressive, then came down here to see if they could bullshit a couple of gold-diggers into a shag.

He felt a robust arm slide round his shoulders and give him a hard squeeze.

"Hey, lighten up my friend. What's wrong?" Darion asked.

"Hey Darion! Nothing man. Just wondering when you're going to buy me a drink." Richard realised he'd fallen into his habit of imitating whoever he was talking to and picked up Darion's practice of calling everyone "man", as well as some of his bravado.

"Cheeky bastard. Hey barman, give my little nephew a Jaeger Bomb. He's still a virgin but we're gonna get him laid tonight." Darion laughed until his cheeks glowed. As he turned his head away from the barman, inclining towards Richard, the lighting caught him, changing him from angel to demon.

Oh no, thought Richard. Any idea of having a quick little drink had just evaporated.

70 - ECONOMIC VALUE

"But the money must come out of the real economy," Richard whined. He was quite drunk by now. The party that had been drinking the Cristal had long gone off to their presumed shagfest. Richard had just succeeded in starting a drunken argument about the merits of what that party had been discussing.

"So what? So what!?" Quinton said. "All money comes out of the real economy, and then it goes back in again, round and round. It circulates." He staggered slightly and had to steady himself against the bar. Quinton was rather noteworthy among drinkers. He could start staggering after only four pints but still be in no worse shape another ten pints later. At present he was somewhere between those two numbers, with a few Jaeger Bombs thrown in for good measure.

"Round and round it goes, where it ends up nobody knows."

"Jeff! Hey, how's things?" Quinton asked, addressing the rotund stranger who had just butted in.

"Round and round it goes..." the stranger repeated, staggering quite obviously.

"We know perfectly well where it goes in your case. The Goddess

Aphrodite and her girls get whatever you can't drink."

"Money well spent. Furthermore, it's her 'secret' and mine too, so don't blab about it," the large drunk replied. He turned his head with difficulty, as though some sort of internal struggle for control of his nervous system was taking place. Finally his eyes began to focus on someone or something in the distance. A moment later, he rolled off to investigate whatever had drawn his attention.

"Jeff Shaw, great guy. One of our best project managers."

Richard didn't reply. He didn't know Jeff but had heard of him. He was aware of feelings of jealousy. He also felt his privacy at "the club" was somehow compromised. He felt vulnerable and jealous when he should be strong and indifferent. He closed his eyes and tried to recover his composure.

"Anyway, where were we?" Quinton asked.

"Going round and round," Richard replied, opening his eyes again. His smart-ass answer helped him recover his sangfroid.

"Ah yes, Arbitrage; that's it. You were saying how useless it is."

"Yes." Richard couldn't think what point he was trying to make. "Yes, but most economic activity is about trading things that have real value. Person A makes something that person B needs, and they trade using money as a store of the value of each other's contribution."

"Yes," agreed Quinton.

"But what value does arbitrage have?"

"It makes sure that everything that is traded is traded at the right price."

"But these price differences exist only for a tiny fraction of a second. Why do they need to get so handsomely paid for such a futile activity as that?"

"It's progress. People always did get paid for that sort of thing. Only difference is that now the times are down to minute fractions instead of days or hours."

"But there is no room for actual thought or bargaining to align prices any more. The person with the quickest computer wins every time. It has no economic value, it's just sucking real money out of the real economy somewhere. It's theft."

Quinton looked as though he was trying to remember something: "You know who else differentiated between the real economy and the financial world, and accused the financial world of theft?"

"No. Hit me with it."

"Adolf-bloody-Hitler."

"Fuck off."

"Not joking. Of course he blamed the Jews for running the financial world and everything was all their fault for stealing from..."

Darion and Steve reappeared.

"Hey, what's all this crap about theft and stealing?" Darion said. "You made Michael Turner nervous. He's just slunk off home."

"It seems like VirtuBank accidentally hired a couple of intellectuals, Darion," said Steve. "We can't have people thinking, you know. It might cause trouble. There could be a revolution."

"Yeah, try not to cause a revolution my friends," Darion advised. "Have another drink to kill off those surplus brain cells. Tonight we have to go look for some chicas."

Next day, Richard didn't remember if he, Darion, or anyone else had succeeded in encountering any chicas, and he didn't recall making any progress in his own mind about the value of electronic arbitrage. All he knew was that his head hurt, he felt ill, and he had to get himself to work. He knew the others would be there no matter what. In that respect, as well as many others, they were remarkable people.

71 - LOYAL TO BOTH

Weber had not met Alexei in person. In spite of the cover his unwitting gay accomplices provided him, he liked to keep a distance from his operational people and rarely met any of them. He could get information to and from them by other means.

He realised he was taking a risk because Alexei was his Ace of Spades – his most important operative ever – but he wanted to meet Alexei in person and make sure Richard was telling the truth about the Zima file. He wanted to make sure Richard had not accidentally exposed his operation to Mitchell, or, since Mitchell no longer existed, to Mitchell's people.

He was painfully aware of the CCTV cameras that were all around in Central London. Admittedly, the police would most likely use CCTV for dealing with anti-social behaviour and pickpockets. That was what they said it was for. But Weber couldn't believe it. Even if he did believe that was the primary intention, he knew that if they got wind of something bigger, they would have video evidence to hand. It was OK to meet Richard outside. Richard was a nobody. Someone somewhere might know something about Alexei, and it wouldn't help either of them to be seen together in public.

So he'd weighed up his options and made the unusual decision of inviting Alexei to a suite in the Dorchester. It had cost a lot, but he intended to claim it on expenses one way or another. He'd done his best to make it seem that the purpose of the meeting was to buy or sell Russian artwork.

They spoke in Russian, using the formal "вы» (Viy) to address each other, as though they were strangers. Indeed they were strangers and the situation called for formality.

"Alexei, you informed me that Richard had sent a file which you suspected I gave him instead of allowing you to install it yourself."

"That's right. I couldn't understand what you were playing at."

"I was not playing at all. When you told me about it I thought that Richard had created that file himself. It turns out he got it from someone else."

Weber didn't tell Alexei he also originally thought he himself had triggered Richard into action by giving him the code word, or someone else had known that word. There was no need for Alexei to know about that. It might frighten him. He might feel threatened – and if he felt threatened it might cause him to question his loyalty. That was what could happen to operatives. They would save their own skins first.

"Someone else? Our leaky comrade in Chennai?"

"No. Someone who was, and perhaps has alerted others who still are, on our tail thanks to our leaky comrade from Chennai. I need you to tell me what exactly happened to this file that Richard sent. That will give me an idea if we need to abort the operation or not."

"Abort!? This is all this Richard's fault. When you first told me about him I said we should have him removed."

"I was worried about Richard from the very start. But only in the sense that I thought he would be of no use to us. We had other 'volunteers' just like him and very few of them were of any use. Remember that Richard has been loyal to our cause since the seventies. Unfortunately a lot of things have changed since then."

"Yes, a lot of things. I lived in two completely different countries myself. They just happened to be in the same geographical location."

"Exactly so. I remain loyal to both though." Weber stared accusingly at Alexei.

"Yes, I understand. I am from a different generation. There were things that we wanted to change, but I was not fooled by all this..."

He looked around as though trying to find the right word or phrase to express what he was not fooled by. As though the word or phrase was hidden in the exotic trappings of Weber's suite. It was hard to find the right language with which to criticise capitalism in this luxurious environment. Perhaps the words were able to hide themselves somewhere among the Japanese porcelain dishes, or were deflected by the French crystal chandelier, or were buried in the patterns of the Chinese rug. Alexei had to refocus his thoughts and start again.

"I have not been fooled by all this globalisation," he managed to say at last. He found it easier to blame globalisation, rather than anything else. Was there an element of racism in his attitude? He would not admit it to himself.

"Globalisation. Yes," Weber agreed, thinking how he had believed in internationalism as a young Thalmann Pioneer. Globalisation, internationalism: were they so completely different? "Yes, many things changed for these activists in UK too. They all turned out to be pretty useless. I presume you fixed Richard's mistake though?"

"Yes. Of course."

"How were you able to do it?"

"I made sure that no one saw his file. Luckily it came through to me just as we were going to lunch. Apart from me, Germain and Dmitri, there were only a handful of people ccd. I just told Germain and Dmitri to delete the email. They trust my judgement when it comes to software deployments so they just deleted it without question. I explained to them that I did not want shit like that getting into the system and I was going to have a word with dev."

"Germain allows you to make these judgements for him as a VirtuBank employee?"

Alexei was momentarily puzzled. "Oh, yes, as a VirtuBank employee. He has no idea of the work I do for you."

"He trusts you implicitly? A cosy arrangement."

"It's known as delegation. Western enterprises cannot operate with the same levels of paranoia that you might be used to at the Bureau."

"Hmph," Weber grunted through tightly pursed lips, but he let the insult slip.

"On the other hand, I am Dmitri's boss and he would not question my judgement either. Anyway, I emailed the rest of the people ccd immediately. I told them that a virus had been detected."

"But that's all done automatically surely – virus checking?"

"Of course, but sometimes the automatic virus checkers can't deal with a new virus or new variant. So, I told them that a virus had been detected and they were to stop using their laptops at once in case they were infected. I then phoned and convinced them that they did indeed have the virus."

"How could you do that?"

"Easy. I just ask them a few questions. Get them to rummage around on their PCs and then sound concerned when they find the file that I'm supposedly looking for. There are lots of stupid files in Windows with stupid names that might sound suspect."

"And then?"

"I re-emphasised that they were to stop using their PCs completely until I had a good look. So then I go to have a good look at their PCs and delete the email. It was not difficult."

"So the email that Richard sent was not intercepted by anyone? No one would be able to confirm that he was involved in any plot?"

"He looked, and still looks, completely clean. Also, he managed to send it from someone else's PC somehow. I left that original email in case we need to muddy the water even more at some point."

Weber considered for a moment. "What will they make of the fact that an email that was sent from someone's laptop never got to any of the people that it was sent to?"

"I don't care what they make of it. It's confusing that's all. Richard never sent anything. Whoever was supposed to watch for an email from him never saw it. That's all that matters."

"Yes, I understand." Weber paused, then added: "So it seems that the person who got Richard to send the file never achieved anything. That file simply disappeared – as though Richard did not understand what it was or did not want to be involved."

Weber was still undecided. Did Richard look completely clean? What if someone was following up on Mitchell? It was still unclear to Weber whether Mitchell had been working for MI5 or for himself. At length he said: "You did well, Alexei. We will continue with our operation here."

Weber knew that he could afford to abort the operation at RCB and continue with the same plan at other VirtuBank projects. But RCB was a tier one London bank. It was too good a target.

72 - MISINFORMATION

There was an email from HR stating that, following the inquest, the funeral of Andy Mitchell had now taken place, and that it had been a solemn and dignified affair. VirtuBank had made a contribution to a mental health charity on behalf of the family.

That's interesting, thought Richard. He wondered if they actually went to the bother of staging a funeral. Surely not. They would need a whole cast of actors to stand and watch an empty box go into the ground.

He skyped Darion. "Why didn't any of us lot get invited to the funeral?"

"What funeral?" Darion skyped back.

"Mitchell – read email from HR"

"Oh – busy now. Read later."

"OK."

He tried Steve.

"Why didn't any of us lot get invited to the funeral?"

"It was private I guess. Family only."

"Hmm, OK. Are you in HQ today?"

"Yes."

Richard realised that, deep down, nobody had cared enough to think about the coroner's inquest or funeral until it had happened. Supposedly happened. If only he'd thought about it himself, he might have been able to cause some embarrassment to whoever was sending out this misinformation.

But a bit of embarrassment would not reveal anything to him. For the cost of an email or two, VirtuBank had allowed their investigator to disappear suddenly and without trace.

Richard closed his eyes and swore at himself. It was Weber who had told him that Mitchell was in it for himself. It was Weber who'd said that Mitchell had been MI5 but had gone off the rails and wanted to have software installed that would divert funds directly to his own account. Was Weber telling the truth?

What about Melanie? The lovely Melanie that he had fallen out with last time they spoke. Melanie might have been Mitchell's accomplice. It could be that she organised and staged the whole "Sally" event. Did she know what she was doing when she passed the envelope to him? Or was she another innocent stooge like himself? That mattered. That mattered a lot. It had taken him a long time to get round to it, but now he would have to find out one way or the other.

73 - DANGEROUS

Richard wasn't surprised, but he was still somehow upset that Melanie hadn't wanted to come round to his flat to see him; as though that was likely even before they had fallen out. If he wanted to see her tonight, he would have to go to the club like every other customer.

So here he was again, back waiting to go into the fake room with the fake furniture and fake girlfriend. It would be a different fake room this time, but the same fake girlfriend. Except that Melanie was nowhere to be seen. He'd looked all over for her. In a moment of jealousy, he realised she was probably with another customer.

"Hi." It was the petite girl with the pointy tits and the open-fronted leather skirt.

"Hi," Richard replied politely.

"You look such a sweet man, you've got such a kind face." After telling Richard how kind his face was, her mouth went into a little pout. She looked up at him intently and blinked slowly at him.

"How would you like me to sit on it?" Before Richard had time to fully realise what she'd told him she wanted to sit on, she stepped even closer to him, and touched his arm. He was engulfed in her perfume; a sweet caramel fragrance he could almost taste. She kept her head tilted up while her eyes lowered and took an interest in his mouth. They seemed satisfied with what they found there and so resumed their job of looking up at him and drowning his gaze in their blue depths, and then her red-painted mouth began moving to tell an intimate secret. "I saw you and your 'girlfriend' talking about me the other day." She ran her index finger of her right hand delicately down his chest, biting her lower lip, and added: "Did you know you were blushing? Seems to me you got quite excited."

"I, I..." Richard cursed himself for stammering. He didn't know what to say. Of course he hadn't been blushing, had he? Why on earth was he still like a stupid schoolboy when a pretty girl talked to him? Or in this case, a pretty girl who was, according to Melanie, a complete bitch.

"I can guess what she told you about me. You must think I'm really bad, but I can be a good girl too. Don't worry, honey. I'll be much more gentle with you. When I'm good, I'm very, very good," she cooed. "That guy deserved what he got, believe me. He likes it. He also likes being my pay piggy now. Honestly." The index finger had been removed from his chest and had found its way onto her bottom lip. It moved from the corner of her open mouth into the centre as the pout reappeared and gently sucked it in. She placed her other hand softly on his chest to feel his heart thumping. The finger hidden in her mouth reappeared, and the mouth itself seemed surprised, for she held it open, either in amazement or laughing silently at him. Then the same finger that was performing all the tricks was held upright so her tongue could lick from bottom to top. "Mmm, I taste yummy," she announced. "Would you like to taste me, maybe kiss me? Look how nice my lips are." The finger was reinserted and then slowly drawn out, as though the fact she was sucking at it made it difficult pull out. Once she'd successfully managed to withdraw the finger, she made a kissing action at him.

"Yes, but... "

She spoke slowly and dreamily, murmuring languidly, "No, only very special customers get to kiss my lips. But look... " She pushed her lips right out at him again and made another kiss at him. "I have another puckered up little place for you to kiss. Can you guess?"

She gave him a moment to guess. Now his heart was beating really hard. He wasn't saying anything. She continued: "My pretty little pampered butt hole is all squeaky clean and perfumed to perfection. When I'm on your face you can lick and kiss me there as much as you like. You can pretend it's my cute little puckered up lips, and if you practise on me down there, then maybe one day... "

Richard was embarrassed to realise her dirty talk was turning him on like crazy.

Her left hand was still occupied with sensing how hard his heart was beating, and the index finger of that hand had decided to play with his nipple, so she had to use the other hand to reach round his neck and pull his head down towards her pointy little tits. Her soft little hand so easily and so gently twisted him round so his ear was near her open mouth. "Come on then. Let's find a room."

"Let go of him, Lana." It was Melanie. "He doesn't want to have anything to do with you."

Lana scowled at her and pushed herself slowly, insolently, away from Richard, keeping her index finger pressed on his sternum. Then she turned her back on him and swayed away, her long legs carefully measuring every step, criss-crossing to keep her balanced in spite of the vicious spikes she wore. A few paces away, she looked back over her shoulder to see if he was still watching her. He was; so she raised an eyebrow at him and smiled enigmatically. Then, turning away from him again, she pulled the skirt right up so he could see her completely nude bottom as she resumed her slinking, leather skirt rucked up like a belt clicking from side to side with the movement of her hips.

"Pay no attention to her, Richard. She really is a little bitch."

The little bitch stood with her legs apart, her bottom sticking out. She had placed a hand on each of her buttocks and was pulling them up, opening them at Richard. She looked straight ahead, ignoring him, as though not interested in whether he was watching or not. She knew that somebody, somewhere in the club would've caught some, or all, of her performance and would be interested. That was all that mattered. Pretty soon she would be toying with whoever that was, and then she would be leading him down to the special room. She clearly loved this work.

74 - LIES

So Melanie had rescued him from a terrible fate and now at last they were together in one of the rooms. This one was in the style of a playroom, with a rocking horse and a swing.

"I don't want to talk about him any more," she was saying. She got off the bed and sat down on the sofa, distancing herself from Richard, who was still standing near the door.

"But I need to know," Richard pleaded.

"I want to forget about this whole thing. It's because of men like Mitchell that I'm working in a place like this. Men who lie and cheat and use you without you even knowing what they're up to."

"I never lied or cheated. You should trust me." As soon as he said it he realised how feeble that sounded. Richard hoped he didn't sound like a wimp. Girls like Melanie only looked up to men who were prepared to lie and cheat.

"I don't know if I can trust you or not, Richard."

"And I don't know if I can trust you either. One thing is clear. Mitchell tried to dupe me into installing software that would take money from the bank and deposit it in his own account. He pretended to be dead so he could get me to do it and you helped him dupe me."

"All I did was pass on an envelope."

Richard pursed his lips. Perhaps that was all. If so, how could she possibly have known what was in the envelope, and what Mitchell was up to? But what about the open door of his flat? Someone had opened the door with the keys. And the only time when Richard's keys were not on his person was when he left them in a locker in Aphrodite's Secret. Had Melanie arranged for someone to use the master key of the locker to get hold of them and make a copy? It was an awkward question. He was going to have to ask it.

"Listen, I know he fooled you into doing a lot of things. You passed on the envelope for him; you got him a copy of my keys. None of that matters. That's all under control now."

"I got him what?" Melanie's eyes were open wide.

"My keys. Someone has a copy of them. It could only be him, and it could only have happened when I left them here."

"How dare you say that! How dare you accuse me... "

"OK. I didn't mean to say it was you. But who else could it be? How else could he have got them?"

"How should I know? I didn't even know he had your keys! What makes you say he had your keys?"

"Someone opened the door of my flat." The only problem was that Richard couldn't be absolutely certain that he hadn't left the door open himself.

"Someone opened the door of your flat. What do you mean?"

"I mean someone broke in, when I was away. I came back and found the door open."

"Are you sure you didn't leave it open yourself?"

"Pretty sure."

"Pretty sure? And you come round here accusing me of stealing your keys and copying them?"

He didn't know where to go with this any more. Why was he

being such a complete dick again? As soon as he had seen her he wanted to make up with her. But instead, here he was blurting out the most extravagant accusations.

"OK, never mind the keys. Let's get back to Mitchell. One thing is sure – he tried to dupe me into committing fraud on his behalf."

"Do you actually know that? Did you test the software?"

Wow! That was a remarkably astute question! How could she understand something like that – something that he had dismissed as unimportant. He had simply believed Weber. But why would Weber lie? Actually it wasn't important to know this just for the purpose of deciding if Mitchell's software was fraudulent or not. It was important to know because it was still impossible to determine if he had been working for MI5, or was just a criminal.

But suddenly the effort of making these decisions nauseated him. He decided instead that Melanie's remarkable insight was no more than sticking up for Mitchell. A wave of jealous rage overwhelmed him.

"You liked him, didn't you?" he snapped. "You liked him, that's what it comes down to."

Melanie sulked silently. Richard was dismayed. This time he had really upset her with his outburst. But at length it seemed that Melanie had decided she could bear to reveal something to him, even though he was infuriating her. Perhaps she did it as revenge, to show Richard he didn't compare well with Mitchell: "He was fun," she said. "He spent absolutely loads of money on me, no questions asked. I bought that little car with the money he gave me."

"He gave you enough money for a car?" Richard was astounded.

"A lot of the people who come here are absolutely minted. Some of them don't care what happens to their money. It's easy come, easy go. Besides, it's not a great car. It didn't cost that much."

"Looks OK to me," Richard said angrily.

"How do you know what it looks like? Have you been following me?"

"No, of course not," he lied.

"Someone did though. I'm pretty sure of it. A taxi. It freaked me and Angie out."

"Well it wasn't me." He was already tired of lying. "Anyway, this has got nothing to do with Mitchell duping me and duping you too." He didn't much care now if he found out the truth or not. He realised he didn't want to fall out with Melanie and decided to pretend that Mitchell had duped her too, whether he had or not.

Suddenly Melanie was crying. "I had no idea what was in that envelope. He told me that you needed the envelope urgently for work. I knew he was in some sort of danger, though he didn't tell me what that was. He just kept telling me that his job was dangerous and that he might need to go abroad and keep a low profile for a few weeks. I know he'd already had to do that a couple of times before – go abroad and hide." She hesitated, and then continued: "He gave me the envelope and told me to get it to you while he went abroad. He told me that as soon as I got the software to you I would be paid. That was all I needed to know. Then, when I heard he'd committed suicide, well, I wasn't sure... I never did get paid."

Richard could understand now, or rather he clutched at the opportunity to understand and reconcile with her. "Oh Melanie!" he said. "He fooled both of us."

"Yes," she agreed. She twirled a strand of hair through her fingers thoughtfully. "It must've been so easy for him to fool a silly girl like me. I thought he was a special customer but all the time he was just manipulating me. It turns out that Sally was his favourite and this envelope trick he involved you and me in was just a scam. I feel so let down."

"Listen. I'm so sorry about some of the things I've said recently. If it's any help to you, I won't let you down like he did. You know I really like you." Richard cringed at himself. He was sounding more and more wimpy now, and he hadn't spent anything like the sort of money on her that Mitchell had. He had no right to ask her questions about Mitchell.

Melanie stood up and went towards him. "You know, I wasn't

sure what to think about you at first, but I liked staying with you the other night. In the end I was frightened of him, I'm still frightened. Maybe his envelope still has other nasty surprises waiting for us," she said in a small voice.

Richard stepped towards her until they were standing close. "I can protect you. I'm sure the envelope won't cause any more surprises. I got it all tidied up before any damage was done." He knew he was lying, but he hoped this was what she wanted to hear.

And then Richard found he was holding Melanie in his arms. He hoped that she would fall for the lie of his protective embrace.

Melanie laid her head on his shoulder, letting him protect her.

75 - THE PEOPLE'S LIBERATION

Weber had invited Richard to his apartment again.

"To be honest, we had lost interest in your idea. Everyone had lost interest. By the nineties, even in the eighties, none of the old activists had very much belief left. We didn't believe that it was worth waking any of them up. We were very badly funded and found that it was a waste of effort trying to get any of the sleepers to wake up. So we let sleeping dogs lie."

"So perhaps I would never have heard of Zima, ever again?"

"Quite likely. As I explained before, it came about a bit by accident."

"Yes."

"But not entirely by accident. I was still only handling a handful of sleepers like yourself that had volunteered services through a loose affiliation to various left-wing parties or organisations. But one day I was offered sponsorship from what seemed to be an obscure part of the Russian Ministry of Foreign Affairs. There were some fussy negotiations, and sponsorship was given."

"Why did they do that?"

"It was the fact that you were at VirtuBank that drew their

attention to me in the first place. We, like many 'terrorist' organisations, had realised that cyber war was the future, and having someone in your position might be helpful in that regard."

Weber went to his bookcase and removed a small book. He flicked the book open and pulled out a yellowing piece of paper. It was a newspaper clipping.

"*The People's Liberation Daily*, a Chinese propaganda rag, says: 'An adversary wishing to destroy the United States only has to mess up with the computer systems of its banks by high-tech means.'"

Weber replaced the yellowing paper and snapped the book shut and added, "That article is from the mid-nineties. Of course, we all know that the internet is crawling with Chinese hackers. Has been for years now."

"I know. Not just Chinese. There have been loads of cyber attacks. Some of the most damaging ones are assumed to come from official governments. You've probably heard about Stuxnet?"

"Remind me," said Weber, somewhat wearily, unable to hide his lack of enthusiasm.

Richard was in his element now. He explained eagerly: "The computer worm, probably created by an official US or Israeli agency which was supposed to sabotage Iran's nuclear facilities."

"Oh yes, I remember."

"There are other examples," Richard continued. "A denial-of-service attack on Estonia, assumed to be Russian in origin, countless break-ins to NATO servers, assumed to be Chinese – "

"Exactly so," Weber interrupted impatiently. "None of these attacks have had any lasting impact." He said it as though this annoyed him, and took a breath to regain some composure before continuing: "In the end though, attacks like that can only happen to systems that are connected to the internet. Or if something is embedded in the firmware of equipment before it gets shipped. For the latter to happen, you need the co-operation of the manufacturer."

Richard thrust himself forward, sitting on the edge of the seat.

"It's difficult to attack software systems that are well protected from the web and which are more dynamic than pre-shipped firmware."

"Exactly. So of course, the agency I mentioned was quite excited by your idea. They liked the thought that they could activate someone on the inside of a bank at any moment, but they had no specific idea what to do with such a person. Their 'high-tech' activities up to that point were more based on denial-of-service attacks, viruses, etc. But with your idea they could – "

Richard interrupted. "I find it a bit scary that this group was able to find me."

"Don't worry, they didn't find you. I found you, and I was always connected to you. Of course, what you should be scared of, is if anyone else has wind of your plan."

"Well, we know that Mitchell had wind of it."

"It seems that he had not sniffed the wind hard enough, and I think no one else is sniffing now."

"Hopefully."

"From my point of view, I'm happy enough if you do nothing."

"I'm happy to do nothing. I'm quite good at it," Richard grinned, relieved.

Weber was not grinning. He was quite annoyed.

"Don't screw up again!" Weber's eyes were malicious. He wanted to hurt Richard. "Mitchell didn't catch you because Alexei mopped up after you."

Richard could see Weber's face was twisted in anger, almost as though he was in pain. Weber was so angry he was stuttering and stumbling over his words. Suddenly Richard felt sick. *Alexei!* Weber knew Alexei; that was why he was stuttering. *How or why did Weber know Alexei?* He knew he would have to try not to react. There would be plenty of time to think later.

"The plan… the plan is much as it was before. I will call on you to activate it in a similar way to before but we are not quite ready."

"OK. I thought you said I should do nothing?" There was a

strange look on Weber's face; almost a look of horror. Richard realised deep down how scared he was of this reptilian oddball.

"Do nothing until required." Weber was still angry, a little flustered.

"OK. When the time comes I'll be ready " Richard hoped this show of enthusiasm would convince Weber he hadn't noticed him mentioning Alexei.

"Exactly so, yes." Weber's eyes narrowed. He stared hard at Richard. It was uncomfortable. Eventually he continued: "Mitchell, or someone advising him, probably imagined how our software would work. His bait software was also going to slot into an interface such as currency rates. But our software is much more ingenious than most people would imagine."

"I tried to imagine how it would work myself," Richard admitted.

"Have no doubt, Richard, that when I call on you to implement the operation, it will be what you have been waiting for. Will you be ready for that, or do you have doubts?"

"Doubts? Why should I have doubts?"

"This will be an action of historical significance. It will trigger the collapse of capitalism in its present form and pave the way for the sort of society that you dream of. Do you still dream, Richard?"

The word "dream" energised Richard. It surged through him like a drug. He remembered catching his reflection in the mirror recently. He had been surprised, disgusted, and horrified to see how the skin round his throat was beginning to sag loosely. Age was withering him.

This was his last chance of the dream he'd waited years for. The chance that had gone forever and now, by magic, had reappeared, sitting in front of him in the form of Weber. Weber was offering him one last chance that he must grasp with both hands.

"Yes. Of course. And I will be happy to see these dreams finally made real."

Weber seemed satisfied with that. "So... Now I will tell you a bit about how it will work. The reason it sits in the interface, where it does, is so that it is always active – there are a lot of currency rates and other rate changes every day coming from Reuters, Bloomberg, the European Central Bank etc. It means, for a start, that it is not suspicious that the program is always doing something."

"Of course."

"And what it is doing is very clever. It is writing its own programs."

"That's impossible," Richard stated flatly. It crossed his mind that Weber was just some sort of fantasist. If so, he was going to be disappointed in the Zima project yet again, perhaps for the final time.

"It's an exaggeration. It does not use its own intelligence to write its own programs. We tell it what to write. We send data. Now, data is not as carefully monitored as software, so it is relatively easy to get it into the system without it having to go through all sorts of security checking. Our data is marked in such a way that the program, which is looking out for it, will realise we are sending a piece of code hidden in the data. It uses each piece to gradually stitch together a much bigger, much more sophisticated program: the program that will do the actual damage."

"Wait, you're going too fast. Some of the data that is coming into the system via the interface has a marker telling the Zima program to use that to build another program. So you get this other program into the system and bypass all the security we have in place. Is that right?" Instead of being disappointed Richard was amazed.

"Exactly so. What appear to be just currency rates or other data are mapped onto what turns out to be code."

Richard could understand that this would be possible. It would not be easy though. It would need a team of programmers and testers. It would also need someone in the bank for various reasons, not least to get a feed in from an external source that was not what it was supposed to be. For example, a feed that was not the actual Reuters one but a copy, with some extra data fed in every now and then, hidden within the real data.

"Imagine you are a builder, and you are making a huge fortress with your bricks. But all the time the bricks themselves are changing what you are building. The fortress is still there. It still looks rock-solid. But inside... inside is a huge living monster that can smash apart the fortress at any moment."

"That sounds very dramatic Weber. Like a fantasy story."

Weber smiled ruefully. "If you say so. It's not a fantasy though, it's simply logic. But perhaps the analogy I used just now does not permit you to imagine how bricks would use themselves to build something, or how that something would be materially different from what bricks normally build, or how no one would notice until too late."

"Software is extremely complex. Almost like a living organism. There must be a big team of developers back in Russia or somewhere that can develop and test this. What if some normal data gets interpreted as code and the program goes wrong?"

"All I can say is we have a very good team."

"So you can more or less write any programs you like into the bank's live system!"

"Yes... and what will happen when it is all activated suddenly is that every funds transfer in and out of the bank, every transaction, will be for the wrong amount or the wrong payee or just somehow wrong. But it will still be correct enough to be processed into the financial system. That is the key point. It will spread uncertainty about the reliability of banking and value of assets in the same way as the credit crunch did, but this time it will take only hours to bring about a new credit crunch. There will be no time to save the system. As you know, Richard, money is an illusory concept. It relies on everybody having faith in its promise. If that faith is destroyed, so too is the value. Money itself will cease to have any meaning."

76 - THE LESS DESERVING

Richard had not expected this. It would be more devastating than a nuclear bomb. Destroying money would destroy everything. Millions would starve. Civilisation would be set back hundreds of years. How could new social structures possibly be put in place quickly enough to prevent devastation? Richard had wanted revolution, but he wanted progress. He had vaguely imagined an organised surgical strike at an undeserving top echelon of society, removing them and replacing them. He had imagined a flattening of the hierarchy. What Weber was proposing would leave no basis to rebuild on.

Now that he had seen into the abyss, Richard wanted to pull back from the edge. All this – everything – would be destroyed. Much as he hated some of it, still there was plenty in it that worked, plenty that was good.

This was the problem with revolution. Either it destroyed much of the workings of the previous system, ending in failed states, or it retained the working parts of the old system and its supposed success was ironically due to the fact it had not brought proper or lasting change.

Weber was merely assuming that once you smash something up, something better appears in its place. But the second law of thermodynamics contradicts that idea – once you smash something up, it will not come back together in any coherent form. You need to suck effort and energy into a system to maintain structure within it.

You wouldn't fix a computer by taking a baseball bat to it. Why would you expect to fix social problems by smashing everything up?

Richard had to finally admit to something that had nagged his thoughts for a long time. In the years since he had been an activist, everything had changed. There was a different zeitgeist. He had grown up in an age influenced by the radicalism of the sixties and seventies but had matured in the post-Reagan/Thatcher era. Some of the ideas that had influenced his thinking really had been disproved.

Richard saw Weber for what he was: a clever and effective operative, organising the resources of various cells at arm's length to bring about the change he desired. But as to what that change would be... He seemed to have no interest in that mere detail. He seemed to rely entirely on faith that it would all work out for the good of his cause. He was a type of religious zealot.

Moments ago he had so eagerly assured Weber he wanted to be part of this, but that was before Weber had explained it. It turned out Richard had not made up his mind. He absolutely had to stop Weber. But how? Could he persuade Weber that instead of wrecking the whole financial system, the software could be used to produce a more nuanced result so it was targeted against particular individuals or organisations that could be identified as... as what? ... less deserving?

He was grateful when Weber showed him out. It felt like he was escaping.

77 - FORCED MOVES

Richard was thinking about his options to back out of Zima. All the worrying he'd done about Mitchell was of no consequence, it was Weber that worried him.

If he simply quit VirtuBank, would Weber still be able to carry out his plan? Maybe not; someone had to be there to push the software through and then connect the interface to a false feed. So Weber would not be happy if Richard quit. He would still have plenty of people at VirtuBank in Chennai, as he had mentioned, but no one in the vital position within RCB. He would only have people in dev. He would then have to get one of his dev people into Richard's position so the plan could go ahead. Then Weber's plan would succeed. Richard probably wouldn't halt the plan just by quitting VirtuBank. It was unlikely, given the level of resources and determination Weber had.

What would Weber do about him if he quit now? Let him stroll casually away, with no hard feelings? He would not want someone who knew as much as he did, and who was evidently no longer committed to the cause, on the loose. Richard was therefore trapped in VirtuBank. He had no option but to stay and appear to be helping Weber, until he could come up with something.

Another possibility would be to persuade Weber the plan was too dangerous, that it should be reduced in scope, or that it should be more carefully targeted. However, that would require Weber to be open to persuasion. If he was not, it would expose the fact that he, Richard, was not committed, every bit as much as walking away.

There was another, far simpler way of stopping him. An email to some of the bank's big cheeses would do it. He had email addresses for quite a lot of the guys who would understand what was going on if he explained. They could easily put a stop to it. Any of the guys that had been in the conference overlooking the Thames would do. But then Richard himself would be found out in the investigation. Even with plea bargaining, he could end up in jail, or on the run somewhere, either from the law or Weber... or both.

78 - AN END TO IT

Of course, if things got really hopeless, he could always kill himself.

He had narrowly avoided whatever trap Mitchell had nearly caught him in. Mitchell could have been trying to expose him as a saboteur or he could have been trying to use him to line his own pockets. Either way, Richard might have had to get out of the UK and run for it. By now he might be hiding in a favela, unable to sleep at night because all his money was in a rolled-up wad underneath his pillow.

But after that lucky escape, he now had Weber to deal with. Fortunately, Weber's plan wasn't going to happen just yet. Richard still had time.

Mitchell, Weber... all of these people he was involved with were simply trying to use each other for their own ends. Their own, supposedly, noble ends.

He himself had used Srini. The very fact he believed himself to be right, and to be serving a greater purpose, had made him do it. The more wonderful men believed their objective to be the more atrocities they were prepared to inflict to achieve it.

It was just as well Alexei had mopped up for him. At least now he didn't have to worry about whatever Mitchell was up to.

Richard tried to imagine where in the world he could escape to with no money, no Melanie, nothing. He couldn't think of anywhere safe. He thanked his lucky stars that Alexei had...

Wait a minute! "Mopped up" – where did that come from? Those were Weber's words. Alexei hadn't mopped up, he had simply blocked the Zima pack. That was what VirtuBank employed him to do – check and block any poor-quality software packs.

It dawned on Richard those words were accurate. Alexei had mopped up – and Weber knew about it. In his anxiety about Weber's plane he'd forgotten to question how Weber had known Alexei's name. Weber and Alexei were working together. Alexei had mopped up because Alexei was Weber's real Zima contact in the bank. Mitchell's software... it was probably genuine. It was probably designed to flush him, Richard, out as a saboteur. But whether it was or not didn't matter as much as the fact Weber and Alexei were working together.

Richard knew where his thoughts would take him next. His selfish thoughts of self-preservation. This meant that he himself was still in the clear. He was not guilty of attempted sabotage. If he could get an anonymous message to the bank, he could have the whole Zima project stopped and no one but Weber, and perhaps Alexei too, would know who betrayed them.

79 - DESTRUCTION

Weber went over to the tall Georgian window of his apartment and looked out. He was wearing a grey hooded robe and, standing motionless, he almost gave the impression of being a monk deep in contemplation of theological mysteries.

But he was not deep in contemplation. He was seething with rage. He couldn't believe his stupidity. Why had he got angry with Richard and blurted out Alexei's name? It was the stupidest thing he'd ever done! Had Richard really not noticed?

Right from the start, he'd decided his experience with other sleepers showed they were no good. Any time he tried to use them, they got caught out. So instead of using him at VirtuBank, he'd got people in to replace him. Richard was therefore completely expendable.

It was time to decide what to do with him. Weber stared out into the street, almost in a trance, wondering if he had been right to take Richard more and more into his confidence. Like other amateurs, he was likely to become a liability. He had been lucky until now, but he had nearly blown the whole operation by believing in Mitchell and confirming Mitchell's suspicions.

Mitchell's software had turned out to be just a simple program that diverted funds into his own account. That didn't mean that he had gone rogue. More than likely, he was MI5. More than likely it was an account specially set up to make it easy to show where the funds had come from, so they could put them back after Richard had been caught. Or, after as many Zima people as possible had been caught.

Weber had the resources to have Richard "tidied up". The kindest option would be to get Alexei to get him moved to another project. But the kindest option was not always the best one. The best option would be the one that protected himself, the project and Alexei.

He had felt quite friendly towards Richard, but there were more important things at stake than feelings of vague friendship.

Weber had betrayed the likes of Richard many times in the past. It made him feel stronger. It gave him credibility and deflected attention from who or what he really was. If those sorts of people suffered, it was of no consequence. Weber was someone who had no friends and no need of friends. Those that encountered him had to ensure their fate was aligned with his or suffer the consequences. Logan was not the only person who had met with a violent end just because there was something suspicious about his activity.

He was in a grim mood. He was angry with himself and wanted to lash out. He knew his anger had to fester or find release. He had been in this unstable mood many times before and had discovered a cure.

He walked out of his living room and along the hallway into the gym. It was in semi-darkness, lit only by a small light above a full-length wall mirror to his right. He didn't switch the main lights on. The first thing he did was slam a left hook into a heavy punch-bag.

"Violence is always the solution in the end," he said aloud. "It's just a question of deciding how and when to use it." He threw another punch with his right, shaking the solid wooden frame from which the bag was suspended.

"It may surprise you to know that even here, in this quiet street of pretty stucco houses, a man was blown to pieces. It happened in the late seventies; soon after I moved in." He caught sight of himself in the mirror, letting his arms hang loosely for a moment before slamming another punch into the bag.

"A Middle Eastern terrorist group managed to blow up a minor Iranian diplomat."

He ducked away from a couple of imaginary blows. "The blast blew all the leaves off some nearby lime trees and left bits of the diplomat's entrails dangling from the branches."

He shook his arms down and twisted his neck around a couple of times.

"It was gruesome enough but completely futile. What did it accomplish?" he asked, turning to his left-hand side, where another object was hanging in the shadows, within its own wooden frame. It looked like some sort of enormous chrysalis. Indeed it wriggled as though the emergence of a giant butterfly was imminent. But it was not a chrysalis. It was a man, encased in an old straitjacket and suspended by a robust chain which connected to thick leather bands round his ankles. Apart from the straitjacket, a blindfold and a leather thong, he was naked.

"I want you to consider the efficacy of violence; to experience it for yourself. Are you ready to begin?"

There was no answer, for the man was gagged.

"I like the way you're struggling. That is most entertaining," Weber told the man. "It may make me go easy. Or it may encourage me to greater efforts. Who knows?"

Weber turned to the wall behind him and picked a wide leather belt from among various items that were hanging from hooks.

"A few days after the incident there was no sign that it had ever happened. Everything had been tidied up and restored to normal."

He ran the belt through his hands, caressing it. "I imagine you're hoping that it will be the same for you. That you will recover from this experience within a few days."

Weber's face twisted into a grimace as he took a wide swing at the man's buttocks with the belt. There was an explosive slapping noise and the grimace transformed into a satisfied grin.

"Violence can solve otherwise difficult problems. Alexander the Great, for example, solved the problem of the Gordian Knot simply by slicing through it with a swipe of his sword. And now I'm going to slice some welts in your stupid faggot bottom with a variety of implements designed for the purpose. Do you understand?"

The man's upside-down head nodded vigorously. He had stopped struggling. The cocoon was rotating slowly until his erection, encased in a tight leather pouch, was facing towards Weber.

"Violence needs to be used carefully, correctly," Weber said, waiting until the man had swung back to his original position before administering another swipe to his buttocks. "I'm sure you appreciate that."

There was more nodding.

"You should be grateful that I declined the opportunity to strike you where it hurts most. I did not want to soil my belt by having it come into contact with that ridiculous object."

The man's cheek twitched.

"We were talking about terrorism, weren't we?" Weber mused. "Of course, back in those days, the IRA was a bigger threat to the authorities here in London than Islamists. They caused pandemonium back in the days when they had access to money raised in the USA. The explosion at the bandstand in Regent's Park, for instance, and the Baltic Exchange incident in the City."

Weber took another swipe.

"That one caused a lot of disruption. Commercial insurance rates in London jumped. There was talk that London property and businesses would become uninsurable."

Another swipe.

"But even that incident ended up as an irrelevance within a year or two."

Another swipe.

"Uninsurable? Imagine! Property in London is a rock-solid international grade investment. I'm fortunate that this property here in Leinster Terrace is in my own name." Weber said it smugly; it was one of the most satisfactory parts of his cover.

He returned to the wall and replaced the leather flogger with a long thin crop, then turned back towards his victim, flexing the crop in his hands. He administered a series of quick swishing strokes back and forward across the man's defenceless buttocks.

"London is resilient as well as big. It is well able to absorb any damage that a few bombs might inflict. As you may know, during the war the Nazis poured wave after wave of bombs onto the docks, warehouses and the old working-class slums in the East End in the hope of causing material damage, and of destroying morale and perhaps instigating class warfare."

Weber paused. By now his victim's buttocks were red and marked with lines from the crop. He needed to change tactic – so the pain would be drawn out for him to savour. He poured wave after wave of swishing blows onto the man's thighs.

"Are you following me?" He waited for the man to nod, seemingly with some effort. "All that happened was that the working classes forgot about the class struggle and became ever more patriotic. London soaked up bombs that could've been used instead to destroy the RAF's airfields. Just as you have soaked up blows that could have left your bottom bleeding like a raw steak." He paused. "Do you see what I mean?"

The man nodded again.

Weber decided to descend into a deeper level of hell.

"Of course …" He paused, and then the air seemed to hiss and crackle as he took an almighty swing at his target. He waited a moment to observe the chrysalis jerk wildly, caused by a series of rapid, forced breaths.

"Ultimately weapons that could destroy London do exist. Just as I have a weapon here that could rip your flesh away, leaving only bone. Do you want me to try it?"

He took this new weapon into his left hand from the selection on the wall.

The man shook his head from side to side frantically, causing his whole body to vibrate and yank at the chains attached to his ankle straps. Weber, inserting the crop, which he still held in his right hand, between the mask and the man's face, used it to lever it aside, allowing his victim to see.

"Look," he said, dangling the implement in front of the man's eyes. It was an ugly looking thing, a type of cat-o'-nine-tails with spidery barbs at the end of each tail that would rip away flesh with each blow.

Weber could see panic in the man's eyes, but he calmly resumed his monologue, as though it was a bedtime story for a child.

"During the Cold War, London was presumed to be a prime target and a sitting duck. You are a prime target and a sitting duck too, don't you agree?"

The man shook his head even more frantically and pleaded with his eyes.

Weber lashed at the man again and again. He held the ugly flesh ripper in his left hand while delivering blow after furious blow at the man's naked bottom with the crop in his right hand.

And then the crop was discarded and the flesh ripper taken into Weber's right hand. Black stars moved in a blur through the air and froze into focus. Something like a metallic spider bit into white flesh and flew away again, leaving a red hole from which a trail of blood dripped.

Red on White.

Weber was no longer in control. All he saw were colours: black, red, white. All his focus was on something deep within the colours.

Suddenly a voice shouted out:

"Stop!"

80 - WORST CASE

Callan was attending a meeting. It wasn't a VirtuBank meeting. He wasn't playing at being a software manager; he was doing his real job. The other person in the meeting was Mark Osbourne.

"By the way, before we get started, have we heard from *Snowman* yet?"

"Nothing, not a word," Callan replied. He could see his boss was losing his temper. Osbourne was not a pleasant prospect when he lost his temper.

"But surely he must be in touch with the saboteurs by now?"

"He must be. Either that, or it's just not happening."

"You know what, we should've done this the old-fashioned way," Osbourne stated.

Callan didn't know exactly what Osbourne was referring to when he said, "old-fashioned way". They had done it the way they thought best, using fewest resources and likely to get best results. He had been there since the start, with Hamilton Denton, who had had a string of successes. So much so that he was now happily retired and basking in the glory of knighthood as Sir Hamilton Denton. He sighed. There was so much to do these days with so few resources. Did he really have to explain this to Osbourne? It seemed he did.

"Maybe," Callan said. "But the *Winter* project is hardly a pressing matter at present. It's been going on for years. We had a tip-off from inside Russia that *Snowman* was going to be activated but then our source was discredited. He sent us a whole pile of misinformation that wasted a good deal of our time."

Osbourne's frown grew deeper. "What's the worst-case scenario?" he barked.

"We think the whole thing will turn out to be just a bunch of amateur activists fooling around with some banking software. Our best guess is that, even if the plot succeeds, it will only have a limited effect and can be quickly mopped up at that point."

"Mmm. Meanwhile we have ISIS and all manner of threats jumping out of the woodwork. But what if they're not amateurs? What if they come up with something a bit more clever than we expect?"

"Hardly likely. Let's arrange to discuss it with Dr Skinner next week and see what he thinks of our chances of success. I'm guessing Skinner will explain it all to us in terms of his mumbo jumbo. It will all be due to state or phase transition or something. Meanwhile we'd better get on with the agenda. First item is from the orange dossier."

81 - MUSHROOMS

Weber stopped in mid-swing, his mind in confusion as redness and blackness flew away from him into the corners of the room.

"Master," the voice added quickly.

Weber had frozen, torso twisted round, right arm extended ready to deliver the next blow. He looked past a weight-lifting machine and an exercise bicycle into a dark corner of the dimly lit room, where a large dog-like creature was sitting.

"I am Master here. I'll decide when to stop." Weber strode over to the dog-creature and kicked it soundly. It whimpered and spoke again. This time there was panic in its voice.

"No, please, Master, he's had enough now. You must stop."

Weber looked at the dog-creature and then at the bloody cocoon with contempt. He was back in the real world again. Or rather, the place where a man pretending to be a dog had brought him back to. However, his fury had not been vented and he was not ready to let go of that other place yet.

"We can never back away from this" – he kicked the dog-creature – "ultimate" – kick – "threat" – kick – "of violence." He stood over the whimpering creature. "Now that we have got to this stage, the threat of mutually assured destruction is all we have to stop ourselves being totally wiped from the map. Do you understand?"

There was silence.

Weber shuddered. He had really lost it that time. Why the fuck had he become angry? The topic. This topic was poison to him. He imagined the scene: if it had come to nuclear war, then, while London was disappearing in a mushroom cloud, so too would Moscow, along with Leningrad, Vladivostok and hundreds of other targets across the eleven time zones of the USSR.

"Everybody needs to understand this."

"OK, Master. Yes," the dog-creature whimpered, in a barely audible whisper.

"Imagine where this folly would lead us. Imagine!" Weber saw it in the darkness, almost like a flickering cine projection. Where

New York had once stood, he could see an enormous, turbulent pillar of smoke powering its way upwards, with the apparent purpose of transporting the souls of twenty million now-deceased inhabitants directly to heaven. Only it would fail in a boiling cacophony of vaporised chaos folding back on itself, creating the cap of a mushroom cloud infused with lightning and hell-fire.

"Yes, Master."

"His stupid naivety could destroy the world. Never let him hand out his propaganda bullshit again. Especially not in the club. Never."

"Never, Master," repeated the creature.

"Get him out of here," he ordered. "And do it quietly. I don't want to hear or see this freak ever again."

The dog-creature bowed. "Thank you, Master. You have been most kind. It is a pleasure to serve you."

Weber tossed the flesh ripper away. The servant creature would ensure everything was cleared up, and return to his flat in Acton. The cocoon creature might need treatment. Weber's connections at the club would ensure that something could be done for him at a private clinic in Holborn.

Weber strode back to the living room and collapsed into an armchair. At last, he felt better, his thoughts clearer. But his fantasies of nuclear catastrophe continued to their conclusion.

That war, the Cold War, was a war with no winners. Consequently, it was a war that was never fought.

And then – and this was what he needed clarity for, so he could think about it properly – Weber's thoughts turned to the financial weapon he was about to unleash. Would its destructive power also be too great? Who would be left standing to reap the reward?

Targets must be chosen carefully. Weapons too. There is no point in fighting a war you cannot win. There is no point in winning a war if you don't gain from it. He had thought it through many, many times. It had all been discussed in the Bureau. The weapon was appropriate; the right people would gain.

Those societies that had too much icing and too little cake would be worst affected; those that relied too much on a top-heavy financial system; those that relied too much on advertising which created false markets or over-inflated them; those that created huge imbalances between the rich and poor; they would be the ones that would be worst affected. The ones that relied on tangible, primary economic activity, such as agriculture, fishing and mining would gain. Russia itself would gain. Perhaps that was why, in spite of the chaos of policy decisions back at the Bureau, and a lack of ideological conviction, there was still enough support in the right places for his operation.

Weber adhered to another theory about the Cold War which influenced his thinking. The Soviet Union had kept capitalism in check. It had forced Western capitalism to provide adequately for their working classes in order to win the battle against the USSR. But as soon as they had won they showed their true colours. Social mobility had ground to a halt; the difference between rich and poor had grown ever greater. The overconsumption of raw materials, including oil, had created a situation in which a medievalist Islam had come to influence the world stage, quite undeservedly.

All of this could be rectified if Richard did not upset his plans for the greater good. The ends that he wanted to achieve were too important to allow any more mistakes. If the plan worked, much of the civilised world might be reduced to barter for a time, but just long enough to blast away all the overblown superstructure that capitalism had built to weigh down the real economy. Then Russia would be ready to save civilisation again. They had stood as a bulwark many times. They had forced the Mongols back. They had stood against Islamic Constantinople. They had defeated Napoleon and Hitler. Now they would defeat this insane form of capitalism.

Weber stood up and went back to the window. He was relieved Richard still thought of himself as the one who would deploy Zima.

It proved that Richard had not understood what he meant when he accidentally mentioned Alexei tidying up. Thanks to Alexei, Richard was now squeaky clean. Whatever Mitchell had thought the word Zima might mean, it had proved to mean nothing.

On the one hand, Richard had screwed up. He had fallen for Mitchell's trick. On the other hand, he had dealt with it quite well. He had come out of the interrogation process in Moscow with no sign he was anything other than what he said he was – an employee of VirtuBank who had secretly pledged to help his socialist party as a student.

Furthermore, Richard had inadvertently deflected the attention of MI5 away from Chennai.

It was surely someone in Chennai who had screwed up initially, who had caused VirtuBank to appoint Mitchell in the first place. In an ideal world, it would be good to find out who that screw-up in Chennai was and deal with him. But how on earth could he do that?

What if he got someone else sent to Chennai to check up on the guys there? It was hard enough getting anyone in there. Getting a new person with the right commitment and knowledge... impossible. Alexei was the only one he could trust, and he was needed in RCB itself.

Expendable people were the most useful of all. Richard was about to make himself useful. He could get Alexei to send Richard to Chennai. Alexei could think of a pretext to have him sent there on VirtuBank business. There, he could find who had leaked something and if it was deliberate. If anyone was deliberately leaking information, then the whole plan would be in danger. It was imperative to have any such person eradicated. He would have to give Richard the names of his operatives. Otherwise, Richard would be looking for a needle in a haystack, as Mitchell had been.

He picked up his mobile phone and inserted a new SIM card into it. He dialled Alexei's number.

"Alexei, who is playing?"

"Zenith."

"Good. Can you get Richard sent to Chennai?"

"Personally, no. Germain makes those decisions."

"Germain. The one that delegates so many things to you?"

"Yes."

"But if you suggest to Germain that Richard has to go to Chennai for such and such a reason he will just rubber-stamp it?"

"Probably, yes. I can say that we are not happy with the packs that we are getting from Chennai and we need him to go and review quality control. I'm pretty sure he would send him unless he wants to go himself."

"Exactly. Suggest that to Germain as soon as possible."

82 - DEVELOPMENT

If ever a city deserves to be described as a teeming cesspit, it is Chennai. Huge, sprawling, disorganised, with beggars everywhere; it is a truly unpleasant city.

Richard didn't have to worry about that too much though. He had come straight from the airport by taxi to a five-star hotel in the Velachery district. The check-in process had taken twenty rather disorganised but friendly minutes, after which an attractive Indian lady in a sari introduced herself, along with two uniformed male porters who accompanied her. It was her job to show him the way to his room, and the job of the porters to carry his bags as she did so. The pleasant lady pointed out the bars and restaurants of the hotel as they made their way to the lift. She informed him the fitness room and pool were on the first floor and the panorama bar on the eighth floor. Glittering, gold-coloured lettering alongside the numbers "1" and "8" in the lift provided further evidence her information was accurate.

Alone at last, and away from all the hustle and bustle, the inefficiency, and the over-politeness, Richard would be able to gather his thoughts together at last. He turned the air conditioning down and discovered his thoughts did not interest him much. They could wait till later to be gathered together. Something to do with finding out who was who for Weber, and who was doing what. In addition to that, he had his real job; making sure dev were providing good-quality releases. Not to mention the question of what he should do to save the world. Or failing that, to save his own hide. It was all a jumble, but it could wait until he was ready. Meanwhile, he flicked the TV on and lay on the bed.

However, it turned out, even though he was jet-lagged and tired out, he couldn't stop trying to think about what was going on. On autopilot, his mind back-tracked through recent events. First of all, Germain had asked him if he wanted to go to Chennai to sort out some issues with quality control in dev. He hadn't hesitated too long. He had jumped at the chance. There were various reasons why he had jumped. Firstly, it might be easier to think what to do about Weber, and to plan an escape from the situation. Secondly, it was a good opportunity in itself. Just to get away from his humdrum routine in London would be good. Thirdly, VirtuBank were quite generous in their allocation of hotel rooms. He would be staying in a double room in at least a four-star hotel (it turned out they had put him in a double room in a five-star hotel). He immediately imagined that Melanie might like to come for a holiday. Unfortunately, Melanie's phone seemed to be out of order and she hadn't replied to his email. Much as he wanted her to join him, there had been no time to nip out to Aphrodite's to ask her in person; his flight had been arranged for the next day. A next day during which he barely had time to go to a clinic to ask for malaria pills before catching his flight. The clinic reassured him the malaria pills shouldn't be necessary so long as he was careful, but they sold him a travel pack with various pills anyway. Then he was on the plane.

But, just before that, as he was waiting at the airport, he got a call from Weber.

"Who's playing?"

"Zenith."

"Write these names down."

"Klaus, are you sure? I'm in an airport lounge. There must be CCTV!?"

"These are our people. I want you to check them out for me. Do you have a pen?"

"Pen, yes." Richard got a pen and paper out to write the names down.

"Don't let anyone see these three names collected together in one place. Use your utmost discretion."

"OK. I'm writing them all on one piece of paper right now though."

"I'm giving you a big list of names. Inside that list are my three people. I will tell you which ones they are at the end. Make sure that you don't identify those three together at any time."

Weber read out a list of twenty names and Richard wrote them down.

"Don't write these numbers. The ones that actually concern us are three, eleven and fifteen. Can you remember that without writing it?"

"Yes: three, el..."

Weber interrupted angrily, "Don't sit there chanting those numbers and waving your list around."

"No, I won't. I will memorise as much as possible." It was incredible. Now Richard had the names of Weber's people in Chennai. It was like winning the lottery! But of course, Richard reminded himself, he was supposed to be on Weber's side. He had been on Weber's side for almost forty years, in theory. In practice, it turned out he didn't know whose side he was on or why.

He flicked the TV off again and opened the door to look from his balcony. The heat and humidity wrapped round him, forcing him to take deep breaths of the slightly fetid air.

The hotel gardens were well tended and contained a delightful-looking pool. Beyond that lay the ramshackle mess of the city with its thronging populace in all its vibrancy and squalor. Richard pictured the beggars he had seen on one street corner with their imploring faces and postures of supplication. His Infiniti slipped past them as though, beyond the tinted windows and comfortable air conditioning of the chauffeur-driven limousine, they existed in another dimension, of no more significance to human existence than the pack of mangy, stray dogs that lived among them.

Some of his colleagues gave generously to beggars, but Richard never gave a penny, no matter what. Here poverty was a bottomless pit. No acts of individual generosity were going to alleviate it. Revolution? Perhaps one day people like these would be so angered that they would rise up, but Richard was vaguely aware of the cultural and religious framework that maintained balance in spite of extreme inequality. In any case, it would have to be the revolution to end all revolutions to reach into the wretchedness and squalor of these uneducated and hopeless people who lived virtually as equals to stray animals.

What really defined him now? While he had been sleeping, he had also been working. It was real work for real banks. He understood the system a lot better now than he did back in the simplistic days when he was studying politics and sociology.

At one time he defined himself as a political activist, and had understood the world in terms fed to him by his lecturers and fellow students. He hadn't consciously redefined himself, but he was a different person now.

He went back into his room, closing the door behind him, and resolved to get some proper sleep before having to face another day.

In spite of being tired, Richard couldn't sleep. His mind was churning round and round. There wasn't enough time left to think though. Now any action or inaction would have consequences. All that was required for evil to prevail was that good men do nothing. He didn't want to do nothing, but he had no idea what to do.

Weber hadn't mentioned Alexei. But he didn't need to mention him. Alexei was not in Chennai. He had given him names three, eleven and fifteen – Balaragunathan, Satheesh and Santosh. But never any mention that they were working with Alexei. That he was part of the team. Why not? It was clear Weber still didn't trust him. Therefore, he was still in danger from him.

Furthermore, Weber would use Alexei to deploy the Zima code. He himself was surplus to requirements, apart from this little wild-goose chase he'd been sent on. Did it really matter to Weber if this wild-goose chase was successful or not?

For years he'd complacently assumed he knew his own mind and was prepared to act for what he believed in. When it came to the crunch, he didn't know what he believed in. Or perhaps he was expecting an outcome that precisely suited what he believed in, and any variation was unacceptable.

It had come to the point when he had to do something. His own neck was on the line.

He had all the information he needed to go to the newspapers, claim he was a freelance journalist and ask for payment.

He could throw Weber and Alexei to the dogs and warn the banks about the whole operation via the newspapers. Weber had a big organisation and would go after him. But newspapers had deep pockets, and they might negotiate some of the payment from the bank, or banks... they had even deeper pockets.

Or he could go direct to the banks anonymously. Perhaps, for example, he could claim he was a private investigator who was investigating Mitchell (Why? ... On behalf of his wife, that's why). He could say he had accidentally uncovered a plot...

He started to draft a letter:

I have accidentally uncovered a plot while acting as a private investigator on a divorce case. I have information about the plot that will enable you to prevent the damage it will cause. This information will be worth billions to you.

I can pinpoint software and outline what it will do. I can identify people and name names.

Please do not act on my information until I tell you it is complete. You still have some time to play with.

Pay me in instalments for each piece of information I provide.

As a gesture that you believe me and wish to proceed put £5000 in this account...

The first piece of information I will provide is that Mitchell, who I believe was originally investigating this area, did not commit suicide but was involved in a separate plot to subvert the original plot for personal gain. I have documents relating to the purchase of property to be financed by this scam.

He read through it again. Not great; he would have to come back to it. Why would anyone believe he was anything other than a nutcase? It would need to be much more convincing. Also, he needed a bank account first, for the money to go into. An account that could not be traced back to him. He had no idea how to do that.

Only once he reread it did he realise the implications.

Mitchell, who I believe was originally investigating this area, did not commit suicide but was involved in a separate plot to subvert the original plot for personal gain. I have documents showing he is still alive and others relating to the purchase of property to be financed by this scam.

Could it be that Mitchell had been trying to use him to trap Weber? Something seemed to slither away from him into the shadows. He rubbed his eyes. There was nothing there, just a solid wall – nowhere for the nematodes, maggots and other writhing parasites that had suddenly appeared as a vibrating mass – to disappear into. They had disappeared into the gaps between their vibrations, leaving a sudden white pain which throbbed away gradually.

83 - A BETTER WAY

Callan picked up the phone. It was Osbourne.

"Jim, let's cancel the meeting next week. Put your VirtuBank hat on and get our man back to safety. I don't think we're achieving anything by keeping this project going. I want to abort and rethink the whole thing."

"But what if it's all up and running? What if it's close to completion?"

"Even assuming you're right and the saboteurs are up and running, there must be a better way of doing this. Don't forget that Logan disappeared off the face of the earth in Moscow and Mitchell killed himself. But worse than that, I've just received information that shows our man is in immediate danger."

84 - GLOBAL COMPETENCY

A company limousine picked Richard up from the hotel and delivered him directly to VirtuBank's development centre, where he was greeted by Sanjay, Global Competency Lead for Core Product Development.

VirtuBank's development centre in Chennai was housed in a sprawling building in the Egmore district. As Richard walked along a murky corridor, the scale of his task became apparent. Whoever designed this building had an evident liking for straight lines and repetitive features, which were gloomily picked out by sickly strip lighting. To add to everyone's misery, there was no air conditioning, just grubby looking ceiling fans which turned too slowly to be effective, circulating staleness and dust in a leisurely fashion. Workers were crammed behind tiny desks with obsolete terminals. Each desk was packed into a tiny cubicle made from a flimsy, ramshackle system of dividing walls.

It was common for employees to work from eight a.m. to seven p.m. or even later. There was a lot of pressure to work long hard hours because, just outside the door, there were four more people clamouring for each job. Not just any old people; graduates who had studied long into the night, every night for their degrees, who were now keen to get proper work experience. On the other hand, once they had a foot in the door, everyone was keen to get on. If VirtuBank didn't keep giving the new entrants some sort of pay rise, they could head across the road to a rival software company. This was quite a frequent occurrence, resulting in a high turnover of staff and difficulties in ensuring continuity of the work in progress. It was one of the problems Germain had told him to get a handle on. He had to remind himself not to be too bothered about getting a handle on Germain's brief, but to concentrate on extricating himself from Weber. It would be useful to know as much as possible about Weber's operation here.

So how am I going to do this? How to find out who's doing what here? And what exactly does Weber need to know about numbers three, eleven and fifteen? What brought them to someone's attention and put Mitchell on their case? Perhaps they've stayed an unusually long time compared with the others?

Richard met Sanjay in the canteen for lunch. There was no meat on the menu, but the vegetarian dishes were excellent. He remembered to buy a can of cola instead of trusting the local water, hoping he would not have to rely on the extra strong pills he had bought in case of "Delhi Belly".

"I'm thinking that at any moment you must be expecting revolution," Sanjay remarked in his sing-song accent.

"What!?" Richard dropped his fork in surprise. He scrambled it back into his fumbling fingers as Sanjay continued.

"Yes. Prices are so very high in Europe. When I went to London and also Geneva, I was very totally shocked. How anyone can able to live in such conditions? It is nothing but painful."

"I don't understand. What do you mean?" Richard was relieved to realise that any reference to revolution was purely generic.

"See – it is so incredibly expensive there. Here, anyone on street can able to beg for just three rupees a day and they will live. There – I don't know how it could be possible."

Now that he understood what Sanjay was saying, Richard was getting annoyed.

"But we don't want people begging in the streets. We have a welfare state."

"So incredibly expensive. Better to let people beg if they want to. If prices are so very low, then it takes hardly any effort."

There were a few moments of silence as Richard tried to contemplate a diplomatic answer that would permit him to challenge this whole idea. It was self-evident that higher wages were a good thing, surely, even if prices were higher too. If wages were low then... only people who already had money, people who did not rely on wages, would be well off. As the difference between rich and poor expanded, social mobility declined. Perhaps there then came a point where the poor are so detached from the others that they no longer matter to anyone. Particularly if the cost of maintaining them was so tiny. They become a different species. Pond life.

"British Empire; thank goodness it finished. We should have joined with Nazis. Their symbol was same as our one you know."

Richard wondered if he was being deliberately wound-up. He scrutinised his tormentor's face and found no evidence he was.

"You mean the swastika?"

"Yes. Svastika."

"But you couldn't join Hitler and the Nazis. Their whole ideology was racist. In the end they would consider you Indians to be 'untermenschen'."

"What about their Japanese allies? Were they untermenschen?"

"I don't know. I know that the Axis powers didn't cooperate very closely."

"Also, we Indians are truly Aryan. That is why they were using svastika."

"But surely..." Richard was lost for words.

"Anyway, we are glad now British Empire is gone."

85 - CHANCES

It had been a pretty unproductive day both in terms of what Weber wanted and in terms of what Germain wanted him to achieve. It was nearly time to go home to the hotel.

A Skype message popped up on Richard's laptop. Darion!

"Hey man, fancy a drink?"

"I can't. I'm in Chennai."

"That's why I asked. I'm in the Westin Velachery. Just got here."

"Great, I'm in the Westin too. OK, see you in the bar."

"OK. I'm in the lounge bar already. See you soon."

Well there he was! Darion himself, lounging on a big old comfy wicker chair in colonial style. He was dressed in white flannels, sitting back, with his extended legs crossed at the ankles, a glass of beer snuggled in his big old, relaxed-looking hand. All that was missing was the pith helmet and elephant gun. There was a copy of the Financial Times, which had obviously been leafed through by Darion's large, impatient hands and left in a state of disarray on the coffee table.

"Hey man, what took you so long? I drank your beer already."

"Darion you rogue. What are you pretending to do here?"

"I'm making sure that everything is working properly. No one but me can do it." Darion grinned widely.

"It's about time someone did that. What can I get you?"

"Just sit down man. They have a waiter. Look he's coming over now."

***

For once, Richard found himself in a serious discussion with Darion. It could've been that after two or three beers they had switched to Black Label and were drinking it straight.

"All over the world people are the same. I mean ordinary people man, not politicians or whatever."

"Well yeah, I agree. But there are big cultural differences too," Richard replied.

"Yes, but if you ignore that. It's when power gets transferred to a smart alec elite that the problems happen. They get out of touch man."

"Did you hear that asshole the other day?"

"Which asshole? There are so many assholes man, I can't tell which one you mean."

"The guy in The Slicker. He kept calling everyone pond life. What a pompous ass."

"Oh, you mean the super City trader guy? Him and his mate hired some good suits for the night and went out to look for a shag. They knew nothing, those guys. Yes, they were assholes."

"I would put them up against a wall and shoot them if I got the chance."

"Would you? Well good for you bro, but you know what? That's the worst solution of all. You're old enough to remember the French Revolution..."

Richard waited patiently for Darion to stop giggling at his own joke and to continue talking.

"... but what did it really achieve? The pompous elite quickly re-established itself. The Terror was some kind of lottery: you pull a winning ticket, you avoid Madame Guillotine. A whole lot of the people that got killed in the Terror were the original revolutionaries."

"Well, yes but..."

"Hey! We don't have to worry anyway, my friend. Look at this. Big opportunities coming up." Darion reached for the copy of the

Financial Times he'd been reading earlier. He held the paper up, folded haphazardly, and pointed at one of the articles at the bottom of the front page.

"Goldman Sachs is recruiting again. Big time. It could be time to go and make some real money. The crisis is over my friend. We have a chance now."

His eyes twinkled and he grinned as though he was trying to win first prize in a grinning competition.

Richard was suddenly in a sombre mood. He felt guilty that he often tried to toughen up his mind by forcing himself to think of killing Steve, Darion or other colleagues for the sake of revolution. Darion was a great guy; cheerful, happy-go-lucky; all he wanted were chances in life, and he was the sort of person who could take them. Chances. Chances were not always fair or right, but they helped people like Darion. People like him deserved their luck. Luck was another of those things that so few revolutionaries understood or wanted.

Ordinary people; maybe that was the key. Any system that gives more power to "ordinary people" would be a good system. Was that system the market economy? The market economy reduced men's objectives to the banality of the mundane – making a better mousetrap, selling more shampoo. That was its very strength. People could strive and struggle with each other to make tiny improvements in innovation without directly harming each other. And in the end, all their struggling would produce something of lasting value.

What about the problem of overproduction and overconsumption of finite resources? It seemed markets were not able to signal quickly enough to prevent finite resources from being used up. That was debatable though. It would only be proved right if and when we ran out of oil or copper or whatever, with no suitable replacement.

86 - MERVEILLEUSES

Someone had taken his hot desk today. He was directed instead to the desk Mitchell had used.

He sat down at Mitchell's desk and opened the drawer. There was a glossy brochure of RCB's forecast for the Indian stock market for next year. The introduction expressed the fund manager's optimism for growth prospects, which, according to the forecast, would be driven by a rapidly increasing population of mostly young people.

The whole world economy was just a giant Ponzi scheme requiring huge population increases to keep it going. At some point this could not continue. The trust manager's optimism was based on a fundamental and irresolvable problem. Billions of people would live in even more cramped conditions for the sake of moving the lines on some graphs a few percentage points higher. Annoyed, Richard clumsily tossed the brochure back into the drawer so that it fanned out, releasing a photograph that had been concealed between its pages. It span out and fell on the floor.

It was a picture of London. Probably somewhere in Bloomsbury.

***

His mobile rang.

"Richard? Just through customs, be with you shortly. I'd like to have our meeting immediately."

It was Callan! What the hell!? Richard was worried. Had he done something wrong? Why would Callan fly halfway around the world and rush from the airport just to have a meeting with him?

"Richard, are you there? Can you hear me?"

"Yes. I can hear you."

"Get a staff car and meet me back at your hotel ASAP."

But Richard wasn't paying attention to whatever Callan was saying. He was transfixed by the picture of Bloomsbury. He recognised one of the buildings unexpectedly well. Wasn't it a clinic of some sort? He stared at it, feeling himself being sucked back in time and into the photograph.

"Do you understand, Richard?" Callan's voice sounded terse.

Suddenly Richard was feeling very strange. It was nothing to do with Callan bossing him around. It was something far worse. He took some deep breaths. Something far worse, and yet maybe connected to Callan as well. He really didn't feel good at all. Strange; he felt a very strange feeling, of being in two places at once. He lurched out of the building and got into a waiting staff car.

"Westin Hotel Velachery."

By now there were jagged lights flashing on the periphery of his vision. The lights zig-zagged elusively, twisting like an adder inside his head, but insubstantial, electric. Metallic butterflies tumbled in front of his eyes, blinding him. He could barely make out the crowds that had stopped the taxi from moving. They seemed to be just some sort of seething, throbbing movement.

No, no, no, no!

The serpent was getting closer. Something seemed to split apart in his head. They knew everything! How could he escape? Where could he hide from them?

There was a huge explosion in the sky. Heavy drops of water started hitting the windscreen. The driver switched the wipers on at full speed to try to clear the view, but rain lashed down like a waterfall and was simply sloshed from side to side by the wipers. The taxi was moving again as the crowds ran for cover, scattering in all directions. All around, the falling water was pelting down on streets which had already turned into shallow rivers. An early monsoon.

They were on a wide boulevard now, travelling at a decent speed. Richard looked behind, out of the rear window.

"How long has that car behind been following us?"

"No one is following." The driver grinned and waggled his head.

He looked again. The black Lexus was still there. Is the driver deliberately allowing himself to be followed?

They turned in at the hotel entrance, but the Lexus went straight on. Once again it seemed he was in a panic for no reason. But then the Lexus stopped. The driver seemed to make some sort of signal to his own driver. It looked like a thumbs up; a friendly gesture. But why make any gesture?

He threw the passenger door open and ran into reception.

Upstairs in his room, he threw things into his suitcase as quickly as he could.

He struggled against splendours that were too marvellous to contemplate. Struggled to stay in the real world so that he could complete the mundane task of getting his bag packed so he could escape before he fell into the trap.

The jagged lights were sometimes like a wonderful kaleidoscope. Sometimes they made it look as though there was a hole in his vision which was a portal to a new level of consciousness, full of possibility edged with fear.

The air tasted metallic. The room was crawling with exotic caterpillars, dragonflies, serpents...

87 - FLIGHT

He had to run, now, before it was too late. This time he was convinced of it. Callan was the one trying to kill him. Or maybe one of the ones trying to kill him.

He had to get to Frankfurt. There was something or someone there who was a friend, he was sure of it.

It had only taken minutes for him to throw all his things into his suitcase. Now everything felt clearer, more real. He headed to the lift. No, not the lift! Turning round abruptly, he went to the emergency exit and began running down the stairs, trying to go quickly but without making a lot of noise. He knew the emergency exit would take him back into the lobby, and he also knew the opening was at the side of the reception desk that was hidden from the lobby bar. Nevertheless, to get to the exit, he would need to pass in front of the door into the lobby bar.

The last flight of stairs already – soon he was going to have to cross the lobby to get to the exit. Callan would be in the lobby bar, probably looking towards reception, waiting for Richard to join him. Running will just draw attention to myself. Same if I walk too briskly. Just try to walk normally.

He was opening the cab door. In the cab now. The taxi driver was putting his suitcase in the boot. Why was he taking so long? Richard glanced at the hotel entrance expecting to see Callan coming out, walking towards him, enraged. But there was no one there except one of the bellboys.

At last the driver was opening the cab door and settling behind the wheel. "Airport!" Richard snapped.

88 - AWOL

At the airport, Richard bought a ticket to London via Amsterdam. He hoped that would keep Callan from realising where he was going. His plan was to get off at Amsterdam and get to Frankfurt by train. Why Frankfurt? There was a reason. Richard just hadn't remembered it yet.

In Schiphol airport, he withdrew as much as he could from a cash machine. When he switched his phone off flight mode, he saw there were three messages from Callan.

"Waiting in the lobby bar. Where are you?"

"Richard, almost an hour now. Lobby bar."

"Where have you gone? Hotel tells me you left without checking out and your room is empty. Get back and meet me or you will face disciplinary action."

There was a voicemail message too. Richard played it and heard Callan's voice say: "Richard. I don't know where you are or what you're up to. You're going to be sacked for this. I guess you know that though."

Callan was right – Richard knew that already. Getting sacked was the least of his worries. Staying alive was his main concern.

He got the train to Frankfurt. As the train was arriving at Cologne station, a horrible thought struck him. The phone! He took the SIM card out and examined it. It seemed normal but he wasn't satisfied. He went to the toilet for privacy and took the phone apart. It seemed normal too but, there again, he had no idea what he was looking for. He decided he should keep the SIM card but buy a new phone. He smashed the phone into fragments and threw them away at Cologne station, feeling guilty about being so paranoid.

Once he got to Frankfurt, he checked into one of the vaguely sleazy hotels in the red-light district near the station. At thirty euros a night, he could stay there for a while... and then what?

He would need to figure out what the hell he was doing in Frankfurt, and soon.

89 - OPHIDIAN DELIRIUM

A couple of days had passed. At night the dreams were getting worse. Almost unbearable.

And now he was dreaming about Mitchell. Mitchell was in his hotel room back in Helsinki. No, he wasn't in the room yet. He was standing outside, on the balcony. Then he swept the curtain aside and stepped into the room. He switched the TV on and watched himself on an old video recording that kept breaking up.

But the curtains weren't the curtains of his hotel room. They were curtains round a hospital bed in which he was sleeping. There was a doctor standing alongside. Mitchell spoke to the doctor.

"I'm glad I'm dead. Glad to be out of it," he said.

The doctor didn't reply but took Mitchell by the arm and led him out of the door.

There was someone else in the room too. He stood there for a moment before speaking.

"Do you know who you are?" he asked.

"No."

"You are Richard."

"Do you know who I am?"

"No."

"I am Richard."

***

Sometimes he would wake up, relieved that what had seemed so real and terrifying had turned out to be just a dream, yet again. But even when he was awake, he was constantly aware he felt somehow different, as though the dreams would soon break through into reality and swap places with it.

He had started to keep a diary to try to keep track of everything. He hoped it would help him to understand what was real and what was not. He had no idea what had made him suddenly take off and flee to Frankfurt. Callan was trying to kill him. Callan! Why Callan? Why was he so sure of this crazy thought? Was there anyone he thought wasn't trying to kill him? He worried that he must've had a nervous breakdown. It must be paranoid schizophrenia. The realisation that was a real possibility was so deeply concerning that...

Anyway, he only had enough cash to hold out here for three weeks. He'd taken every penny he could from his current account, up to his overdraft limit. By now all his standing orders would be bouncing. That was of no consequence at all in his situation. His situation? What situation? He didn't even know what had made him do this. Reading back through his diary on the third day gave him no insight into what was going on. Only that he was feeling deeply anxious and had no idea what he was doing. There would come a point when the loony bin or suicide would be his only options.

The way the streets intersected in Frankfurt revealing gleaming skyscrapers, symbols of banking power, gave him an odd feeling too. He'd written about it in his diary. Walking through the streets at night, it seemed as though the skyscrapers were watching him. The red eye of the Commerzbank, in particular, followed him wherever he went. The red eye that looked down from the mast of the tallest building in Germany. He was hidden from its gaze as he walked along a row of buildings in streets that were parallel to it. But on reaching a junction there was no shelter; he was caught in its inquiring glare. Sometimes, at certain intersections, he found himself caught in the force field generated by several of these skyscrapers. They knew of his guilt. They knew he was a fugitive.

And then on the third night his madness could no longer be denied. He saw something which he had already seen, yet he saw it for the first time. In Niddastrasse there was a young man sitting on the pavement. He was propped up against a lamppost; made angelic by its light. He held a small viper in his right hand and was encouraging it to bite into the flesh of his left arm. Now the snake hallucinations were palpable; happening when he was awake, not just in dreams.

The entire universe was revealing itself as a vibration resonating with his nervous system; a wriggling, writhing collection of maggots and parasites. In the empty space between their movement there was something hidden. Suddenly it emerged. It burst out as jagged shark's teeth sawing into his vision at crazy angles, disappearing to reappear somewhere adjacent but impossible to determine.

Fractals fizzed at the edges of his consciousness and focussed pain into the centre of his mind, into the dark triangular shape of the reptilian mind – into the pineal eye. It was from this anguish that a dreadful creature began emerging, oozing from the deepest recess of remembrance. Its jewelled, lozenge-shaped head glittered, scintillated and transformed, as though made of liquid fire, and the eye that is always in darkness observed it in horror.

Richard clenched his fists and breathed deeply. He felt faint and utterly defenceless. What could he do to stop this? Perhaps it was time to take himself to hospital. Would Callan let him live if he admitted himself to a mental hospital? Surely Callan wasn't going to bother to kill a lunatic?

He screwed up his eyes and wondered if he should use the full capacity of his lungs to roar or scream in anguish. No. He breathed out calmly. Not yet. He would breathe. He would get control of his breathing. He dared to look back at the young man again.

It wasn't a snake. It was a syringe. The syringe kept turning back into a snake unless he made a deliberate effort to calm himself and focus.

And then a memory began uncoiling in his mind. A memory of something important. A syringe. A doctor. Something important but hidden.

90 - ICONS

Weber had just finished unpacking another consignment of original icons shipped in from Russia. He could get hold of relics of historical and religious significance if necessary. Most of the time it was not necessary though. Any third-rate tat would do, even replicas. Of course, there was a limit to how far he was prepared to plunder Russia, and a limit on what he was allowed to obtain. These particular items were for his own use. So they were going to be well looked after. He had carefully placed the three precious objects side by side on a velvet cover on his rosewood coffee table.

He was satisfied with his life, with the lavish lifestyle. He liked to be surrounded by nice things. And why not? He was an important person, up there with the likes of Kim Philby. And, like Philby, he was right under the noses of the people who were supposed to sniff him out. Why couldn't they do it? Maybe it was because, as a significant London art dealer, he inhabited the same world as all sorts of movers and shakers. The sort of people that simply couldn't conceive of such a thing. He wore a camouflage made from the spirits of the literati and intelligentsia.

His politics were overtly left wing too, and overtly hypocritical. Except they were not hypocritical. He really was changing the world. He was soon to be a Hero of the New Revolution.

91 - THROUGH THE LOOKING GLASS

Faces floated upwards on the left. Long lines of almost-motionless people stood and waited for four sets of moving stairs to transport them. Two of the lines were sliding upwards, and two were drifting steadily downwards – all at an angle of approximately forty degrees. Richard held on to a rubber handrail and allowed himself to drift.

Above him a wide, semi-circular ceiling spanned all four lines. The ceiling, which was comprised of long, thin, gold-coloured beams, converged below in the distance and splayed out above him, going backwards into infinity. Between each column of people there were handrail belts separated by a brown laminate-covered area from which monumental, evenly spaced lamps stood vertically. They glowed dimly, marking out Richard's downward progress, as though it was necessary to measure this to understand that he was travelling at constant velocity. It normally took about two minutes to complete this process and get down to the platform of Dmitrovskaya Metro Station. But that day the process was indistinct, like a memory which would not reveal itself. It had become infinite.

Then Richard was falling.

The golden vaulting had darkened and shrunk inwards. There was no longer a sense of up or down and everything was narrower, wrapping round in a circle. No roof, no floor; just walls – walls made of brick covered in moss.

He was falling into a deep, dark tunnel.

At the end of the tunnel there was a light; a perfect circle of light, like a small silver coin. Except the coin was expanding rapidly, into a disc, into a crash-landing on the moon...

...and then it exploded, enveloping him in light. When he blinked, he saw he was floating high above a patchwork of fields. He had not been falling, but rising. The tunnel was a tall brick chimney, which dropped away below him as he continued rising into cloud.

Far away to his left, an aeroplane was making its way from the east.

And then, as his eyes focussed, the cloud solidified and he could see that what he had thought was cloud was a white wall. He was in a little, windowless room with no door. The walls were all plain white. On a desk in front of him there was a folder. He remembered trying to read it before. It was a story about a man called Callan. In the story, Callan had another name. Everyone had another name.

There was no dialogue in the story. Richard had to imagine the dialogue himself.

***

He is trying to move through the geometry of the city unseen. But the skyscrapers are all around. They are there, looking down at him with their red eyes, casting their gaze directly into the streets he walks through. He has to get back to the hotel. This other person that he feels he is can remember something.

He writes an entry in his diary to describe the incident.

Then the other person writes something important in his diary. Richard closes the diary and shuts his eyes, slumping back in the bed, relaxed. At last he has remembered something important and recorded it. He knows who he can get help from.

The chimney is already far below. Occasionally clouds slip past, casting their shadows on the fields below. He continues drifting upwards, towards a thicker layer of cloud, and into it, surrounded by white mist.

When the mist clears he is sitting in a small room, seated at a desk. In front of him are folders and documents. Some of these are stamped with grandiose insignia.

After a little while he opens his diary again, wanting to bask in this new knowledge.

Humpty Dumpty sat on a wall.

Humpty Dumpty had a great fall.

All the king's horses and all the king's men

Couldn't put Humpty together again...

Get him to help. Get help now.

92 - UNTHINKABLE

Osbourne was concluding the meeting by giving Callan a bit of a lecture.

"We have to think of everything. What is the point of thinking, of having intelligence, if you have to limit it? If you have to tell yourself that some things are 'unthinkable' because of moral constraints?"

Callan wondered what naïve statement he'd made to be on the receiving end of this particular tirade at this particular time. He was as much a bastard as anyone in this business.

93 - ON HOLD

At last Richard had remembered. He pulled his suitcase out of the wardrobe and opened it. The lining was detachable. He felt underneath and pulled out an envelope.

Yes! This was the emergency procedure! He pulled the contents of the envelope out and spread them on the bed. A photo of VirtuBank and an advert for 100,000 assorted cassettes including Max Bygraves, Des O'Connor etc.

He started decrypting the advert. After ten minutes he was puzzled. After twenty he had completed decrypting. He checked it again in case he'd missed something. But no, he had done it properly. It was *All In The Golden Afternoon*, the prefatory poem of *Alice In Wonderland*. Then two more sentences: "Where Have All The Good Times Gone?" and "This Is The End, Beautiful Friend." How on earth was that supposed to help him?

Richard sighed. Perhaps it was time to end it all in the way Mitchell had done. Where had all the good times gone? There had never been any good times. His whole life had been spent waiting for this one opportunity. It was the end. This one opportunity that had turned everything to dust. The one good thing in his life had been Melanie. But he hadn't heard from Melanie for weeks. Her number had been unobtainable ever since that time he'd lied to her. It couldn't be that she'd known he was lying, so why had she just disappeared?

The desire to get back in touch with her nagged at him again. A desire and longing that ached; a loneliness like the bleakest empti-ness. Deep down he knew it would never happen. There was no way of contacting her now. He'd already tried everything he could think of. The last time he had contacted Aphrodite's Secret he had been told that she didn't work there any more, which was hardly surprising because she hated the place. He idly wondered if she really had worked there anyway or if it was all just a cover. Had he ever seen her with any other clients? He shrugged and made a face for his own benefit. Who cared about that? If it was a cover then she had only had sex with him as part of her job. She was still just a prostitute. He was still just in love with a prostitute. Just in love. Just a prostitute. Just. Still.

He ruefully remembered the times they'd had together. He had paid for her every time, apart from that one time. But the conversa-tions they had had – they had been real. And then he remembered something. He remembered she had told him she was a coffee addict and had to have a coffee and cake every day at three p.m. She went to the same posh cafe every day.

He tried to transport himself back to that fake room and get hold of the name. No, not the fake room, his own room; and it was a funny name. Someone from Greek mythology. The trouble was it was too obscure. He would never remember it. She was giggling. He remembered her giggling.

But it was obvious, she was giggling about something. Incest?

No one needed a memory nowadays. Google was your memory. He got on his phone and googled "incest in Greek mythology". A few moments later he had the name. It came back to him as soon as he saw it: "Myra Hindley – Myrrha". And then the phone number. It would be twenty to three in the UK. He couldn't wait any longer. He got on Skype and phoned the UK.

A rather posh voice sang the name of the cafe at him: "Myrrha's."

"Hello, I'd like to speak to one of your regular customers. Her name's Melanie." He imagined whoever was on the other end would be rather taken aback. He had been unable to subdue the excitement in his voice. He must sound like a nuisance caller. "It's important," he added, trying to control his voice better and hoping "it's important" would be an acceptable explanation.

There was a long pause. He wondered if he'd given the right name. Melanie was her real name, wasn't it, not a working name? He was pretty sure about that.

"Actually," he blurted out, realising it was still only twenty to three, "she normally has coffee at three p.m. Perhaps I can leave a message for her to call me back."

"Can I ask who's calling?"

"It's…" Richard wondered if he should say his name. Firstly because Melanie might not want to hear from him; secondly because he didn't want to give any clues about who he was to anyone. He was that paranoid. "Just tell her it's a friend of Andy's. It's very important though. Maybe I could just leave a message for her to call me back," he repeated, hoping it made him sound more reasonable, more like the sort of person the cafe's customers would have dealings with.

"I'll see if she's here at present," said the voice with an icy formality.

The lady, by her tone, had told him in no uncertain terms that he was fortunate indeed she was humouring him. Richard felt like such scum to be interrupting the proceedings at an establishment where his superiors had important things to do, such as drink expensive coffee.

Richard was kept on hold until he'd gone past the point of hope, past boredom and anger, and had resigned himself to defeat. To being told that it was not a proper thing to interrupt the clientele and that he would have to come in in person if he needed to speak to anyone there, or being told Melanie knew who was calling and had no intention of speaking to him.

"Richard?" It was Melanie! She'd already guessed it was him and even sounded pleased!

"Yes!"

"Where are you? What's happening?"

94 - THE DISAPPEARED

"He's disappeared. We have no idea where he is. Presumably some-where in Europe."

"Europe's quite a big place," Osbourne said, doing what he imagined was his Robert de Niro face; nodding sagely while push-ing his lower lip out by tightening his upper one.

Callan grunted in agreement, half appreciating the semi-humor-ous, sarcastic remark.

"In that case this whole thing has effectively been aborted. We should have a meeting to review what went wrong and decide what to do next."

"What about *Snowman*?"

"I don't think we should waste resources chasing after him."

"But you wanted to bring him in because he's in danger."

"We have to hope, for his sake, that if he can hide from us he can hide from them too. The problem is, apart from us, there is absolutely no one on earth he can trust."

95 - THE ROSEN GARTEN

"I'm in Frankfurt. I need help. People have been trying to kill me and..." Richard didn't know how to finish what he was saying. He'd said too much already. Melanie would think he was raving mad and hang up.

"OK Richard. If I can help I will. Where are you staying?"

"The Rosen Garten."

"Keep calm. I'll get the first flight and meet you in your hotel. Which room number?"

"117."

"OK. I'll be there before midnight."

Richard hung up. He was amazed. Melanie was coming to see him! But he was also worried. There must be some dreadful reason. Why would she drop everything just to see a poor lost lunatic in Frankfurt? Why had he trusted her with the hotel and room number?

***

Melanie felt slightly over-dressed in terms of quality of designer label and under-dressed in terms of skirt length as she stepped out of her taxi. The Rosen Garten was OK. It was respectable enough for a tourist-class hotel in the red-light district of Frankfurt. But there she was, still dressed for Knightsbridge, wearing a short Chanel skirt and with a Miu Miu bag slung over her shoulder. She caught a glimpse of what looked like a drunk street prostitute at the corner of the road and shuddered. So, putting on what she thought was a brave face, she lifted her chin up, and took a few clippy steps to drag her Globe-Trotter travel bag into the lobby and get off the street as quickly as possible. The effect, in the eyes of the rest of the street, who saw a spoilt young lady with her nose in the air, was to enhance the notion a snobby rich bitch had invaded their territory.

***

Richard watched Melanie go into the Rosen Garten from a window of the bar across the street. He'd decided to get the hell out of the hotel and wait to see who turned up to meet him. If it was Callan, or anyone other than Melanie, then he would be on his way. He'd checked out and taken all his things just in case.

He had called for the bill as soon as he saw her pull up in the cab, but now she was already back out and was looking up and down the street anxiously. There was no time to waste! He dumped a pile of cash on his table and rushed out of the bar.

She was already climbing into a cab as Richard rushed into the street.

"Melanie!" She didn't hear him. She was wearing a frown and struggling to push her bag into the back seat.

"MELANIE!" She looked up. He crossed the street quickly and joined her. "Sorry, I had to check out. I, er, I..." What excuse did he have for this? "I wanted to change to a better hotel to meet you in."

"Oh, Richard, I'm so glad you're here. I was so worried when they told me you'd checked out." She paused, waiting for a reply, but Richard said nothing. He had no further explanation.

"Why don't we go to my hotel?" she suggested.

They got hold of a cab and soon Richard found himself in the considerably plusher surroundings of the Steigenberger Frankfurter Hof.

"Melanie, I think I'm going mad." Richard sat on a stool in the corner of Melanie's room, while she occupied a grandiose easy chair nearby.

"Of course you're not going mad." Her voice was calm but she looked worried.

"I think people are trying to kill me. I've started to have hallucinations and I'm beginning to think I don't know what's real and what's imaginary any more. I think Humpty Dumpty is an important person and he's going to help me. The last straw was when I saw that snake..."

"Stop, Richard. Stop!"

Richard stopped, surprised. He was hurting her with his madness! How could he expect Melanie, a nice cute girl like Melanie, to help him? He should just forget it and go to hospital. So it was all the more surprising to him when she said: "Believe it or not, there could be an explanation for all of this. I don't know what it is. But I'm involved in all this stuff too, though I have even less idea of what's going on than you."

Richard didn't know what to say, so he said nothing. Melanie continued: "Let's begin with Helsinki. What do you remember about Helsinki last July?"

"Nothing much, just that I got drunk with Mitchell."

"And you remember I was there too? We had rather a nice time together, didn't we?"

"Yes, of course. I remember you had brown hair and green eyes then and what turned out to be a temporary tattoo on your thigh."

"Mitchell recruited me to run errands for him and seduce people. One of the people I seduced was you."

"Yes, I always thought that incident was too good to be true. So it was all for Mitchell."

"Too good to be true? It was still true though. I actually like you for some reason. Besides, we're two pieces of a jigsaw. We can help each other get out of this mess regardless of who else is involved or why."

"Sounds too good to be true."

"Any idea why Mitchell got me to seduce you in Helsinki?"

"None."

"I know exactly why. He wanted me to steal some documents and photographs."

"What!?"

"I stole them from you and from him too. You see, I gave him the originals that I stole but I have photographs of everything."

"Why would you do that? Surely if Mitchell found out you would've been in deep shit?"

"But he didn't find out. Why would he find out?"

"So why did you do it?"

"Andy had a hold on me that you can't imagine. But you know what?"

"Go on."

"I think Andy himself was a kind of victim. These people are disgusting. They use each other. Game theory – everything is just a game. They hurt themselves of course, but so long as they can hurt you even more, they will bear the pain."

"So long as they win?"

"Yes. Mitchell was an expert in manipulating people – charming and evil. One day he would offer money, the next he would threaten to tell my folks that I worked…" She broke off and said softly, "where I worked…" Then she resumed more confidently, "I wanted to get as much on Mitchell as he had on me in the hope it would help break his grip on me one day."

"So you kept a copy of the stuff you stole from me."

"Trouble is, I don't know what it is. It looks like an advert for some Chinese stuff and a couple of photos. Some old guy and a place in London. I decided that it would be useful for me to keep tabs on you in case I needed you. I imagine you know why it's important."

"Yes, it's important. I hope. I won't know until I look at it more closely. But then what happened? After stealing that stuff, why did Mitchell decide to get you to give me the envelope?"

"He didn't."

"What!?" Richard's head swarmed with paranoia.

"That was MI5 too. They gave me all that stuff along with a cock and bull story about Mitchell. Mitchell was already dead before they came to me with it."

"Oh fuck. So…"

"Richard, let's move on from this. You called me. All we know is that we're in deep shit. The document I stole must be the key to this."

"Or another layer of the hell that we're descending into."

"Let's start with the pictures. I guess you know why they're important. I have printouts in my bag." She laid her bag on the bed to open it.

"Why were you expecting an envelope anyway?" she asked, holding up the first picture and squinting at it.

"Oh shit. You don't know that? In that case, I can't tell you."

"OK. Let's leave it at that for now."

There were nasty interrogators and there were nice ones. Richard knew that. Sooner or later he would tell Melanie everything. He could hardly resist already. Richard watched her placing the photographs carefully on the bed. He loved how her eyes looked so intently at them.

"So…" She tilted her head to one side.

In that cute pose Richard was more interested in her than the photographs.

"Just have a look and see if this gives us any clues," she said, reminding him of the task.

Richard stood up. His eyes widened in horror. The first photograph was that building! The one in Bloomsbury, London! The second was a man with glasses and a doctor's coat.

"Oh my god!" Suddenly Callan was there, asking him to sign something. Was it Callan or someone else? Back in Chennai. No, here in the hotel. The flashing lights were back. His ears were ringing. He staggered into the en suite and threw up into the toilet.

96 - AN UNINVITED GUEST

"OK", said Osbourne, "no need for formalities. We know why we're here. Let's get started." He looked enquiringly round at the two other participants, Dr Skinner and Callan.

At that, the door opened and Ray Hannaford poked his head into the room. He looked round the door and said, "Mind if I join you? My department has an interest in this case."

Osbourne groaned inwardly but kept an impassive look on his face. Now he was going to be out-ranked in his own meeting. Quite a sensitive meeting at that.

"I think it's best if we keep things tight. I didn't think you had any interest in this case," he replied, but Hannaford was already letting himself into the room.

"On the contrary," said Hannaford assertively. He closed the door and sat down immediately.

Osbourne pictured himself manhandling Hannaford out of the room to get rid of him, but he couldn't do that. It was just wishful thinking. His best shot was an awkward question: "What exactly is your interest, may I ask?"

"I'd like to hear what Dr Skinner has to say about the techniques he's using, that's all."

Osbourne stared ahead for a moment. There was nothing he could do. Hannaford was here to stay.

"OK. Let's review the situation. Callan, tell us what the hell's going on."

Callan cleared his throat. "I'll briefly summarise the history and then we can discuss the current situation."

Osbourne nodded wisely. Dr Skinner didn't nod. He looked a little like a rabbit caught in the headlights.

"So, our man, codenamed *Snowman*, came to us many years ago. Hamilton Denton was in charge of him. I was involved too at that early stage. He told us about a plot of his own devising. It was an extremely vague plot, but in any case he had now changed his mind and had come up with a counter-plot for which he needed our help. Perhaps you could put it the other way round – that he was offering to help us. No matter, we came up with a mutually beneficial plan. In return for our helping him, he would help us."

"This all sounds terribly nebulous. Can you be more specific?" Hannaford asked.

"OK. *Snowman* had been a revolutionary socialist and had offered, through his Party, to be used to perform some act of sabotage if and when he ever got into a position to do so. He had now completely rethought his position and wanted us to use him to catch whoever contacted him to implement the plan. Hamilton loved the idea. He always liked anything a bit off-beat. He also took the decision not to force anything but to allow the plan to develop as originally intended."

"Sounds a bit dangerous." Hannaford interjected

"The beauty was, it wasn't going to cost much. All we had to do was rely on *Snowman* to contact us when he was contacted by the other side."

"Still..."

"Two things were wrong. First, *Snowman* wasn't confident of his ability to get deeply involved in a plot in which he was really on our side. Secondly, he had to be confident that we were on his side and would and could help him. That's when Hamilton decided to try some experimental work of Dr Skinner. I think it's best if the doctor would explain it."

"Yes." Dr Skinner still looked like a frightened rabbit. "I had been doing some research for some time into, let's call them 'mind control techniques', whereby the subject could exist in two states and switch between them. Call them state A and state B. When in state A, he would not be aware of his state B personality, and vice versa. Nevertheless, he would have some subconscious control over which state was desirable for him to be in at any one time. This is not a quick or easy process; it's a difficult thing to do. It requires the subject to momentarily shift out of either state so that he is completely detached from his ego. It's a bit like the sort of meditation Buddhists do to try to reach a state of nirvana. I decided to use the term 'phase transition' to describe the process – "

"Yes, OK," Hannaford interrupted gruffly. "Seems like a lot of trouble to go to just for this *Snowman* chap."

"Don't you realise, this is a common problem for many of our field people, not just amateurs? I had been working on it for many years before *Snowman* came along."

"Yes," Callan interrupted. "*Snowman* seemed an ideal guinea pig. He wasn't subject to hostile conditions. He was safe with us, here in UK."

"Indeed," said Dr Skinner. "If you don't mind, I'd like to give you some more background into the techniques."

97 - A MAN MAY NOT KNOW

"Richard!" Melanie let out a squeal of horror. She wished she hadn't – screaming wouldn't help, but she couldn't control herself. She held her hands over her mouth as though that was what was required to prevent herself from screaming even more.

Richard was having some sort of seizure. His hands were shaking as he tried to steady himself by holding onto the basin. His eyes glazed over and he slumped onto the floor, bumping his head against the toilet bowl on the way and ending up in an awkward heap.

"Richard! Richard!" Melanie cried. In an instant she was trying to roll him over into the recovery position. She tried to feel for a pulse while glancing over at the bedside phone. "Should I just phone for a doctor immediately?" His pulse was OK. It was hers that was racing.

"Melanie?" Richard was confused. "What happened?" He was trying to roll back over and sit up. He lurched into a sitting position and rested his head back against the wall.

"Oh, thank god, Richard! Are you OK?"

"I think so. What happened?"

"We were just looking at some pictures and you seemed to have some sort of fit."

"Pictures? What pictures?"

"You don't remember?"

"No."

"You don't remember the photographs at all?"

"No. Can I see them again?"

"Not now." She got up and tidied the pictures back into her bag. "I think it might be dangerous for some reason."

"What if you just describe them to me? Maybe I'll remember. I don't know why I fainted just now."

"It was just a picture of a place in London. A place in Bedford Avenue, according to the writing on the back."

"Bedford Avenue? I used to know that place. I used to go there but then, I think…" Richard's voice faltered. "I think something bad happened to me there and I stopped going."

"Something bad?"

"I was bitten by a snake or something. I had a terrible fever. I wonder… did I end up in the hospital for tropical diseases? I don't know, Melanie. What about the other picture?"

"It's a doctor. Dr Skinner has been written on the back of the picture. It says 'Dr Skinner 020 7946 0975'. He's an oldish guy with a thin face and black-rimmed glasses – "

"Jesus Christ!" Richard cried out. "I remember him! I remember! A man may not know his own mind."

"That's what it says at the bottom of the reverse of the photo. 'A man may not know his own mind'."

98 - A GREAT SUCCESS

Dr Skinner was continuing with his explanation. "At University I did a PhD in multiple personalities. Shortly after joining the Service I came across a study into bilingualism. It got me thinking. I began to wonder if, in the same way that bilingual people can transfer from one language to another, and think in either but obviously not both simultaneously, people would be able to temporarily suppress whole areas of their personality and beliefs. If so, that would protect them in situations where they were not supposed to reveal information."

Hannaford's eyebrows shot up in surprise. Osbourne noticed this and scowled.

Callan interrupted eagerly. "The technique was a great success. *Snowman* is able to separate his personality into two. He was taught how to do this by Dr Skinner. However, he was not supposed to be aware of this ability and was supposed only to be able to switch from one to the other by following Dr Skinner's instructions. It turned out that he spontaneously began to reconcile the two parts of his personality."

"Can we stop there with all this theory please?" Osbourne interrupted. "We should get to the nitty-gritty of the *Snowman* case, not the theory behind it." It was evident to him that all this information was new to Hannaford. If he didn't already know it, now was not the time for him to find out.

99 - ALWAYS TOMORROW

Richard remembered Dr Skinner.

"It was him... he did something." Richard was confused again. "Tortured me with a snake? No, it doesn't make sense. He cured me, I think. He must've cured me after I was bitten by the snake." He looked at Melanie in anguish. "I don't know what happened."

"Are you feeling OK now, anyway?"

Richard nodded.

"Come back into the room. We should get some sleep. There's always tomorrow."

"Hmm, there's been a couple of times recently when there wasn't going to be a tomorrow," he said.

100 - CHINESE MASKS

They slept together without having sex. They were too exhausted for any intimacy at all. The bed was large enough for them to sleep a little distance apart. Melanie ordered breakfast to be delivered to the room next morning. Over breakfast she asked: "How about the advert? What do you think it is?"

"Probably just one of my messages."

"Your messages?"

Oh! That's it! thought Richard. I knew Melanie would catch me out. But we were on the same side, with Mitchell anyway... except I was on Weber's side. I was pretending to be on Mitchell's side and Melanie was really on...

"Well, do you want to tell me what it's about?" Melanie prompted.

"I don't think it's anything important." Richard was relieved that he was still in the clear. She must think it was a message to Mitchell.

"Here, tell me all about it." She thrust the message at him eagerly.

"Oh, OK," he sighed. "I need to decipher it first if it's what I think it is." He was still going to be OK. He could just make up any old message to Mitchell and tell her that's what it was. "I need time to do that."

"OK. Do it while I go for a shower."

"OK." Richard wondered what message he could make up. "Having a lovely time in Helsinki, wish you were here" amused him for a moment. But for some reason he was intrigued. He couldn't remember an advert like this one. An advert for antique Chinese masks. This advert sounded much too interesting. He would've been flooded with enquiries if this had ever been put in the paper. He began decoding.

101 - STATE B

"Dr Skinner, take us back to the last session with *Snowman*. How did it go?" Osbourne asked.

Dr Skinner pursed his lips. This was what he'd been dreading. He didn't know where to begin.

"You went to Helsinki with Mitchell to reinforce the treatment. Am I correct?"

Dr Skinner shook his head.

"No, after the initial treatment I have had no further contact with *Snowman*. In fact, I am not permitted to contact him because I am likely to remind him of the treatment and cause it to unravel."

"So Mitchell did everything on his own. What about the consent forms? I couldn't find the electronic copies on file."

"No, there were no consent forms this time. Erm..." Everyone was staring at him. "We couldn't snap him out of state B so..."

"Just remind me. What's state B?" Osbourne interrupted to ask. "I get confused."

"State B is when he's not aware that he's working for us. He's acting purely as a revolutionary."

"Gentlemen, I need to leave you to it. I have another meeting to attend," Hannaford said abruptly.

Callan was annoyed that Hannaford had invited himself to their meeting and then not even had the courtesy to stay to the end.

***

But Hannaford didn't want to waste more time on this. He really did have another meeting and he'd already heard enough. He'd heard that, by their own admission, they'd spent years helping a saboteur. They weren't doing it by accident either; it was deliberate. They seemed to know what they were doing, except that it was going wrong. He was aware that somewhere else in the organisation, they'd been trying to stop this *Snowman* chap.

Hannaford left the room determined to find out who or what was the source of the misinformation.

102 - DECODING

After five minutes he was bored. This was just more nonsense. There was a date, then a bit of incomprehensible mumbo jumbo stating that: "This agreement between the parties below has been reached on this date dd/mm/yy."

There was a superscript (1), the note of which stated that substantive evidence in the form of audio and visual records and paper documents would be held in perpetuity even after the death of the signatories. The records would be held at a place known to the principal signatory and would be made available to the secondary signatory on request. Then Her Majesty's Government of Great Britain and Northern Ireland was mentioned, for no apparent reason. He stopped decoding. He was starting to get a headache again.

He reached for his diary. He had the overwhelming feeling that this time he was going to write something important.

103 - CONSENT

"Where was I?" Dr Skinner asked. "Oh yes. State A is his normal state. Apart, that is, from the inability to remember state B. Now –" he hesitated again, not happy to reveal this. "We couldn't get him to switch to state A to sign the consent forms."

"We always switch him back to 'A', otherwise consent doesn't really mean anything," Callan explained to Osbourne.

"So... The thing is, it's become more and more difficult for us to keep the two states separate over the years, so we've had to introduce more and more phobias to block off certain memories of certain events." Dr Skinner was visibly flustered. "Normally we switch him to 'A' and get him to write a statement in his own handwriting. This time we couldn't do it. But he signed our typewritten document."

"But you're saying he was still in state B at the time?"

"Yes, probably, according to Mitchell. It was all we could do."

"Christ. It's against protocol. Furthermore, what guarantee do we have that he will ever flip back?" Osbourne asked.

Osbourne was edging closer to the sort of questions that the rabbit was so frightened of, but luckily for Skinner, Osbourne had only asked it rhetorically. The meeting broke up and Skinner fled the room unscathed.

104 - LOST

Richard wrote in the diary, so lost in thought he had no awareness of his surroundings, no awareness even that he was writing. He was writing about something important that Mitchell had told him. He was writing almost as though Mitchell was there dictating it. He had fallen into an unreal world and was being held there by someone, but he could still escape and rejoin Mitchell to carry out the original plan.

A noise behind disturbed him, making him look round in alarm. It was only Melanie coming out of the shower room wearing a towel round her head, but otherwise naked.

She sat down with her back to him, fussing with herself in the mirror. He watched dumbly. He had once gone to a Japanese Kabuki. Melanie was like that; her mannerisms and movements were like an actor in an incomprehensible play.

Suddenly he had the thought she had just materialised there at that moment and he had no idea who she was.

Worse than that, she was not just a stranger, but some sort of blank with no past. Suspicion insinuated itself into his thoughts, settling into the darkest place in his mind. He continued to watch, wondering if his faith in her was misplaced.

Melanie continued to fuss with herself in the mirror, apparently unaware of being watched, as Richard began to wonder if she had been one of the people who had betrayed him. Wonder who had been involved in the attempts to kill him. Wonder why he had decided to run away to Frankfurt and why Melanie had decided to join him as soon as he'd suggested it.

105 - AN INTERRUPTION

The solid wooden door of Osbourne's office received several loud raps from Callan's knuckles before he opened it. "Sorry to interrupt," he said.

"Come in, you're not interrupting," Osbourne replied. Callan let himself into the office and sat down.

"I've been in contact with Hamilton Denton about leaving *Snowman* to his own devices. He was not at all happy about the idea."

"Hamilton-fucking-Denton. This whole mess is his fault in the first place. We should never have let him get his way over this. Do you remember the arguments we had about it?"

"Of course I do. MI5 wouldn't touch it with a bargepole."

"But we got badgered into it just because Hamilton personally thought it was a good idea and he knew Skinner wanted a guinea pig."

"Anyway, never mind all that now. No point crying over spilt milk. Hamilton has just deigned to inform me that there was an emergency procedure that should jolt him out of state B."

"We have to find him first," Osbourne retorted.

"We're MI fucking nine for Christ's sake! We should be capable of finding him soon!"

"I'm not so sure. From Schiphol he could've gone anywhere in the world if his new friends helped him get false ID."

"Goddamnit. We should've implanted a chip in the bastard, like the one in my dog. He's been so much trouble."

Snowman or your dog? Callan wondered. He didn't bother to say it. He rarely joked and this was not a good time. Instead he said: "Except we decided not to in case anyone interrogated him. It would be a death sentence."

"Yes, OK, I know. Let's get hold of Dr Skinner and find out how this emergency procedure works."

106 - SUPERNOVA

Dr Skinner had been dragged into Callan's office at a moment's notice. "It's about *Snowman*," Callan began. "We tried to bring him back, but he disappeared."

He knew he was going to have to tell Callan more than he had got away with previously. Somehow, he would have to resist telling him too much. So far his explanation of the techniques hadn't been entirely honest. It was true the studies into bilingualism had helped him, but he hadn't mentioned the splitting of Richard's personality had been achieved by extremely traumatic techniques with origins in Nazi Germany. Experiments which had the side effect of inducing schizophrenia in normal subjects. Mitchell had found out about this shortly before Helsinki and had become a nuisance.

"Yes, I believe so." He hoped he sounded sympathetic.

"There is apparently an emergency procedure to get him back to his senses. If we can initiate that, he'll realise what the hell is going on and come back to us."

"We can't do anything now. If he's disappeared, it's too late."

"Then why the hell didn't you tell us about it before?" Callan shouted.

"How am I supposed to know what you know and don't know?"

"You developed this. You should have kept everyone fully informed."

"Sir Hamilton decided who should know what."

He also managed to avoid mentioning that, although there had been an emergency procedure when Denton had planned the project, now there wasn't one. As soon as he had realised Richard was stuck in state B in Helsinki and the emergency procedure wouldn't work either, he'd panicked. He'd tricked Mitchell into stealing the required documents from Richard and replacing them with meaningless duds. That way his name wouldn't be connected to any enquiry into what happened to Richard. Richard would almost certainly go through with the sabotage plan, and then his whole personality would begin to collapse in on itself like a supernova. When that happened, he didn't want photographs and documents that could be traced back to him to be found.

In those final moments, Richard would find himself with no friends, no idea who he was and a growing awareness of misdeeds, real or imagined, that had been committed against him.

Though much of his work was based on Nazi experiments, Skinner had believed the improved techniques and drugs he had used should have given superior results to theirs. In any case, they had not been doing proper science, whereas he had. But it seemed, from recent evidence, his techniques were not going to prove any better than theirs. If that turned out to be the case, he knew what was likely to happen. In the last few hours of confusion and terror, Richard would probably kill anyone he came into contact with, before committing suicide.

107 - UNRAVELLING

Richard returned to the diary and recoiled when he saw what was written there:

> THERE IS A KEY
> Melanie is illusion.
> She is imaginary.
> She does not exist.
> She is not real.
> She is not alive.
> She cannot die.
> There is another you.
> She is another(.)
> (you.)
> She is the key
> that you must unlock
> to be free.

He had no recollection of writing this. He tried to overcome his confusion, but instead another vivid image burst into his consciousness. He was in the bathroom with Melanie. Water was gushing from the showerhead but Melanie was not showering. She was collapsed in a heap. Swirls of red water were billowing around her pale, lifeless body and draining down the plughole.

And then he was back in the room looking at the diary. There was more writing on the next page:

I am walking along a narrow path in the mist. The path is difficult and hilly. There are rocks under which scorpions hide. Occasionally a brightly coloured serpent slithers away at the edge of my vision and vanishes.

After a while I become aware that a shadowy figure is walking nearby on another path. He is a step behind me a few yards away to my right.

Our paths are coming closer. Now I can see him quite clearly. I realise that he looks exactly like me.

But he is not me. I am me.

I looked away for a moment. Something glitters and disappears behind a rock, distracting me. The person is now in front of me to my right. I wonder how he has overtaken me so quickly and without me noticing. It is clear that now I am him and he is me.

Then I am talking to Mitchell. Mitchell is saying something important. He is saying:

"Take this key. It will open my desk drawer. In there you will find all the remaining instructions."

I don't know what to say. It is not for me to speak to Mitchell nor he to me. I feel that the other man is disappointed or angry but what can I do? Mitchell spoke to me and it's not my fault. I take the key. Then I am alone again in the desert. I look for the key but I cannot find it. I look for the person who was talking to Mitchell who seemed to be me. He is gone. There is only mist.

Richard looked blankly at what he had written. This felt important; it would make everything all right somehow. If only Melanie wasn't bleeding to death in the shower, this might have been the clue he had needed. Perhaps it was not too late. He could still phone an ambulance. And when he discovered what this writing meant, it would make everything all right. But how could it make any everything all right? It was meaningless nonsense.

Richard turned the page. There was more:

As soon as he left, I took the key and wrapped it carefully. I put it into some kind of bag or sack, concealed inside a gap that cannot be seen.

"What are you doing?"

Richard spun round in confusion. It was Melanie! A new Melanie, not the one still lying in the shower basin. He opened his mouth to speak but no words came out.

"Are you OK? You seemed to be almost in a trance just now." Melanie was tucking some stray hairs into her towel turban.

"I, I'm OK," he stuttered. He struggled to understand which universe he was living in: the one where he had discovered that disturbing poem and Melanie was dying in the shower, or this one where things were far from perfect, but at least more normal.

"Can I see what you've been writing?"

"No!"

He had said it too quickly, too anxiously and too angrily. A quick glance down had told him what was written on the page was really there. So what was written on the other page must be there too, and he had no explanation for it. All he knew was that she mustn't see the poem.

"Just a bit of it. You..."

"No! Get away from me!"

Melanie shrunk away from him, visibly shocked, perhaps even scared.

"Sorry, I just need to..." he began, but was unable to finish. Suddenly he was blinded by bright, jagged shards of light that crackled with electricity. They fizzed outwards explosively and wriggled like lightning. For a moment it felt as though the entire universe was a vast, vibrating mass of living energy with death hiding in the negative spaces behind the illusion. He knew that soon the flickering positive and negative energies would switch places permanently and he would cross the border to join Mitchell. And now there was a voice telling him what to do. He would cross and take Melanie with him.

He thought of the exercises he used to do. Who would he be prepared to kill? Would he be able to kill her? Yes, if he had to, he would – and Mitchell's voice was telling him that he would have to. Someone had betrayed him.

He shook his head.

Betrayed him? But no one had. He was too tired. Too confused. He closed his eyes and held his head in his hands.

Someone was whispering now, incessantly whispering something about scissors or a knife, scissors or a knife.

He didn't want to listen to this imaginary Mitchell. He didn't want to do this. There must be something else he could do? He looked round in confusion. He saw Melanie backing away from him, looking very scared and confused.

Something else? Yes, he could finish deciphering the document.

108 - POLITICAL MASTERS

Osbourne was sitting at his desk wondering what to do with a messy situation that one of his people had got into in Yemen when Hannaford burst into his office. His surprise turned to annoyance when Hannaford announced: "I'm going to arrange for a full investigation into this whole affair."

"Which whole affair?" Osbourne asked, genuinely nonplussed and still thinking of Yemen.

"*Snowman*. I don't think anyone above Denton is aware of the work of Dr Skinner. That is not acceptable."

"What's going on here? Denton didn't need to tell you. You're the same level as him. All he had to do is pass it upwards."

"But now that I do know, I know that he didn't pass it upwards."

"Oh, I see. I wasn't aware of that. Obviously it should have gone upwards."

"Yes, our political masters should have known. There are several aspects. First, in spite of appearances, we have been trying to move away from a Cold War mentality in our relations with Russia, but somehow bureaucrats on both sides of the divide keep picking at old wounds. Secondly, the precise nature of Skinner's experimental methods should have been made available to scrutiny. We have a code of ethics to uphold. Finally, and for this reason I have had Skinner suspended and placed under house arrest, we believe that some of the people involved in this project have tried to abort it in a most unethical way. Mitchell's suicide was no accident. I have evidence that Skinner himself more or less guaranteed it. There are indications that he was trying to have *Snowman* killed too. You will have to face the committee yourself to give answers to all of the questions."

Osbourne was speechless.

"Of course, Osbourne, I hope that you will cooperate and be able to give us satisfactory answers immediately. If so, I'd like you to continue with your work on this project. We absolutely must get it under control. But I have to tell you that it's not looking good for Skinner. I have been refused permission to have anyone else suspended as yet, but any evidence Skinner gives that ties you in with his behaviour will force me to suspend you too."

109 - ALL THE KING'S MEN

Richard continued decoding patiently. He knew that he mustn't get distracted again.

As well as whole lot of legalistic mumbo jumbo about Her Majesty's Government, his name had suddenly popped out, and then, a few moments later, the name "Hamilton Denton".

"Oh Christ," he said aloud. He held his hands up to his head. He didn't know which way this was going to go. He really didn't know whose side he was on – but this was going to tell him. His memory was already anticipating something very strange. Something slithering in and out of his consciousness.

110 - COMPLEX

Richard sat back in relief. He felt much better. Much less confused. Firstly, because he'd managed to decode several pages of complex documentation, but, more importantly, the documentation finally showed him who he was and what had been going on.

He had managed to overcome his memory block too. Well nearly – memories that had been associated with fear and thereby suppressed, felt as though they might be attainable soon. Everything was going to be OK after all! Even the strange story about the shadow people made some sort of sense now. Someone known as Humpty Dumpty was going to help him.

"Melanie, do you have some scissors or a knife, or maybe a steel nail file?"

"Why?"

"I've remembered something important."

Melanie gave him her nail file and he tipped the contents of his suitcase onto the floor. He used the nail file to unscrew the handle and then shook the case until a small key emerged from between the foam padding and the outer material.

"It's probably identical to the key you gave me. Mitchell had already given this to me in Helsinki but somehow I'd forgotten."

"How is that possible?"

"Everything is explained in this document. I'll read it to you in a moment. It ties in with a little story that I've just written. I think that little story and your document have just prevented me from going completely off my rocker."

"So the document's important?"

"Yes, and also Humpty Dumpty is going to help me. Or, as it said in the document, Hamilton Denton."

"Wow. This is crazy."

"You've no idea how crazy it felt just a few minutes ago. I hope I'm coming together again. We need to go and see Hamilton Denton."

"Who's that?"

"I'm not sure. I can't remember properly, but according to the document he's my emergency contact. I must have had some sort of subconscious knowledge of this, which is what made me come to Frankfurt. For some reason he lives here. And if I seem to go into a trance again, best get away from me. You've no idea what… in fact I've no idea either… it's just that I don't think I'm fully in control."

"Well, let's just have a rest for a bit and think."

111 - CHINESE WHISPERS

"Before we relax too much, can you tell me why you decided to help me?"

"I was there in Helsinki."

"Yes, I know. I remember rolling around in bed with you."

"No, not then. That was when I stole the documents. I was also there when Mitchell was trying to get you to sign some other documents. I didn't take part. I don't know why he wanted me there. Perhaps he felt he was doing something wrong and needed moral support."

"Hmm, well, anyway, I just found out something very strange. I don't know if you're already aware of this or not."

"What?"

"So…" Richard picked up his decrypted document and waved it in the air. "It begins with a kind of confession that I was intending to cause damage to the United Kingdom, and/or the Global Banking System, but had come to realise that this was not necessary or desirable. After a great deal of thought I had come to the conclusion that democracy was a better way of effecting change. Particularly in view of the fact that the process of democracy in the UK and our allies involves scientific, technical and economic research as well as political freedom of expression.

"Secondly, I had come to realise that if I was ever contacted it was probable that I would have to go through with the plans my handler had devised or else be killed to protect my handler's identity.

"Therefore, in return for the protection of Her Majesty's Government, I would agree to help them. In particular, to help trap or expose any person or persons who made contact with me to carry out the plan.

"However, being aware that I would need to act in a duplicitous way in the course of this task, and having no expertise or ability in this, I would agree to a programme of mind alteration in order to help me accomplish it."

He read out the relevant parts:

> *While under the influence of the drugs, hypnosis and other mind-altering techniques, the aforementioned will be absolved of responsibility for actions including acting, engaging in, or encouraging others to act or engage in:*
>
> *Terrorism*
> *Sabotage*
> *Subversion*
> *Similar acts normally considered to be counter to the interests of HMG*
>
> *The mind control techniques are to begin on this day xx xx 201x and will be reinforced once per year or as required.*

"These techniques are supposed to allow me to switch between two states of consciousness," he explained.

"In state B, my personality was limited by means of deep hypnosis and drugs administered by Dr Skinner. By associating certain thoughts with phobias, this prevented me remembering certain people, facts or places.

"The techniques I was trained to use enabled me to switch back to state A in order to pass information back. In this state I would be fully aware of all memories and personality traits."

He looked up at Melanie.

"Well, that certainly worked. I was interrogated in Moscow and gave nothing away. I was completely unaware that I had anything to give away."

He paused; something was puzzling him.

"I guess I must still be in state B because I still don't remember any of this stuff even though I can see it here in black and white."

He paused again, wondering if this was all a clever plot to get him to confess and give Weber away.

"I'm so confused now," said Melanie. "Did Mitchell know any of this? Am I the only one that thought you were just an ordinary guy that got caught up in things by accident?"

"I'm caught up in all this deliberately. You're the one who's in this by accident. Why did you decide to get involved with me?"

"I told you already. Mitchell had a hold on me. When he died I thought I was free. But then his friends got in touch and I knew then that I wasn't free."

"How did you know the documents were valuable?"

"I didn't, but they were all I had. Anyway, never mind any of that just now. It must be such a relief for you to know that you're not going mad and you're on the side of the good guys."

"I'm not on the side of any good guys. I have no idea who the good guys are. I don't know how vivid my memory of this document should be, but my recollection of it is absolutely non-existent. I can't imagine how this can really have anything to do with me."

"It will probably take time. Go for a shower now. Let's just relax." Melanie's eyes looked straight at him. It was that look that said she knew best.

***

When Richard came out of the shower, he found Melanie had turned herself into a present. She was all packaged up in stockings and underwear with ribbons and bows. The packaging was silky or transparent and made the product even more enticing. Ready to be unpacked.

She was still standing at the mirror holding her head this way and that way coquettishly while fussing round her neck with a soft brush. She smiled at him and came to him, dropping the brush on the floor. She took his hands and led them to the ribbons on either side of her panties. There wasn't much unpacking to do before Richard found himself on his back on the bed with Melanie ready to impale herself on him. She leaned forward, enclosing him in a curtain of hair, and kissed him. Hot breath blew out of her nostrils and then she leaned back, pushing down with her hips.

"Ow! You're so big today!" she said.

No bloody wonder, Richard thought. But he was so busy being ravaged that he couldn't speak. He wasn't going to be able to hold back for long. She twisted on him and all of a sudden he was juddering and it was all over.

"Richard!" she said, playfully scolding him. "That was naughty. Why didn't you tell me?"

"Sorry, I couldn't speak. You were... just fantastic"

"Never mind. There's always a next time," she said, lying beside him. She seemed quite content even though he was a bit embarrassed by his performance, or lack thereof. At his age, his problem was that it normally took ages. Quite the reverse of what had just happened.

112 - HUMPTY DUMPTY

There was a splurging noise from Richard's laptop – a Skype noise.

Richard wiped with a tissue while he went to have a look. It was Steve.

"I just heard you're coming back to RCB. Well done!"

Richard wasn't sure if he should answer or not. He'd been ignoring all Skype messages ever since Chennai. Steve? Why Steve? Why now? Steve was a good mate and a good colleague but... What the hell, he and Melanie were working with MI5. The sabotage stuff was all gone somehow, as though by magic.

"Hi Steve. Don't know. I got into trouble in Chennai."

"No worries mate. There was a wild rumour about that. You missed a great party last night."

"Party?"

"Yes, RCB go-live."

What!? RCB! There was at least two weeks to go before go-live.

"Go-live? Ahead of schedule?"

"Yes. Rescheduled last month."

"Currency rates live too?"

"No. We switch the interface on in two hours."

"Can you delay it? I mean, I suspect a problem."

"No, not a chance. The rumour was that you had a big problem in Chennai. Drink or something upset you. You're not back yet. I don't know what scope you'll have if they reinstate you here."

"OK, thanks Steve. Thanks for the info."

"Let's meet up somewhere sometime for a few beers."

"Good man. Say hi to Darion and the others. Must go..."

He shouted through to the en suite where Melanie was taking another shower: "Melanie, while you've been fucking my brains out, we should have been trying to save the world. We need to get word out and we only have two hours to do it."

"Are you serious? Who do we contact? I might be able to get Callan."

"No! Not Callan. I think it was Callan that tried to have me killed in the Moscow Metro."

"Then who?" Melanie came out of the shower, hastily drying herself.

"Humpty Dumpty."

113 - TOGETHER AGAIN

Sir Hamilton had been easy to find. The mobile number in the contract went straight through to him and he gave his address immediately. He had security at his gated house but it only took moments. Now they were sitting in his lounge while he spoke on the phone to Callan.

Richard still didn't understand if he was just being paranoid about Callan, but he felt very uneasy that Sir Hamilton was putting his trust in him. So either Callan is OK after all, or the global financial system is going to be wrecked fifteen minutes from now, he thought, looking at his watch as he listened to Sir Hamilton talking to Callan on the phone.

Sir Hamilton hung up. "It's all in hand. I gave him the names of Weber, Alexei and the guys in Chennai. We've stopped all go-lives of VirtuBank projects until all releases of code are double-checked. We've also alerted other software houses and financial institutions to do the same."

Richard heaved a sigh of relief. He and Melanie exchanged a glance.

"Sir Hamilton. I still have no idea what was going on, to be quite honest. In fact I hardly know who I am, let alone what was going on," Richard said.

"That's hardly surprising, Richard. I'm sorry you had to go through this. Let me get you a drink while I explain. Tea? Something stronger?"

"Tea will do."

"We'll break out the champagne if the financial system's still intact in thirty minutes' time."

Richard nodded.

"So, where to begin?" He turned to Melanie. "I retired soon after this project was initiated. I moved to Frankfurt to be near my daughter, but because of the personal nature of this project, and, above all, the fact that I'm the emergency contact, I've been getting regular updates. Richard came to us in 2011. It was his own idea for us to use him as bait to catch whoever contacted him. We couldn't afford resources to keep an eye on him for month after month so we decided to try our experimental mind control techniques.

"At first we were confident this would work. But we had to keep refreshing every now and then. Mitchell performed that procedure. Over time we found it was becoming more difficult to keep his two identities separate. To counter this we had to bury him under more and more phobias. Then it became more difficult for him to switch from state A to state B. I'm talking about states, you understand, where A was his normal state, and B his undercover state.

"We realised no one was getting in touch with him, but simply thought no one was interested. Then we got information from a source in Russia, late in 2012, that someone was running with his idea anyway. His handler, whoever it was, could see where his career was taking him and had got a plan together to use his idea without involving Richard.

"We were amazed at our stupidity. We'd signalled a deadly sabotage plan to the enemy but now had no way of tracking it.

"Richard himself was apparently stuck in state B and responding in an unstable way to our techniques to switch back. Of course, there was supposed to be a safeguard whereby we could get him back to normal in an emergency situation. The emergency code was "A man may not know his own mind." That was supposed to allow us to activate a neural pathway that would override anything else. He himself had mental safeguards that should allow him to remember me but to dislike or even be afraid of Mitchell and Callan.

"But Mitchell reported back that 'A man may not know his own mind' had become one of Richard's own pet quotes. We realised that he had somehow disassociated it from the purpose we had assigned and it was unlikely to work. In any case, in state B, Richard might still help us. Mitchell was told not to push too hard to get him to switch because if Richard got stuck in state A, he would be no use to us at all. So we left him in state B believing that he would be contacted. Only once that had happened would it be useful for us to get him back. So, knowing this, we did everything we could to get the enemy to change his mind, contact him and make use of him after all."

Melanie had a question. "But why didn't you just get someone to keep a close eye on him and report back to you?"

"Adding someone else into the mix, you for example, just makes them a target for the other side. So they have to be at arm's length from Richard and from us. It's of limited value."

Melanie interrupted angrily. "But I was in the mix. I mixed myself up in all this. You knew I was in danger and you did nothing."

"Whatever you did was your own business. As you just admitted, you mixed yourself up in this and we were under no obligation to assist you, even if we had known you had done that."

Melanie opened her mouth to object but Sir Hamilton ignored her and continued: "Furthermore, a few months ago, we tried to get permission to keep tabs on him. But we had wasted a lot of time and money observing him in the early part of 2013 when there were no results. Late in 2013 our contact in Russia seemed to have been discredited, so we had zero credibility. We had promised that all the costs for this project would be in the set-up. We exceeded the original budget fourfold because we ended up having to spend such a lot on additional costs that were not part of the set-up.

"When he volunteered himself to go to Moscow, we managed to get permission to send Logan to organise things out there and see who he would meet. But Logan disappeared and that operation was a cock-up. As far as we knew he met no one. That's it. The rest you know. Typical British story of cock-up and muddling through, I suppose."

"What about Moscow?" Richard was still not sure what level of paranoia was appropriate. He was supposed to trust Hump, wasn't he? That's why the nursery rhyme had been attached to something of great meaning in his memory. It was some kind of escape tunnel. Only his mind still wasn't coming back together. He had no awareness of this person who had this idea to switch sides and had signed the documents all those years ago. "Someone tried to have me killed in Savelovskaya Metro station."

Sir Hamilton looked grave. "We'll have to look into that in due course."

"What if it was Callan?"

"Callan?" Sir Hamilton stared straight ahead. All banking and financial services had been alerted to freeze software updates until further notice. The agency had alerted not just VirtuBank but everyone they could think of in financial services and every software company in that sector. Except that Callan had personally volunteered to inform VirtuBank.

He snatched up the receiver, at the same time checking his watch. "Give me VirtuBank's number," he barked at Richard.

Richard dictated the number and Hamilton tapped it into the phone.

"I need to speak to – " He flapped a beckoning hand at Richard.

"Germain Stoltz."

"Germain Stoltz." There was a pause while he was transferred. "Germain! Can you confirm that the RCB project has been halted? No, no I'm not a journalist. You'll have to take my word. I know Callan, Jim Callan, if that's any help to you. You need to tell me now. I'm afraid we only have five minutes to confirm everything's OK."

There was a long silence from Sir Hamilton.

It seemed to Richard that his worst fears were confirmed. Callan had tried to kill him in the Metro because Callan was part of the plot. Callan had got Logan sent to Moscow so he would be captured and killed too.

Then Sir Hamilton took in a deep breath and let it out again.

"OK. Can you give me the number of someone to speak to at VirtuBank HQ? I need to check that a general order went out.... It did? OK. I still want to speak to someone personally." He turned and gave a thumbs up sign to Richard as he put the receiver down, then immediately began dialling again.

"Kevin Webb please.... Kevin? I need to double-check that Callan was in touch with you earlier to put all go-live projects on hold and hold back software releases until very stringent tests have been done.... They have? ... Good. That's OK then. Oh, so RCB will let you know immediately." He looked at his watch. Thirty seconds to go-live. "In that case, can I hang on? ... Yes, put me on hold." He continued to look at his watch for two more minutes. "So, nothing changed at RCB and nothing abnormal reported by them. Good. I hope that's it then. Panic over." He put the receiver down smiling. "It's OK." he said to Richard. "At least we know Callan's on our side. It was probably just a random nutcase that tried to kill you in Moscow."

"By the way," Richard said. "I forgot to mention, Weber gave me some clue as to how the software would work."

"We can pass that information on later. In the meantime, let's celebrate. I have a 1999 Grand Cru. I think I should crack it open."

At that moment Hamilton's mobile rang. He answered and listened. His face went grey. He nodded his head a few times and said "Yes" occasionally, then hung up.

"That was Hannaford. He said we have been lucky to get away with this. Furthermore, that none of it would have happened if we had not made it happen and it was all somewhat pointless."

"But Weber... we caught Weber. That wasn't pointless surely?"

"To the powers-that-be, that's a moot point," Hamilton said sadly. "Apparently we are going to make our ambassador apologise to Russia, they are going to apologise to us, and that will be that."

"Good God," Melanie said quietly. "People risked their lives and their sanity and this is all we got."

"He also mentioned that Dr Skinner is currently in jail awaiting trial for a number of serious crimes."

"What on earth is going on?"

"I don't know. But as far as I'm concerned, this was a successful project. I have absolute faith that we did the right thing. I will ask what Dr Skinner is charged with during the debriefing and I'll be making a very strong case for our project. Obviously Callan is in the clear, so... Let's get our coats and go."

114 - A REVOLUTION BETRAYED

Weber was looking out of his Georgian window again. He could hear a helicopter in the distance. It was quite common to hear a helicopter in London. Other than that, the street was quiet, as usual. Three tourists looking at a map, no one else. Perhaps they were looking for J.M. Barrie's house. It was just on the corner. Perhaps they were looking for the façade that had been made to look like a real three-storey Georgian building, but was actually just a wall hiding the underground. That too was quite popular with tourists.

Two burly men had just got out of a parked car a block down the road. Weber was still lost in thought as they walked back down the street towards Kensington Gardens. He was thinking about the operations at RCB, National Shanghai Investment Bank, First Delaware Industrial and three more, slightly smaller banks, in Europe. By now the software bomb would have exploded in all of those locations at once. As the muddled transactions made their way into the financial system, it would surely be enough to bring about a catastrophic financial collapse.

How many years had he been doing this now? Too many. He could've retired already. None of his operations had ever been detected. His connections to various international socialist groups had always been indirect. The way he liked to think of it was that he had always been disconnected from his connections. Nowadays, as the director of a lucrative art business, he had the perfect cover.

Never mind that the agency had to buy back many of the artworks itself; it meant that he was undetectable. He amused himself by thinking this plan would be something to tell the grandchildren, assuming he could trace the little bastards.

The doorbell rang.

Weber realised his mistake too late. At first he had underestimated Richard, then he had ignored him, then he had inexplicably told him nearly everything, believing for a brief moment that he would be useful, as well as committed to the cause.

The helicopter suddenly seemed very near. He wondered if its thermal image camera could already see him standing there looking out the window. He remembered his mistake in mentioning Alexei. He continued to look out of the window, imagining that something similar was happening outside Alexei's house, and in Chennai. A police van had just blocked the narrow exit to Bayswater Road. Two more police vans were pulling up on the opposite side of the road.

And Weber also wondered if Richard had ever known what he wanted. He wondered whether Richard had ever properly decided his intentions or not.

115 - UNDER OBSERVATION

"Come."

Osbourne sat down and Hannaford continued, "I have to prepare a document for the Permanent Secretary. He has, of course, assured me that the document and details of this case will never be made public."

"I've heard that one before."

"Yes, well. I have to do it anyway. So let's get the facts right first of all. I'll do my best to show everything in a positive light."

"Of course."

"*Snowman* came to us offering information. The initial idea was to use him in an experiment to split his personality for his own protection."

"Correct."

"However, nothing happened. We realised that his handler was probably implementing our plan without *Snowman* and it was therefore vital to catch whoever that was. So we came up with the idea of forcing the handler into contact with him. We took advantage of *Snowman*'s dual state to try to convince him that he had written the software for the plan himself and we also signalled this very convincingly to his handler."

"So we believed."

"But *Snowman*, for reasons that we don't fully understand, lost the plot."

"He was obviously confused."

"Well, we simply don't know. Mitchell killed himself almost as soon as that was supposedly put in place."

"Yes, thanks to Skinner."

"And Mitchell had already screwed things up further by sending an email that must have made it seem like he was the handler."

"Yes." Osbourne bounced his head a couple of times in agreement.

"So then we decided we could still get away with it because, even assuming *Snowman* thought Mitchell was his handler, we just needed to force the real handler into contact. As soon as that happened, we believed, *Snowman* would remember to switch states and reveal all. But it didn't happen like that."

"Yes, we knew *Snowman* was having trouble switching states but we hadn't realised the implications," Osbourne agreed.

"We discovered there was an emergency procedure but, in the end, even that was unsuccessful."

"Yes, even now *Snowman* is stuck in one state with unstable flashbacks and a lot of confusion."

"If there is an investigation, this is something they will focus on. We've been left with a highly unethical and undesirable outcome.

We've now discovered that some of Skinner's work was based on Nazi experiments that inevitably led to the subjects becoming a danger to themselves and others, just as a violent schizophrenic would be."

"We have him under observation and hope that Skinner's improvements to the Nazis' work will help. Actually, he doesn't seem terribly bad."

"Hmm, not yet. It's too early to say if he has entered what the Nazis called the 'third phase' yet."

"We need to keep him under observation and give him all the help we can."

"He is under observation. If only we had some idea what might be helpful, there might some point to it," said Hannaford, drily.

116 - POSTSCRIPT

Richard had been in hospital for a week. He was making good progress. The nurses assured him he would be his old self pretty soon.

The varicose veins in his foot had cleared up too. Probably, he'd never even had varicose veins. His shoes had probably just been too tight or something.

He would be interested to find out who or what his old self had been. "A man may not know his own mind," he said to himself aloud, fully aware that he was using the phrase that was supposed to be part of an emergency procedure to help him snap out of state B. Fully aware that it had no effect.

He knew that when Mitchell had tried the "phase transition" techniques in Helsinki, they hadn't worked. He was going to have to relearn them but was worried this might not be possible. He wondered if, as a "different" person, he would have the ability he originally had to do this.

That Dr Skinner had been arrested under Hannaford's orders

had been confirmed. Firstly, Skinner was charged with giving Mitchell (under false pretences) the drugs that caused him to commit suicide. Secondly, the techniques of mind control Skinner had devised were far from ethical and, when he believed the project would totally unravel, he had tried to cover his tracks. Finally, though, it was speculation. It was believed Skinner, with no direct access to Richard, had used Russian contacts to spread misinformation to MI9, hoping they'd kill him'

He shuddered to think how close he'd come to death. Death or madness. If Melanie had not brought his contract, and the emergency document she had kept after replacing it with Skinner's meaningless dud, he would have killed himself. In fact, he had only just deciphered it in time to prevent himself killing her. If that had happened, suicide would have been his only option. However, although that document had given him enough information to avoid that catastrophe at that moment, he was still far from his normal self.

In fact, he was troubled about becoming his "normal self" again. For one thing, he had to be kept under careful observation in case he was going to unravel and become dangerous, as Dr Skinner had supposed. Furthermore, some of the things he had believed in his current state were true. He didn't want to find that his carefully-thought-out beliefs would disappear for no reason. What if it is true that only a wider distribution of capital will make a fairer society? What if it's true that social change is controlled and limited by democratic processes and revolution is the only way of breaking free?

Revolution might still be necessary and possible. It wouldn't have to be bloody revolution. It could be a revolution of ideas; like the first and second Industrial Revolutions. But these are rare events, after which wealth becomes even more concentrated in the hands of the few. No doubt, one day, better minds than his would solve all those problems.

It was too bad Melanie hadn't popped in to visit him. Of course, she probably wasn't allowed to, because he was being kept in a secure unit for his own safety.

He looked at his foot again. It looked much better. The varicose veins would need to wait.

The nightmares were not getting better though. Sometimes he would wake up with an after-image present in the room with him. An image of snakes, or maggots, or worst of all, Melanie in the shower with clouds of blood swirling around her. It was difficult to believe that this last event had not actually happened.

Suddenly it felt as though he had been stabbed through the heart – he had to take a deep breath and clench his fists tight. He had just realised that for the first time in memory he had no particular objective or purpose in life.

He wrote in his diary:

Sometimes I'm excited. Sometimes I'm terrified.

Acknowledgements

I want to thank:

Iain Pattison for telling me that I had thrown my story away. He was right. In fact, at that point, I had 35,000 words of non-story.

Caitlin Collins for reading and advice.

Lee Dickinson for extraordinarily detailed and observant editing. I needed all the guidance and help I could get!

Graham Miles for taking a horrible rough sketch for the cover artwork and turning it into a masterpiece.

I should also mention that the Moscow, of sometime around 2013, described in the book, has been drastically improved since. Nearly all the grunge and mess described has been tidied up. The streets are now paved, not with gold, but sparkling granite.

I apologise to Russia for making the bad guy Russian. Unfortunately, the idea expressed somewhere in the book, that we are trying to improve relations with Russia behind the scenes is still, in 2019, wishful thinking. Hopefully, our diplomats will begin to do this eventually. I guess they have tied us in too closely with some of Russia's rivals and enemies for this to be an easy process.

Lightning Source UK Ltd.
Milton Keynes UK
UKHW011532291219
356066UK00001B/53/P